Praise for *THE ART OF BURNING HEATHER*

"A compassionate and hilarious must-read for anyone who has ever broken a cycle and broken free. Donalson's trademark wit shines."

—Jeneva Rose, #1 *New York Times* bestselling author

"*The Art of Burning Heather* is a story full of sweeping scenery, hilarious women, and hunky Scots. A beautiful and fragile exploration of love and identity that will sweep you away to the cliffs of Scotland. Donalson takes us by the hand and tenderly guides us through those universal experiences, and some unexpected ones too. Donalson left her heart on the page. It takes talent, courage, and good wit to unpack a broken heart, and Donalson delivers."

—Stacey McEwan, *New York Times* and *USA Today* bestselling author of *A Forbidden Alchemy*

"It felt like I was there, on a seaside cliff in a Scottish Highland town, holding my heart in my hands, determined and clever and full of grit. A stunning debut with complex characters, wrapped in sizzling banter and kilted spice."

—Anna Przy, bestselling author of *Keep It Up, Cutie*

"A story as beautiful as it is gut wrenching, this debut fiction novel introduces you to complicated women trying to love in the only way they know how—for better or for worse. A heart-on-your-sleeve kind of tale that will have you booking a trip to the Scottish Highlands and begging for another sweeping adventure penned by Donalson."

—Summer N. England, author of *The Impossible Garden of Clara Thorne*

THE ART OF BURNING HEATHER

ALSO BY DEVRIE BRYNN DONALSON

Nonfiction

You're Gonna Die Alone (& Other Excellent News)

THE ART OF BURNING HEATHER

a novel

Devrie Brynn Donalson

This is a work of fiction. Names, characters, organizations, places, events, and incidents are either products of the author's imagination or are used fictitiously. Otherwise, any resemblance to actual persons, living or dead, is purely coincidental.

Published by Montlake, Seattle
www.apub.com

EU product safety contact:
Amazon Media EU S. à r.l.
38, avenue John F. Kennedy, L-1855 Luxembourg
amazonpublishing-gpsr@amazon.com

ISBN-13: 9781662527852 (paperback)
ISBN-13: 9781662527838 (digital)

Cover design by Mumtaz Mustafa
Cover image: © Devon and Cornwall Photography / Getty

Printed in the United States of America

To the wild women,
especially mine.
May you forever be free.

CONTENT WARNING

This is a story about people who live complicated, regretful, courageous, hopeful lives—and, as such, it merits content warnings for the following:

Ableism
Fatphobia
Body dysmorphia
Emotional manipulation and abuse
Discussions of homophobia
Discussions of domestic violence

I have been a bairn, a boy, a man
grown wild by the sea
salted heart
windblown touch
surefoot, feral
creed

Had I been told my crescent love
lost moonlight to eclipse
would I laugh
'fore I had known
budding rose's
hips

I have been a bairn, a boy, a man
gone wanderin' from the sea
now bloomin' rose
I call her home
lily, valley
free

—Callum McDonnell, *Untitled*

1

Twenty years ago
Scotland

"You'll catch your death, Delilah!"

Delilah MacDonald kept running.

"Young lady, *get back here*!"

But her mother's voice was fading as the endless green-and-rust streaks of the Scottish wild rose in front of her, daring her to go and go until she found where the world ended. Her cheeks stung as her pigtails whipped around her face, and still Delilah's heart soared. She closed her eyes and threw her head back, laughing as the distance grew. She was only nine years old, but she knew the difference between being trapped and being free.

Delilah opened her eyes just in time to see the cliff's end. Rocky earth bit into her palms and knees as she dropped and skidded to a stop with inches to spare, sending pebbles bouncing down the sheer stone face toward the slate colored sea. She listened to them fall until she couldn't hear them anymore.

"Holy SHIT!" Delilah shouted. She sat on her knees, clasped her face in her hands, and cackled into the sky—because she had just cheated death *and* because she was not supposed to say *shit*.

Someone spoke behind her. "I thought Americans weren't keen on swearing."

She froze.

"You're bleeding," they said.

She spun around to find a boy, his head cocked to one side. He was skinny and short with wavy reddish hair sticking in every direction, but what stood out were his eyes. They were yellow, or maybe something like gold? Delilah had never seen eyes like those before.

He raised an eyebrow. "And I think you almost just died."

"Yeah, well, I didn't die, did I?" She was glad her mom wasn't around to call for an attitude adjustment. "I'm perfectly alive."

The boy smirked and walked toward her all confident, even though he was smaller than she was. When her mom and grandma had taken her shopping for this trip, they'd given her another lecture about needing bigger jeans. *No boy wants to date a girl that's bigger than him, Delilah.* Sometimes she looked at her thighs and wondered if a boy with bigger legs even existed.

His Scottish accent was thick. "Running with your eyes closed is a stupid thing to do."

"Following girls like a super creep is pretty stupid, too." She got to her feet and made a show of looking down at him, but he just stuck out his weirdly big hand.

"I'm Lachlan."

Delilah scanned the bulky camera on his hip and his warm boots—nothing like the knock-off Converse with her big toe poking through that she'd snuck into her suitcase. His smile turned his eyes warm, like the honey Auntie Maureen—no, wait, Auntie *Mo*—liked to have in her tea.

"I'm Delilah." She went to shake his hand but pulled hers back when she saw the blood smeared across her palm.

"Yeah," he said as he observed her shocked reaction. "Did I mention that you're bleeding?"

Worry shot through her. Blood was dripping from her knees in red paths through the soft hairs on her legs and staining her new white socks. She shrugged like it was no big deal.

"It's not that bad."

"You should see your face."

Okay, that was just *rude.*

"What is your proble—" Delilah started, but then remembered grabbing her cheeks before she knew she'd be smearing blood around. She must have looked like she'd just fought a bear or something! She rubbed her palms against the dark fabric of her shorts. "My mom is gonna kill me!"

"Why?"

She could *not* deal with this tonight—the last night before they had to go back to Los Angeles. The last night for her to be happy, unless she ruined everything by pissing her mom off. Delilah kneeled and rubbed her hands against a patch of damp grass.

"Because!" she cried. "Just look at me!"

Lachlan, the strange boy with the strange eyes, stood just above her with his hand still reaching down. "I am looking at you. Let me help you up."

"I can do it myself."

"I bet you can," he said, but he didn't withdraw.

Delilah hesitated. "My hand is gross."

"I don't mind."

She felt like crying when he pulled her off the ground, but it wasn't because of the way her hand hurt. He took a water bottle out of some pocket and poured it over a corner of his jacket.

"Here. Try this."

Delilah rubbed the jacket against her face super hard. "Did I get it?"

Lachlan tilted his head again. "Almost."

He stepped closer than Delilah remembered ever being to a boy before and took the jacket to press it against her cheek. Delilah went still, like a bee had landed on her. One time, when she had pneumonia and her parents were super worried, her mom had taken a cold wash-cloth and touched her face the same gentle way through the night until her fever broke.

He moved to her hands, and she realized this probably wasn't good. What the heck was she doing letting a stranger give her a freaking sponge bath in the wilderness?

She snatched the jacket back. "I can do it *myself.*"

Lachlan gave her a weird look. "I know you can."

Her skin got hot. "You don't know me at all."

"Not yet." He shrugged. "But we have the whole walk back."

"It's not a far walk."

"I know a longer way."

Normally, Delilah didn't have trouble speaking her mind. She knew exactly what she thought, which was a big problem for her, actually. *Be polite, Delilah!* But something about Lachlan was making her brain do things she didn't have words for. She wished Chloe were there. She and Delilah would make a pillow fort with Aunt Mo's old quilt and whisper way past their bedtime until they figured out what was happening with this odd boy Delilah had found in the wild—just like they always did when Chloe had a new secret boyfriend.

But her best friend wasn't there, so Delilah agreed to take the long way home in the hope of figuring him out. But as they walked, and he asked her if she knew any movie stars back in California, and she asked him if he had a pet sheep there in Scotland, she forgot about finding answers. She told him about how she wanted to be an artist someday, like Frida Kahlo with all her colors, and he told her about how he wanted to take photos to remember everything, all the time—and she didn't feel like he was a puzzle to solve or a game to beat for once. She was busy feeling, not thinking. Usually, Delilah was always thinking.

She gasped as they came over a hill and pointed to a sprawling purply-pink meadow that looked so bright beside the gray sea and sky. "What is that?"

Lachlan followed her finger. "What, the flowers? Wild heather."

"Wow," she whispered, and the sound got lost in the wind. She turned to find Lachlan watching her with that weird look again.

"What? Is there still blood on my face?" She touched a cheek.

"No, no, your face is fine," he said, grinning. "It's just beautiful."

Delilah looked back to the lush blanket of tiny blooms covering the ground. "Yeah, it really is. Hey! You should take a picture! This has gotta count as something to remember, right?" The camera shuttered as she knelt to pluck a stem that wouldn't come free. She watched a bud open into a small magenta colored bloom between her fingertips, like it had been waiting just for her. She tugged again. "These flowers are freaking tough!"

Lachlan's cheeks were stained the color of crushed berries. "As tough as they are lovely."

Delilah liked that. She straightened. "I wonder if they have these back home." Then the thought of home cut through the moment, and she could hear the clock ticking in her mind. *"Crap!"* She grabbed Lachlan's wrist. "We have to go!"

They ran, and too soon they were standing on the path to the bright red front door of the funny little cottage where her aunt was going to live now.

She toed the gravel with her shoe. "Well. I guess this is the last time you'll see me."

For a second, Delilah and Lachlan just sort of stared at each other in this way that felt like a balloon about to pop, so she started walking fast up the path without saying anything else.

"Wait!" Lachlan called. "Let me take your picture!"

Delilah stopped on a stepstone right in the middle of a patch of heather she hadn't noticed before she'd met Lachlan.

"Why would you want to take my picture?" she shouted over the gusting chill.

"To remember!"

"Should I smile?"

"Just be yourself!" Lachlan raised the camera to his eye.

Herself. For the first time since she was very small, Delilah didn't think about how much she hated being in pictures. She threw both her arms out and roared into the Highlands' winter winds. The camera flashed.

Her mother's voice yelled from the cottage. "Delilah? *What in God's name?*"

She flinched. "You better go!"

Lachlan hesitated with a furrowed brow before he darted off, and she felt happy and sad at once. He was barely out of sight when the door swung open.

"Delilah, just look at you! You're a disaster."

2

Mo

Now
Fearnhall, Scotland

As a general rule, Mo McDonnell did not believe in looking back. You make your choices and keep on moving. It's best not to linger.

But now and then, she had a dream.

That morning, Mo had jolted awake from chasing a girl through a field of purple flowers, melting green Popsicles on checkered linoleum floors, and a black stallion in a circle of white petals.

She was 90 percent sure it meant nothing, but the possibility stoked something in Mo's soul back to life.

She paced back and forth in front of her glowing laptop.

It was nearly the twentieth anniversary of her move to Scotland. Perhaps that was why she'd dreamed of her niece, Delilah. Or maybe it was the moment the photo fluttered to the ground like an autumn leaf when the old magnet holding it had run out of juice. Mo had nearly missed the glossy corner jutting out from under the fridge.

She'd nearly missed what was happening now.

A hard knock on the door yanked her back into the room.

"Oi, Mo! Tell me you're decent!"

Mo threw herself into the kitchen chair and clicked frantically to wake the now-sleeping laptop. "Uh, yeah," she yelled back. "Come in!"

The doorknob rattled, accompanied by a muffled, *"Fuck me, these gloves."*

Her screen brightened with a rainbow wheel spinning in its center. Mo silently willed technology to work for her, just this once.

"Lend us a hand?"

"Whaaat?" She did feel guilty leaving him in the cold, but she needed to buy herself time. "I can't hear you! The rain!"

"Oh, aye," he mumbled. *"The raaain."*

The wheel vanished and her draft reappeared. She held her breath with her finger hovering over the trackpad.

She could turn back now and nothing would change. She would be safe.

Or . . .

Lachlan ducked inside from the black night in a flurry of frosty air—so unlike the skin-and-bones boy who'd first knocked at her cottage many years before. Mo slammed the laptop shut and stood, toppling her chair in her bid to seem casual.

His golden eyes narrowed as he stepped out of a heavy boot with a knowing smirk. "If you're struck by lightning before morning, shall I clear your internet history?"

Mo's shoulders bunched by her ears. "Guilty pleasure videos."

He shrugged off his jacket. "Which ones?"

Mo thought of a lie. "Soldiers coming home."

He tutted. "Propaganda."

"Like I said. *Guilty.*"

Lachlan shook out his thick, auburn hair and held his woolly cap over his heart. "The ones with the dogs get me every time."

Mo released her held breath. "Me too."

"So, what's it gonna be tonight?" He mimed great concern for the chair he'd recently refinished as he set it back on its feet. "Battleship? Or Scrabble?"

Mo set out two whisky glasses. "I've had enough of war for one evening."

He squatted beside the crackling fireplace and ran his fingers along the stack of board games. "Battleship it is."

3

DELI

Los Angeles

Deli MacDonald watched the blood trace a path down her foot and collect into a dark, glistening drop before it splattered against the white bathroom tile. She sighed, but it came out just like her mother's, so she sucked it back into her face as quickly as possible.

Deli repositioned the shop's communal tweezers in her hand, prepared to contract a tweezer-borne infection not seen since the freezing of the ice caps, and hissed as the metallic edge slipped against the brittle sliver of glass that had pierced straight through her sneaker. Dropping a vase and paying the price was a rookie mistake, but Deli had been distracted.

Too distracted.

She dabbed the wound with a piddly wad of single-ply toilet paper and collapsed backward with a frustrated grunt as she slid her phone from her apron—still open to the last text from Trey, which she'd read when the vase now in her foot was in her hand.

I can't wait to see you tonight.

She read Trey's words again as she felt her cheeks stain pink. After half a lifetime of knowing and loving the boy she'd met when they were teenagers, Deli MacDonald had a *feeling.*

It was almost time, and she would finally be done waiting.

She opened a new text to Chloe.

Ugh, Chlo. Literally all he has to do is text me and I end up dropping everything and bleeding out.

Chloe wrote back in an instant.

Are you okay??

Deli rubbed at a bit of gunk on her screen.

There's a vase in my foot.

She sent a screenshot of Trey's text to her lifelong BFF.

Am I crazy for feeling like it's happening? I know Trey and I talk every day, but not like this.

Deli played back the last six months of hazy push and pull between her and Trey in her head while she waited. She had begun to think Chloe might not respond when her phone chimed.

Has he brought up the kiss yet?

The words landed like a blow to her stomach.

No . . .

Deli studied the screen, waiting for her best friend to respond. A minute passed. Then another. Chloe probably needed more context.

> But that's what I'm talking about, you know? He's going to. He's ready to talk about it . . . about us. He just needed time.

She watched the three dots of Chloe's response appear and disappear as a newly familiar unease pulsed alongside her heart. In twenty-five years of friendship, they'd never run out of things to say. Not until recently.

Something in Deli's chest wilted, just a little, as she tapped on a new text from her mother.

> Delilah, we're here early. Please come as soon as possible. Your grandmother is already half a glass of wine in, and I'd like to get this over with.

Deli's good foot tapped against the floor. Their reservation wasn't for another thirty minutes.

> Be there soon, Mom.

Chloe's response came through.

> I guess. I just think if it was going to happen for you, it would have already happened.

Her eyes watered as a fresh bead of blood quivered and fell to the ground. Chloe texted again with a link to a slinky backless dress that didn't come in Deli's size.

> Do you think Jared will like me in this? I want to blow his mind for V Day.

Deli tried to turn off the unexpected and deeply uncool feelings that had been more and more common, and think. She filed the name *Jared* into her brain under "Chloe's Boyfriends."

From the moment Deli and Chloe met on the kickball court in first grade, they'd spent most lunches under their special sycamore tree, giggling while they braided each other's hair and dreamed about make-believe worlds. The lunch tree was a magical haven for the two little girls, where impossible things felt real and growing up felt far away. Then, in third grade, Brayden broke Chloe's heart when he didn't give her a special valentine, and Deli had run to the bathroom to stuff her pockets with paper towels. Beneath where "C + D = BFFS" had been carved into the bark—the precursor to a collection of carved hearts with Chloe's and a boy's initials that would all eventually be scratched out—Deli held Chloe's hand while she cried until her nose was rubbed raw. She'd learned to keep a travel pack of the tissues with lotion baked into them on her person at all times.

Since then there had been so many "lunch trees": café tables, parked cars, beaches, and bedrooms—any place that had been turned holy by the sacred bond of girls' friendships.

For Deli, there was a stretch of curb in a high school parking lot—where she and Chloe had waited for their rides home, coloring in the checkers on their shoes—that had been sanctified with the first whisper of Trey's name.

Deli reacted to the link for the dress with a heart and typed back:

He'll die! See you in a few!

She checked the time and checked her email.

Her foot stopped tapping. She had one new message from *Maureen McDonnell.*

Deli hadn't spoken to her aunt in nearly twenty years. Had she missed all her other family members' attempts to reach her? Had Grandma Rosemary finally succumbed to one of the many illnesses she insisted she was plagued with, and some poor EMT was currently trying to scrub her industrial-strength red lipstick off his face after giving her mouth-to-mouth?

> To: Delilah MacDonald
> From: Maureen McDonnell
> Subject: Happy Holidays!
>
> Hi!
>
> Sorry for the late season's greetings, but I was just thinking of you. Big day, huh? Hope you're thriving in life!
>
> Love,
> Aunt Mo

Heat pricked her ears. When she was little, Deli had gotten in trouble at school for writing *McDonnell* instead of *MacDonald* as her last name on her homework, angry that her mom had married someone with a name so close to Auntie Mo's but not the same.

But I just want to be like Grandma and Auntie Mo! she'd cried.

Well, you're not, her mother had said. *You're just like me.*

Deli scrolled to the bottom of the email and clicked on the first of two attachments.

It was a photo of a little girl in front of a cottage's red door under a blanket of heavy clouds as smoke curled from the chimney in the slanted roof. The girl's belly poked out over the shorts bunching between her thighs. Her knees and socks were stained with something dark, and her head was thrown back in a laugh or a yell as the wind tugged at her tangled pigtails. Deli touched the screen with her fingertip. She didn't remember it being taken.

She hadn't thought about that little girl for a long, long time.

In the second photo, a group of people laughed in a pub with twinkling lights in front of a bar decorated with a string of ornament-dotted tinsel. Despite the great family fallout that had all but erased Aunt Mo's face from memory, Deli still recognized her round cheeks and wide smile.

A towering man squeezed Aunt Mo's shoulder with a considerable hand. His smile crinkled the soft spray of freckles that crested his nose and disappeared into the stubble that matched his auburn hair, tousled into messy waves. Behind the sort of eyelashes women coveted but only men seemed to be born with, eyes the color of molten amber glowed with warmth. Something in Deli's head fluttered against her memory, like a bird desperate to escape.

She could have sworn she *knew* those eyes from somewhere.

Deli's boss pounded on the bathroom door as another text came through.

"Deli, quit roosting. The sooner you get to dinner, the sooner you can come back, and we need every second before D-Day V-Day. Plus, Carol has to pee."

Behind Paola, Carol shouted, "We're about to have a situation, kid."

"One second!" Deli called, imagining their seventy-eight-year-old delivery driver in her leopard-print spandex outfit, dancing from foot to foot with her fuzzy pen tucked behind her ear.

Trey had just texted a photo of himself in the mirror—his sun-kissed skin and hair glowing against his cool gaze as he grinned in an expensive olive-green sport coat.

Is this the right color?

Deli forgot all about the pain in her foot and the golden-eyed man in a country far away.

She wedged a new wad of toilet paper into her sock and limped to the mirror.

Two weeks of no sleep and treating iced coffee like a food group had taken its toll. Staring back at Deli was not the reflection of a twenty-nine-year-old spring chicken, but the sallow visage of a haunting swamp witch who had come to claim a mortal soul. Normally, Deli embraced swamp witchery, and Paola had long since stopped cringing at the slept-in ponytails and nacho-cheese stains on the apron of her best designer. But now Deli needed to be cute, and swamp witches were notoriously unsexy.

She tugged at the corners of her eyes and watched the wrinkles there smooth out and then reform when she released the tired skin. She could hear her mother's voice: *I told you to wear sunblock, Delilah. What type of retinol are you using, Delilah?* She reached for the dry shampoo nestled in her bag next to her new dress and doused her head in a powdery cloud, then wrapped a paper towel around her finger to scrub at her teeth. She rubbed at the lily pollen staining her forehead, ditched the apron and sweatshirt she'd been wearing for two days to liberally apply deodorant, then slipped into the olive-green dress. She tied the ribbon around the middle into a bow, coaxing her waist out of hiding, and stood back for one last look.

Staring at herself in the mirror, Deli practiced her game face, tugging at the fabric as it tried to bunch. Then she slipped out the back of the flower shop. The bathroom door slammed in her wake as Carol shouted, "You look bangin', kid!"

Deli got in her car and took a deep breath, bracing to face her family.

And to face the man she'd been secretly in love with for half of her life.

4

Deli

"There's my girl."

Trey Evans held out his hand, and Deli felt the expected gravitational shift tug her feet faster—like she wasn't bound to the earth's core, but to his.

Trey wasn't the small-town quarterback or the local-hero type. He was cunning and sharp—the guy who taught you how to roll a cigarette or convinced you to skip class while he slipped through a back door. He'd had mousy brown hair and pale skin when Deli met him as a teenage transplant to LA, but after years in California his colors had bled into each other in that sun-kissed surfer-boy way that begged for summer romance. And when he spoke, his Georgia accent was *almost* imperceptible—unless he wanted to drip through a person like sweet tea and stick them to his purpose.

Deli limped across the parking lot as he stepped out of shadow. His gaze left a trail of goosebumps in its wake as he scanned her from head to toe. For the thousandth time in her life, Deli's head lightened and her heart quickened at the sight of him, the sound of him, the way she didn't feel real until he walked into a room.

"Wow," Trey said as the icy touch of his attention flicked from her lips to her eyes to her lips again. While the rest of him was warm, his eyes were rounds of wild tundra. "Just . . . *wow.*"

It wasn't convenient—her love for Trey Evans—but Deli had been quietly beholden to him since the day they'd met as kids. But she'd become an expert at forcing the blush from her face under his watching, hungry eyes. She knew to hide her hope over the promise of stolen moments.

She'd almost gotten over him once.

About six months before, Deli had finally started to believe she could move on. Even though she'd loved him for so long, and even though there had been so many moments Trey touched her or looked at her or spoke to her the way only lovers did, it had started to hurt too much. But if she told him how badly she wanted to be more than friends, she knew she might lose him entirely.

Every time she plucked up the nerve to say *You see it, too, right? You love me, too, right?* she'd have a vision of their lives buckling under the weight of an anvil with *love* scrawled across it in messy letters that she'd dropped into the fragile arms of their friendship, and she'd chicken out. She couldn't live without Trey's good-morning texts, or his calls from LA traffic, or his refrigerator he let her stock with her favorite gin. She wouldn't recognize herself in a universe where Trey Evans wasn't the first person she wanted to tell things to. She didn't want to know what life would be like if she broke it all.

So Deli had decided it would be better to remind herself it wasn't meant to be instead of entertaining hope when they watched movies on her couch or sang along to their favorite songs driving down the PCH. It was better to cage her heart until it stopped struggling than let it run itself into the ground chasing a man who'd only admitted to loving her in her head. Deli needed to move on. And she'd gotten so, so close.

Then Trey Evans had kissed her.

It was a Tuesday. Deli had been trying so hard to move on, so she hadn't answered the phone when he called, just like the day before.

She'd left every other text unanswered. And it was brutal, but it was working—she'd been trying for months.

She had just gotten into her pajamas. There was a knock on her door. And out of nowhere, there he was, holding his phone to his ear and holding Deli to his eyes like dry ice. Her phone rang in her robe pocket.

She could hear her own heartbeat as she answered. "Hello?"

Deli's voice echoed small and tinny through Trey's phone. He was breathing too fast.

"I called," he said, voice low. "You didn't answer."

Her heart rattled its bars. "Is everything alright?"

"I just . . ." He stopped. Goosebumps rippled across her skin. "I needed to tell you something."

They stood on either side of the threshold, unmoving mirrors of each other, like a fox and a mouse before one of them decides to run. She took a deep breath.

"Wha—"

Then he was kissing her. It was over before she knew what was happening, and she was still in shock as the door swung closed behind him. Deli stood there tracing her lips with her fingertips and listening to her jailbroken heart's thudding joy for a long, long time.

Trey never brought it up again.

So neither had she. And since then, she had been waiting.

Six months later, he was so handsome it nearly hurt as he pulled her in for a hug and held her body against his for a significant moment longer than he usually did.

"You ready for this?" he asked into Deli's hair, and she mentally prayed a thank you to the god of dry shampoo. She closed her eyes and tried to press the feeling of his breath on her neck into the pages of her memory, like the petals of a camellia pressed into the journal on her nightstand.

"I couldn't do it without you."

He looked down and grinned as his accent slipped into his voice. "It's just your family. You'd survive."

"Please, my family loves you more than me."

A montage flashed through her mind—fourteen-year-old Trey laughing beside the barbecue with her dad, seventeen-year-old Trey bringing sunflowers for the Thanksgiving table, twenty-five-year-old Trey dancing to Frank Sinatra in the living room with Grandma Rosemary.

Trey laughed softly. "I love them, too."

"Then you can sit by my mother. We're—" Deli checked her phone—there was another text demanding to know where she was. She looked back to the moonglow of Trey's watching eyes. "Um . . . three minutes late. And she's already in a *mood*."

"Oh God, a *mood*?" Trey swept her arm up. "We've gotta move!"

As Trey led her toward the restaurant, her hand around his arm in the olive coat he'd bought to match her dress, Deli MacDonald knew again that love was a strange thing. It could be one person's burning sun but live in another person's shadow. Love wasn't a thing you could call on demand. It decided when the time was right. It didn't like to be rushed.

So, just like she had for so many years, Deli fell into step with the boy who'd slipped her heart into his pocket. She could be patient another day. Always another day.

Any minute now, he'll be ready, she thought. *Any second now, I'll know.*

5

Deli

Deli and Trey stepped inside Mama Mia's. The lasagna-scented air hit them like an Italian grandma's saucepot.

She straightened a drooping peppermint carnation in the cheap hostess-stand arrangement and cleared her throat. "Reservation for MacDonald?"

The hostess tapped manicured nails against the glass of her phone.

Trey spoke behind her. "I believe our party is already here and seated."

At the sound of *his* voice, the girl looked up and threw a hand over her mouth—eyes going wide with recognition. A few years after Trey's breakout acting role on a long-running soap opera, he was booking better and better projects and awing more and more hostesses.

The girl giggled beneath her hand. "Um, follow me."

She led them down a narrow, winding hallway of red-and-white-checkered wallpaper, black-and-white photos of Italian celebrities, and more Catholic paraphernalia than the Vatican's gift shop. The hostess darted away as they arrived at the coveted Pope Table—the epitome of class and decorum at Mama Mia's and the only table you had to reserve in advance.

A ghastly attempt at a papier-mâché bust of some forgotten pope spun under a plexiglass box in the center of the round table, warping the reflections of Deli's parents and grandmother where they sat in various states of agitation. Her mother, Lorraine, shifted to face her, and she could feel the threat of unpleasantness in the air like static electricity. Deli's eyes flicked through the clues—Grandma Rosemary's nearly empty wineglass, her father's soft chin as he contemplated the ceiling, her mother's steepled fingers with baby-pink acrylics touching at the tips. Deli stood a little straighter without choosing to.

Lorraine's smile didn't touch her eyes. "Oh, Delilah! You've decided to join us!"

Delilah. Deli sighed in her head as she sat next to Trey. Her mother had chosen a pretty, princess name for the pink-ballet-slippered daughter Deli never became.

"Sorry, Mom," Deli said, snuffing out the tension in her voice with sincerity. "Work's been rough. Valentine's Day."

Lorraine let out a scoffing sort of laugh, shifting her gaze around the table to call the small group to attention. "I'm always amazed people spend so much money to have someone plop some flowers in a vase. I mean, just go to the store, get a reasonably priced bouquet, and put them in water yourself. It's laziness, right?"

Trey looked nervously down while Deli's dad, John, looked nervously up—comrades in silence. Grandma Rosemary caught Deli's eye for a beat, then pursed her lips. "Please, Lorraine—"

"It's *Laurie*, Mom."

"Well, whatever your name is, I've seen you try to 'plop some flowers in a vase,' and we both know they end up looking like hockey sticks jockeying for space in a garbage can."

Lorraine rolled her eyes. "*All* flower 'arrangements' look like that."

Deli loved her work. She understood flowers in a way she couldn't explain—the truth of their meaning and sentiment. While other people wrote in ink, Deli could write in petals. She knew how to transform a person's intention into an arrangement and send it as a physical declaration. Her designs communicated so clearly that it seemed impossible, but she did it so well she'd gained a knot of loyal customers who swore Deli could work magic. Each bloom was a sentence in a carefully penned letter, each color or petal a confession, each thorn or stem a curse. She didn't know how or why, but Deli seemed to have been born knowing a secret language, and she dearly cherished its poetry.

"Well, Mom, it *is* an art form."

Her mother's smile went stale. She moved on. "And where is Chloe?"

Deli swallowed down the sick, hot feeling at the base of her throat as she realized she'd never heard back. "I'm sure Chlo's on her way."

"Bless her heart," Grandma Rosemary chimed in. "She's just a *doll*, that girl."

"Sure is, Grandma."

Trey shifted in his seat and pressed his leg against hers under the table. It caught Deli off guard, and as his eyes found hers, a betraying heat blotted her skin.

"Um, are you *Trey Evans*? I'm, like, *such* a fan!"

The hostess was back, standing in the entry to the Pope Table's divine alcove with her hands clasped together beneath her chin. Deli watched Trey flip the switch that transformed him from the sandy, sly boy she loved to a professional late-night talk show guest. He beamed at her, and her fake eyelashes fluttered like scared caterpillars caught in a mean gust.

"I just love you in *Chestnut Gardens*, like . . . you're definitely the hottest guy on that show. Seriously, all my friends agree that you're the hottest one, and—"

"Darling, ask for your photo and move along." Grandma Rosemary's voice cut through the fan's sentence like a knife.

Deli's mom looked appalled. *"Jesus Christ, Mom!"*

Grandma Rosemary's eyes flicked to Deli's before she tipped her glass to her lips and waved dismissively. Lorraine snatched the stemware from her mother's hand, effectively stopping her from a rather graphic attempt to get every last drop.

"I'm sure Trey won't mind," Lorraine said with a smile.

"No, no, that's okay . . ." the poor girl mumbled. She backed out of the claustrophobic room, well and truly Rosemarried.

The pope spun around steadfastly, but if Rosemary felt any shame, it stayed between her, God, and a vanished merlot.

Deli scanned Trey's face for discomfort as their server stepped lightly into the room. "Can I get you another glass of wine?"

Rosemary calmly said, "Yes," while Lorraine nearly shouted, *"No!"*

Lorraine forced a smile. "My mother should not be served another drop. And I'll take whatever has the most alcohol."

"Sure," the waitress said, "and your food will be out shortly."

Deli wondered which family-style meals had been ordered in the few minutes she and Trey had been late.

"You know what, *Lorraine*?" Grandma Rosemary sighed as she slowly refolded the cloth napkin in her lap.

Deli's mom hated being called *Lorraine*, so Deli referred to her as such, exclusively. As long as Deli was *Delilah*, Laurie MacDonald would be *Lorraine*. Deli wasn't exactly proud of it, but a vindictive gremlin danced a jig in her brain whenever her grandmother used *Lorraine* instead of *Laurie*, too.

Lorraine answered, "What, Mom?"

"You should consider that I'll be *dead* someday. And you'll wish you had been kinder to your mother."

Lorraine's eyes narrowed and her hands balled into fists as she glared at her mother. Rosemary simply pantomimed fear and shared a worried look with His Holiness before crossing herself.

Trey's eyes went wide. Deli tried and failed to smother a cough from wine gone down the wrong pipe, and she felt her mom's attention snap to her like a rubber band.

"Are you okay?" Trey scooted his water toward Deli and patted her back. Deli's awareness split between her mother's ramping anger and the new place Trey was touching her. "Here," he said. "Drink."

The waitress breezed in as Deli was catching her breath, and left a fresh glass of red in front of Lorraine. Deli's father appeared to be counting the cobwebs.

A small, dangerous smile tugged at Lorraine's artificially plumped lips. "Can we dispense with the drama, Delilah?"

Deli looked down. "I was just choking."

Chloe's special ringtone sounded from Deli's bag. She rushed to find it, filled with sudden visions of car crashes and axe murderers causing her BFF's demise.

"Put your phone away, Delilah." Baby-pink nails tapped impatiently on the table. "Don't be rude."

Grandma Rosemary snaked a hand toward Lorraine's wineglass and dragged it back toward her, winking at Deli over her mom's shoulder.

"I . . ." Deli began, but she trailed off as she read Chloe's message.

Hey. So sorry, I'm not gonna make it tonight.

Deli squinted into the blue light and typed back.

Oh, that's okay. Are you alright?? Do you need anything?

Her mother spoke more loudly. Sharply. "Delilah?"

"Who's hungry?" Their waitress materialized and lowered a heaping bowl of noodles onto the table. "Fettuccine Alfredo?"

John came to life like a Chuck E. Cheese animatronic with a finger in the air. He reached for the jumbo serving spoon and smiled at Lorraine. "I'll take a scoop! Pasta, honey?"

The cresting confrontation in Lorraine's face sputtered and died as she turned to her husband to loudly declare, "You know I'm trying to be *good*, John . . ."

As they all filled their plates under the welcome distraction of her mother's tirade against carbs, Deli realized how very tired she was. She took deep breaths through her nose. She should have just stayed at the shop instead of stealing a few hours to try to celebrate before she had to work late into the night. She'd be there till the sun came up, writing love notes from one valentine to another and sending them off with red roses, again and again.

Trey's hand found her thigh.

"Hi," he whispered.

"Hi," Deli whispered back.

"How's your lasagna?"

She still hadn't tasted the forkful she'd managed to grab from one of the family-style platters. "Not sure." She chuckled weakly. "How's your fettuccine?"

"Saucy."

She felt like every bit of her had been reverse-big-banged and was now coiled, thrumming and threatening to explode, under his palm. She willed her voice to stay nonchalant. "Saucy is . . . good."

His grin grew wider. "Saucy . . . is *great.*"

No one knew that Trey was touching her under the table, teasing goosebumps into her skin. For one tenuous moment, it was just the two of them together in the swirling chaos of the night. A team.

Chloe's chime sounded again.

I'm fine. Just came down with something. Hope you have a good night!

Deli couldn't count the number of times she'd gone over everything she'd said or done in the last six months, searching for the moment she'd messed up and upset Chloe enough for things to change. She summoned the list in her head again and started at the top.

Trey interrupted her inventory of possible mistakes. "Hey? Are you okay?"

"Yeah," she said. She clung to the feeling of Trey noticing her when no one else did. "It's just Chloe."

Trey rolled his eyes. "What now?"

A wilted petal in Deli's heart broke away. "She's sick."

Before Trey could respond, Lorraine's voice made them both jump.

"MOM!"

Lorraine's eyes were glued to Grandma Rosemary's red lipstick, left like a neon sign on the rim of her freshly empty wineglass. Lorraine lurched for the evidence, shaking the table with the effort and sending Deli's half-empty glass teetering in what felt like slow motion to empty its contents into her lap.

Lorraine turned toward the sound of Trey's chair screeching against the floor as he kicked away from the splattering scarlet mess. She took in the blossoming stain on Deli's brand-new dress, never to be worn again.

"Well, that's never been my favorite dress of yours, darling. Perhaps your grandmother will buy you a more flattering one, considering she's to blame."

Deli closed her eyes and wondered whether her mother would have noticed it was new eventually. She stood and slipped down the hallway. She thought someone might follow her, but when she looked over her shoulder, she was alone.

Her footsteps echoed in the bathroom as she felt the first traitor-tears start to well.

"Hey," someone said from behind her. "Need some help?"

6

Deli

"That's not great."

Their waitress stood with hip cocked and bubbly water in hand, taking in the wine splattered across Deli's lap.

"No," Deli sighed. "I suppose it's not."

"I can get it out. It's my magic power."

"I got it." Deli smiled as she took the glass. "But thank you so much for this."

She nearly recoiled at the unexpected touch on her forearm as the stranger gave her a gentle squeeze. Their eyes met in the mirror.

"Hey. Who cares what they think of you?"

Deli had no idea what she was talking about. "What?"

Her reflection stared as the waitress smiled softly with something like . . . pity?

"Club soda will take care of that quick," she said, then backed into the hallway.

Deli took a steadying breath in the stark, cool room—all dark stone and bronze hardware, despite the riot of color and sound muffled just beyond the metal door.

She locked eyes with her reflection and tucked a strand of hair behind her ear. A balloon filled in her stomach, and she swallowed it down. It was easy enough to do. "It's almost over, Delilah." Her voice wasn't kind, but she didn't need kindness. "Keep it together."

As Deli wove back toward her table with a damp skirt, a roar of laughter and music erupting from a nearby table stopped her in her tracks. A little girl with unbrushed curls tumbling from a crooked crown stood in her chair over a single birthday cupcake. In the flickering light, while her family sang, that girl looked wild and free. Deli blinked very hard, turned, and kept walking toward her own family.

She found her dad scribbling a signature on the check. He folded up the glasses that were perched on the tip of his nose.

She refused to sound crestfallen. She smiled. "Oh, no dessert?"

Her mom looked up. "We knew you had to get back, what with Valentine's Day being tomorrow." Deli's foot pulsed painfully. "And it's not like any of us girls need the extra calories. Unless Trey is still hungry?"

"Me?" Trey asked. "Oh, no. I'm good."

"Great." Lorraine smiled as she pointed toward the exit. "We have to drop Little Miss Lush here off at home." Grandma Rosemary shooed the comment away with a papery hand like she was swatting at a fly.

On her way out, Grandma Rosemary squeezed Deli's shoulder and slipped an envelope into her hand with a wink. "You know, when I was your age I already had two children, a marriage, and a career. I want you to think about your life and reach your goals. Use that to get there." She nodded toward the envelope and took Deli's hand, the way she only did when she was a few glasses of wine in. "I have a very good plastic surgeon, if you'd like to get a little something. You know, to stay competitive." Grandma Rosemary whispered the last word with a quick flick of her eyes to Trey slipping on his coat over Deli's shoulder.

Deli knew Grandma Rosemary was simply from a different time. She barely felt the sting that used to raise welts on her heart. "Thanks, Grandma. I'll keep that in mind. Love you."

"Alright, darling. Alright." She patted Deli's arm and moved into the hallway.

John and Lorraine MacDonald were probably already in the parking lot.

Deli struggled to get her coat on, until Trey picked up the dangling arm and held it out for her to find.

"I don't know what you were so worried about," Trey said from behind her. "That was a *delight*."

"A huge success!" She turned to face him. "I'd love to do it again."

"Is tomorrow too soon?"

They were interrupted by their waitress carrying a single cupcake with a lone candle.

Tears threatened to wash away Deli's composure. "Did you . . . ?"

Trey teased his robber's smile. "I may have mentioned it. We *are* here to celebrate you, right?" He held the cupcake between the two of them. "Make a wish."

Deli hoped beyond hope that one small flame could carry the weight of so much wishing. She blew, eyes closed, acutely aware of her breath on Trey's fingers.

Then the cupcake collided with her face.

"You *ass*!" She laughed.

Trey danced away laughing as she tried to snatch the smooshed cupcake in his hand. She bent to study her face in the twirling plexiglass box and licked a wide circle in the frosting. "Trey, check. Did I get it all?" She spun around.

He was standing close. Too close.

"No." He set the ruined cupcake down without looking away from her, coaxing a chill with his voice like dark satin gliding across her skin. The kiddish sparkle in his eyes was gone. They simmered silvered blue. "You didn't."

They were alone in the private corner of the restaurant. The air between them hummed with the things they'd never said. He raised his hand, head barely tilting, and caught her face in his fingers as she went still. Trey's thumb traced the place where she had attempted to rub away the mess, so slowly it felt like torture.

Deli looked up while he learned the shape of her lips, and she knew it was impossible she was the only one thinking the things she was thinking. He held her so softly, fingertips against blushing cheek, like he was afraid he might hurt her. He *had* kissed her. She hadn't made that up.

She didn't know when the gap between their bodies had gotten so small. Deli's heart raced, desperate for an answer—to know what Trey wanted—and she felt the silly thing buckle in her chest as she looked to his eyes for clarity but found misty fog.

"Deli . . ." Trey whispered.

Is this it? she thought.

Splintered bits of shattering glass exploded around their feet—so loud in a room where Deli could hear her own blood in her ears. It jerked them back from the edge. They took a clumsy step away from each other.

"*So* sorry about that!" Their waitress made a *whoopsie* face. "Dropped a glass!"

Trey flipped on his million-dollar smile.

"No problem at all!" he drawled. "We were just on our way out."

"Have a good night!" She stayed hovering in the doorway until Deli and Trey shuffled down the hallway and spilled out into the winter air.

Deli sucked in a massive gulp of night and cold, and hard panic chased off her love-drunk stupor. She didn't look back as she walked toward her car, searching her brain for protocol on how to act with your longtime friend after he'd kissed you once, acted like he hadn't, then done . . . whatever the hell *that* had been. She hit the unlock button on her car once, twice, three times.

Trey caught her wrist and spun her toward him in the middle of the empty parking lot.

It all felt too real. Too fragile.

"I have to get back to work," she said in a rush.

"Come over tomorrow." Everything sounded underwater. A strange shadow crossed Trey's face. "After your shift. There's something I . . . Just come over."

"I'm off at three," she managed.

"See you at five."

"Okay."

Trey wrapped Deli in his arms, and she stiffened—thinking about all the ways tomorrow night could ruin things—but she forced the thoughts away and melted into him to bury her face into his shoulder.

"Tomorrow," he murmured against her ear. Then he strode toward his car and looked back at her with one hand on the handle. "Oh, and Deli?"

"Yeah?"

He smiled under a perfect cone of streetlight.

"Happy birthday."

7

Deli

Valentine's Day passed in a whirlwind of chaos, flinging stems, and zero counter space. At 3:00 p.m. Paola locked the door and slowly extended one fist into the sky while the girls made weary whooping sounds and collapsed onto whatever could hold their weight. Deli snuck out, limping on feet that hadn't seen rest in weeks, and she sat in her idling car. She checked her phone. Chloe still hadn't returned her voicemail or her many texts.

In all the years they'd been friends, Deli and Chloe had only spent two birthdays apart. The first when Deli had pneumonia for Chloe's seventh birthday, and the second when Chloe missed her connecting flight on her way to celebrate Deli's twenty-first during her semester abroad in Spain.

People said friendships changed as you got older—that sometimes they just faded. But that couldn't be true of Deli and Chloe. They weren't just friends. They would forever be two little girls giggling in the shade of a sycamore, even when they were old and gray and so touched by time no one would believe the photos of them when they were young. Sisterhood was much more than who was born in the same family. They had grown up together and been each other's witness for all the life they could remember. Chloe was Deli's sister.

Chloe wouldn't fade.

Deli watched the screen in her palm, hoping for her best friend's name to pop up. Instead, she got a text from her mother.

Delilah—I need you to come by after work today. It's important. Love, Mom.

Deli let her head fall against the headrest.

Okay, Mom.

She fished ibuprofen out of the purse pocket she let them loosely roll around in.

It's efficient! she'd once said while Trey looked on, disgusted.

It's chaos.

She popped three into her mouth and sped toward her apartment, newly sure she hated all her clothes. Twenty minutes later, Deli stared at the mess left from trying fifteen outfit options, wishing she could have sent pics of them to Chloe for help. She chose a little black dress that hung off her hips in just the right way, grabbed her keys, and hobbled to her car. By the time her slingback heels clicked against the hardwood floors of her childhood home, it was 4:15 p.m.

"Mom?" Deli searched through the house until she reached the kitchen and stopped to pull an errant guard petal from the deep red and sterling silver Valentine's roses her dad had sent her mom as a re-creation of their wedding flowers. She always wondered if they knew what they'd chosen—one rose whispering of *shame*, the other declaring *love at first sight*. It left a sour taste in her mouth.

She found Lorraine in the backyard, basking in the sun of a Los Angeles February, complete with Pamela Anderson hair in a hot-pink towel and giant cat-eye sunglasses obscuring most of her face. Her nipples, however, were on full display.

Deli held her hand up to block the Mother Breasts. "Oh, come on!"

Lorraine smooshed them together with a pout. "Oh please. You used to love these, Delilah."

Deli's lip curled against her will. "What do you need, Mom?"

"Your birthday presents just arrived today—that package on the counter. So sorry I was too busy to wrap it."

Deli hadn't noticed the lack of a gift from her parents the night before. She slipped the cardboard box on the counter into her bag and turned to go.

"Open it, Delilah!" Lorraine called as she continued melting into her lawn chair.

Deli ripped open the package and saw a thick black-and-yellow book titled *Dating For Dummies*, and a series of memories thudded into her mind like darts, echoing through her head. Her grandmother's voice—*Girls your age should be married, Delilah.* Chloe's saying, *If it was going to happen for you, it would have happened by now.* She squeezed her eyes shut and pressed her fingers to her temples.

"Do you like it?"

Deli jumped three feet in the air at her mother's voice behind her. She turned, clutching the book to her chest, and found Lorraine tucking the edge of a towel into itself under her arm, looking uncharacteristically timid.

"I just wanted to get you something that really felt like *you*."

Deli glanced at the dating guide in her arms, fighting to keep her face neutral and voice positive. "Like me?"

"Well, yes . . ." A strange note of real concern touched her mother's words. "I thought . . . Aren't you looking for someone?"

Deli watched her mother revert into an unsure, self-conscious girl—like she so often did—and Deli's anger drowned under a wave of responsibility. She had her role to play.

"Thanks, Mom. That's really considerate. I'll give it a read."

Lorraine's voice was pulled thin with fragile sincerity. "I just want you to be happy, Delilah."

Deli's stomach tightened and churned at the naked, trembling wanting of her mother—the minefield routinely laid for Deli alone. "I know, Mom. I am happy."

"If you could be realistic and move on from Trey, you could be."

Deli stared, stunned by the words so casually fired, like they weren't an arrow aimed at a heart.

Lorraine mistook her silence for agreement and beamed, clapping her hands together and pointing one stiletto acrylic back at the box. "There's another present!"

Deli repeated her mother's advice over and over in her head as her hand moved robotically. *Be realistic*—such a nonchalant admittance that, to Lorraine, her daughter had no hope of winning a boy she loved. She pulled a plastic-wrapped box set of the first five seasons of *The Highlander* from the package. Grandma Rosemary and her mother had talked her ear off about their favorite show so many times, and every time, Deli expressed that she had absolutely zero interest.

Yet she stood in her childhood kitchen, clutching her hurt feelings and a kilt-wrapped reminder that she should be more like *them* to her chest as a birthday gift.

"*The Highlander* is the best, Delilah. You're going to love it. It's my and Grandma's favorite show."

"So *thoughtful*," Deli managed through a clenched smile.

Lorraine drifted to the fridge and removed a bottle of rosé, making little *wee* sounds as she wrestled the cork before palming an unopened pile of mail on the counter. Deli slipped the gifts into her bag as her phone rang.

"It's Grandma," Deli said.

Her mother's eyes went wide. She shook her head and whispered, "Don't tell her you're here! I'm not here!"

Deli answered the call. Before she could say hello, her grandmother was off to the races.

"Delilah? It's Grandma Rosemary. Listen, I believe I have a nasty case of malaria."

Deli took a deep breath and summoned the patience she kept on a shelf marked just for her grandmother's eccentricity. "Grandma, it's very unlikely you have malaria." She exchanged a look with Lorraine.

"Well, if it's not malaria, it's Ebola, Delilah. Your mother's phone is going to voicemail—*so* typical. I think you need to take me to the hospital."

Deli mouthed *Ebola* and *hospital* to her mother, who held a finger gun to her temple and mimed pulling the trigger. "Grandma, you haven't traveled beyond Beverly Hills in ten years. There's no way you have Ebola."

"I got takeout from a Jamaican restaurant last week. How do you kno—"

"No, Grandma," Deli interrupted, horrified. "Absolutely not."

There was a brief, tense silence. Her grandmother sighed in a very familiar way.

"Fine," she said, then she hung up.

Deli shook her head. Lorraine sighed, too, blissfully oblivious to how indistinguishable the sound was from her own mother's. "How many rare diseases are we up to now, do you think?"

Deli stared at the ceiling, trying to average how often Grandma Rosemary diagnosed herself with something terrible on any given week. "Gotta be five hundred plus."

"At least," Lorraine said, dropping her eyes back to the stack of mail in her hand. Deli soaked in the camaraderie of being the only two people Rosemary McDonnell called to insist she had mad cow disease. It was a strange club. But they had each other.

"What the *hell*?"

The tone in Lorraine's voice snapped Deli's head up, scanning for the cause so she could snuff it out. Lorraine squinted at a photo pinned against the envelope it had come in. There were Royal Mail stamps next to a return address.

"What is it, Mom?"

Laurie shot her a withering look that sent a spike of panic up her spine. "It's just something *my sister* sent. God knows why."

Deli thought of the email with photos of a place that felt so far away. If she closed her eyes, she could almost smell the sea-salted wild. "Aunt Mo?"

"Aunt *Maureen*," her mother practically growled. "But why she thought I'd want a reminder of her abandoning us for that horrid town, I'll never know."

Lorraine tossed the envelope and its contents in the garbage and turned to rummage in the refrigerator. Deli knew it was a bad idea, but she slid the trash open as quietly as possible and lifted the envelope.

There were the same two photos Aunt Mo had emailed her, but with a handwritten note. She ran her finger along the edge of the photo of her as a child and slid it behind the stack as quietly as she could to examine the next. Again, Deli's eyes were pulled to the man beside Aunt Mo in the pub. His shoulders were broad, and his sleeves were rolled to reveal skin both freckled and tanned. Deli's gaze caught on his forearms and his hands. Then his eyes—like pooling honey—pure and warm. She felt the thing in the rafters of her memory beat its wings for freedom as she slipped the note out of the pile.

Aunt Mo's handwriting was scrawled across thick paper. Deli hadn't seen that looping cursive in so long. She began to read.

Dear Laurie,

I know this is out of the blue, but I—

Her mother's pink claws nearly scored her nose as Lorraine tore the mail from Deli's hands. Her eyes were too close, burning with a cold fury. The frozen dread that had so often glued Deli's feet to the floor of this house held her still again.

Her mother's voice was a blade. "That woman is *not* a part of our family, Delilah. Understand?"

Deli's mind raced to calculate her options and outcomes, but there was really only one choice. She would calm her mother's rage, repair the fraying wire that threatened to burn things down, and quiet the part of Deli that whispered words like *unfair* and *why.*

"I'm sorry, Mom. You're right, of course. I barely even remember her."

Lorraine examined her daughter's expression—a warden searching for signs of dissent. She tore everything from Aunt Mo in two and shoved the pile back into the trash. Her eyes narrowed, scanning Deli's body for the first time. "Why are you dressed like that?"

"I have plans tonight."

Lorraine's lips pressed together. "So I'm wasting your time?"

It was too late. "No, Mom. You're no—"

"Fine." Her mother cut her off, tone final. "Just go."

Her mom gripped the bottle of rosé by the neck and paused long enough to look up at her with watery eyes before they turned dark and she returned to the backyard. Deli stood in the empty kitchen. She silently pieced through the garbage until she found the mail from Aunt Mo. Wet coffee grounds slid off the glossy photos without much harm, but the note was now an illegible kaleidoscope of fountain ink and dark roast. She shook off the mess and slipped the photos into her bag, then held her flattened hand at eye level and counted until it stopped shaking. She opened the fridge and slid her mother's last bottle of wine into the tote to jostle around with the kilted actors and humiliating tome.

Sometimes her family made her want to run away, like she was a little girl.

Happy birthday to me, she thought, squaring her shoulders and moving toward the door. Some family you were born with, but some you got to choose.

And Trey was waiting to choose her.

8

Deli

"Hey, this is Chloe! Leave a message, and I'll text you back."

Deli waited for the beep of Chloe's voicemail while the stoplight outside Trey's building tinted her dashboard red.

"Hey, Chlo. I don't know if you saw my texts, but I'm here and I'm sort of freaking out. Are you okay?" She was dreading asking the next question. "Did I do something to upset you? If I did, I'm really sorry. Please call me back. I'm getting worried."

She set the phone down and spied the shiny corner of a photo peeking from her bag in the passenger seat. Deli twisted to grab her emergency floral design kit and fished out the clear tape. She lined up the torn edges of a pub far away and of the little girl she'd been the best she could, and taped the backs. She checked the clock: 5:03.

Deli chased away the gnawing feeling in her gut. It didn't matter if her mother or her best friend or everyone she worked with didn't think Trey would ever love her. It didn't matter that other people didn't understand their timing or their chemistry. It didn't matter if the stars wouldn't align or the planets were in retrograde.

They didn't know him like she did. No one knew him like she did.

At 5:07, Deli was knocking on Trey's door. It swung open with a gust that rustled the fabric around her calves, and there was Trey—Trey, with his smooth chest so tan against the white button-up, his eyes glinting the same blue-gray of his sport coat.

"There's my girl."

"Wow," Deli said, nearly swaying on her feet. "You *do* clean up nice."

"Me? Look at you! Where's this girl been hiding?" He wrapped his arms around her waist and made a sound of exertion in her ear as he struggled to pick her up.

"Put me down, Trey!"

He set her down as she tugged at the sleeves on her dress and forced a chuckle, hoping he hadn't heard the edge of sudden panic in her voice. Trey stepped backward into the apartment, gesturing with a hand.

The smell of sundried tomatoes, garlic, and cream wafting from the stove chased the beginnings of an unpleasant thought from her mind. Trey beamed at her and nodded. "Your favorite."

It was her Grandma Rosemary's Tuscan chicken recipe—not that Grandma Rosemary had made it in many years, but Deli must have cooked it for Trey a thousand times.

His apartment was even more meticulous than normal. Not a thing was out of place except an eruption of royal blue, indigo, and electric aqua petals on the table.

Her fingertips brushed a few of the vibrant blooms. "Delphinium?"

Trey's Southern drawl and grin lifted his voice. "That's the one you like, right?"

Delphinium *was* her favorite—a joyous endorsement of *lightness, hilarity*, and *wit.* It was a flower for the *openhearted.* She hoped finding it for the first time between her and Trey was a good sign. "I can't believe you remembered."

"Of course I remembered. I listen to you, Deli." He made a mock-hurt face, like she'd accused him of something awful. A little game, just for her.

"Is that right?" Deli tried to cover the blush in her cheeks behind her bag as she lifted it over her head and set it on the counter.

Trey watched her from the corner where the countertops met, hands braced against the smooth tile, head dipped just slightly. She felt the snow-blinding touch of his eyes move up and down her body. Heat leaped to highlight its wake on her skin.

She wished she remembered what it *felt* like when he'd kissed her. It had happened so fast.

"You know I listen to you," Trey said.

His gaze sent Deli's blood rushing through her chest, her fingers, her lips. It was completely unreasonable how quickly Trey Evans could undo her.

He glanced toward the stove. "I'm not sure if I made the sauce right?"

"I have to taste it."

Trey stilled but didn't pull away as Deli squeezed into the space beside him and their arms brushed. She forced herself not to stare at the spot where their bodies shared warmth.

Deli wished she'd found another word for *taste* as she retrieved a spoon in the kitchen she knew by heart, dipped it into the sauce, and raised it to her mouth. She could barely stand the intensity as Trey watched her move, their bodies inches apart.

"What do you think?"

Deli slipped the spoon into her mouth. It tasted mostly of hot cream and acrid burned garlic, but she couldn't tell him. He was waiting with a look so vulnerable she rarely ever saw it—a glimpse of a little boy who was desperate for praise.

There was nothing she wouldn't do to make him feel alright. "It's perfect."

"Do you remember the first time you made this for me, Deli?" He was still whispering, their bodies still so close together and so charged he could shock her with his touch. "We were only, what? Seventeen? We were at my house and were gonna order pizza."

Deli remembered the way Trey's father had stormed into the room, red-faced and screaming while he waved Trey's English test in his face, like it had happened that afternoon.

"He was so mean to you."

"Mmhmm." Trey nodded. "And you said, *Don't worry. You can come to my house.*"

Deli smiled at the memory. *"And I'll make you something better than pizza.'"*

In silence louder than Deli had ever heard, Trey reached up and tucked an errant strand of hair behind her ear. Shivers rippled across her skin like a shock wave as his fingertips danced at the place her cheekbone met her hairline. She could feel her pulse in her lips.

"You've always known exactly the right thing to say, Deli. That's why you're my best friend. There's no one like you."

Her phone's buzz from somewhere deep in the bag on the counter ended the moment. Trey pulled back and slipped his hand in his pocket as she took a few halting steps away from him, doing all she could to keep from gasping for air. She reached for the bottle of wine set out next to two empty glasses on the counter. "Shall I?"

"Hmm?" Trey looked up from his shoes and blanched. "No!" He lurched toward her. "No, that's, uh . . . Don't open that." Trey noticed his hand hovering between them and ran it sheepishly through his tousled hair. "It's supposed to pair perfectly with dinner."

The man never stocked his fridge with two different types of beer, much less wine to pair with the dinner he was cooking. Her heart pounded with the newness of him.

"Apologies, my good sommelier." She gave a panic-move half bow. "Luckily, I snatched a bottle from Lorraine that pairs perfectly with the end of long weeks." The contents of the tote shifted as she pulled the bottle free. She spied a missed call from her grandmother on her screen as *Dating For Dummies* and the box set of *The Highlander* slid onto the sparkling tile.

Adrenaline shot through her as Trey picked up the book and Deli realized what was about to happen.

"What's this?"

"Trey. Give it." He held it high above their heads as she reached for it.

"*Dating For Dummies*?"

She came off her tiptoes and stared at a single fingerprint marring his spotless stainless steel fridge. "Just . . . some motherly advice."

Deli watched foggy, jumbled emotions collide in Trey's eyes like clouds vying for sky. His smile vanished.

"You haven't *met* someone, have you?"

Heat prickled up her neck. "I'm not exactly trying to date right now."

"A shame."

His words nearly knocked the air out of her. She took in every detail of him, desperate to find and repair the invisible thing tainting the night with such strangeness. She spoke slowly and softly. "What do you mean, 'a shame'?"

Trey did not speak softly at all. "It was a *joke*."

Jealousy had always been a weird color on Trey. In the fifteen years that they'd lived their lives side by side, there had been a few moments when Deli had managed to wrestle her feelings for him into a jar, set them on a shelf, and have a crush on someone else. But whenever she even mentioned the name of another boy, Trey's hurt would crystalize into envy.

It didn't matter that Trey had countless flings that never quite reached a labeling level. Deli wasn't capable of loving without offering her whole heart, so she was not allowed to want someone else.

If he hadn't kissed her, she might have thought it was unfair. But she knew his jealousy was proof of life for the thing she wanted most in the world.

Good, she thought. *Jealousy is a good sign.*

Trey didn't meet her eyes as he tossed the book onto the counter. Instead, he grabbed the box set of *The Highlander*, with its strapping, shirtless man wrapped in tartan on the cover. He held it up between them and glared at her. "Do you watch this, Delilah?"

Deli flinched at the name.

The gift skidded across the counter with an indignant flick of Trey's wrist. "I can't believe you watch this *garbage*."

Her mind was racing, trying to pin down the thing going wrong and right it. Trey was a complicated person. He didn't always *act* in alignment with what he *felt*. It was far from the first time Deli had to pick through the rubble of a moment to find evidence of what was really upsetting him.

But, standing in his kitchen on sore feet as the sauce thickened into gravy, Deli couldn't quite draw a straight line between their secret kiss, her favorite things, his whispered memories, and . . . the evils of *The Highlander*?

She reached for humor and hoped it would soothe whatever was roiling just under Trey's skin. She really put some mustard on the words. "Oh, yeah. A man in a kilt? Wielding a sword? *Mmm*, Mama! Sign me up!"

He looked at her like he'd never been more disappointed in someone in his life, and then he saw the photo—roughly taped back together, peeking out from the bag. She made a sort of involuntary move toward it, but Trey was faster. He pinched it between his fingers, scanning the cheery strangers in a holiday card, and his eyes snagged on something.

Someone.

"Who is this?" His fingernail creased the fragile paper near the man behind Aunt Mo.

"I don't know. It's just a picture my aunt sent."

He glared at her as she tried to stay calm. She couldn't blame him. Of course he was upset finding a taped-together photo with an admittedly gorgeous man he'd never seen right before he was going to lay his heart on the line. She elaborated, hoping to comfort. "I have no idea who that is, Trey. And I don't care."

Trey looked from Deli to the photo, to the box set, and said, "This is beneath you, *Delilah*."

Deli—truly baffled as she watched the night slip away from her—held on to the silence, hoping he'd say something that made it all simple and silly and salvageable.

He relented in a pent-up breath. "It gives women false expectations. Like, what? If I can't toss a tree over my shoulder or swordfight in a skirt, I'm not man enough?" Deli looked at him like he'd sprouted a banana out of the top of his head, which seemed to strengthen his resolve. He threw his hands in the air and crossed them over his chest. "It's simple, Deli. It's a double standard. A ridiculous fantasy."

His mercurial eyes bored into her, searching for combat over his bizarre fixation on nameless women craving the rugged touch of an imaginary kilted woodchopper. But Deli knew the rare storms of his anger weren't really *him*. She tilted her head to listen, because what Trey actually needed was for her to listen.

Deli watched the pink of his hands go white against the cool tile as he squeezed his eyes closed. Then he was there, his arms wrapping under hers and around her body, his fists balled against her lower back as he buried his face in her shoulder.

"I'm sorry," Trey whispered into her hair. Deli's arms hovered at strange angles on either side of him, halfway between hanging and hugging him in return. She could feel the heat of his breath on her neck—the tension in the way he held her—as she brought her arms to rest over his shoulders.

"It's alright, Trey." She stroked his head—his highlighted hair stiff with product instead of the sea salt of their younger years.

Trey began to sway, so gently at first Deli wasn't sure if she was imagining it, until they were dancing together. In the quiet of the moment, of just two people dancing in a little kitchen, their whispered words felt right. It all felt right. And she realized what Trey was trying to say underneath it all. Deli let him hold on to her, rocking back and forth, for a long time before she spoke. He just needed a little push.

"Why did you invite me over tonight?"

The dancing stopped. Trey pulled back and looked down, one clenched fist still pressing against her back, and she watched a desperate sadness flood him.

She'd been too scared to say she was in love with him—too scared to ask about the kiss. Too scared to risk losing him altogether. Maybe she'd been scared her whole life. But there, in his kitchen, on Valentine's Day, while Trey was searching and failing to find the words himself, Deli MacDonald decided she could be brave. She could be brave for him.

"Trey?"

He didn't respond. A muscle in his jaw moved.

"You don't need to worry about anyone else, especially not an imaginary Scottish dreamboat." She counted to three, and jumped. "I only want . . . *you.*"

Deli would never know how much time actually passed in the moments that followed—Trey's mouth opening to speak, his hand coming up to touch her face, then his eyes sliding past her to the flowers on the table and the wine on the counter. Had it been a second or an hour since Deli flinched at the sound of his watch chiming so close to her ear, or the moment he scanned the notification and went still? Time seemed to stop as he stepped away from her in one smooth motion and left her hand hovering in the space where they were just touching.

"Deli . . ." It sounded like something inside him was trying to keep the words from escaping. "We're just . . . we're just *friends.*"

Deli felt the world drop out from under her while Trey watched her standing motionless in his home, waiting for a response that wouldn't come.

Just friends. How could she have gotten it so wrong?

Trey paced in a tiny line in the kitchen, muttering and glancing her way before he turned with a pleading look.

"Please, Deli. You're . . . We're perfect as we are. Why do we have to change anything?"

It didn't make any sense. Why would he *do* all of it—the food and the wine and the flowers and *the kiss*—if he didn't want her? Why errands and families and five-hour phone calls if he didn't love her? Trey reached for her. Deli backed away.

He made a sound like a wounded animal. "Deli, please. *Please.* I can't. I just *can't.*"

Blue petals fell onto the cold metal table. Beads of condensation slid down the wine she wasn't allowed to touch.

"Why did you invite me over tonight, Trey?"

Trey moved like he was going to hold her face, but Deli recoiled, turning her head and squeezing her eyes closed. Desperation strung his voice tight.

"Deli, please—"

"Why?" She didn't recognize her own voice—so thin and rough with the effort of holding back her broken heart.

Trey ran his hands over his face and into his hair, leaning backward against the refrigerator with anguished eyes. Deli spoke methodically, like they were just two people trying to solve a riddle. "It's Valentine's Day. I'm wearing heels."

"I know, I—"

"What about yesterday?" Indignance and shame burned in her cheeks. "That . . . stupid cupcake?"

He buried his face in his hands.

"Something *has* changed between us, though—right, Trey?" She hated herself for begging, but she hated herself more for being on the verge of losing him. "I mean, why did you *kiss* me?"

Trey's stilted breath came in small bursts between periods of silence as he pressed his palms into his eyes. Then he smoothed his hair as he took a deep breath, looked up, and returned her gaze. The frantic confusion in his eyes fled and left behind cool, hard stone. He stood straight, tugging at each sleeve one at a time.

And Deli MacDonald watched the man she was in love with decide something.

"You're right," he said. "Something has changed."

He set his jaw.

"I've fallen in love."

She couldn't breathe. Couldn't think.

"I've fallen in love with Scarlett."

9

Deli

Deli plumbed the fresh shipwreck of her heart, combing through the years, minutes, *seconds* for the moments she'd made into something more. How could she have been so stupid?

Her mouth moved uselessly. She tried again. "Scarlett?"

Deli kept a catalog of tones Trey used with different people. He answered her with the one he used for strangers. "Yes. Scarlett."

The name shone dully, like she'd heard it before. It had been a long time since Deli had asked in depth about anyone Trey was seeing. They were always young, beautiful, promising, and doomed to fail. In the end, it only hurt her to know. So she'd stopped asking, and he'd stopped telling in any real detail, and she never committed them to memory. He'd certainly never mentioned anyone serious. Deli thought Scarlett might have been the name he mentioned one night walking tipsily together after a long dinner. Yes, that had to be it. She'd made a joke about the board game Clue.

Miss Scarlet in the kitchen with the knife.

"So . . . this is all for *her.*" It wasn't a question, and Trey didn't respond. Deli nodded slowly. "Sure," she said. "Of course it is."

She mechanically packed up the scattered contents of her bag.

Trey cleared his throat behind her. "Deli, can we talk more about this later? I feel like there's more to say."

She never wanted to be anywhere near this moment again. "Better to say it now."

"It's just . . ." He glanced at the clock.

Oh, she thought as it hit her . . . *Oh.* She mustered the will to look at him.

"She's . . . ?"

Trey hung his head. It was answer enough.

"Okay. Okay, I'm leaving." Deli wanted to sound dignified, but her voice betrayed her pain and she choked out the last word. Everything was swirling around in her head, too bright and too loud. She moved for the door. She'd been so *sure* as she walked in.

Her feet throbbed as she touched the handle, but a thought broke through the surface and stopped her. "Wait. You didn't actually answer my question. Why did you invite me here tonight?"

His eyes flicked to his watch, looking torn. Deli recognized the battle he was fighting in his mind between pushing her away and trying to care for her. His shoulders sagged and his rigid posture faltered. It plucked the chord in Deli's chest.

"I . . ." He took a breath as he worked his jaw and started again. "I wanted you to tell me that I—that *this*—was good enough."

Her brows drew together. "That *what* was good enough, Trey?"

His eyes abandoned hers. "I needed you to tell me . . . um, that when I asked Scarlett to be my girlfriend tonight, she would say yes. That it would be okay." He met her gaze. "That *I* would be okay."

Trey flinched at the scoff she failed to smother with her hand.

He made a frustrated sound. "Okay, alright. I guess I just needed you, Deli. I needed you to tell me that I . . . made the sauce right."

Deli felt like she was a million miles away—like she was watching herself in a horrible glass dream.

"Deli, please—I know I should have told you about . . ." Trey didn't say her name. "And I probably shouldn't have asked you to come over here. I just didn't want things to change between us. You know?"

She could only imagine what her face looked like. "You didn't want things to *change* between us?"

Trey's ears burned red. "You're my best friend, Deli, and I needed you. I knew you'd come. You always do. And I don't know what I'm doing."

She'd been so close once. *So close.* And then he'd kissed her, and she'd been too spineless to do anything about it. He'd put his heart on the line with that kiss, and she'd said nothing. What had she expected him to do? Wait for her forever?

It wouldn't be fair to punish Trey for her insecurity. Her *mistake.*

So, standing in the threshold of *his* door, Deli finally did the brave thing. "The sauce is awful. Start over. More salt, red pepper flakes, lemon juice. Taste it as you go."

Trey caught the door behind her looking more miserable than she'd ever seen him, but she couldn't feel it the way she usually did.

"Please, Deli," he begged. "*Please.* I can't lose you."

And just like that, Deli saw her life unfold—thirty-five, in the same apartment, at the same job, with the same wanting, aching heart that had never been brave enough to yell into the wind. She saw Trey with a thousand more anonymous girls who never aged—girls he would spend sparkling evenings and glittering summers with—before coming home to lay his head in Deli's lap and call her his best friend.

There would be nothing glittering in Deli MacDonald's world. Just long stretches of darkness, desperate for the thin moments Trey's sun would eclipse her life as she made order out of the chaos of his heart so he could leave again.

"Trey? I'm in love with you."

Trey's face cemented in a mask of surprise. His chest began to rise and fall faster. He took a step toward her—full of purpose and urgent. "Deli, I—"

But his apartment's buzzer struck him silent.

Deli knew she was out of time. She chose her last question and hoped against hope he'd say the right thing. "Do you *notice* me, Trey?"

Trey looked like he might cry. "Deli, I *need* you."

Her eyes flushed with tears as the buzzer went again, and she reached inside and pressed the button to unlock the gate. "Don't forget the lemon."

Neither of them looked away as the door clicked shut between them.

Deli forced her feet to move. She couldn't sob in Trey Evans's hallway. She would make it to the elevator, even if she was carrying all the pieces of her heart in her hands. She rocked back and forth, holding her middle and pressing the call button over and over so she could fall apart.

A girl who looked like she belonged on a red carpet—all legs and golden hair tumbling over smooth skin—stared at Deli in surprise as the elevator doors parted. Deli knew who she was. Who she had to be.

"Sorry!" Scarlett said as she tried to step around the spot where Deli was glued to the floor and shimmy past her into the hallway. "God, I swear, I'm always in the way."

Deli scraped up a smile as they swapped places. She watched Scarlett smooth her crimson dress and square her shoulders, and Deli could imagine them together. She could see Scarlett beside Trey for their glittering mornings, glittering dinners, glittering moments of simple, wonderful things.

The glittering girl stared down the hallway and whispered to herself, "Okay, Scar. It's just another night."

This was the person Trey loved. The elevator dinged, and the doors began to close.

"You look beautiful," Deli said. She hoped it was what Scarlett needed to feel brave.

Scarlett's smile nearly knocked Deli to the ground. "Thank you!" She waved as she disappeared. "So do you!"

The elevator began to move, and Deli began to sob.

10

Deli

Deli sat alone in her car, choking through the sort of crying that would leave a hangover. She hadn't anticipated the way seeing a missed call from her mom would make her chest lurch, and it set another rogue sob free.

Her finger hovered over the call button. For a second, she wanted nothing more in the world than to call back, wait for her mom's voice, and fall to pieces. But right beside the raw, Trey-shaped injury, her Lorraine-shaped scar twinged in an old, warning way.

Deli needed her best friend. Her call log showed Chloe's name beside all the calls she hadn't answered. The texts remained ignored. Deli couldn't stop herself from opening social media to Chloe's page, hoping to find a sign of life and put the quiet fear that something awful was happening to rest.

A new post showed Chloe, shining sheet of caramel hair and hazel eyes, glued to a guy tagged in the photo as *Jared* as they toasted drinks on a sunny pier somewhere. The next photo was of Chloe in a hotel bathrobe, holding up a peace sign while sitting crisscross on a bed covered in red rose petals. In the next, they held hands at an expensive dinner. Chloe was stunning in the satin dress she'd sent Deli a picture of the day before—the day she was too sick to make it to Deli's birthday.

The caption read *"Last-minute getaway in Santa Barbara with my Valentine."*

Deli stared at the screen.

Get up, go inside, and cope, Delilah, she thought after a very long moment. *Stupid girl.*

Deli could still feel the shard of glass as she limped her way through her dingy, pastel apartment complex with her small pile of things cradled in her arms. She stood in the doorway of her home feeling like a voyeur of a life that belonged to someone else—like she was waiting to be invited in. The silence boomed in her aching head. She dropped her bag and grabbed the remote, desperate to drown out the roar of her thoughts, the silent howl of her pain. She flipped through episodes of multiple shows, but each one felt like a different grain of sandpaper on her skin. The box set of *The Highlander* lay abandoned where it had fallen out of the bag by the door.

Mindless. Predictable. Completely void of reality. Exactly what was needed by a heart just blindsided and mangled by things all too real.

Deli popped in a disc. As the piercing voice of *The Highlander*'s theme song welled in her quiet apartment, she felt a single screw in the too-small grip of her heart give way.

She thought of a slanting cottage far away, nestled on a cliffside dotted with knots of purple heather.

The final note echoed, and suddenly Deli's apartment was full of grunting, ripping fabric, and the high, feminine keening of *"Hamish! Oh, Hamish, yes!"*

The man on screen responsible for the squealing had a mane of dirty-blond hair just past his shoulders that met the lone tartan sash adorning his oiled chest. His muscles looked earned, not chiseled out of a suburbanite by a professional nutritionist and trainer. And his jade eyes belied a man who had plenty of source material to pull from while filming his most oily moments on the show.

Deli went to Google.

Hamish was played by a man named Billy S. Burns—born in an actual small town in Scotland. She clicked through photos of him smiling on red carpets, posing on the covers of magazines, and laughing as some reporter or another blushed at his side. She privately admitted—with great embarrassment—that perhaps her mother and grandmother did have a point about the appeal.

The cries of *"Hamish, YES, MY GOD!"* continued as she closed her laptop and pulled her knees to her chest—her carefully chosen heels still cutting painfully into tender, swollen feet. As she was lulled to sleep with a whirl of kilts, clashing swords, and accusations of witchcraft in a world that was nothing like the life she'd just blown to pieces, she tried not to think about how different things would be now that she wouldn't hear from Trey in the morning. She tried not to think about how she had one best friend who had felt the need to lie and ditch her after months of off-and-on tension, and another whom she'd admitted to being in love with while he was in love with someone else. She tried not to think about her favorite flowers in his only vase.

Deli tried not to think about Trey Evans at all.

She dreamed of being fourteen years old on the beach, squinting against the afternoon light as a boy with sandy hair and sandy skin tugged her by the wrist toward the water. They laughed as he looked back with a sly, crinkled grin—his eyes the same color as the last wisp of cloud in the sky.

Deli woke to the sound of her own labored breathing against the booming laughter that poured from her television. A tear cut across the bridge of her nose and sank into the cushion as a ragged breath tore out of her, followed by another, and another, until the sun began to rise.

Then she got up, got ready, and put on her sneakers for work.

11

Deli

On February 15, Deli turned her key in the back door of the flower shop and nearly swung it into a baggy-eyed Paola bending over buckets. One look from her lovely boss—who had made a safe place for her full of magic—and the threadbare patch over Deli's foolish heart began to give.

Paola reached toward her, her dark hair and golden-brown skin so much like a sunflower. "Oh, mija, what happened?"

Deli pushed past her with her head down. "Don't. Please. I can't."

Her throat was hoarse from crying as she balanced on a mound of thorny rose stems left under her station from the day before—when they'd all been too tired to do the big shop clean after the Valentine's Day onslaught. As she dragged her first bucket toward her, pain radiated in her bones. And the pain in her heart?

One time, Deli and Trey were watching one of those ominous nature documentaries, and she turned it off after a small gazelle was separated from its herd—lost and scared in a world too harsh to survive without the other gazelles it had counted on its whole life.

It's too sad, she'd said.

Trey had looked at her, baffled. *It's life, Deli. Some things die.*

In the shop, only Sarah was cleaning as Paola returned to crunching numbers in her office, trying to be casual as she poked her head out to watch Deli now and then with a furrowed brow. Deli was glad it was Sarah beside her. Sarah was gentle and a person of nuance. After years of listening to the will-they-won't-they saga, Sarah still understood that Trey and Deli were a complicated thing. She wouldn't poke or prod or whisper, *I told you so.*

Sarah knew a lost gazelle was too sad a thing to watch.

Deli's coffee from the day before had long since gone cold, but it had a lid to keep the bits of flora out of it, and that was something. As she lined up her many orders going to women whose men had forgotten to send flowers, she sipped and swept an arm across her station—sending stems, wires, and tape to the floor in a waterfall of Valentine's Day fallout. A perfect, bloodred tulip clung to the counter. In an arrangement, it would be a *declaration of love* or a plea of *believe me.* Deli reached for it, unsure of why she'd cast it aside, until she peeled back a petal and found the fine layer of soft blue rot underneath.

Deli made the first order on her stack—two dozen red roses—and checked the card message with a pen poised in her hand.

> Baby,
>
> I can't wait to run away with you.
>
> XOXO,
> Big Papa
>
> P.S. Sorry I'm late, but you're the
> one getting red roses.

Irritation prickled her skin. She pulled the next order on her stack on instinct. The same man was sending a different woman a tiny cluster of three white roses in a plastic vase—one of the cheapest arrangements they offered.

To My Gorgeous Wife,

Thank you for the best 15 years of my life. You make me a better man. I owe everything to you.

Love,
Your Hubby

A sudden and consuming anger swelled within Deli. The white roses he'd chosen were meant to say *I am worthy of you.* If she sent it, *knowing* the inexplicable way her flowers whispered truths, she'd be a part of it. Deli imagined the wife who lay next to Big Papa and watched him breathe—the wife who probably cursed her intuition for the unsureness that ate at her bones.

She filled a new vase and gathered red carnations (*my heart breaks*), snapdragons (*deception*), yellow carnations (*disdain*), gladiolus (*you pierced my heart*), geranium (*stupidity*), hydrangea (*indifference*), yellow lilies (*lies*), and anemones (*forsaken*). As a final touch, she placed the red tulip to rot just out of sight. Altogether, it said *He's in love with someone else.*

Instead of Big Papa's message in the card, Deli wrote, simply, *Believe me.*

By the end of the day, a wife who'd spent fifteen years taking care of a man who sent roses to another woman would open the door to a bouquet Deli had filled with meaning. And that wife would *know.*

Good, Deli thought, wiping her hands on her apron as she watched Carol load it up and drive away. *She deserves to know.*

About an hour before the shop closed, the bells on the front door chimed. Sarah's bubblegum pink voice was cheery as she greeted the backlit figure tapping his foot at the counter. "Good afternoon, sir. How can I help you?"

The man jabbed a finger at Deli's friend. "You really fucked up."

Deli's hands stilled. Sarah didn't do well with conflict, and she was small and young. After many years of working in a flower shop where men were the most common customers and few believed this "women's work" was worth respecting—especially if the woman was someone they thought they could intimidate—Deli knew what was coming next. She heard the smallest quiver in Sarah's response. "I'm sorry, sir. Can yo—"

"Sorry, oh *sorry*!" He cut her off to mock her, mimicking her high voice. "Sorry's not gonna cut it. I don't know what you people did, but one second I'm ordering my wife overpriced, shitty flowers, and the next she's screaming in my face, completely hysterical, holding some ugly thing *you* delivered to her, shrieking, *I know! I know! I know!*"

He slapped his hand against the counter so loudly Sarah jumped. Formal looking papers were balled up in his fist.

"You delivered the wrong thing and *a divorce*, you stupid b—"

Deli "tripped" and threw a vase at the man's feet, fuming at the injustice. It was so incredible to feel something *else* besides the thrumming hurt that she smiled as the sound of shattering glass swallowed Big Papa's slur and sent him leaping back. Sarah turned slowly, with her shoulders next to her ears, to find Deli standing behind her with her empty hands still curled in the shape of the vase-turned-projectile.

Deli glared at the man, unblinking. "Oops."

"I'll . . . I'll get the broom," Sarah said, but Deli stopped her.

"Actually, can you please check on the vendor out back?"

There was no vendor waiting for them, but Sarah got the message and nodded, teary eyed as she walked straight out the back door.

The man glowered. "Are you the manager?"

Deli raised an eyebrow. "Are you *Big Papa*?"

Big Papa's nostrils flared as he took a step back. "Read my lips, *girl*. I want a refund."

Deli MacDonald had been called far worse than *girl* by worse people, and she'd always kept her cool. She'd stood right there while men projected their failings, belittling and cruel, while demanding her services, and it hadn't blipped her radar. But when Big Papa called her friend *bitch*, and called her *girl*, she got an idea. Everything about her had been hurting, until she felt the hot lick of anger, and she thought, for just a second, *Maybe I can burn it all away.*

That was all it took.

"What did your wife think of her flowers? I made them just for her."

"You?" His face mottled crimson. "Do you have any idea what you've done?"

Deli shrugged, completely detached from what was going to happen to her now that she'd made her choices. She was sick of men who saw lost gazelles and licked their teeth.

"My guess is, I saved your wife forty sexless years of her only life spent bleaching the skid marks out of your undies."

Splotchy patches of blue joined Big Papa's bright red face. He looked like a rotting thing. "Come say that to my face, you *fat, ugly bitch*."

Deli didn't hesitate as she stepped through the gate. Glass crunched under her foot.

"DELILAH!" Paola reached them from the back of the shop in record time. "Wait for me in my office."

"Bu—"

"NOW."

Deli stalked through the shop and slammed the office door, muffling the sound of Big Papa's yelling while Paola tried to talk him down, and nearly rattling a photo off the wall. It showed Paola and her daughters, visiting the home Paola had grown up in in Mexico and flanked by her smiling parents, and Deli felt a sick surge of guilt for endangering Paola's business with her impulsive recklessness. By the time Paola returned, the heat of Deli's anger had died and left behind soot-filled spaces for her misery to reclaim. She slid down the wall and wept as Paola closed the door behind her, snagged the tissues off her desk, and slid down the wall, too.

"Deli, honey, *what happened*?"

Deli told her boss everything, and Paola listened as she ran her nails over Deli's back—just the way Deli's mom used to when she was very small and Lorraine hadn't started paying for expensive manicures yet. When Deli had recounted the way Trey made her wonder if he'd ever kissed her, the way Trey had begged her to let them stay the same while he loved someone else, had let her confess her heart and then leave—Paola took a breath and said, "Deli, I think it's time you take a break."

Deli blew her nose into her tenth tissue. "I already took my fifteen minutes."

"That's not what I mean, Deli. You're almost thirty years old, and you're working your life away in a flower shop that's not yours. Where are you gonna go from here?"

"It's a good flower shop. It matters to people."

"Yes, it does, and it will matter to people whether you're here or not. *You* are not supposed to get stuck here."

Deli pretended to really consider taking time off—like it wouldn't be severing her last tether to someone she could count on to be there when they said they would. "I think I want to stay at the shop. I'm already feeling better. See?" She smiled as big as she could.

Paola did not. "I'm afraid it's not your choice."

There it was. The last of her herd, disappearing on the horizon.

Deli blinked in disbelief. "You're . . . you're firing me?"

Paola's eyes were soft, but her voice was unyielding. "You just nearly started a fistfight with a customer. You went rogue on the arrangement."

"It was just a mistake, Paola. *One* mistake—"

Paola's skin was warm as she placed a hand on Deli's arm. "You don't make mistakes. Plus, you said *skid marks*."

"But . . . he made Sarah cry! And you *know* how often we see men cheat like that—*fifteen* years they'd been married, Paola. Didn't she deserve to know? Didn't *he* deserve to—"

"It's not fair, I know." Paola squeezed Deli's arm, and Deli remembered that Paola knew more than most about being married to a man who sent roses to another address.

"I'm sorry," Deli said, unsure which of her apology-worthy antics she was referring to. She'd never been fired before. She didn't mess up like that. She didn't *fail.* "Please, Paola—"

"That marks the second vase of mine you've killed in a week—and one you've tried to steal, if you count the vase in your foot." She held a hand up at Deli's attempt to interject. "You've been distracted, Deli. And more importantly, it doesn't fit you anymore. This job, this place—you need something new."

"I don't want to go." Another thing she'd broken, slipping through her fingers.

Paola pulled Deli into her arms. "Sometimes things are done with us before we're done with them."

Deli surveyed the landscape of her life—so vastly different from what it had been just twenty-four hours before. Paola didn't need her anymore, Trey had Scarlett, her family was . . . her family, and something was really, really wrong with Chloe. She peeled herself from the ground and left the office.

Deli hung up her apron for the last time and wondered how she'd gotten there.

"Delilah? There's more for you out there." Paola's eyes welled. "Take a leap. Go find it."

Deli wasn't sure if the sound she made as she left was a laugh or a cry or somewhere in between, but she knew it was a goodbye to the woman who had once gone far from home in search of something more. Paola had created a place of belonging for so many. Loneliness threatened to knock Deli off her feet as she felt the places she'd always belonged growing thin. She tossed her things in her car and slammed the trunk closed to find Sarah waiting and wringing her hands.

"You're leaving?"

Deli nodded. "Yeah."

Sarah looked her over, worry creasing her creaseless forehead. "Are you feeling okay?"

"No," Deli whispered. "Headache."

"Oh, um . . . what happened?"

"I sabotaged his marriage."

"I didn't mean with that asshat. Thank you for that, by the way."

Deli shrugged her shoulders.

"I meant what happened with . . . with Trey?"

"He, you know . . ." Deli tried to say it simply. "He *didn't.*"

Sarah's jaw moved back and forth and her fingers wrapped around her wrist, twisting the skin. "So . . ." she said. "He's still pretending you're just friends?"

"He wasn't pretending," Deli said as she slid into her car. "I was."

Sarah put one hand on the door and leaned down. "No, Deli. *You* weren't."

Deli stuck the key in the ignition, impatient. She had to leave to do . . . What *was* she going to do now? "I'll see you later, Sarah."

Sarah's words came out in a jumble. "I know it's not my place, and if I'm crossing a line you can hate me forever—but I've been watching you two for a long time, and I think I know why Trey doesn't get it. He's always had you—being there for him. Like, Trey has no idea what his life is like without you in it. He makes you act like a girlfriend, but he doesn't know the difference. He doesn't *know.* The one time you actually started to move on, he freaked out." She raised her eyebrows. "Deli . . . I think he needs to *lose* you."

Trey's voice, so clear it felt cruel, rang in her memory. *I knew you'd come.*

She thought of her family—the way they beckoned for Deli and the way she always responded, despite how little they seemed to notice.

She thought of her best friend—after a lifetime of counting on Deli to meet her at the lunch tree with tissues in her pockets—suddenly *gone.*

Things had gone so bad, so quickly. Whatever she and Trey had been twenty-four hours before was already buried. How was Deli supposed to wake up in the same bed, put on the same clothes, drive the same streets, and live the same day over and over again—like she hadn't just seen something precious die?

Then Deli thought quite suddenly of a torn photograph and an envelope full of money with her name written in her Grandma's loopy script. She thought of her aunt—once a woman Deli loved so much her cheeks would ache from laughing together—far away from the mother and grandmother who always seemed to *need.* And Chloe, who had never had to learn what to do when your best friend vanished.

It wasn't just Trey who believed Deli would come when they called.

An idea was churning in her head.

"Sarah," Deli said, "you're a *genius.*"

"What are you gonna do?"

Deli felt a thrill as the words rolled around in her mouth. Maybe her life *could* be glued back together. Maybe she could fix it.

She grinned.

"Disappear."

12

Mo

Five thousand miles away from Los Angeles, Mo McDonnell stared at her computer.

> From: Delilah MacDonald
> To: Maureen McDonnell
> Subject: See you soon, Aunt Mo! (PLEASE?)
>
> Hi, Aunt Mo. It's me, Deli. I know I haven't seen you in a really long time and this is really out of the blue, but I'm coming to visit. Well, I'm hoping I can come visit. Just for a little while?
>
> I arrive Tuesday, I think. Or Thursday? Crap. I can't remember. I'll forward you the details when I have a second.
>
> Anyway, I hope it's okay. I understand if not, but I don't have a Plan B yet, and I think you might be able to help me.

See you soon?
Deli

P.S. Thanks for the holiday card!

Lachlan knocked softly and peeked his head inside. When it came to Lachlan, things were always easy. Mo cherished ease.

"So, what's the big surprise, Mo?" He lowered himself into a kitchen chair.

She slid him the whisky she'd poured before he arrived, adjusted her reading glasses, and cleared her throat.

"Hi, Aunt Mo . . ."

Lachlan listened calmly until she'd finished.

"So, your niece is coming here."

"In two days, apparently," Mo said.

"For how long?"

"No idea."

"What does she want?"

"No idea."

They leaned back in their chairs and fell into comfortable silence, lost in their own thoughts about the stranger and her inevitable arrival from the land of palm trees. A bright yellow daffodil—the first thing to grow in the garden in twenty years—glowed cheerily in a bud vase between them.

Lachlan spun his glass against the table. "One question."

"Shoot."

"This niece of yours. Is she a respectable lass?"

"No idea."

Lachlan shook his head with a sigh. "She'll be a wild woman, then, like you?"

Mo smiled a wicked smile. "God, I hope so."

"A shame."

"Isn't it?"

Lachlan squeezed Mo's shoulder and raised his whisky in a toast. A sly grin played on his lips. "To the wild women."

"To the wild women."

"Slàinte," they said together.

The sound of their glasses clinking was swallowed up in the crackling fire and heavy rain of the inky Scottish night.

13

Laurie

I'm going to Scotland. I'm not sure when I'll be back or if I'll have reception. Sorry for the late notice, Mom. But I need to do this. I'll see you soon! Love you!

Laurie imagined her sister's gloating face as her only daughter was swallowed into Maureen's viper nest.

That snake bitch!

"John!" she shrieked, beckoning her husband from his hideaway. "Get in here!" Her voice came out so high there was only an infinitesimal chance her aging husband, who'd missed more and more of her summonses lately, actually heard her. She dropped her pitch, seething. "NOW!"

The recliner chair's mechanisms complained as he shifted his weight forward, and she returned to the text from Delilah. She'd been obtuse to think *she* was the only one who'd received the unexpected letter and unsolicited photos, or that there wasn't a worse intention behind them—considering they'd come from the sister who'd stolen the only inheritance their absent father had left behind.

Clearly, Maureen wouldn't be happy until she'd taken everything Laurie had. Even her daughter.

John moseyed down the hallway. "What was that, honey? I couldn't quite hear you."

"It appears our daughter is abandoning us." She shoved her phone out in front of her and watched his eyes moving slowly back and forth. "Did you know about this?"

John pushed his glasses back up his nose to sit squarely in front of his emerald eyes. Occasionally, Laurie would catch a glimpse of those eyes in a certain light and be sent back in time. She would be twenty-two again, swept off her feet by the man of her dreams, who made her laugh until little crumbs of mascara ran down her cheeks with her tears. But now she was in her fifties, the man she'd fallen in love with was losing his hearing and his hair, and she resented the eyes he'd given their daughter—eyes wielded in defiance against Laurie since the day Delilah, currently abandoning her on a plane, was born.

John drew a tedious breath and tutted the way he did when he was *pondering* something. "I didn't know, but I'm having difficulty grasping the crisis here."

"Our *daughter* is being manipulated by my sister." Her lip curled on the last word.

"Her aunt?" John asked casually—like it was an innocent enough thought. Like he wasn't talking about the sister who'd been her best friend once—who'd promised not to *leave*. Like he wasn't talking about the biggest heartbreak of Laurie's life.

"Yes, *darling*." She seized her phone. "*Her aunt*, whom she hasn't seen in twenty years because *her aunt* stole *my* inheritance and disappeared into the woods of a sad, soaking, gray little country full of toothless men in skirts."

Her husband blinked at her. "And you're worried our daughter might . . . *fall* for one of the toothless, soggy men in skirts?"

If there was one thing Laurie *wasn't* worried about, it was that her daughter might actually manage to find an honest-to-god relationship. She'd been pining after that Trey for so long sometimes Laurie would see Delilah's eyes follow the boy around a room and feel nauseous. It was impossible to understand how Delilah could love Trey so entirely but refuse to make the needed changes to appeal to him. Laurie had even purchased Delilah a gym membership for Christmas last year. She didn't think she'd gone once. Watching her daughter approach thirty without a dating history or any real hope for happiness kept Laurie up at night sometimes. She was running out of ways to help.

She took a deep breath, trying to center herself as the hum of hot, sharp worry grew anyway. "No, John. I'm not worried about Delilah and her . . . love life. I'm worried that my sister will fill her head with poison until my daughter hates me."

John rubbed his chin. "That doesn't sound like your sister."

Laurie could feel the rage gathering just under her skin, buzzing like bees in her skull. She glared at her husband, barely contained.

John pulled his glasses off and pinched the bridge of his nose. "Okay. Your sister is a snake. But Deli is not easily swayed."

They were too much alike, John and her daughter. They got along too easily. They never fought. It put Laurie on edge, and it made John an unreliable ally at best and a traitor at worst. She tilted her chin up in challenge, daring him to take Delilah's side.

He sighed. "You're right, dear. Of course you're right."

Laurie smiled in her small victory, clipping her tone. "And are you going to stop her?"

"How?"

She fought to keep from falling into what John called her "Preschool Teacher Voice." "Talk. To. Your. Daughter."

John rubbed his glasses against his shirt, no doubt adding more micro-scratches to the lenses. Laurie bought him a microfiber cloth months ago, but she'd never seen him use it. Even when she gave him everything he needed, the man would still do things the wrong way.

"I can try, darling, but I don't know how much I can do. She has a mind of her own."

"Yes." Laurie waved a dismissive hand and returned to her screen. "You've made quite sure of that."

As John began back down the hallway, Laurie opened her recently called list and stabbed at the name at the top. She fumed as the phone rang.

"Hello?"

Laurie sat up a bit straighter. "Mom?"

"You called my house, Lorraine. Were you expecting someone else?"

Laurie suppressed the urge to scream for the thousandth time that no one called her *Lorraine*. "Delilah has left the country without so much as a note." She heard the rustling of blankets as her mother sat up in bed. "She's run away." Laurie paused. "To *Scotland.*"

Her mother sucked in a breath. *"Maureen?"*

"Yes."

"No!" Rosemary McDonnell was wide awake. "That *bitch*!"

That, Laurie thought as her husband shook his head in retreat—so slightly he probably thought she wouldn't notice—*is more like it.*

14

Lachlan

Lachlan Scott was trying to be optimistic.

He wished he had been born reckless or happy-go-lucky. But he wasn't his brother. He had responsibilities. He had people who relied on him.

He had people to protect.

Lachlan remembered the day he'd met Delilah and taken her photo—the day he watched a fearless girl run into the wind and felt a twist of jealousy, wonder, and something foreign rush his heart. That day felt like an important one—like things might change forever.

But they didn't. Delilah had gone as quickly as she'd come.

He couldn't say it to Mo, but he wasn't excited for an unexpected visitor from Los Angeles coming to their village for an undisclosed amount of time and for an undisclosed reason—probably to touch magic rocks that didn't exist.

"Ready!" Mo called from under the tumbling things in her closet.

"Ready?" he called.

"Be there in forty-five seconds!"

"I'll hold you to it."

Lachlan set a forty-five-second timer on his watch and started toward his old Land Rover. He thought, not for the first time, how very lucky he'd been to find Mo—or for her to find him.

He'd been barely thirteen when the long-lost daughter of Callum McDonnell claimed the family home. When she first offered to pay him to come by and weed the garden, chop firewood, or repaint a door, he'd been a kid thankful for the chance to stash away some money. He didn't realize she was perfectly capable of doing everything on her own, and that he probably slowed the processes down. He didn't realize she was giving him shelter from the storm of his father and home.

Mo was a stalwart friend. And as Lachlan became an adult, he understood what she had given him, despite what she had been denied by her family.

But there were more ways to be family than blood.

So Lachlan made sure the weeds were pulled in the garden that he had never seen bloom, and the heather-sown path was shoveled when it snowed. He polished the old wooden furniture. He made sure the fire stayed warm.

The night Mo read him the email, the small hope he saw in her eyes had sunk his heart with dread. Lachlan knew better than anyone how quickly Delilah would run from their dying town once she'd had a real taste. He knew what it was to have your family abandon you. Mo had been so betrayed by hers that she'd run *to* their crumbling hamlet and spent years trying to get back on her feet, but she'd never fully recovered. Those people had wounded his friend in an irreparable way.

The women in Mo's family had ever only reached out to take. Never to comfort, never to embrace or offer a helping hand.

No one was going to leave Mo behind in pieces. Not again. And whoever Delilah MacDonald might have been twenty years before, she was one of *them* now.

It was Lachlan's turn to be Mo's shelter, even if she couldn't smell the storm gathering.

"Hey," Mo huffed as she heaved herself into the Defender. "What was my time?"

Lachlan looked down. "Forty seconds."

"Damnit!"

Lachlan grinned as he turned the keys. "You're early, Mo. That's a win."

"I said forty-*five* seconds. I hate being wrong. I'm often late, but I'm never wrong."

"That," Lachlan said as he eased the car forward in case there was an unfortunately short sheep beyond the bonnet, "I know. I should get a second watch dedicated to Mo-Time that runs half an hour behind."

"Finally." She rubbed her hands together to warm them. "I always said you were a bright boy. It's nice to see you living up to your potential."

"My father would be elated."

Mo gave him a sideways look, and Lachlan felt the familiar press of being under her observation. Mo might have been a little messy and a little-always late, but she'd never missed a single thing that mattered.

"Speaking of—" she began.

"It's fine."

"Lachlan, I really don't mind."

He was about to tell her *again* that he didn't want her to sacrifice time with her niece to help him with his family obligations, but a plan began to grow. If he was going to protect Mo, he would need to separate them. He would need to get enough time with Delilah to suss her out and, more importantly, scare her off.

"Actually, if you really don't mind, I've got a lot going on, and she's been a little needier lately—"

"Done." Mo nodded.

"Are you sure?"

"I wouldn't offer if I wasn't sure, Lachlan. Now, stop asking and start driving. We've got shopping to do."

"Aye, Captain."

Lachlan turned onto the road to Edinburgh as he turned over his plan in his head. He'd get this woman alone and find the reason for her sudden arrival—be it to dig through the floorboards for a secret inheritance or pry open a long-locked door in Mo's life. Lachlan would find the truth.

And when she proved to be a rotten apple flung from a poisoned tree, he'd make her wish she'd never come to Fearnhall. He'd make her life so intensely unpleasant she'd go running back to where she came from before she could break Mo's heart.

15

Deli

Deli collapsed into her train seat, rubbing her ankles and remembering the days she couldn't gauge her hydration level from her eye bags.

A peal of squealing laughter tugged her attention across the aisle. A boy no older than twenty stood on the platform with a lopsided smile as he pressed his hand to the glass. The young woman opposite Deli giggled as he finished writing something in the dust. The train began to roll, and he jogged alongside the girl's window until he ran out of platform. Right before he was out of sight, Deli saw him mouth the words *I love you*.

Well, she thought, swallowing a lump as she logged on to the train's Wi-Fi, *good for them.*

Two message alerts obscured her phone's wallpaper of her and Trey at a New Year's party a few years before—hair mussed and cheeks aglow with champagne. Her arms were flung over his shoulders and his were wrapped lazily around her hips while they laughed. Chloe had taken it.

The first text was from her mother.

Delilah, I am shocked and disappointed by your choice. I'm worried sick! You know my sister is not a good person. And what will Grandma think? Did you even call her? You need to come home.

For one staggering moment, Deli was gripped with the compulsion to get off at the next stop and turn around—to apologize for her selfishness and accept all the relationships she'd ruined. Her eyes stung as she clicked on the next message from her dad.

Go get 'em, kid.

It was just enough to keep her on the train.

Deli checked her texts, calls, and socials for anything from Chloe, and each sent a new spike of worry through her heart. The unnamed problem felt like constant, low wind in a house that wasn't meant to be empty—whistling through the windows and drafty hallways, calling for someone who should have been home. *So dramatic, Delilah,* she thought, but still. Chloe's absence was never completely silent.

And Trey . . . Deli hadn't spoken to him since she'd told him she loved him and he'd told her he was in love with someone else. She hadn't told him she was leaving, and so far, he hadn't noticed, even though they'd never gone this long without talking. She put her phone screen-down on the tray in front of her and buried her face in her hands, exhausted.

Deli woke with a start only a few stops from hers, on a train much less crowded than it had been when she boarded. The girl across the aisle who had seemed so in love was gone. Lush countryside blurred by as a sunray poured through the window, covering the empty seat with a sheet of golden light. It lit the words the boy had written in the dust—scrawled across the glass in messy, large letters.

I miss you already!

Flashes of her life with Trey came to her in a sudden, uncontrollable supercut—learning her favorite song of the week on guitar, laughing beside her at their high school graduation, holding her hand at her grandfather's funeral—each with their shining moments of intimacy. Then came the horrible scenes from the night at Trey's—whispering apologies into her neck before he turned cold and said Scarlett's name.

Deli reached for her passport and gingerly slipped the photos from between the pages. She wondered if anyone else ever looked at pictures of their childhood selves and felt they were peering in on someone else's memories—on some child they'd never known. She remembered the cottage and shady images of Scotland, but she didn't remember ever being the girl with bloody knees and a fierce cry.

Her Aunt Mo had gone away so long ago Deli couldn't remember why. Her mom and grandma always recoiled and snapped when she asked, leaving her with some invisible welt or another. Now Deli tapped her fingertip lightly against the woman's picture and wondered how much time it took before the people you once cherished became strangers.

Of course, staring at a tiny Aunt Mo didn't *feel* like staring at a stranger, despite the great purge of Aunt Mo photos that came when they'd returned to California without her. But staring at the ocher-eyed man beside her didn't feel like looking at a stranger, either, and that was impossible.

Deli and Aunt Mo had managed to exchange two more emails with bare details—which train to catch and where to get off, arrival date and flight number—but that was all they'd had time for before Deli's phone was in airplane mode. The other passengers getting off at her stop had begun to gather at the train doors. By the time Deli was standing on the platform with all her bags, she'd lost one wheel, run over two feet (belonging to different doomed locals who had tried to assist), and broken what felt like three sweats. She wiped her upper lip and smoothed her flyaways as a man with white hair and kind eyes smiled.

"Do you need a hand with those bags?"

She tossed a glance at the station doors, glowing with the cool winter sunlight. "No, no. I'll be fine, thank you. I think my aunt is here."

He nodded at the wheel clutched in her left hand. "Your aunt must be a strong woman."

Deli swallowed. "I hope so."

She was hoping so many things she couldn't bring herself to say out loud, but if everything went okay, she should be on her way home to people who missed her in no time. Nerves gripped her as she wheeled her way toward the exit.

Deli figured it was the shock of the cold air that stole her breath as she stepped into the Scottish Highlands—not the dark mountains rising on either side of the tracks that instantly made her feel like magic was a thing she could reach out and pluck from the sky, and she was always meant to pluck it. And it definitely, probably, wasn't the honey-eyed man with wind-tossed waves of burnt umber, standing in a fairy-tale land holding a piece of cardboard with *DELILAH* written in deliberate strokes.

He was studying his watch with a furrowed brow and such intensity he startled when Deli said, "Um, that's me."

He whipped his head up, and Deli was struck with a sense of déjà vu so potent it reached into her mouth and stole the words she'd been about to say—like a dirty thief made of time and trickery. His square jaw was peppered with reddish stubble over the cranberry flush in his cheeks. And his *eyes*—like sunlit amber or hazel glass. During her *Twilight* phase, she would have swooned for the color alone.

He blinked down at her, jaw closed tight. Deli pointed at the sign in his hands with one finger and tugged her scarf up with the other hand, hoping to cover the mutinous blush she could feel climbing her skin under his scrutiny.

She cleared her throat and nodded toward the name she couldn't bring herself to claim.

"I think I'm the one you've been waiting for?"

16

Deli

Soft color spread across the stranger's cheeks as the chill nipped at their skin.

He looked down at the sign and back. "Delilah MacDonald?"

The way his accent rolled her name almost made it sound like it wasn't hers. "Yeah, that's me. And you are?"

"I'm your ride."

He reached for the handle of the larger of her two suitcases, but she pulled it back and glanced around the parking lot. "I'm not supposed to get in the car with strangers. Where's my aunt?"

"She's sent me to collect you. She's a busy lady."

Deli looked him up and down with pursed lips. "Fine, but if you kill me, she won't be too busy to kill you back. I'm sure she'll clear her schedule."

"I don't doubt it. Come on, then. Let's get you to the cottage." He turned and walked toward the lot without waiting for her to respond. She hurried after him, dragging her haphazardly packed luggage and shivering as the Scottish air cut through the denim jacket she'd thrown on at the last minute. He glanced over his shoulder and smirked.

"What?" She caught up to him beside a classic Land Rover Defender covered in mud.

He popped open the back and leaned against the truck while he took his time sweeping his gaze from her head to her toes. A casting of goosebumps crawled up her arms. He seemed to be wafting waves of, somehow, dislike. Clouds of breath escaped him as he chuckled, and Deli felt spiritual hackles rise like an angry porcupine at the unearned attitude.

He finally said, "Nice jacket."

"Thanks, it's vintage." It was from Target, but what did he know?

"Bold choice for this climate."

"I run hot." Deli fought to keep her tone civil as she pushed past him and dropped her massive backpack into the cargo space with a grunt, suppressing a full-body shiver. "You never even told me your name."

"Well, Delilah—"

"Deli."

He blinked at her. "What?"

"No one calls me Delilah. I go by Deli." She crossed her arms over her chest and widened her stance in a way she hoped was signaling dominance or something. He must have been six foot two? Three?

Goliath sounded judgy. "Deli?"

"Yes. Deli."

"Huh." He shook his head and muttered something under his breath that sounded a lot like *nonsense.*

"What was that?" she said.

"Nothing."

She snagged her carry-on off the handle of her smaller suitcase and crushed it against her chest before he hoisted the thing into the back like she hadn't had to sit on it to get it to close. Deli knew, in her heart of hearts, that it would be ridiculous for two adults to meet and become instant nemeses. He must have been having a bad day, or she was reading him wrong, or heartbreak had stolen her social graces swiftly away and replaced them with the nuance of a teenager.

"Hey, are you hungry, *Deli*?" he asked. "Strangest thing, I'm suddenly craving cold cuts." The corner of his mouth twitched as he waited for her reaction.

She felt her lips contract like she was trying to keep a marble against her teeth as she fought back the overwhelming urge to say something childish.

"Bravo. Deli, cold cuts. A true master of comedy."

He radiated smugness as he reached for her last bag.

Deli very much failed to rise above and slapped at his hand. "No thanks, Chuckles. I don't need your help."

He shrugged and disappeared around the side of the Land Rover as she planted her feet to hoist. There were two neon tags left on the handles from the flight with the word **HEAVY** and drawings of stick men throwing their backs out.

Deli didn't recognize the sound that came out of her as she barely lifted it a few inches and let it fall. She could hear his glee in the silence that followed. Then he whistled like he was calling a dog.

She tried for another suitcase deposit—hoping whatever adrenaline helped mothers lift cars off their babies could also be channeled by great irritation at a stranger. Her foot slipped in the gravel, and she caught herself funny-bone first against the frame of the filthy bumper.

He whistled again, followed with some clicks and *"Here, girl!"*

"You've got to be kidding me," Deli growled, stalking around to face him. FunnyGuy McReachShelf stood beside the Land Rover with his arms across his chest and one foot propped on the step. He raised an eyebrow and jerked his head toward the open door.

Deli's jaw dropped. "You think I'm gonna *drive* this thing?"

"No." He used the same tone she remembered from preschool. "I value my life. You're in Scotland. This is the passenger's side. Do me the honor of getting in so I can load your portable clothing boutique and we can get on with it?"

Maybe it was jet lag. Maybe it was the look on his face. Maybe it was one too many men in a week standing in front of her saying something repellent. Deli didn't know exactly where her inspiration came from, but in the coming days, she wouldn't be proud of what happened next.

She used a caveman voice. "Ooh! Big boy want heavy! Silly woman! She no lift!"

Deli climbed past him and plopped into the seat, slamming the door and grinning into her scarf, temporarily triumphant. The cab shook as her luggage—which could, admittedly, fill a studio apartment in Manhattan—landed in the back. Then the least pleasant thirtysomething in Scotland slid into the cab next to her and clicked his seat belt into place.

"Well then, *Deli*," he said as he pulled keys out of his pocket. The way he said her name now, like it was an insult to call someone on a playground, made her want to flick him in the eye. "Are you ready?"

Deli leaned forward and yoinked the keys from his hand, dangled them in the air, and stashed them in her fist. "As a general rule, I don't let anyone whose email signature is probably 'Fee fi fo fum' drive me into the woods."

He narrowed his eyes, clearly evaluating whether he could steal the keys back without it escalating into the inspiration for a true crime podcast. He sighed and fell back against his seat to stare at the ceiling.

Deli smiled. "Especially without their name."

He held his hand palm up for the keys. "Lachlan."

"Lachlan what?"

"Lachlan Scott."

They stared at each other for a beat before she started chuckling.

His tone was flat. "Something funny?"

"Lachlan Scott?" she asked.

"Yes?" His lips pressed into a line.

"Lachlan Scott?" she repeated.

"Are you broken?"

"Your name literally means Scotland Land of Lakes."

He blinked slowly, like he was trying to befriend a cat. "And?"

"I'll take cold cuts over America Military Bald Eagle. What? Was William Wallace taken?" He glared at her as she lifted her fist in the air and whisper-shouted, *"Freeeedommmm!"*

Deli relished the irritated look on his face as she dropped the keys into his palm with a satisfying jingle. The engine roared to life while she clicked her seat belt.

"Big words from a girl who named herself after lunch meat." He punched a few buttons on the radio.

She could be an adult again tomorrow. "You started it. Seriously, though, I heard the Highland roads are pretty gnarly, and I'm not so good with heights. So it would be great if you could just go slo—AHHH!"

She was cut off by her own scream as Lachlan pressed his foot to the floor.

17

Lachlan

Lachlan had been sure he'd gotten the train's arrival time wrong. He'd double- and triple-checked, but he was still watching the minutes tick by on his watch, guilt stricken at the thought of leaving Mo's niece stranded somewhere.

That was why he was caught off guard when she spoke to him. Though he couldn't blame distraction for the next bit, when the sight of Delilah MacDonald—with raven hair in a lopsided ponytail and eyes that scattered the light—had stuttered his mind, too.

She was, he noted with distrust, beautiful.

Lachlan was also surprised to find himself holding his breath—waiting for her to remember the elusive, unreal feeling from the scrap of their childhoods. He could recall it like he was still hiding on the other side of a mossy stone wall, listening to angry voices as Delilah disappeared behind the bright red door. By the time he realized he was staring blankly and hadn't spoken to her yet, he was already on the back foot.

Not ideal. He had a plan to execute.

In hindsight, Lachlan *did* wonder if he'd gone a bit too hard with the acidity out of the gate. There was being strategically unpleasant as a means of making Fearnhall as inhospitable as possible, then there was, well, being petulant. But right about the time he thought he might have taken it too far, Deli had gone full Neanderthal and stolen his keys. She might as well have grabbed him by the collar and hauled him so far over the line they were both hurtling down a cliffside of churlish dislike and bickering.

He feared there was no coming back from there.

So Lachlan grinned and took another turn with too much speed, sending Deli's hand flat against the window as she hissed.

"Can you NOT?"

"What?" He feigned innocence. "Drive?"

"Like you have a death wish," Deli said. Her face seemed a bit paler than when she'd gotten in. "Can you not drive like you have a death wish?"

"I'll do my best." He hit the gas.

She tried for the silent treatment, though it neither bothered Lachlan nor lasted very long. The closer they got to Mo's, the closer her face got to the window. He started hearing small sounds of wonder at each new curve in the road's reveal. Lachlan didn't realize he'd slowed way down until a sedan sped past him at a straight stretch of road.

"You . . ." He cleared his throat. "Erm, you alright?"

She shot him a distrustful look, which, he supposed, was earned. "Yeah, I just . . . didn't remember it being so beautiful."

Lachlan bent down a bit to peer over the wheel and scan the horizon for the object of her fascination, but everything was ordinary. "What's so beautiful?"

Deli gave a disbelieving laugh. "Are you kidding? *Everything*."

He watched the blurring scenery flicker in the light of her eyes until he had to look back to the road. He supposed the contrast of the ferns gone rust with frost against the black stone and streaks of green was, in its cold, lonely way, remarkable. He wasn't sure how long it had been since he noticed the magnificence of winter.

"Oh my god, there it is!" Deli pressed a fingertip to the windscreen, leaving a smudge he'd have to wipe clean, as she pointed to

Mo's cottage at the end of her narrow road. Mo's car was still gone. She hadn't returned from helping his mother yet. Deli's voice trailed into a whisper. "It's been so long . . ."

Lachlan quite suddenly felt his heartbeat in his chest as he pulled up alongside the stone path leading to Mo's door—too fast and too hard, for no reason at all.

He turned off the ignition. "When was the last time you were here?"

She turned to smile at him, her first real smile since she'd arrived by his calculation, and he felt the oddest sensation—like a wee tether was buried in his chest, tugging him *toward.*

"About twenty years ago." Deli opened the door with an excited *"Eee!"* and stepped onto the first stone of the path. She was laughing as she turned to look at him.

There they were, in the same places they'd been so many years before. Lachlan hadn't felt like a boy in so long it would be many weeks before he could name the way his heart thudded in his ears and ballooned in his chest as he watched Deli laughing into the wind—like maybe that day *had* been significant after all.

Instead, he felt his blood rush and his world narrow, and Lachlan Scott decided that Deli MacDonald was a bigger problem than he'd prepared for.

He'd expected her to make quick work of Mo's trust, considering how dearly his friend wanted to reconnect with her long-lost niece. He *hadn't* expected it to work well on him. From what he'd heard, neither of the other two wayward McDonnells could be described as charming or warm or open. But as he watched Deli kneel in front of the cottage for the first time in twenty years, Lachlan knew there was a true threat in Mo's life.

Deli's face changed to tender concern as she touched a stem and a few papery, graying buds crumbled off the dead ground cover Lachlan had repeatedly asked Mo to let him replace. She stood as he approached with one of her bags.

"No, no, I'll take it. I'm perfectly capable, thanks."

Lachlan eyed the uneven stones, the missing wheel, and her outstretched hand. "I think it's best if I just carry it—don't want to chip the pave stones—"

Deli rolled her eyes, grabbed the handle, and jerked before Lachlan could let go—wobbling like a Chihuahua losing a battle of tug with a Great Dane. His hand found her waist to steady her on instinct, and Lachlan felt a bolt of lightning crackle through him at the spot. Deli scowled up at him. His brain stuttered.

"Careful," he said in a quiet breath.

She looked uncertain. "I . . ." Deli began, then she closed her eyes, took a beat, and reopened them, entirely clear of the unsureness he'd seen. "I wouldn't have to be careful if you weren't so stubborn."

Sense came back to Lachlan in a rush. "*Me*, stubborn?"

"They're my bags!" She waved her hands in the air at nothing in particular.

"Yes, and you packed, what? Gold bars? Dead bodies?"

"Ugh!"

Lachlan lifted the bag easily and held it behind him as Deli made a grab for the handle. She blinked—once, twice, three times—then turned on her heel and stomped toward the door.

"Aunt Mo? Aunt Mo, it's me!"

Lachlan took his time ferrying the rest of her luggage to the doorstep while she continued to knock, whistling as he went, savoring the small increases in volume and manufactured cheeriness each time Deli called for a woman who wasn't home. He cleared his throat behind her and watched her shoulders go rigid. She turned, lips flat in a line.

He smiled as wide as he could and began to angle past her. "Exsqueeeeze me."

She scoffed. "She's clearly not home. And what makes you think *my aunt* would open the door for you and not me, anyway?"

"I may not be the princess of this particular castle . . ." He held up his fist and opened it to let the cottage keys he'd had on his key chain since he was fourteen jingle as they dangled from his fingertip. "But I *am* the groundskeeper. Now, if you'll excuse me, milady." He gave a small curtsy and reached for the lock as Deli shuffled behind him.

"How *do* you know my Aunt Mo, *Lachlan?*" She said his name like it was an alias.

"We've been pals a long time." Lachlan noted the knob had come a bit loose and made a mental note to come back with his tools as he opened the door. It gave a cheery squeak, and he made a note to fix that, too. "Careful of Beans," he said as he reached in for the light switch.

Deli looked baffled. "Careful of . . . what?"

Mo's no-good, excellent calico cat tried to shoot past him, but Lachlan was ready. He managed to scoop Beans up under the belly and hoist him into the air, his little cat legs still wheeling. Lachlan held the creature up with both hands as he waited for the cat's yowl of protest to fade into a prolonged, incensed note of what he assumed was a string of curse words in Beans's native tongue.

"This is Beans," he said as Beans continued to make a sound like an accordion on its deathbed. "Sir Beans McGee, if we're using titles."

Deli's eyes went wide. She abandoned their mutual hostility and closed in on the cat, who, mutinously, dropped the prisoner of war act and went straight to purring.

Deli scritched his lower jaw with both hands. "Beans, you are a perfect thing."

"He's an escape artist and a liar."

Beans reprised his sad song as Lachlan tucked him like a rugby ball and stepped inside with his back against the door. He swept his feline-free arm toward the place he, too, called home, in a way. "Welcome to McDonnell Cottage."

Deli's breath caught and her step halted. Her eyes dropped to the threshold. She took a long breath before crossing and only looked up when she'd made it a few steps inside.

Lachlan observed carefully. Deli took in the simple living room, handmade table and chairs, and threadbare quilt that hung over the back of the low sofa—a favorite perch of Beans's. Thus far, her delight and dislike had been visible the instant they appeared—but now Lachlan found himself struggling to know what she was thinking. All of a sudden she was . . . cloudy.

"Huh." She ran her fingers across the back of a kitchen chair.

"Huh?" He moved to lock Beans in jail while he finished getting Deli settled—a contested battle of dexterity and will as he tossed the cat toward Mo's mattress and retreated. A fuzzy paw chased his foot from under the door. Lachlan turned and found Deli standing in front of the robin's-egg blue refrigerator, examining the photos, notes, street art, and postcards from Mo's many adventures.

He watched vigilantly as she combed through the snapshots of a life she'd never borne witness to. He knew it wasn't fair that she'd been kept away as a child, but where had she been as an adult? Lachlan chased pity away with facts—no one knew why Deli was here now, and he couldn't imagine it brought anything but bad tidings.

"Who's this?" Deli squinted as she coaxed Mo's lone photo of Beth out from under its magnet. He was across the small space in an instant, plucking the precious thing from her hand and wedging himself between her body and the rest of Mo's memories.

She stared at him with her mouth agape.

"Erm, can I get you a drink?" He opened the cabinet without needing to move.

"Excuse you?" She reached for the photo behind his back. He held it over their heads as Deli stood on tiptoes, aware of how ridiculous he was being.

"Sorry," he mumbled, ashamed but committed to his protective panic maneuver. "It's . . . private."

Deli blinked up at him. "Are you serious? Give it to me."

"I, erm . . ." Lachlan couldn't think of a better explanation than the truth, and the truth wasn't his to share. "No."

For a flash, he thought he saw pain shadow her features, then they settled into stone. "Where is my aunt?"

He chewed the inside of his cheek. Saying Mo was busy with a favor for *him* would probably be the wrong thing to say. "She had an errand."

"An errand," Deli repeated, walking pointedly to the door and tugging in a suitcase. "Right."

Lachlan realized in a jolt he'd abandoned the chore. He hid the photo of Mo and Beth under a postcard from Japan and turned to do the heavy lifting, but a look from Deli glued his feet to the ground.

"I said . . ." She drew her words out slowly. Her tone grew patronizing. Venomous. Lachlan had only ever heard her mother's voice from behind a door, but in his memory, Deli sounded just like her. "I would do it *myself.* Got it?"

There was his first bit of hard proof.

"Fine, struggle all you like." Lachlan crossed the room and began building a fire in Mo's old fireplace, more for her than for Deli, as she'd be home any minute. He prepped kindling and listened to the sounds of exertion coming from the impossible woman hauling in her baggage until her boots appeared beside him. One toe, complete with a hole in the cheap material, tapped.

"Which room is mine?" she demanded.

Lachlan returned to the fire, stoking a small ember. "Neither."

"You know what? I don't appreciate your attitude, and I think you're an ass."

Lachlan raised a brow, eyes glued to his work as smoke began to twist in small tendrils from the pile. "Is that right?"

"Yeah, that's *right.* And you know what else?" She waited. When he didn't react, she shoved his leg with her boot. It didn't do anything—Lachlan had excellent balance—but it was irritating. "My aunt *invited me here*, bucko."

"That," Lachlan said, slowly meeting her eyes, his narrowed to match, "is not exactly true, now . . . is it?"

Fire caught as he rose to his feet, and she tilted her chin up to keep his gaze. Gravel popped outside. Mo honked an exuberant greeting on her horn as she pulled up to the cottage.

A smirk tugged at Deli's lips. "You should probably go. *Family* reunion."

"Nah," he said, low enough that Mo couldn't hear him as she pulled something from the boot and slammed the lid. The thought of leaving Mo unguarded and unaware of how quickly Deli had dropped the sincere act made his stomach drop. "I think I'll stay awhile."

"Delilah!" He could hear the smile in Mo's voice as Deli flinched at her full name.

"Go on, *Delilah*," he said.

She hesitated like she was loath to turn her back, but faced the doorway as Mo appeared, beaming, with matching bathrobes held up in each hand. She looked between Deli and Lachlan, radiating joy.

"Oh, I can already tell." Mo chuckled. "This is gonna be *great!*"

18

Mo

Mo McDonnell knew instantly, the way flowers know to bloom, that a piece of her heart had come home.

"Aunt Mo!" Her niece threw herself into Mo's arms, and Mo hugged her as tightly as she could, bathrobes and all. "I go by Deli now."

"Deli . . ." Mo rolled the name around in her mouth, remembering the little girl who acted as Mo's champion when she herself had declared her own name. *It's Auntie MO now, Grandma! Not Auntie Maureen.* "I *love* it."

"Really?" Deli asked.

Mo saw Lachlan glowering over Deli's head before his attention snapped to the ceiling.

"Deli is an excellent name." Mo kicked the cottage door closed behind her. Beans cried from her bedroom as she draped the bathrobes across the back of the sofa. "Did you get to meet both of my boys?"

"Uhhh," Deli said as Lachlan very pointedly looked elsewhere.

"Lachlan?" He looked guilty. She crossed the open living space to her bedroom and released a furry flash of calico. "And Sir Beans?"

Beans went straight to Deli and rubbed against her combat boots until his fur stood up with electricity. Deli scooped him into her arms.

"Beans and I are already great pals," she said into the top of his head before she kissed him and he nuzzled her face.

Mo couldn't smile any wider. "I'm afraid Beans has stolen your charisma crown, Lachlan."

Lachlan looked at her like he'd been called on in class from a dead sleep. Deli eyed him over Beans's eyebrow whiskers and mumbled, "Just barely."

Huh, Mo thought. "Did Lachlan give you the tour?"

"No, he must have forgotten that part," Deli said, a little too sweetly.

He grumbled and dropped to a knee to examine the fire. "Hadn't gotten around to it."

Mo pushed open the door to the second bedroom, a little thing with a simple bed, dresser, and nightstand—adorned with a vase of daffodils. "This is your room!"

"Wow, *mine?*" Deli put too much emphasis on the last word, and Lachlan muttered something under his breath.

She couldn't believe Deli was there. "All yours. As long as you'd like."

Lachlan dropped the fire poker with a clatter.

She showed Deli the shared bathroom and her room, then brought her back to the common space that was half kitchen, half living room while Lachlan sipped a glass of water broodily near the sink.

"And now, the best part . . ." Mo swung open the door to the back garden.

"Wow." Deli gasped as Mo followed her out. Her face transformed with wonder as she beheld the true, untapped beauty of the Scottish Highlands, and Mo *saw* it—that spark. Deli was still Deli.

"I know, right?" Mo took in the scene through Deli's eyes, like she had when she first arrived in her thirtieth year.

Standing in the garden, they were dwarfed by soaring slopes disappearing into the dove gray clouds. Snowcaps faded into streaks of iron, charcoal, and sage as silver threads of crystal water braided together, running down the mountainside into babbling creeks that cut deep lines through the tall grasses. Still pools of cool water mirrored the peaks and sky. A handful of sheep dotted the mountain face, and gulls called from somewhere they couldn't see. The air smelled of sea salt and wet earth.

Mo never got sick of it all. "Bit of a trek to get here, but you can't beat the view."

"You said it." Deli laughed and twirled in a circle. Behind her, Mrs. Peevis emerged from her shelter with a polite moo, and Deli shrieked, "Is that a Highland cow?"

"Meet Mrs. Peevis, a.k.a. my pet Peeve."

Deli stared at her. "That . . . is *so effing good*, dude."

Mo nodded sagely. "Peevie loves making friends. Just watch the horns."

Lachlan stepped beside Mo as Deli jogged toward Mrs. Peevis. She pivoted her attention. "What's up with you?"

"What? Nothing!"

"Mhmm."

He crossed his arms over his chest, an inch from pouty. They watched Deli bend at the waist to be eye to eye with the cow, her tone bright but too far away to hear words.

"So . . . did she tell you why she's come to Scotland?"

Mo shrugged. "I didn't ask."

"Seems like an important thing to know."

A raindrop fell on Mo's shoe. "It will come out when she's ready."

"Of course." Lachlan was failing to sound casual. "I just hope she's not into something dangerous."

Deli plucked a dandelion and tucked it into the cow's fur. Mo nodded toward her. "Observe, the evil mastermind at work."

Lachlan stewed quietly for a minute more. Mo made a mental note to put out her quilt on Deli's bed before night. Mo's Gran had made it for her little boy, Callum, who had grown up and kept it safe for two little girls named Lorraine and Maureen to wrap up in against the cold.

It was soft and stained from a long history of being right in the middle of real-life moments, but it was still sturdy. It was still warm.

For the first time, Mo McDonnell could wrap herself around her niece and keep her warm and safe. She didn't know why Deli had come, but she didn't care. She didn't care if Deli left her stained or worn down.

Mo wouldn't waste her second chance.

Lachlan cleared his throat. "How did it go today?"

"Pretty good." Mo spoke evenly. "She's joined the puzzle club."

"Puzzle club?"

"Apparently puzzling is *the* activity, and the club is exclusive."

Lachlan's tone went dark. "Good for her."

"Lachlan—"

"Did she ask after me?"

Mo hesitated, wishing the truth wouldn't sting. "She asked after William."

"Of course she did."

"It's okay, Lachlan. It's okay to feel—"

He sniffed hard and squared his shoulders. "I'm fine."

"You don't have to be fi—"

"Mo, I'm fine. Just like always. Please." His eyes softened with his plea. "Leave it be."

They were tracing the same well-worn circles. Lachlan picked at a callus on his palm. Another raindrop landed on Mo's shoulder as he made a bored clicking sound with his tongue.

"Seriously, you've got a weird energy about you today, Lachlan."

"It's going to rain," he announced, and practically did an about-face to disappear into the cottage. She heard the squeaky gate on the fireplace open.

"Aunt Mo!" Deli had a flower tucked behind her ear and many more crowning Peeve. "Your life rules!"

Mo grinned as Deli started back toward her, amazed at how much better her life had become in one day. She heard Lachlan turn on the kitchen sink. "It's got its perks!"

"Seriously," Deli said as she neared the cottage. She stopped about ten feet away and knelt to cradle a daffodil bloom. Deli smiled up at Mo, sunnier than the flower. "Daffodils."

"Funniest thing, I planted an entire flower garden when I moved in, but everything—and I do mean *everything*—I planted died. Didn't matter when, or which, or what season. I tried for years before I gave up. Then, last week, boom. A daffodil." Mo gestured toward the many new patches of yellow. "Now they're growing like weeds!"

"New beginnings," Deli said, running a thumb along a petal.

"What?"

She stood, wiping her palms on her jeans. "Daffodils say *new beginnings.*"

Flowers know to bloom, Mo thought.

"For real, though," Deli said, turning again to take in the scene—so different from the dusty blues and orange haze of Los Angeles. "I can't believe this looks exactly how they make it seem on *The Highlander*!"

A glass shattered in her sink, followed by a curse. The sky opened up and doused the two women in a sudden torrent.

By the time they'd run inside, both giggling as Deli shrugged out of her drenched denim jacket and holey boots (both things Mo internally vowed to improve), Lachlan was emerging from the bathroom, smoothing a plaster around his finger.

Mo stole his hand as he tried to cover it with the other. "Lachlan! What happened?"

"I was just being careless. I broke your glass, Mo. I'll replace it."

"Nonsense," she said, patting his uninjured palm. "The glass deserved it. It tried to pick a fight with my favorite mug just this morning."

Lachlan didn't smile. It sent a stabbing feeling through Mo's heart.

"Are . . . um, are you sure you're okay, Lachlan?" Deli asked, her voice suddenly small.

Lachlan's head jerked up, eyes trained on Deli like a deer in headlights. "Yes."

A tense silence bloomed. Mo clapped her hands and snatched the bathrobes off the sofa. "Deli, tell me you like to swim?"

Deli and Mo slipped into their rooms to change. When they emerged, Lachlan was gone.

"Guess he had somewhere to be." Mo shrugged, slipping her feet into grippy shoes. "Just like us."

"Yeah." Deli touched her denim jacket—no longer in a ball, but hanging on the back of the cushy chair, drying in front of the fire. "I guess so. Wait, where are *we* going?"

Mo grinned. "Where the wild women go."

19

Deli

Aunt Mo cupped her hands around her mouth and called over the crash of a small wave, "It's good for you!"

"That *cannot* be true!"

Deli's voice was swallowed up by the sea. She clutched her robe around her body, shivering in a bathing suit on a rocky Scottish beach in February. It had only taken them a harrowing climb down the rickety staircase protruding from the sheer face of the cottage's cliffside to get there. Beside her, Aunt Mo's robe and swimsuit were folded neatly on a fallen tree that called the crescent sliver of coastline home.

Deli wondered for the first time if the whole Scotland thing had been, perhaps, too impulsive. Maybe her mom had a point, and she should have stayed instead of drowning in the frigid water on day one. Maybe she should have stayed with Trey.

Trey.

She set her jaw against the cold. Back home she'd have to sew a life together out of the scraps of the one she'd ruined. She was here to get enough distance so she could see the whole picture—find a way to fix all the things that went wrong. This was the only place Deli could think of to go that wasn't a part of the massive knot she needed to untangle. She could figure out how to repair whatever had happened with Chloe. And

Trey . . . She couldn't just *stop* loving him after so many years because of one bad night and one wrong girlfriend. Love didn't quit that easy. And neither did she.

And maybe, she thought, *they'll miss me.*

Deli's aunt was a pale circle topped with an orange knit cap bobbing and beckoning in the water, and Deli hugged her matching cap to her chest with dread. "Wild swimming," as Aunt Mo had explained, was a tradition for all new arrivals in Scotland to get in touch with the land.

Though you're welcome to keep the suit on, she'd said. *Leave the full monty for the pros.* Then she'd left Deli shivering speechlessly on the shore as she stepped out of her suit and splashed into the sea.

Deli knew what her mother and grandma thought about Aunt Mo's general being, but she remembered feeling like her aunt was her favorite person in the room before she'd gone away. Plus, Aunt Mo had excellent taste in pet names, which almost made up for her taste in friends. Deli tugged her cap over her hair.

This is a fine way to die, she thought as she waded into the icy water toward the woman she hoped was kindred. By the time she was closing in, she was numb from the neck down.

Aunt Mo swam toward her. "Glad to see you've got it in ya!"

"Got what in me?" Deli managed through her trembling jaw.

Aunt Mo winked. "What it takes." Maybe Deli's mom was right, and the aunt she remembered as a little kooky was truly one french fry short of a Happy Meal. Aunt Mo spun in a circle, grinning. "You get used to it. It's good for circulation."

Deli tried to breathe through the cold. "Is losing feeling in your nipples good for circulation too? Cuz that happened three minutes ago."

Aunt Mo laughed. "No, but it does wonders for your character."

Deli forced a smile. "Oh, good. More character development."

Aunt Mo's eyes narrowed so slightly Deli thought she might have missed it, flicking across points in Deli's face. She suddenly remembered how it felt when she was little and Aunt Mo was the only adult in the room who truly *noticed* her.

She wasn't sure she liked being noticed anymore.

"Is everything alright, Deli?" There was such an unexpected sincereness in Aunt Mo's question Deli sucked in salt water and began to cough. Aunt Mo frowned. "I think this was enough for your first dip. You've gotta take it in doses. Head on in and I'll be right behind you. Take this for me?"

She handed Deli her hat and dipped completely under the water.

Deli swam in and scrambled through the rocky sand for her robe. She was trying to squeeze every drop of salt water from her hair when Aunt Mo called from behind her, "Toss me that towel?"

Aunt Mo emerged from the ocean completely nude, like Aphrodite being born from a clamshell.

When Deli's mother was sunbathing, it was an act of striving—displaying her triumph over her body's pursuit of softness, and there was always a sharp undercurrent of comparison. Like whenever Lorraine's body was on display, Deli was being stripped down, too.

Aunt Mo, on the other hand, might not have even known she was naked. Her body was rippling and relaxed, soft and gentle—moving like she was still playing in the waves. There was no comparison or competition, only ease and joy. There was just . . . *being*.

Something in Deli's head whispered, *Run*.

"Is there something in my teeth?" Aunt Mo smiled and tied her dripping hair up into a knot on her head.

"Sorry!" Deli squeezed her eyes shut and tossed the towel. "Here! Sorry!"

"Oh, please, it's only a body. We've all got one, and they all change."

If someone had asked Deli to choose the person least likely to be her grandmother's daughter, she would have chosen this pink-nosed, tangle-haired, barefoot woman who hadn't asked Deli a single question about her sudden arrival at the edge of the world.

The climb back up the cliffside was a smidge less harrowing since the rain had stopped. At the top, Aunt Mo suddenly took Deli's hand. She had the same freckle above her right eye that Deli did.

"I'm so glad you're here, Deli. I am *so* glad you're here."

Deli's smile turned to cardboard on her face. Aunt Mo had said it so casually. Like it wasn't an intimate moment. Like it was an everyday sort of thing to do.

Deli fumbled for words. "I, um. Can I have a minute?"

"I'll go start a bath for you. One must dethaw post-dipping."

Deli watched her aunt walk happily back toward her cottage, pausing only to marvel as a gull flew overhead. Despite the cold making a play for her bones, Deli took a deep breath and faced the sea.

She thought she might have come out here before, when she was a kid. In fact, she thought she might have almost fallen. She took a big step back.

Deli didn't know how long she stood there listening to the water rush in and out of the rocks below, stirring up fine sand that settled between each push and pull of the tide—counting the number of days it had been since she'd spoken to Chloe. She sifted through what she knew about her connection with Trey—the kiss, the desperate way he looked at her moments before his new girlfriend would take Deli's place.

She stared at the hands she used to pull a feeling from the air, translate it into flowers, and send it off as a clear message to someone needing an apology, an answer, a reminder of their worthiness to be loved.

Deli didn't know if she was making a huge mistake or if she'd find her answers. She didn't know how long it would take.

But as she started back for the little cottage completely empty of the people she'd chosen to build a life beside, Deli *did* know, for the sake of love, she had to try.

20

Mo

"Peevie is fed!" Deli hopped on one foot just outside the back door, wrestling a wellie with one hand. In the other, she clutched a tall stem covered in what looked like maroon feathers. "Can you believe this?"

"Another one?" Mo asked. It was the third type of flower that had popped up in the garden that had previously been a graveyard since Deli's arrival days before. "Is that Amaranthus?"

Deli raised an eyebrow and blew a strand of dark hair out of her eyes. "Impressive flower knowledge, Aunt Mo."

"Comes with the job." Mo gestured to the event coordinating documents she needed for the wedding she was working that weekend spread across the kitchen table.

"Amaranthus is good for good friends. It's a silly, everlasting thing, you know?" Deli exhaled as she plopped onto the chair beside Mo. Somehow Beans was already purring in her lap. He materialized wherever Deli sat down so quickly Mo had begun to wonder if he'd learned to teleport.

"Huh, what about the others?" Mo gestured toward the garden.

"The new little purple ones I think are a type of primrose, and there are marigolds of some sort. They're both . . ." Deli's eyes went far away for a second—a habit Mo had clocked more than once. "They aren't happy flowers. They say *neglected merit, childhood,* and *pain. Grief.*"

Everlasting friendship, silliness, neglect, childhood, and grief.

"Well, this little cottage has seen a lot of life." Mo patted the table fondly. "Perhaps it wants to tell its story."

The look on Deli's face—so quick Mo almost missed it—broke Mo's heart.

She watched as Deli whispered things to Beans. He stood on her lap as tall as his legs went to boop her head with a silly kitty grin. Mo noticed the round orange flower tucked into Deli's pocket and was struck with inspiration.

"Wait, I have something I think you'd love, Deli." Mo headed for her bookshelf and found the one she was searching for. Its binding had started to fray from time.

Deli brightened as she read the cover. "*A Guide to Flowers and Language*?"

"I picked it up at a flea market in Paris years and years ago. Never really looked through it. Maybe it was always meant for you."

Deli flipped through the pages and stopped on an intricate drawing of a Scottish marigold. *"Grief, despair, pain,"* she muttered, nodding as her fingertip ran along the text. Then her eyebrows knit together and her hand stopped moving. "Huh."

"Huh?" Mo asked.

"It says they also stand for *grace, healing,* and . . ." She hesitated.

"And?"

Deli tried valiantly, but Mo heard the sadness choking her up. *"Constructive loss."*

"Constructive loss," Mo echoed.

Sir Beans's purr and the quiet crackle of a dying fire filled the space left by their silence. Mo returned to her planning, committed to her decision to let Deli come out with her truth on her own, despite the agony it was causing the meddling auntie inside her. In the week since Deli's arrival, they'd caught up about some things—almost all of them pertaining to Mo's life. She'd learned there were many topics that she couldn't ask about if she didn't want Deli to shut down and withdraw, retreating to her bedroom and claiming jet lag. Mo had a small list scribbled on a paper in her nightstand.

Don't ask about: family, work, friends, love life.

She also had a list of safe topics.

Totally okay: religion, politics, and different combinations of carbs and cheese.

"Aunt Mo?"

At the sight of the tears building in Deli's eyes, Mo had to mentally tackle the part of her that wanted to leap up and gather Deli into her arms. She tried to look unshaken as she set her pen down and pushed her glasses on top of her head. "What's up, buddy?"

Deli's voice was small as she began to cry. "Do you know that show *The Highlander*?"

Over the next three hours, Deli told Mo about the life she'd left. She told her of Chloe (Mo was unimpressed), and of Trey (Mo was *deeply* unimpressed), and of the many years Deli had spent as his partner (though Deli didn't describe it that way) before the night he'd kissed her. Then she explained what had happened just a week before, on Valentine's Day.

"You'd just emailed me. And that stupid show was on cuz my mom—never mind. I just thought if I could kind of . . . I don't know, go somewhere so far away Trey couldn't show up when I don't answer his calls, maybe he'd . . ." Deli dropped her head into her hands. Mo simply waited until her niece took a big breath. "I'm just so tired, Aunt Mo. I need some space, so I can see it all from above. Then I'll figure out the things I missed, and I can fix it."

Mo wondered if Deli knew what she'd really come to Fearnhall for, or if Mo could help her find it.

"I see," she said, passing Deli her third cup of tea and second packet of tissues. "And if Trey were to call, professing his love and asking for you to come home, would you?"

Deli picked at her nail polish. "Yes."

Mo sat and blew out a long, slow breath. It was a difficult thing, knowing how to share wisdom earned over time with someone too young to have learned it in a way that didn't hurt. She suspected sharing her perspective on Trey, Chloe, and the root of all of it—*their* family—would only send Deli running back to them faster and sooner. There was a time in her life she would have done the same.

But that didn't mean Mo couldn't give time a helping hand.

There was magic waiting for McDonnell women who came back, and it had called Deli here, just like it had called Mo. There was joy to be found. There was freedom. She thought of Lachlan—another kid she'd loved so long and dearly wanted freedom for, too.

Thus far, Mo had kept the well-meaning residents of Fearnhall at bay, despite their loving and insistent attempts to swing by and meet Mo's long-lost niece. But now Mo was doing some plotting, and she'd need coconspirators. She tapped her fingers against the table and quirked an eyebrow. "Do you know what we need?"

Deli sniffled. "What?"

Mo grinned, grabbed her phone, and held it to her ear as it rang.

Lachlan answered, accompanied by the familiar sound of lively conversation and clinking glass. "Alright, Mo?"

"Hey, come pick us up. Just give Douggie the keys. He'll babysit."

Lachlan made a groaning sound as she clicked end.

"Deli MacDonald, we need a night out. And I know the perfect place."

She sent Deli to her room to do a quick change out of her muddy leggings and tearstained top while Mo listened for the sound of Lachlan's tires outside over the "getting ready music" Deli played from her phone. It took him much longer to walk to the cottage from his truck after he'd parked than it usually did. He paused in the doorway, glancing through the living room like a vampire waiting on an invitation, until Beans made a play for the space between his boots.

"You're letting Beans out and cold air in, Lachlan."

He made a show of checking his watch. Beans yelled in the crook of his arm. "I need to get back, Mo. Can we hurry?"

"Should I put on makeup for wherever we're going?" Deli shouted from the bathroom.

"No," Lachlan said as Mo said, "Sure!"

He pressed his lips into a line and shifted from foot to foot until Beans sank a prison-break bite into his hand.

"Jesus!" Lachlan dropped the cat as he examined his unbroken skin. "Evil legume!"

Mo grinned. "Funny, he says the same thing about you."

Deli emerged from her room in a fresh sweater and jeans, squeezing her arms into the same sad denim jacket she'd been hang drying in the humidity since the first day it got wet.

"Isn't that still a bit damp?" Mo asked.

"Oh, it's no big deal." Deli's smile didn't reach her eyes. "It's the only one I brought."

"Lachlan." Mo turned to him. "Can you grab the jacket from the closet behind you? The old leather one."

He frowned. "The leather one?"

Mo answered him with a very rare glint. "Absolutely."

"It's fine, really!" Deli interjected, her eyes moving between them. "I don't need it!"

"Lachlan," Mo said flatly. "The jacket. Please."

Lachlan pulled it from the closet it had hung in for many, many years.

Deli's eyes narrowed as she snatched it from his hand. "Thanks."

He grunted in response as Deli slipped into it like it was always meant to be hers. Mo wondered if, perhaps, it was.

Lachlan was glaring at her niece like she'd torn up his favorite baseball card. "Oi," Mo called, snapping him out of it. "Is *it* happening?"

Lachlan sighed but nodded.

"Well then, what are we waiting for?" She jostled Deli toward the door. "We've got a show to catch!"

21

Lachlan

Lachlan watched Deli being jostled in the back seat of his Defender as she refreshed her phone in the dark. He made a mental tick on his running list of successful irritations accomplished thus far.

"Is there service anywhere around here?" she asked through the turbulence.

"At the pub!" Mo hadn't dropped the impish look in her eye since he picked them up. When he'd lost the round of poker that had given Mo the unilateral right to call on him as designated driver for a year's time, he hadn't anticipated Deli. He didn't want her in his truck, much less his home.

They drove down the narrow street, flanked on one side by the dark sea. At the very end, across from a dock anchoring small fishing boats rising and falling with the waves, stood The Wallflower's Crown. Warm light flickered through amber windows like the moonlight catching on the crests of dark water as Lachlan parked. He'd had another row with William a few months before about solutions for the rapidly approaching crisis point between upkeep and income. He tried not to fixate on the energy bill.

Deli climbed out and stood with her toes pressed against the small retaining wall, as close to the water as she could be. She stared out and up, taking in the moon and the pricks of starlight dappling the dark bay with their reflection—safe with mountains standing guard on either side. Her breath escaped in a small cloud as she exhaled a simple, "Oh."

He didn't realize how close he'd gotten to her until he whispered, "What are you looking at?"

She shook her head. "There are so many stars."

Deli's eyes glimmered with silver light. The air smelled like salt and rain.

Lachlan turned on his heel and stomped toward his father's—well, *his*—pub.

Mo and Deli were met with an eruption of cheers. Lachlan slipped into his place behind the bar and watched, only half listening to the patrons he poured for.

"There ye are, lass!" Douglas wrapped Mo in a hug, his potbelly complementing his shiny bald head. "Ye promise us the beauty and wiles of another mysterious McDonnell woman, and make us wait for days?

"And *you.*" Douglas placed his hands on Deli's shoulders. He had to look up to meet her eyeline. Lachlan strained to hear the conversation over the din of the pub. "Indeed, a classic Hollywood beauty. I can't believe they let you leave!"

Deli beamed as she gripped his forearms in a sort of comrade's embrace. Lachlan's jaw tightened. "They practically kicked me out! Too pale, no tolerance for heat, not for the big screen."

"Shite, all of it. I'm Douglas."

"A man of taste. I like that about you, Douglas."

Douglas smirked at Mo. "She can stay."

"She's welcome as long as she likes," Mo said. Deli's gaze flicked up to Mo's, and Lachlan's heart pounded with urgency.

Blair tugged on Douglas from behind. "Give her some room or you'll scare her off, Douglas."

He stared up at Blair's six feet of height and waterfall of dark copper hair.

"No, *Blaaaair*," Douglas said, dragging out her name. "My new bestie and I are bonding. She'll be stayin' forever, I'll have you know."

Lachlan pulled the wrong tap, dumped the glass, and started over.

"Come off it, Douglas," Blair said, "or she'll be gone by the morning."

Deli grinned. "Douglas doesn't scare me."

"Wait till you see him dance. It gives my children nightmares," Blair said.

"Bollocks! The wee ones love Uncle Douggie!"

"You're the monster under their bed, Douglas."

Douglas's smile was wide enough to show the gap of his missing tooth. "Jealousy looks good on you, Red!"

"In your dreams, Douggie!"

Blair wrapped an arm around Deli and guided her to a table with many of the same people Lachlan had known his whole life—who'd patronized The Wallflower, as it was known by most, when he was small enough to weave between the table legs and pluck lost coins from the cracks in the wooden floor. Graham leaned close to ask Deli a question as he gestured toward the bar, his long salt-and-pepper dreadlocks sweeping her knee. He straightened and called, "Oi, Lachlan! A gin and tonic with lime!"

Deli followed Graham's gaze and caught Lachlan's eye.

Graham's wide smile changed to a frown. "Did you hear me, brother?"

Lachlan blinked hard and began to move. "Gin and tonic, you got it."

When he turned back to the bar top with gin in his hand, Mo was sitting on the barstool across from him. "So. What do you think?"

Lachlan shrugged. "It's a good turnout."

She rolled her eyes. "You know that's not what I mean."

He set the gin and tonic on the bar and reached for a pint glass. "I don't presume to ever know what you mean, Mo."

She caught the pint of Guinness he slid across the surface he polished every morning, just like his father used to. "What do you think of Deli?"

There was very little Lachlan had ever successfully hidden from Mo, even as an adult, but he was trying. He focused on pouring another pint no one asked for. "I barely know her."

"Lachlan Scott, look at me." Mo's tactical mum voice worked. He slowly met her eyes and sighed.

"She's fine, Mo."

"Fine?"

He clung to his indifference. "Fine."

She frowned. "Lachlan, 'fine' is how you describe Douglas's cooking."

"His cooking is fine."

"You were on the toilet for a week."

"And I'm stronger for it."

Mo narrowed her eyes. "What aren't you telling me?" A peal of laughter from Deli's table reached them, and he looked toward her, then back to Mo. She softened her tone, leaned closer, and asked again, "What aren't you telling me?"

Mo's Guinness sloshed over the edge of her glass as Douglas collided into her from behind, wrapping his hands around her middle and plopping his head on her shoulder. "Look alive, Mo! It's time!"

He grabbed Deli's gin and tonic and twirled away. Graham dimmed the overhead lights as Hannah hung the holiday bulbs in a square over the fireplace to make the stage. Blair and her partner, Andrew, moved chairs and tables into place as Douglas held up a plastic Tesco's bag and shouted "Prepare thyselves, fools!" before disappearing into the bathroom.

Lachlan hadn't really believed Talent Show Night would stick when he'd agreed to it—considering the same motley crew of folks who'd known each other their entire lives would be performing each month.

But he'd underestimated their boredom, and now he'd seen Mo juggle and Douglas do . . . whatever Douglas did about twelve times.

Mo's eyes went wide with delight. "Douglas is first?"

Lachlan reached over the bar and plucked a clipboard off a nail on the wall. "Aye, *and* he'll be performing a double feature tonight."

Deli was helping Graham move an overstuffed armchair. The few dark wisps that had escaped her bun clung to her face, arcing over her cheekbone like water running downhill.

"If Deli's still around after a double helping of Douglas, nothing will chase her off." Mo watched Deli, too—hope blooming in a barren garden, unaware of a coming frost.

His friend, so kind to so many—so hungry for the family she'd never had—didn't know the killing cold was coming. That she was already here.

As Mo slid off the barstool and headed toward the lumpy sofa, shouting, "Dibs on the couch!"—Lachlan reminded himself why he was doing what he was doing.

Mo had sacrificed her entire world once to put an ocean between her and that family, and Deli was here—still without a reason—building a bloody bridge. And once she did, she would be like everyone else. She would leave. And she would take the very best of Mo with her, stuffed into the pockets of a well-loved leather jacket.

Lachlan had to make sure Deli left before she ever got close.

He had to protect his family.

22

Deli

There were some moments in life, Deli had found, where things were so unlike what you thought they would be that you had to just . . . lean in.

Recounting to Aunt Mo the events leading up to her arrival had been exhausting and quietly shameful. She'd spent the past several days in a sort of half-there daze between the jet lag and the waves of emotion from the compounding trainwrecks of her life.

Nothing felt stable, not even Chloe, which was a new and terrifying feeling. Deli couldn't make her aunt understand the connection, history, and dynamic between her and Trey or her and Chloe—and she knew they both sounded a bit one-dimensional. She didn't have the energy to go into all the tiny details, even though her gaps in information left gaps in empathy for her two closest people. But she was so *tired* of trying to explain herself and her choices under someone's microscope.

Luckily, Aunt Mo didn't ask for reasons or explanations to pick apart like Deli's mom or grandmother would have. She didn't cast judgment. She just . . . listened.

When Aunt Mo said they needed a night out, Deli hadn't pictured a talent show with strangers in a pub owned by a man who might have despised her. She certainly could have never pictured Douglas.

Douglas in his *mini* kilt, doing what he was doing in front of her.

The sounds of a didgeridoo pealed through the small pub, accompanied by ritualistic chanting and synth waves Deli suspected Douglas had composed himself. The man's thin arms were waving bonelessly next to his cue-ball head. He leaped from foot to foot, holding the other aloft like a flamingo and cooing. "Interpretive Dance," he'd called it. What he was interpreting, Deli had no idea. Her best guess was "the exquisite agony of being trapped in a human body." And he was nailing it.

"This is why my kids can't come to Talent Show Night anymore," Blair whispered beside her. They giggled.

In the few minutes she'd had at the pub, Deli had decided she liked nearly everyone there. Apart from the bartender, who seemed to be going after the world record for glowering.

"I feel like I should look away, but I can't," Deli whispered as Douglas writhed. "It's . . . beautiful, but haunting."

"That's Douglas's sweet spot. Ow!"

Hannah, the quiet older woman with silver braids past her chest, mimed a *shhh* with the finger she'd used to poke Blair in the side, then gestured back toward Douglas, who was scooting across the floor like a dog with frustrated anal glands.

Douglas's display came to a close as the yowling instruments receded into the sound of pure synth. He perched on the arm of Graham's chair, chittering like a squirrel, while Graham, the only man in The Wallflower's Crown wearing a full-size kilt, smiled up at him, enthralled.

I'm a tour guide, lass. It's the uniform. Plus, Graham had said, his burnt umber eyes and fiftysomething face lighting up with his smile, *I get more tips this way.*

Cheers erupted as Douglas took a bow with little beads of sweat collecting along his brow. Andrew, Blair's partner, with ash brown hair and soft blue eyes, hooted from the dark.

"Your best by far, Douggie!" Aunt Mo chimed in. "Inspired!"

Douglas stoically walked through the crowd, blowing kisses without smiling, until he disappeared once more into the bathroom.

Graham took to the stage next and displayed his strength, laughing at himself as he picked up heavier and heavier things. For his finale, he snuck behind Lachlan and hoisted him, eliciting a roar from the crowd so loud Deli could have been convinced a hundred people were cheering, not a handful.

Hearing Lachlan really laugh for the first time took her by surprise. It felt like the time Chloe had insisted she try a gravity blanket—heavy, comforting, and sure. His face was so open, and something tugged at the back of her head again like it needed escape, but she couldn't reach it. Their eyes met as Graham set him down, and something caught between them. Then Lachlan shook his head like he was clearing it and shot her a glare that said *What are you looking at?*

Teenage moody ninja assclown, she thought.

Next, Andrew played a dinged-up acoustic guitar so gently Deli almost didn't realize how expertly his fingers flew along the fret.

"Is that how he stole your heart?" Deli asked Blair.

She kept her eyes glued to Andrew with her chin in her hands. "It certainly helped."

When he finished, Blair stood, grabbed his face, and kissed him. He held his guitar out to his side, eyes closed, until Graham took it from his hand, which Andrew then wrapped into Blair's ember hair.

"*That's* why yer kids aren't allowed at Talent Night anymore, ye horny, wee goats!" Douglas called, now in civilian clothes.

Deli turned to smile at Douglas, but Lachlan was right behind him, watching her. In the shadow of the lovers, kissing deeply and unashamed in front of all their friends, his gaze on hers felt intimate. Too intimate. Something molten spread across her collarbone and dripped into her chest.

"Okay, okay!" Aunt Mo jumped up from the couch. "It's intermission! Which means?"

Many voices shouted in unison, "Truth or Drink!"

Blair looped her arm through Deli's as everyone rushed the bar.

"Blair, what the hell is Truth or Drink?"

"Deli," Blair said, her round cheeks still flushed, "it's exactly what it sounds like."

The rules were simple. Everyone got a shot of liquor and a beverage. It was popcorn-style, but if someone had already taken their shot they could sip a drink instead.

"Truth or Drink, Douglas!" Andrew growled over the empty shot glass he'd drained after Blair had asked which of their kids he loved the most. She was still cackling as Andrew pointed at Douglas. "What is the largest animal you could take in hand-to-hand combat to the death?"

Douglas leaned back in his chair and rubbed his chin. "I reckon I could take a kangaroo."

Graham shook his head. "A kangaroo is as big as I am, Douglas."

"Aye, and I've yet to see a day you'd walk out of the ring with me *alive*!"

Graham stood in mock outrage. "Prove it, little man!"

"You've picked a fine night to die, ye great oaf!" Douglas cried and leaped to his feet.

Graham settled back into his seat and pointed two fingers at his eyes, then toward Douglas's.

"Truth or Drink . . ." Douglas held the back of his wrist against his forehead, wiggling his fingers. He pointed behind the bar. "Lachlan."

Lachlan stilled. "I'm not playing."

Douglas shrugged. "Sure you are."

"No, I'm not."

Douglas turned serious. "What do you really want out of life?" A hush fell over the room. Blair stiffened beside Deli.

Lachlan squared his shoulders, his voice going low. "I told you, I'm not playing."

"Is this"—Douglas swirled his pointer finger in the air of the dark pub—"everything you wanted? There's nothing more?"

Aunt Mo set her hand on Douglas's shoulder. "Alright, I think that's—"

"What's that supposed to mean?" Lachlan's hands were pressed flat against the bar, head sunk low between his shoulder blades.

"Has there been no woman since Blair? No leaving since you came home?" He acted unaware of the tension filling the room. "Are you ever gonna give yourself a chance, boy?"

"Douglas." There was no joking left in Blair's tone. "Enough."

"It's fine, Blair," Lachlan said.

"Lachlan, you shouldn't have to—"

"It's fine." Lachlan walked around the bar. Andrew's eyes were fixed on his lap. Blair's chest was blotching. Aunt Mo watched Lachlan with laser focus as he effortlessly picked up a heavy looking chair and set it next to Douglas with a thud. He straddled it and sat slowly, arms crossed over the back. Then he reached over, took Douglas's pint, and growled "Drink," before draining it in one go.

"Attaboy," Graham said, clapping Lachlan on the back as the table released a collective breath.

Lachlan set down the empty glass. "I choose Deli."

Deli's attention snapped up from Lachlan's hands in the instant hush. "Me?"

The intensity of his firelight eyes so close to her felt almost searing. *Focus,* she thought.

"Truth or Drink. What are you doing here?"

Deli swallowed. "What?"

"What, *exactly*, are you doing in Fearnhall, Deli MacDonald?"

Aunt Mo shot Lachlan a sharp look. Deli's head felt fuzzy, and she realized for the first time how many drinks had been purchased for her over the evening. Was she on four? Five?

She smiled. "I'm visiting my aunt."

Lachlan's eyes narrowed. "After twenty years? With no warning? You just fancied a holiday so sudden you couldn't buy a proper coat?"

"Go on, love," Douglas said. "Give us a tale."

"Aye." Lachlan's voice was far colder. "Go on."

"I . . ."

Deli brought her drink to her lips to opt out, but as Lachlan's eyes rolled and he made a move to stand, she lowered the cup. She certainly wasn't going to give Lachlan the satisfaction of seeing her quit. Deli MacDonald didn't quit anything.

Lean in, she thought.

"I'mhereforaboy," she blurted in one word. Lachlan lowered himself back into his chair. "I'm here for a boy."

Over the next twenty minutes, Deli told the circle the truth—not the losing-her-job part or the building anxiety about Chloe or her nagging guilt over leaving her family, but about Trey. How they were soulmates but she'd missed her chance and had to make up for lost time.

"The last time he thought I was moving on, he showed up at my door and kissed me." She watched a muscle in Lachlan's jaw move. "So I just thought, maybe if he missed me . . ."

She trailed off as an unexpected wave of hurt washed over her.

"But why *here*?" Lachlan pushed. "Why Fearnhall?"

Deli felt her cheeks flush. "Um, you guys know that show *The Highlander*?"

Aunt Mo glanced at Lachlan. Deli could have sworn she looked nervous.

"We're generally familiar, yes," Blair said with a cautious smile.

"Uh, right," Deli continued, trying to recover from the chill in the room. "Well, Trey had, like, a chip on his shoulder about hot Scottish men and how they didn't exist and how they made women everywhere have unreasonable expectations, and . . ." She realized she was rambling and was still keenly aware of Lachlan's eyes on her skin. It was like she could feel it, like it was a sunbeam. "Anyway, I thought . . . Aunt Mo had just emailed me, and I thought that it might . . . I don't know, make him *realize*."

"Realize what?" Lachlan asked.

Deli had to force her eyes to his. "Realize that he, um . . . loves me, *too.*"

"So it's a kilt-wearing Scottish hunk you're after?" Douglas asked as he grinned.

"What?" Deli's voice came out high. "No, that's not—"

"Oh, come now." Douglas grabbed her hand. "A little competition does wonders for a man's passions. Give your boy something to *really* worry about." Douglas exchanged a quick look with a few members of the table before he winked at Aunt Mo.

Deli felt very *peered* at, all of a sudden. She wondered how fish survived life being observed through glass their whole lives. Her eyes weren't moving as fast as her brain, and her face was way too hot. "Where's the restroom?"

"Through the wonky archway to the right—careful of the step," Aunt Mo said. "It's easy to fall."

23

Mo

Mo waited for the click of the restroom door.

Graham put a wide brown hand on her shoulder. "That poor girl, Mo. She's in pieces."

She felt like a new heart had moved into her chest—like she could feel Deli's fresh hurt pulsing in the faded shadow of her own. "Love will do that to you."

Blair scoffed. "For the record? I *hate* that knobhead."

"Aye," Andrew echoed. "We hate that knobhead."

"I have a plan." Douglas tapped the tips of his fingers together with a puckish grin.

Mo smiled with relief. "That's why I came to you, Douggie. Whaddya got?"

His eyes took on a twinkle. "Assuming you want to keep her here as long as possible?"

Mo nodded. Lachlan's knuckles turned white around his empty glass.

"I say we sell her on the idea of an oiled fantasy lad as the missing piece in her plan and send her on fool's errands, one by one. We'll buy her time."

"She needs time." Mo knew how difficult it was to see yourself differently—to imagine being happy in a new life. "Deli just needs a chance."

"Then a chance she'll have," Graham said. "I can take her to a games practice. Shouldn't be hard to imagine strapping young bucks there. And Lachlan will be there to show her a good time, eh, Lachlan?"

Lachlan looked pinched, like he was holding back something he very much wanted to say. He barely moved his lips as he said, "Yes, I'll be there, but—"

"She can help me with events," Mo said. "Plenty of groomsmen to be wooed. And Lachlan can have her help around the pub!"

Hannah grinned and nodded. Lachlan let out a low huff.

"Yes, yes," Douglas said. "And I'll have her help Cairn with the sheep feeding."

Mo frowned. "Are you sure, Douggie? *Cairn?*"

Lachlan had been surly since Deli had arrived. Now he looked downright fussy. "I think this is a bad idea, but sheep feeding sounds good for her."

Blair stared hard at Lachlan. "It will all be good for her. *We* will all be good for her."

Mo knew that grieving for her life before Fearnhall was a never-ending task—who her family should have been, who she could have grown old beside. She was content with her lot, but sometimes, just sometimes, she woke up alone in that little house and felt surrounded by ghosts. But moments like this reminded Mo she would never have a shortage of love.

Blair lifted her glass and smiled. "She's one of us, Mo."

"You know what?" Douglas reached for Mo's hand. "She reminds me of *you.*"

Mo blinked back tears and raised her glass. "To time and chance!"

Lachlan stood and returned to his post as the rest of the lot shared a toast.

Her niece arrived just as it ended. Mo didn't like the way her eyes shone, but Deli still smiled.

"Aw! What did I miss?"

24

Lachlan

"Hey, Lachlan, you got any bubbly back there?" Andrew whispered over the bar. "Could you pour the lot a round on me?"

"Sure thing."

Lachlan lined up flutes, lost in thought. Whatever else Trey Evans was, Lachlan knew he was a wee prick. Deli had crossed the world for just the hope of Evans, and it was lost on him.

Lachlan sorted through what he'd learned as he poured champagne. He'd studied Deli's eyes as she answered his question—watched her mouth, searching for a passing shadow of insincerity, but her response felt honest. Deli seemed to be a little tipsy and a little embarrassed, but Lachlan didn't think she was lying.

"Seriously, what did I miss?" Deli swayed slightly on her feet.

Andrew answered her. "You haven't missed anything, Deli. But would you mind if I stole your turn choosing the next truth or drink?"

"Sure," Deli said. "Popcorn, Andrew! Hey, does anyone have the Wi-Fi info?"

Lachlan had always liked Andrew—even when he'd been the annoying best friend of his infuriating little brother. And especially since he'd loved Blair the way Lachlan wasn't meant to.

Andrew mimed a finger over his lips and helped Lachlan pass out glasses while Blair happily played rock paper scissors with Hannah. When they were ready, he addressed the group. His soft voice was resolute.

"Blair? May I interrupt?"

"Yes?" Blair's brows creased in worry. The two of them had been together so long—two kids long—and had never acted so formally in The Wallflower.

Andrew's hand slipped into his pocket. He lowered himself to one knee.

"Truth or Drink, my love?"

Blair's laughter lit up the room. Douglas clapped his hands over his mouth and burst into tears.

Andrew smiled at the woman he loved and asked, "Will you marry me?"

The room fell silent, but it was *full.* Lachlan Scott was struck with pride over how different a silent pub full of *love* could be from a silent pub full of fear. He had worked hard to make it so.

Blair dropped to her knees, grabbed Andrew's face, and said, "Yes, my kind, gentle, silly man. I have loved you every day since the first day, and I intend to keep up my streak. You choose any one of them and I'll marry you on it. As long as it's fun and Douglas gets to teach the kids a choreographed dance."

The small crowd of people Lachlan had grown up beside broke out in cheers, the top note of which was Douglas's high, keening squeal of joy.

Mo smooshed Andrew's and Blair's faces together. "Holy balls, this is THRILLING! Why now?"

Lachlan saw Blair's face drop the way it did when she was hiding something painful. He'd seen it often, once upon a time.

"Mum's gotten a bit of . . . scary health news recently." She ran her fingers through the hair at Andrew's temple before he caught her hand

and kissed it. "We figured, life is short, and the kids *really* want to be flower faeries."

Deli hugged Blair, *really* hugged her—like they'd been friends forever and not just an hour—and Blair's face lit up with warmth.

Lachlan closed his eyes and pressed his fingers into the corners. Deli was careless with her heart—stampeding in with a reckless vulnerability—and she'd be careless with any heart she won. He thought through the silly plan to send Deli on wild goose chases in a bid to make her stay, searching for opportunity. He could use it to his advantage. She'd traipse through their town, sure she'd find a fake boyfriend with each adventure, and end each one alone. He could stoke that disappointment like an ember. Lachlan could build a fire in his sleep.

And he would need to.

"So when's the big day?" Graham asked.

Blair looked at Andrew and raised an eyebrow. He grinned. "One month from today."

Mo mumbled as she rubbed her palms together and stared at the ceiling.

"That is a very short timeline, my lovelies," she said after calculating what Lachlan knew must have been vendors and shipping in her head. "Do you have a pla—"

Blair dropped her hands on Mo's shoulders. "Mo, make our wedding."

Mo laughed—a booming and unashamed thing Lachlan had always loved—then turned, not to him, but to *Deli*, and swept her into a hug.

He knew he'd have something to apologize for—Mo wouldn't see things the way he could. But no one can see the big picture when they're deep in it. He knew the ache that came with realizing family cannot be what you need them to be. He wished hers deserved her.

But Lachlan and Mo weren't nothing. It wasn't perfect, but the family they'd cobbled together in Fearnhall was good.

They didn't need anyone else.

There was another round of drinks ordered and places taken as Blair called for the second half of the talent show. Ten minutes later, Douglas finished his second dance number to the tune of "Under the Sea" from *The Little Mermaid*—chest heaving and hands in a pyramid over his head like a fin. He wore a new mini kilt and a sparkling aqua Speedo.

Hannah plucked the sign-up sheet off the wall and eyed Lachlan. Though it had been years since Hannah had last spoken, she managed to say more with a look than most said with words.

"What? What's that look for?"

Hannah scribbled out her name and rewrote it at the bottom of the sheet under where Mo had scrawled Deli's, taking Deli's place as the show's closer.

Mo appeared at the bar and leaned over it, searching for something. "I need a few of the short tumblers."

He knew exactly where this was going. "No, absolutely not."

"Come on."

"No."

"Got any balls?"

Lachlan patted his pockets. "Fresh out."

"Then it will have to be glasses."

He shook his head. "It's not my fault you never come prepared for this."

"Don't I?" Mo winked as Hannah made a hasty retreat from the bar with an armful of limes.

His jaw dropped. "Hannah, how could you?"

She tossed the limes to Mo one by one in response.

Douglas had commandeered control of the speakers somehow (he'd have to Douglas-proof them later), and "I'm Too Sexy" by Right Said Fred came blaring through as Mo began her show. The small crowd oohed and aahed like they'd never seen Mo juggle limes before.

It was nights like this that made Lachlan feel like spending the rest of his life in this place with these people would be an okay way to live, even if it wasn't always what he'd expected. Even if it wasn't what he'd wanted, once upon a time.

There were many ways to end up alone. He'd be lucky if he had to only endure this one.

"Graham! Hit me!" Mo called. Graham drained his pint and tossed it toward Mo, who caught it and kept juggling.

"Oi!" Lachlan shouted. "You'll be paying for that!"

"Put it on my tab!" Graham called back. Blair tossed a bottle of hand sanitizer from her bag into the mix.

Deli stared at her aunt in open wonder. Blair pulled Deli closer until her cheek rested on Blair's shoulder—their faces peppered with the glow of the colored holiday lights. Blair was really the only woman her age left in Fearnhall, when Lachlan thought about it.

"Thank you, thank you!" Mo said, taking a bow. "Who's next?"

Lachlan consulted the sheet. "Deli."

Deli whipped around, and the jolt that went through him threatened his balance.

Her voice was squeaky. "Me?"

Lachlan swallowed hard. "You."

25

Deli

She'd made so many beautiful things for proposals before—bouquets and centerpieces and installations and archways—but Deli had never actually witnessed one. Blair and Andrew's was simple and honest. They were so obviously best friends.

She kneaded the heel of her palm into her chest to ease a sudden ache.

A moment later she watched her deeply cool aunt juggle stolen goods, and then Lachlan called her name as the next act.

"No, no," she protested, her brain still too fuzzy, "I don't have any talents."

Douglas tugged at her hand. "Methinks the lady doth protest too much! You've a lovely speaking voice, I'm sure you can sing. Andrew can accompany you."

The last time she sang in front of a crowd with anything resembling earnestness was a misguided performance in her junior high talent show of "My Heart Will Go On," complete with ribbon twirling.

Deli smiled and shook her head. "I'm sure I don't know any songs you know, Andrew."

He cocked an ear and plucked a string. "You'll know The Proclaimers."

She did know The Proclaimers. She said, "I don't know The Proclaimers."

Aunt Mo squeezed her arm. "Remember '500 Miles'? We sang it together last time you visited. When I took you into town, just the two of us?"

And suddenly, Deli was swept into a memory, loosed from some dusty corner of her mind. She was a girl, stringy haired and round bellied in the front seat of her aunt's beat-up Jeep. The wind tugged at the window flaps, whistling through the cab while they drove home from the local shops with groceries for Grandma Rosemary's Tuscan chicken—plus Popsicles Aunt Mo had snuck in with a wink.

It had taken a lot of convincing for her mom to let her go run an errand with Aunt Mo alone. *She's a bad influence, Delilah.*

"Auntie?" Deli had asked, lime flavored Popsicle melting down her chin.

"Yeah, buddy?"

"My mom says you're never coming home." Aunt Mo was silent. "Is that true?"

"Delilah, if you need me, I will always be there for you." Aunt Mo reached over and booped Deli on the nose. Her eyes looked wet and shiny, but she was grinning, too. She spun the volume dial on the radio, and a crackly band came through super loud. "This song says it all. But the rule is, we've got to belt it!"

"I don't know it!" Deli protested.

"You'll catch on quick." Aunt Mo laughed, and the two of them sang along. Deli especially liked the *DA DA DA DA* part.

Now she was back in Fearnhall, the same age Aunt Mo had been then.

"I remember," she said in a whisper.

"We'll go slow," Andrew said softly, "Just pull up the lyrics on your phone."

"Right! Phone!" Deli went to the bar. "Do you have the Wi-Fi info?"

"Hmm?" Lachlan turned around like he hadn't heard her at full volume two feet away.

"The Wi-Fi? I need to look up the lyrics for my"—she sighed, resigned—"talent."

He gave her the info. As her phone tried to connect, she tasted lime Popsicles.

"You alright?" Lachlan's voice was softer than she'd heard it before.

"Me?"

"You." He put one hand on the bar top. "Are you alright?"

"Yeah, of course." Deli wasn't sure if she was blushing or just warm. "I'm fine."

He looked doubtful. "You're fine?"

"Yep, I'm always fine."

Lachlan filled a glass with water and set it in front of her. "You're dehydrated."

When she met his gaze this time, it was a soft, dripping thing. Hot fudge on a sundae. Bathwater with lavender. The ice clinked in the glass as she took a long sip of the cool water.

"Sorry they're making you do something for the talent show. I tried to stop them."

"It's okay." Deli smiled. "I actually love this kind of stuff—like karaoke? No one back home will do it with me."

"You do talent shows often?" Lachlan's mouth tugged at one corner.

"Not since I was twelve, and I've wiped that from my brain."

The look he gave her made Deli feel like an ant under a magnifying glass until he spoke with great restraint. "Is there a recording?"

"No. Absolutely not."

His grin bloomed into a smile. "So that's a yes."

"The only copy is in a secure location guarded by a dragon. Count yourself lucky you'll never have to meet her."

"I've slain dragons for less."

Deli smiled, feeling a bit more relaxed than she'd been moments before. Her phone buzzed in her hands as messages from the last week without Wi-Fi at Aunt Mo's began to download. Trey's name erased all thoughts of lyrics from her head. She pulled her phone in closer to her chest and read it, her heart in her throat.

> Hey . . . listen. I think we need to talk. Where have you been? I haven't heard from you.

She beamed at the small victory at the same time her stomach dropped with the knot of *complicated* that came with Trey now. He'd texted her and tried to initiate the conversation—something that had always been Deli's job. Another delayed message came in.

> Also, what was the name of that restaurant you found a while ago? With the rooftop and that one dessert with the strawberries we loved?

Her throat tightened. She'd spent days reading menus and researching restaurants for Trey's last birthday, and he'd waxed poetic about how perfect each bite was, how exquisite the atmosphere. The night had ended with the two of them standing outside his building, holding each other so closely an older man walking his ancient dog had mumbled something about getting a room as he passed.

"Is the Wi-Fi working?" Lachlan asked.

"Perfectly." She struggled to speak around the frog in her throat, coughed into her scarf, and tried again. "Thanks."

"Deli . . ."

She peeled her eyes from her screen and looked up, hastily wiping at a sudden tear.

Lachlan's brow creased. "Are you *sure* you're alright?"

Trey only reached out to her to ask for the details of *their* memories so he could take the girl more worthy than her and make better ones. Now Lachlan, who was the only person in Fearnhall trying to make her feel unwelcome, was looking at her like he *cared*? Her head spun with the gin and the unfairness of it all. What right did he have? Did either of them?

"I said I'm *fine.*" She pushed her empty gin and tonic toward him. "But my glass has been empty for a while."

Lachlan hesitated before turning to pour while Deli looked up the lyrics to the song. He set a drink in front of her and a second glass of water. She rolled her eyes at him.

"Deli!" Andrew tuned up a final string on his guitar. "Are you ready?"

She started to text Chloe, the safety of their friendship wrapping around her shoulders like a favorite blanket, before she remembered that Chloe wasn't acting like Chloe and Deli had been left in the cold. There was another text from her mother, demanding a response.

Deli winced as she drank the gin and tonic down and let the alcohol stand between her and all the things slipping through her fingers. She pushed the full glass of water back at Lachlan, slid off her stool, and cracked her neck.

"Ready!"

26

Mo

Mo McDonnell didn't like to spend her days regretting things—she considered it a waste of good time. But as her niece began to sing, more rattled than Mo had seen her yet, she felt a pang of regret so abrupt it took her breath away.

If Mo was being honest with herself, part of her hesitancy to ask Deli about the details of her arrival had been the fear of what she'd say. She hoped that she could love away the last twenty years of absence. She hoped that she could keep Deli close long enough to rebuild the bridges Mo had burned when she left. She wanted to leave Deli with a permanent way to come back to her. She hoped she wasn't too late.

Mo remembered feeling so adult when she was Deli's age—so on her own in the world. Now she knew how young she had been. She wondered if Deli had any idea how much better was yet to come, or if she felt so much older than she really was, like Mo had.

Andrew played softly and slowly as Deli followed along on her phone. It gave the song a mournful sort of feeling—less like a declaration of love and more like a plea for it. The quiver in Deli's voice shifted from tinny nerves to an urgent, round sound as she sang about a man who would walk five hundred miles to reach his beloved. Douglas laid a hand on Mo's shoulder, his other pressed to his chest.

Before Deli could get through walking five hundred more, she turned to face the fireplace, shoulders bunched as the microphone hung limply at her side. Andrew shot Mo a look and continued to play.

Mo stood.

"Da da da da," she sang.

Lachlan's eyes flashed her way. He nodded once, and his rich voice joined hers. Mo waved her hands to encourage the room.

"Da da da da," came Blair and Douglas.

"*Da da da da,"* Graham joined.

They all sang while Deli did not. *"La da da da da da da da da da da da da daaa."*

Lachlan led the room again as Andrew looped the chorus. Mo wove her way to the fireplace and gently pressed her hand between Deli's shoulder blades.

"You okay?"

Deli's lips were pressed together, silent tears streaming down her face. "I'm fine," she said, forcing her words through the tightness in her throat. "I just think I'm too hard, or too complicated, or . . ." She trailed off.

Mo felt it in her chest. "Honey, what are you talking about?"

"To lo—" Deli looked up at Mo with the same garden-bloom eyes she'd had as a little girl, but the bitter smile was foreign. "Nothing. Sorry, I'm so dramatic." She wiped her eyes. "I'm working on it."

Mo's heart buckled at the knees. "There's nothing to fix."

Deli scoffed. "Tell that to my mother."

I wish I could, Mo thought. The deep knot in her core threatened to unspool as she remembered the way that Rosemary's hands used to tug a brush through Mo's tangles. She forced her guilt back and reached out to touch the tip of Deli's nose. "Come on, buddy," she whispered. "The rule is, we gotta belt it."

Deli laughed weakly and smiled. Mo looped her arm around Deli's waist and spun the two of them around.

"Da da da da!" Deli yelled, rallying. Andrew moved from picking to strumming, and The Wallflower's patrons sang their hearts out. At the end, even though they'd barely made it through a single verse before endlessly looping sounds, the entire pub stood up and clapped. They whooped. They rushed the stage and jostled Deli, hugging away what Mo hoped was the last of her niece's sorrow for the night.

It was hard to stay lonely in a warm place with people who wanted you to be there.

"Alright, you lot!" Lachlan called. "Let's let Celine Dion get some air. Who's next?"

27

Lachlan

Lachlan passed Hannah her sketch pad over the bar.

"You got arts and crafts back there?" Deli leaned with her head in one hand, eyes shiny.

"I store her props for a small fee."

She looked unfocused. "Can I get another drink, please?"

Lachlan tried to distract her. "You were great up there."

"Don't be mean to me." Deli's tone was joking, but her eyes weren't.

"I thought you were," he said, pouring another glass of water.

She took a sip and snarled her lip. "This isn't booze."

"Guess I'm a better backup singer than a bartender."

"If I drink this, will you give me the boozes?"

He fought a smile. "Yes, if you drink that, I'll give you the boozes."

"Okay, booze man, watch and learn." Deli took the water and started swerving back toward the couch.

"Watch and learn . . . how to drink water?" he called.

"I'm gonna be so hydrated *you're* gonna have to pee!" She pumped her fist in the air and collapsed into the couch like she'd struck a mighty blow.

Deli's water sloshed onto Mo's leg as she gestured at Hannah. "What is she doing?"

Mo patted Deli's knee. "Just watch."

Hannah scanned the crowd. Everyone's posture shifted and their attention went either straight to Hannah in hopes of being chosen or straight to the ceiling in hopes she'd pass over them. She pointed one long, slender finger at Blair, who closed her wide brown eyes, smiling. Hannah began to draw furiously, peeking over her paper only to observe her subject.

Lachlan saw the light of Deli's phone glowing in her lap. Her thumbs stopped moving, and her eyes flicked back and forth in the same pattern over and over. A low drumroll began as Graham softly clapped on his legs, building up to the big reveal until Hannah spun the paper around. She'd drawn a big, shaggy dog with a ball in its mouth. Blair squealed and clapped her hands together, nodding furiously.

"We are NOT GETTING A DOG!" Andrew yelled.

"Why not?" demanded Blair. "I already clean up *your* fur every day!"

"You *love* my beard!"

Mo leaned toward Deli. "Hannah can tell what you want most. She can read your heart's desire."

Hannah was scanning the crowd again. Since the start of their Talent Show Nights, Lachlan had witnessed her divine deepest desires ranging from a sink clear of dishes to an Italian vacation—the latter eliciting a rare, coy grin from Cairn as he took in his slim form depicted in a tiny Speedo more befitting of his brother. He'd even seen Hannah draw a small living room with a sofa full of faceless women gathered around the cozy fire. Mo had dismissed his timid attempt to ask who Hannah had drawn in her cottage.

Lachlan glanced at the dusty photo of his family hanging on the wall. Just like Truth or Drink, he never played this game.

Hannah's gaze snagged on Deli, and she frowned. Deli's eyes went wide, and for some reason, Lachlan's heart skipped a beat.

She stood. "Where's the restroom?"

"It hasn't moved since the last time," Lachlan said, already moving to guide her.

"I was just testing you." Deli narrowed her eyes at his approach. "I don't need a fancy escort. I'm hot." Deli shrugged off the jacket and balled it up as she thrust it toward him. "Can you hold this?"

He took it silently. "Deli, are—"

"I'm FINE," she whisper-hissed, poking him in the chest with one angry little finger before disappearing into the restroom.

Lachlan took a deep breath and squeezed his eyes shut. She was a very difficult person. He turned back to the room to find Hannah's finger pointing squarely in his direction.

The blood drained from his face.

"I'm not playing," he said.

But Hannah began to draw.

28

Mo

Mo watched Lachlan's fists clench and release in time with his jaw as Hannah's hand whipped across her sketch pad.

Then there was a crash from the direction of the bathroom, and Lachlan was gone.

"I'm okay!" Deli called from behind Lachlan's frame eclipsing the bathroom door. "Tooootally fine!"

"You're bleeding," Lachlan said.

"'Tis only a flesh wound."

"Bleeding?" Mo rushed to the narrow passageway to the toilet. "Deli, what happened?"

"Is the boozes stronger here? Or is gravity different in Scotland?"

"Here," Lachlan said. Mo couldn't see what was happening.

"Ow!"

"Shh."

Deli huffed. "Don't *shh* me. I'll bleed on you."

"You're already bleeding on me."

"And whose fault is that?"

The surliness in Lachlan's voice was gone—once again gentle and good natured. "I don't mind."

"You're weird." Deli hiccuped. "You're a weird guy."

"I'm also your ride home."

"I don't wanna go home."

"Too bad," he said as he ran the tap for a moment. "You need a nap."

"*You* need a nap." Deli snickered.

Lachlan sighed. "*I'd* love to be napping right now."

"It's too hot to nap in LA."

"Good thing you're in Scotland."

Deli gasped. "Oh my god, *you're right*!"

There had been moments in Mo's life where she was struck with a certain type of knowing. The first time she set foot on Scottish soil, she knew that she'd live there someday. The first time she saw Beth, she knew she'd love her all her life. As she witnessed something blossoming between the two kids she called her family, arguing on the bathroom floor, she knew again.

"Can you walk?" Lachlan asked.

Deli chortled. "Your *butt* can walk."

"Once-in-a-generation comedic gift, you've got there. Let's get you up."

There was a shuffling.

"Everyone okay in there?" Blair asked over Mo's shoulder.

"I believe so," Mo said quietly, "though our Lachlan may have met his match."

A handful of emotions passed over Blair's face. "I hope you're right."

"I'm afraid the talent show is over, though."

"I'm on it." Blair turned to the pub. "Oi, you lot! Closing time! You know the drill!" She rallied everyone into tidying and moving the furniture back, and Mo slipped behind the bar to start washing up. When Deli and Lachlan emerged from the bathroom, his hand hovered over her lower back. Deli had a small trickle of blood dripping from a cut on her forehead.

Mo felt a spike of unfamiliar panic. "What happened?"

Deli grinned and winced as she prodded her face. "You should see the other guy."

"You mean the sink." Lachlan raised his eyebrows at Mo. "The 'other guy' is the sink."

"Yeah, and it's out cold. I said I'm fine, Lachlan!" Deli waved him away. "I just slipped."

"Rolled your ankle and cracked your head, you mean? Once you're outside my pub, you can fall all you want. You're too American. I don't need a lawsuit."

"Aunt Mo, save me," Deli pleaded. "I'm being smothered by the giant off the green beans can."

Lachlan edged her toward the door. "Bit of a stretch."

"A little leafy kilt and an overblown sense of importance?" Deli leaned back and squinted to look at him. "I see no difference."

"First of all, the green bean giant is wearing a mini *toga*—"

"Toh-gay-toh, toh-gah-toh—"

"Secondly"—Lachlan pulled a chair out of Deli's path before she walked straight into it—"I'm wearing jeans."

"*Pffft!* You're all"—she gestured at his body—"tall and hunky and rugged and stuff. And you totally have a kilt. I bet you sleep in it."

"Absolutely no—"

"He does!" Mo called out, unable to help herself. "Nothing but the kilt!"

"REALLY?" Lachlan glared over his shoulder. "*Really*, Mo?"

"Kilts *are* hot," Deli said. "You *are* hot."

Lachlan's back went uncharacteristically stiff as he took a step away from Mo's niece, but just then Deli tripped on something unseen. Before Mo could call her name, Lachlan was there—one arm looped under her back while the other grasped her hand, and he caught her in a classic movie-scene dip. Their faces were inches apart.

"Holy shit," Deli said. "I almost just died."

"You're okay." Lachlan's voice was tight. "You're perfectly alive."

"What were you putting in those drinks?"

"Gin."

"And poison."

"Sure," he said softly, "and poison."

"If you're trying to kill me, you suck at it. You won't get rid of me that easy, Lachlan Scott."

The following beat of silence lingered too long. Deli looked at him strangely before he stood them both up, steadied her with a stiff hand on either arm, and took a full step backward.

"Mo." He turned to face her on his heel like a military maneuver. "Will you lock up? I need to get her home as soon as possible."

Lachlan almost never let anyone close for him, but Mo wasn't about to interject.

"Sure thing, Blair and Andrew can drop me at home afterward."

"Great." Lachlan turned to Deli. "Let's go."

"Oh, uh." Deli looked worriedly at Mo. "Okay?"

Mo smiled. "It's okay, that gives you two kids time to bond."

Lachlan's eyes flared with small panic. "On second thought, let's just lock up now." He raised his voice so the room could hear him. "Don't worry about tidying up, everyone. I'll do it in the morning. Let's all call it a night."

Blair and Douglas hugged Deli and swayed back and forth with her wrapped in their arms before they carried on, leaving Graham to right her as she tilted, with a side-hug so crushing Mo heard Deli squeak. Hannah shuffled out with Graham. Andrew clapped Deli on the back.

"Glad you're with us, Deli," Andrew said. "I think you're here for a reason."

Deli's nose scrunched up like she'd smelled Douglas's cooking. "Yeah, a friggin' boy."

"Let's hope." Andrew chuckled and jogged after his fiancée.

Lachlan helped Mo get Deli into the car on her shaky ankle, leaving puffs of breath in their wake, then opened the passenger door for Mo.

"Wait! My jacket's still inside."

"Go quickly," Lachlan said as he slid into his seat.

Mo unlocked The Wallflower with her own set of keys. She found her coat balled up on the bar top and shook it out, rubbing the familiar leather between her fingers.

The day Mo's father died, she'd collapsed onto the kitchen floor, but she hadn't cried. Not when she got the call, not when his lawyer read that he'd left her the cottage he'd grown up in, and not when her mother and sister had said all the things they could never take back.

Mo didn't fall apart until she opened the cottage's bedroom closet to find her father's jacket hanging with a letter in the pocket addressed to "Momo." She'd slipped on the jacket he'd worn nearly every day of his life, slid down the wall, and read the last things her father would ever tell her. There were still some smudges in the ink where her grief had bled into his confessions.

Hannah's easel caught Mo's eye as Lachlan honked outside. Mo had seen Hannah make up wonderful bullshit plenty of times, but now and then she thought there might be some truth to her claims of reading longings of the heart.

Mo wondered what she'd seen in Lachlan's mind as she reached for the sketchbook. Perhaps a younger version of his parents—though Mo believed Mr. and Mrs. Scott were sick a long while before anyone had noticed. Maybe Lachlan longed only for a strong pint.

What Mo found on the page made her gasp.

Another beep came from outside, somehow angrier than the last.

"Coming!" Mo closed the drawing pad and tucked the secret away. It would find who needed it when they needed it.

Mo McDonnell was a patient woman.

29

Lachlan

Lachlan pulled up to the cottage.

Mo already had her keys out. "You get her inside. I'll go start the hot water."

"I don't feel so good," Deli mumbled with her face pressed against the window.

"Just hold on, I'm coming." Lachlan's boots crunched in the gravel. "Don't you dare be sick in here."

Deli had only been in Fearnhall for a week and was already becoming Mo's crisis.

She looked pitiful as he opened her door. "Lachlan, I'm sorry. I'm sorry I fought your sink."

He wanted to get her inside and leave. "It's fine."

Deli's bottom lip stuck out. "He's a nice sink. He didn't deserve it."

"Can you get out on your own?"

"I think so." Deli shifted her weight to the foot on the ground, but she winced and sucked in her breath.

"Your ankle." He reached for her. "It's worse."

"I just need to walk it off." She took a limping step and pressed her hand to her head. "Ow."

Lachlan sighed. She was stubborn, and someone was going to get hurt. He couldn't allow that. "I'm going to pick you up now."

Deli's eyebrows shot up. "You're going to *pick me up*?"

"Mmhmm."

Her mouth turned to a flat line. "Nope."

"Deli, you can't walk. You might have a concussion—"

"I don't have a concussion."

"That's not what my sink said."

"Well, your sink is a dick. And you don't get it." Deli patted her hips. "I'm dense."

"You're what?"

She shifted her weight and winced again as her eyes brightened and she stuck a finger in the air. "Like a potato!"

He fought a laugh. "I can pick up a potato."

"What about a sack of, like, a million potatoes?"

"Child's play." He moved to lift her.

"No!"

Lachlan straightened and looked her in the eye. "Deli, if you really don't want me to help you, I won't. But if this is pride or . . ." He paused, considering what she might truly be concerned about. "Just let me help you."

"Ugh, fine!" She threw her arms up and let them fall.

He lifted her easily and carried her toward the door.

Deli's puff of breath came out a small, "Oh."

She was warm all over. She even smelled warm, and Lachlan felt warm, too. Her body relaxed in his arms. Lachlan glanced at her, and he regretted it.

A beam of light fell across her face as Mo opened the front door. "The bath is read—"

She stopped short as she registered Lachlan holding Deli in his arms on the doorstep. He felt suddenly mortified—a teenager again.

"Her ankle," he said as heat flared in his cheeks.

"Sure," Mo replied, stepping back to let them squeeze through.

"He made me," Deli said from his arms. "*I* wanted to walk."

"*You* wanted to die limping in the dark."

Mo failed to hide a smirk. "Plenty of time to bicker tomorrow, kids."

He set Deli down as Mo looped an arm around her waist.

She looked over her shoulder. "Can you take Deli early tomorrow? I've got the event, and Douggie said Cairn is in need of assistance."

Deli hiccuped. "Tomorrow?"

Mo wiggled her eyebrows at Lachlan with a grin. "You've got a date at the farm."

"Farm?" Deli said at the same time Lachlan said, "Yes."

Mo winked as she helped Deli through the bathroom door.

It wasn't until Mo called his name that he realized he was still standing in the doorway. He cleared his throat. "Yes?"

"Are you afraid to go home?"

"No."

"Okay," she said. "Because you were in quite the rush twenty minutes ago."

"Right."

"And you're still standing in my living room."

"Right," he said, shifting from one foot to the other. "I'll be off, then."

"Thanks for helping me get her home."

"Of course."

"I've got her from here."

"That's not . . ." he began, but the look on Mo's face stopped him short. "Good night."

"Good night."

She closed the bathroom door behind her, but Lachlan's feet wouldn't move.

He could hear Beans meowing happily. The damn cat hadn't even tried to escape.

"Aunt Mo, help," Deli said. "My shoe is giving me attitude."

Mo laughed. Her *real* laugh, and Lachlan was flooded with such a surprising sense of contentment he almost felt drunk. Then he heard himself chuckling, and he heard his friend counting on the companionship of a woman who was bound to leave, and he sobered immediately.

Lachlan had work to do. He turned to leave, but the fireplace was cold.

First, he'd build a fire.

Then he had work to do.

30

Deli

I'm dead, Deli thought. *I've died and I'm dead.*

Her head was throbbing. She rubbed her eyes and cursed as the skin on her forehead tugged painfully. A knock on the door bounced around the inside of her skull, and she glanced at the window. It wasn't even light outside.

"What?" Deli whined.

Aunt Mo opened the door slowly and poked her face into the slit. "Good morning, Sunshine. You've got to be dressed for a day of farming." Deli stared at her blankly. "Some of the sexiest men in Scotland are wandering shepherds. You deserve to have a little fun. And Lachlan's on his way."

Deli shot up and instantly regretted changing the location of her brain that quickly. "Can I cancel?"

"Cancel on Cairn?" Aunt Mo's eyes widened as she shook her head. "Not if you want them to find your body."

She flopped back onto the bed and pressed the pillow over her face.

Aunt Mo flipped on the lights. "I made breakfast. You can do it."

Deli had no idea what was going on. She hauled herself off the bed and sucked air through her teeth as her limped into the kitchen with, apparently, an ankle injury. "How can I help, Aunt Mo?"

Aunt Mo spun, spatula in hand. “You can’t.”

Deli hobbled determinedly to the stove. “Can I chop something? Set the table? Wow, that smells good.” She plucked a wooden spoon from the milk jug on the counter.

Aunt Mo slapped it with her spatula-turned-sparring-weapon. “Away with you, girl! Let me feed you.”

Deli’s eye twitched. “I want to help.”

“Tough nuggies, kid.”

“Can I make you a cup of tea?” Deli asked.

“Kettle’s already been on.”

“Can I pour you a—”

Aunt Mo produced a steaming mug from the counter behind her and sipped, raising her eyebrows. Deli let out a frustrated huff. Aunt Mo extended a second steaming mug.

Deli snatched it and splashed a bit of tea on the floor.

“Shit, sorry, I’ll get a—”

A squeaking sound cut her off as Aunt Mo’s slippered toes moved back and forth over the spot.

Deli felt very itchy.

“Breakfast will be ready in five.” Aunt Mo went back to her cooking. “You need to be ready in twenty.”

She turned on her heel and stalked back to her bedroom feeling petulant. Aunt Mo was racking up a long list of favors Deli owed. The sooner she could wipe the slate, the less likely Aunt Mo would be to think Deli was a crappy person.

She threw on clothes and shuffled to the mirror, and her jaw fell open. There was a small cut on her forehead surrounded by an angry purplish halo.

“Aunt Mo?” She squinted and dabbed tinted SPF onto the angry mound. “What happened to my face? I look like—”

Deli opened the bathroom door and promptly froze. Lachlan was there, looking down at her—six foot something, fresh faced, and wearing a bright yellow apron tied around his waist that said *Bada Bing*.

"I believe—" he said, holding out a glass of water and a bottle of ibuprofen. She took them without speaking. "—you lost a fight with a sink."

The night came rushing back to her like a tidal wave. The drinks, the talent show, the warmth and laughter, and the proposal. The game. Blair's face when Lachlan came to the table. Deli's embarrassing admission about her reason for being there. The tears she'd cursed alone in the bathroom mirror.

Then the fall. Lachlan, pressing his sleeve to her forehead, his golden eyes searching hers in worry. Her stomach folded with fluttering. No, queasiness.

She just needed grease.

She made a *pfft* sound. "I totally won that fight."

Lachlan mocked her with a smirk. "The *sink* didn't need me to carry it home."

God, he *had* carried her across the actual threshold—full damsel in distress style. Deli's chest flushed red under her sweater.

"If I recall, you *insisted* on picking me up."

"I *insisted* on not having to drive you to the nearest hospital with a broken yankle."

"Yankle?"

"Yankle."

"Are you having a stroke?"

"Yankee ankle!" Mo piped up over the sizzling. "And breakfast is ready!"

Lachlan pointed at Mo and grinned, triumphant.

"Oh, *good one*," Deli murmured, and she tried to barrel by him with visible conviction, but his hand found her back as he shifted to make room.

She could feel the tips of his fingers where they brushed against her like they were burning. For a second, she was back in his arms under the stars, feeling weightless. His eyes—like malted mercury glass—searching hers. Deli had never felt that way—like she could put her whole weight onto someone and trust them to hold her up. Her heartbeat quickened.

It all called for a sausage and some quiet.

Lachlan pulled his hands back and held them up, palms open. He looked timid. "Sorry."

Deli didn't trust Lachlan—so cold one minute, so concerned the next. She limped past him, eyes narrowed. "Mo, can I help you?"

"For god's sake, Deli, sit your ass down before I slap you with a pork link."

Deli sat reluctantly. She tapped her chipped black fingernails against the wood, looking anywhere but at Lachlan.

"Mo, why don't you sit and I'll serve?" Lachlan said.

Aunt Mo glared, gesturing at his body with her spatula. "I only let you set the table because you agreed to put on the apron. Don't push it."

"Shite apron," he mumbled, reaching for the tie behind his back.

Aunt Mo set heaping plates of steaming food in front of them. "Full Scottish."

"Thank you," Lachlan and Deli said in unison. Their eyes met, and Deli remembered to glare. His stare changed as he dropped the innocent act.

Aunt Mo placed a basket in the center of the table. "Blair's bread, Cairn's butter."

"Blair *bakes*?" Deli's mouth watered at the smell.

"Like an angel." Aunt Mo settled down with her plate. Whatever catchphrase was on her apron was swallowed up between her chest and belly.

"And Carn—"

"Cairn," Lachlan corrected.

"Caaiirrnn," she overpronounced, ". . . butters?"

Aunt Mo spooned beans and egg onto her toast. "Cairn is a man of many mysteries. And Douglas's brother."

Deli's brows shot up. "My god, there's two of them?"

Aunt Mo stabbed a mushroom. "Very different people, but brothers nonetheless."

Lachlan sliced a thick slab of bacon with a little too much gusto. He was back to being moodier than a Midwestern teen with a drum set and daddy issues, just like Deli had predicted.

She shoved a bite of baked tomato and poached egg into her mouth and fought the eye roll from the supreme tastiness. "Ohfmygrrd thrs-gurd," she snarfed. Lachlan stared and shook his head. Deli smiled and hoped that there was so much pepper in her teeth.

"Deli, go get your boots on, and be nice to Lachlan. He's taking the time to be an accomplice in our quest." Aunt Mo slid Deli's plate away as she chased her last bite with her fork. "And, Lachlan?" He froze, eyes trained on the table. "Do not abandon my niece in the wild."

"She'd be with Cairn," he mumbled.

She snatched away his plate as he toyed with a sausage bit. "Exactly."

As if on cue, Deli and Lachlan both announced, "I'll do the dishes!"

Aunt Mo rounded on them. "If you two dinguses don't learn to let somebody love you, I'll kill you both! Now, get out of my house."

Turned out, Aunt Mo's apron said *That's Showbiz, Baby!*

Lachlan stomped to the door and shrugged on his jacket. "I'll wait outside."

Deli still had no idea what was happening or why. "Um, Aunt Mo? What exactly am I going to a farm for, again?"

For a second, Deli thought her aunt was looking at her with . . . pity? Then Aunt Mo smiled a puckish smile. "Douggie was right, Deli. Men love a little competition, and there are plenty of boys just like that Hamish who'd love to take you out on the town." She hesitated at Deli's face, and her smile softened. "Hey, pal. You're allowed to have a little fun. It's not like you're gonna fall in love."

"I'm in love with Trey," she said.

"I know. But I am going to be in planning mode all day, and what else are you gonna do? Peevie doesn't need any more flower crowns."

Deli thought to protest, but Aunt Mo was right. Maybe a random farm adventure would get her mind off everything while she waited for time to do its work. She tied her boot as tightly as she could stand. "Okay, I'm off."

"Take my jacket," Aunt Mo said. "It will be freezing."

"I'll be fi—"

"Delilah MacDonald, what did I *just* say about being a dingus?"

The prickle that crawled over Deli's skin as she pulled the leather jacket from its peg didn't feel angry, but it didn't feel good. "Thanks. Wish me luck."

"Good luck, buddy. I hope you get to ride a sheep with a lover into the sunset!"

Deli sighed and climbed into the beat-up Defender, once again alone and at Lachlan's mercy.

31

Deli

Lachlan was brooding as he drove. The landscape around them was cast in pale gray, like someone had turned the saturation down as the night began to yield to day. Streaks of silver blue cut through the muted green-and-charcoal mountains, trickling from unseen places into streams on either side of the road.

Deli touched the glass of the window with her finger. "It's like magic he—AAH!"

Lachlan snickered after cranking the wheel around a corner.

"Would it KILL YOU to drive like a person who values his life?"

He didn't slow down. In the haze of gin and lost memories of her evening at The Wallflower, Lachlan had seemed like a very different man from the one she'd known so far. He'd been warm and caring with the people who gathered in his place. And he'd been so attentive to her . . . almost tender. But he'd been stony over breakfast, and now he was flinging her around the truck while he bordered on giggling.

Deli was sick of whiplash from men who didn't know what they wanted to be. She felt her dislike and distrust of him surge up with her breakfast, and she swallowed. *Fine,* she thought, *I can do whiplash, too . . .*

"So," she asked, inspecting her nails. "You and Blair?"

Lachlan's knuckles tightened on the steering wheel. "That's none of your business."

"What happened there?"

He glanced at her murderously before returning his eyes to the road. "What part of 'none of your business' is hard for you to understand?"

"Seemed tense yesterday . . . when Douglas brought it up."

"It's none of *his* business, either."

"How long ago?" She waited, but Lachlan didn't answer. "Did you two break up?"

"Oh, I don't know, Deli. How long have you been in love with a man who doesn't know you exist?"

She knew Lachlan was just trying to get under her skin, but still, it worked. A little too well. Deli clenched her jaw and sniffed against the hot prickling in her nose as she looked out the window, away from him.

"Doesn't feel too good, does it?" His voice had lost some purpose. Lachlan looked at her nervously. "Deli? I'm sorry. I shouldn't have said that."

Deli's voice was quiet. "Don't worry about it."

"No." His hand twisted on the wheel. "Deli, I didn't mean it."

She channeled her mother and sighed in the exact same way. "It's okay. You're probably right."

Lachlan reached toward her like he might touch her leg, but snapped it back to the wheel, his eyes forward. Deli let the silence tug at him.

He took a big breath. "Love is not my strong suit. I just think . . ." He looked at her, and the combativeness fled again. Lachlan looked suddenly earnest. He looked *sad.* "Never mind."

"What?" she asked.

"Nothing."

The tires hummed along with the wind's current as they cut a path through the rainwater on the road. She heard a bird's morning call and its partner's cheery response, and Deli felt like a cold, thick water was flooding her heart.

Lachlan spoke in a sudden burst. "I just think that if someone is in *love* with you, they should, you know . . . *see you.*" He took a sharp breath and nodded to himself. Deli's annoyance blazed back to life, pushing back the waves.

"Trey sees me." He looked at Deli sideways but didn't respond. Frustration bubbled inside her. "Anyways, it's like you said—what do *you* know about love?"

The shadow of tenderness in his face vanished under haughtiness. "I know I haven't had to run to the other side of the world to make someone *jealous.*"

"That's not what I'm doing."

"Oh right, I forgot, you're also here to what? Avoid your mommy issues?"

Deli's jaw dropped. *"Really?"*

He grinned. "Really."

"Okay, you mammoth babyman." Her nostrils flared as he rolled his eyes. "You wanna talk mommy issues? Why is *my* aunt washing your dishes while you're practicing for your Bitter Divorcé era with me? Where's *your* family?"

When Lachlan didn't respond, she repeated his words. *"Doesn't feel too good, does it?"*

Deli's seat belt locked and squeezed a wheezy sound out of her as Lachlan slammed on the brakes.

"Get out," he said flatly.

She gasped and choked on her spit. "Seriously?"

"Yes."

"You're gonna leave me on the side of the road? Because you lost an argument?"

She jumped as the outline of a man materialized like a ghost through the condensation before he walked away.

Lachlan still wasn't looking at her. "We're here."

"Great." Deli rubbed the goosebumps on her arm. "What did you even tell him about me?"

Lachlan's face split into a Grinch grin. "Don't worry, I told him everything he needs to know."

"That's comforting," she muttered as she wrestled with her seat belt.

"It shouldn't be."

Deli slid out of the ridiculously tall thing Lachlan drove and turned to glare at him one more time. A voice called out behind her, "Before I'm dead? And, Lachlan, have you a minute? There's a fence that needs fixin'."

Deli closed her eyes and took a deep breath. Lachlan made a similar sound in the truck.

It's all for love, she told herself.

Lachlan hung his head as he took the keys out of the ignition. "Aye, Cairn. Whatever you need."

32

Deli

"Cairn Campbell."

The old man didn't extend a hand.

He looked like he'd fallen out of a storybook. Cairn was tall and wiry, with deep, permanent wrinkles. His corduroy trousers hung off his bony hips like a coat hanger. The only things about him that didn't look worn down, worn thin, or weather-beaten were his blue eyes winking under thick white brows.

Cairn looked Deli up and down. "What sort of name is *Deli*?"

He said her name like he'd very much enjoy spitting it into a napkin and feeding it to a dog under the table.

"It's a nickname."

He blinked slowly. "For what? *Delicatessen*?"

Lachlan laughed behind her. Deli's face fell flat. "Something like that, sure, *Cairn.*"

She emphasized *Cairn* just so he might have the chance to reflect on his own name, which she decided sounded like someone started saying one word but accidentally mashed it up with another in their head, creating an embarrassing syllable of shame.

Cairn continued to stare.

She couldn't believe Cairn was Douglas's brother. Douglas, who was practically glitter in a bottle mixed with the charm of an elf king.

There was a small utility buggy behind him with two seats and a minuscule truck bed, like a golf cart with a real, blue-collar job.

A furry bundle in the bed lifted its head.

"EEE!" Deli squealed. "A DOG! Can I pet him?"

Cairn nodded, and Deli jumped at the chance to talk to a border collie, whose silence felt a little less personal. She scritched the dog under both ears.

"You're not a vegetarian, are you, *Deli*?" Cairn asked.

It had to be a trap. "Um, no. Not a vegetarian."

"That's good," Cairn said.

His accent made *good* sound like *güd*. Deli's head throbbed. "Why is that good?"

"Well." Cairn paused to spit something into the grass far too close to where Deli was standing. "I don't want to point to a cute wee lamb and say, 'That's a fine lookin' Sunday roast,' only to have you faint in horror."

Deli's stomach gave an involuntary lurch, and she had to cover her mouth with her hand. He grinned like one of those Krampus elves that run around the streets of small German towns terrorizing children and tourists.

"But you're not a vegetarian," he continued, "so no one's losing consciousness today." He tapped the truck bed with his staff, and the dog hopped out. "Except the Sunday roast. Come on then, hen. Those bonnie bastards won't find themselves!"

So, Lachlan had given Cairn plenty of details. She glared at him until he looked up from under his brow with a smirk. She felt a wet nose nudge into her palm.

"He's nuts, isn't he?" Deli whispered as she looked into the dog's mismatched eyes. He offered one rumbly *rrrruf* in response. Deli sighed. "Yeah, that's what I thought."

"Angus!" Cairn called as he got in the buggy. "Leave young Delicatessen alone, you're standing in the way of true love, ye silly dug!"

Angus barked and ran off as Deli hauled herself in. She was a little sore, body and heart, and she wasn't 100 percent sure she wouldn't puke on Cairn's shoes.

"Don't listen to a word Angus said. He's notorious for talking shite." Cairn flipped switches and pressed buttons. The cab shook as Lachlan hopped into the bed of the buggy.

Then Cairn floored it.

As they climbed over the hills of the farm in a way that felt like flirting with death, Cairn told her about his family's long history on that plot of land. She wondered what it must be like to feel so tied to somewhere—like the earth and your blood were old friends.

They came over a hill to a landscape dotted with puffballs. Deli squealed and clapped.

"Sheep!"

Cairn replied like she'd just awoken from a forty-year coma. "Yes, very good, Deli. Sheep." She rolled her eyes against her will. Cairn chuckled as he stopped the buggy and got out.

"Well?" he called through the glass. "Are you going to leave the poor beasts to starve?"

He tossed handfuls of greenish brown pellets from a heavy bag in Lachlan's hands toward a group of sheep standing in a tight circle. Deli got out and filled her hand without looking at Lachlan. She squatted.

"Here you go, buddy," she cooed at the nearest sheep, holding out a pellet.

Cairn stared. "What *are* you doin'?"

"Feeding the sheep?"

"Out of your hand?"

She looked up at him, confused. "Of course."

"They're livestock, not pets. They're wild animals."

Cairn couldn't ruin sheep for her. She outright refused to let anyone ruin sheep for her.

"They need love and nuggets, too."

He huffed a half laugh. "They're not the only ones needin' love, from what I hear."

Wooowww, she thought as the sheep took a single step forward and let out a low *baaaa.*

"Already got love, thanks," she whispered.

"Yet you're looking for a strapping Scottish lad to sweep you off your feet?" He sucked his teeth. "At least, that's what I hear."

"I'm *here,*" she whispered for the fluff thing's benefit, "because he just needs a little push."

Cairn replied easily, "A man who needs pushin' in love is no man in love."

Deli's incredulous sound was enough to make the sheep bleat in annoyance and run back to the herd. Cairn and Lachlan both gave a low chuckle at her nugget-filled hand held out to nothing.

"You don't know Trey," she snapped as she stood. "Neither of you do."

"No," Cairn said as he tossed another handful of pellets, "but I know I proposed to my Marjorie the night I met her."

Deli had been prepared to engage in a battle of snark with Cairn, but the softness in his voice stopped her short. "Marjorie?"

"Aye. Marjorie."

"Is she . . . ?"

"About ten years ago now. It was pneumonia that took her."

Sometimes, Deli felt like other people's pain was hot and bright and sharp-edged, dangerous and fresh. Cairn's felt like sea glass—worn smooth and familiar with time. It was a grief you slipped into your pocket and turned in your palm. A companion. An old friend.

"I'm sorry you lost her," Deli said softly.

"As am I." Cairn squinted at the sky, watching the sun break through a shifting cloud. "That woman gave love away like her heart was a bottomless well."

Over Cairn's shoulder, Deli watched Lachlan crouch with a handful of pellets as a single sheep got brave and walked toward him. He looked away and held perfectly still until he felt its soft nose in his palm, and he smiled.

A breeze blew through Deli's hair. "It sounds like Marjorie made the world a better place."

Cairn closed his eyes and smiled as the sunbeam warmed his skin. "She made *me* a better place, Deli."

She watched him, transfixed. A moment before, Cairn Campbell had been a classic curmudgeon she couldn't wait to get away from. Now he was a heart laid bare, breaking open his pain like an offering in his palm to *her*—for all intents and purposes, a wild animal.

She felt the sting of shame for her closed-mindedness.

"That's what love does." He patted his chest over his heart twice. "Love makes *us* into a better place. Understand?"

A second and third sheep approached Lachlan where he knelt, still as a statue. Deli looked away, searching for anything that didn't make her want to cry. "Where are all the babies?"

"The wee lambs? Off with your mysterious man who walks these hills, I'm sure." Cairn whistled and slipped back into the buggy as Lachlan tied up the food bag. Deli took one last look at the cluster of sheep and got in.

They drove quietly for a few minutes until Cairn veered off the path without warning and climbed toward a peak through patches of knotted ground cover flecked with dusty purple. Lachlan whooped from the bed as the buggy squealed in protest.

"Can I tell you a secret, Deli?" Cairn didn't wait for her to respond. "I've got no idea what I'm doin' or where I'm goin'!"

That makes two of us, she thought.

She was still quiet after Lachlan and Cairn had repaired a small fence and she and Lachlan were deposited back at the Land Rover without seeing a single hot shepherd.

Lachlan stayed silent. She didn't notice that he drove gently the whole way home.

33

Mo

Mo McDonnell sat at her kitchen table, staring at an empty page. She had an event coming up, and there were things to plan. Timelines. Rentals. Deliveries. But she was distracted.

Having Deli back was the arrival of a crisp breeze after the relentless heat of summer. She was the relief that comes with seeing the first leaves go orange—like the world was turning once again.

Mo's dad had felt like the start of autumn, too.

Then, on a Saturday morning, he died.

That day, Beth's skin was hot as Mo dropped a kiss onto her shoulder and wrapped an arm across her chest while she delivered breakfast to the mosaic tabletop Beth had made while she was in college. Beth always did her morning journaling on the patio with their rescue cat, Riceroni.

"Thank you, love," Beth murmured, distracted. A thrifted silk scarf that still smelled like the cigarettes of another woman held back her strawberry blonde hair.

"You're welcome." Mo spun the plate away a moment before Roni could steal scrambled eggs, eliciting a chastising meow.

Beth looked up with eyes like the oceans on brochures for the Caribbean or Fiji—teal gems that promised rest. She stuck out her bottom lip. "Let kitty have eggs."

It took all Mo's willpower to stay firm. "You know what the vet said."

"Vet, schmet," Beth grumbled as she buried her face into Roni's furry head.

Mo smiled. "And yet?"

The house phone rang in the kitchen.

"Come sit with me," Beth called as Mo went inside.

"Move your plant babies off the shady seat and I will!"

"Deal!"

Mo was still smiling as she reached for the phone. They'd been debating getting rid of the landline altogether since cell phones were making them sort of obsolete, but Beth was sentimental. *It's our phone number,* she'd said, patting the receiver, and Mo had been quietly relieved. Beth often found a way to say things Mo couldn't find words for.

She pinned the phone between her cheek and her shoulder, scooping breakfast onto a plate. "Yaaallow?"

Mo only knew what happened next because Beth told her. When Beth heard the dish shatter against the kitchen floor, she nearly knocked the screen door from its hinges trying to get to her. She found Mo lying on her side on the black-and-white-checkered linoleum floor, her cinnamon hair pooling around her pale face with lips parted and eyes open. The phone lay inches from Mo's hand while the other was curled in a fist between her chin and chest—and she had her knees pulled into her stomach. Beth could hear someone calling out in lilted English before the line went dead.

It took Beth ten minutes to coax a word from her. She was a second from calling an ambulance, when Mo whispered, "My . . . my *dad*?"

Beth lay down on the cool kitchen floor behind Mo and held her. Roni curled up in the crooks of their knees. They lay there for a long time, listening to gentle rustling as the pages in Beth's notebook turned where it sat forgotten on a breezy patio the day Mo's world stopped turning.

Mo stared at the red door of her cottage and returned to the empty page of her notebook, thinking of the moment twenty-some years ago when her life had changed forever, and of the moment a week ago when it had changed again.

She was happier than she'd been in so, so long.

And yet, she had a *feeling.*

So Mo wasn't surprised when she found the emails from the two of them. She could imagine her mother's cherry red nails, slick and glistening, slowly clicking out vitriol.

Maureen, they'd both written. Mo wondered if they'd pulled a muscle hauling out and dusting off so many old classics—calling her ungrateful, vicious, hateful, cruel—or if it had been like riding a bike.

She ignored them. A small part of her hoped that would be the end of it, but the rest of her knew that was a child's wish. She thought of the latest arrival in the garden.

Rhododendron, Deli had said, though she hadn't touched the pink-and-white petals. *They mean* beware.

Mo clicked her pen. *1. Pick up rentals from pub.*

She pressed the words into the notebook so harshly she nearly tore through the page.

The first week that Deli was in Fearnhall, she'd sought the pub's Wi-Fi as often as she could to frantically swipe at her phone screen when she thought no one was watching. If she thought it would have helped at all, Mo might have told her that she was spending a disproportionate amount of energy, time, and brain space on people who didn't seem to be spending any on her. But Mo's job was to love Deli, not make her feel small—even if it hurt to watch.

She had to remind herself of this often.

Once, Blair and Andrew had swung by to present Deli with an orange cake with lemon drizzle to give her "a slice of home." Deli had reacted like she was being handed a suspicious parcel at an airport. She'd offered to "help" them in return, naming potential chores that needed doing with a subtle, feverish look only Mo seemed to notice. By the time Deli was insisting on weeding their garden, Blair threw her hands up, grabbed Deli's face, and said, *Oh, for fuck's sake, can you just let me be your friend?*

That night, Deli went back to the pub and was glued to her phone, rereading text conversations with her friend Chloe. Later, in the wee hours, Mo shot up from a dead sleep and heard Deli crying desperately—the way one does when they are trying with all their might to stop.

Watching such a brilliant girl reject any love that came easy made Mo want to go back in time. She wanted to snatch Deli away before anyone could carve unworthiness into her bones and change Deli's story about herself.

Still, her niece was not bitter. Instead, Deli cared for everybody. Mo woke some mornings to find Beans had been fed and Mrs. Peevis had fresh hay and flowers in her fur. Deli spent hours one day helping Graham set up social media pages for his tour company. Mo pulled up to see Graham posed beside the ocean with his leg propped on the retaining wall and his emerald kilt hiked to tease his rugby-made thigh, sienna and strong in the sunlight. Mo thought proudly of Graham's success, despite the surprise some tourists showed plainly on their faces to find a Black Scottish tour guide, as he rolled a thistle between his fingers and held it in his teeth. Deli snapped photos and directed. *Look over your shoulder at me. Now look out to sea. Now pretend I just told you the funniest joke you've ever heard—now I've whispered a secret—it's scandalous! Good!*

One day, Mo arrived at The Wallflower post–ocean dip (which Deli was not keen on doing again, despite Mo's insistence that it was great for the nerves) and found Lachlan wiping down the bar top as he glared at Douglas and Deli painstakingly bedazzling a mini kilt with rhinestones.

Lachlan slid a small glass of Glenfiddich across the bar as Mo climbed onto a stool.

"They've monopolized that table for hours."

The pub was empty except Graham with a private tour of giggling women.

"How rude."

He made a face. "Do you know what I caught her doing today?"

"Writing your phone number on the bathroom walls?"

"She was"—he hesitated—"dusting."

"Dusting?"

"She stole my rag to dust the picture frames."

Mo gasped. "Not the picture frames!"

"It was *invasive*."

"Didn't she know that dust was *archival*?"

"When I told her to stop, she said I had 'walling-myself-into-my-own-crypt energy.'"

Mo spit some of her whisky on the bar top. "That's very funny."

"I didn't think so."

"Well, crypt keepers aren't famous for their humor." Lachlan scowled at her. "You've mentioned wanting to dust at least three times since January."

"I would have gotten to it."

"And now you don't have to. If you'd just play nice and *tell* her how she can help around here, she wouldn't be stealing your very best dust."

He huffed. "I don't like it."

"Yeah, how dare she see a need and take care of it? What a turd."

After a moment, Lachlan lowered his voice and asked, "Has she heard from anyone back home?"

Mo glanced over her shoulder at her niece, who was laughing with her head thrown back after Douglas had whispered something cheeky. Her phone was on the table, face up, screen dark. Mo's foot tapped against the barstool. "I don't think she's heard anything good."

Lachlan thought he was being subtle when he'd brought firewood to the cottage even though she'd been well stocked, or when he'd put a chalkboard with the Wi-Fi password on the bar despite years of refusing to give it unless specifically asked. But Mo had always seen through him, ever since he was a kid.

Not that it mattered. Lachlan was the sort who needed to learn his mistakes on his own. Mo brought her drink to her lips and swallowed it down with the rest of the things she could see but they couldn't.

Once, Beth had tried to tell Mo a terrible truth—about where Mo's pain was really born—but Mo hadn't listened. She'd needed to learn it on her own.

She hadn't learned it in time.

Everyone said Deli and Mo were so alike.

Mo prayed they were wrong.

34

Deli

By the first week of March, Aunt Mo's garden was growing so wild Deli could almost get lost in it. Every day she took the antique book and a gifted sketchbook from Hannah to document the latest arrivals in a sort of dictionary of her own. She'd even come to love donning her wellies and Aunt Mo's umbrella hat so she could draw under a clear poncho as big as a tent when it rained.

Deli hadn't expected it, but she was having *fun* pretending she belonged in the sleepy Scottish village. She noticed how less frequently her teeth ground as she slept—how much she looked forward to evenings playing games and laughing into the night with Aunt Mo. Deli had even become a sort of temp worker for the town and had been enlisted for all sorts of tasks—from helping Douglas clean out his closet to chasing off seagulls from The Wallflower's dock while Andrew and the other local fishermen unloaded their catch. Graham had taken her on a private tour so she could leave honest reviews on various sites (five stars, across the board). She'd made arrangements from the garden for one of Aunt Mo's coordinating gigs.

Still, Deli carried an ache in her wherever she went. She'd arrived with the hope that her absence would spur a reckoning in Trey, Chloe, maybe even her mom, in a week—neat and tidy. But she'd gotten only guilt trips from Lorraine, she hadn't heard from Trey since the night of the talent show, and she hadn't heard from Chloe at all.

A few days after her adventure in farming, Lachlan pretended to be busy polishing glasses while Deli waited for Blair at the bar and munched on salt-and-vinegar chips. Deli decided to post a video of Mrs. Peevis before the otherworldly mountains, stark and stalwart against the moody sky—and she hoped it might catch someone's attention or stir their imagination. Deli figured there wasn't harm in going along with the town's theory about competition. It seemed outlandish, but it was a distraction from all the *waiting*. So she posted the video, and an embarrassed part of her wished Trey would see it and wonder if someone else was standing behind the camera with Deli, making her laugh in the land of *The Highlander*.

She nearly fell off her stool when her phone lit up with Trey's name.

> Our song came on while I was driving to an audition, and I got a callback You're my good luck charm. I miss you. When are you coming back to me?

Deli's heart pounded as her thumbs hovered over the glowing keyboard. Trey was up late, thinking of her. *Missing* her. She wished she could fall through the screen and be with him, but he'd missed her before. Trey had missed her so much he'd kissed her once, then sprung a secret girlfriend on her.

Missing her was great, but Deli needed Trey to love her.

> Hey you. That's incredible! What was the audition for? I'm so proud of you. But I'm not sure when I'm coming home . . .

She felt the swoosh of the text sending like a drop on a roller coaster. Things were working. She was on the right track. *Soon,* she thought.

Lachlan saw her smiling into her phone as he ran a rag along the counter. He was back to carrying a constant air of annoyance. "Writing love letters?"

Deli was going to win this scrimmage. She raised a superior eyebrow. "Yes, in fact. Trey just wanted to share some good news."

"Did he, aye? And what's that?"

She wasn't sure why she needed to make it bigger than it was. "He has a callback for a major motion picture."

Lachlan whistled in that *big whoop* kind of way. "Shall I call the press?"

It was Blair who saved Deli from saying something regrettable.

She dropped her bag on the bar top. "Lachlan, don't be a fartface. And please bring us two cuppas."

Lachlan grumbled away. Deli passed Blair a chip. "Fartface?"

Blair shrugged. "I have kids."

Deli had sent Chloe two more texts and even tried calling since she'd been in Fearnhall. She'd heard nothing. But Deli and Blair passed two hours eating lunch like they'd known each other their whole lives.

What a thing it was—to marvel at something new, guilt stricken over something that might be lost.

Four cups of tea and three bags of chips later, Blair headed off to grab the "wee yins" from school with a hug and a promise to see each other again soon. Deli waited until she was out of sight to open her phone.

She refreshed the video, checking for likes or comments. There was nothing new. She just needed to be patient. Deli opened her email to find a waiting message from her mother. Her foot tapped against the barstool. She clicked.

To: Delilah MacDonald

From: Lorraine MacDonald

Subject: Doddy

Hi Sweetie,

I saw your video. Glad to see you're safe.

When I was really little, my Gran had a Highland cow named Doddy out there, too. I'm sure that's not Doddy (she said Doddy was the short form of George in Gaelic! George the Coo!), but it brought up fond memories. I remember there were flowers that used to bloom all year long, like magic. I used to make daisy chains for his horns. Gran said as long as "Doddy had his daisies" he couldn't be stolen by the faeries! She used to make them for us, too.

Are you coming home soon? We miss you.

Love,
Mom

Deli had a great-grand-cow named Doddy who'd worn daisies on his horns to keep safe from faeries, no matter the season. It was such an unexpected thing to be given, so sweet and true and sad, she actually stared at her empty hands like they might show her where to put it.

Her eyes drifted to the photo of Lachlan's family on the wall of The Wallflower's Crown. His stern looking father and waifish mother; Lachlan, stoic even at six or seven years old; and a blond, curly-haired little brother standing in front of the door with a big set of keys. She'd dusted it a few days before.

"Oi, Hollywood." Lachlan slid her a glass of water she didn't ask for. "One? You need to hydrate."

"I don't." (She did.)

"Two," he said, ignoring her protests, "I'm meant to take you to the Highland Games practice tomorrow. Are you sure you still want to come? It's just muddy, cold, and sweaty."

She frowned. "Are you trying to convince me not to go?"

"Just want you to know what you're getting yourself into. It's not the sort of place you go to win a man. Can't have you wasting your time, can we?"

Truthfully, Deli agreed. She didn't even *want* to win a man, except the one missing her with her heart in his pocket. But something about Lachlan woke a feeling in her—some passionate refusal to turn away.

"Oh, I'm going." She picked up the glass. "And I'll enchant the most beautiful man there—whether you like it or not." She stared at Lachlan in an unblinking challenge as she tried to chug her water. A trickle ran down the side of her mouth and to her neck.

He smirked. "Enchanting, indeed."

She soaked up the dribble with the neck of her shirt. "You don't even know. I'm the woo-ingest damn thing you ever saw."

He wiped the water off the bar top. "Can't wait."

35

Deli

Lachlan draped a lazy hand over the steering wheel like they weren't chancing death by eighteen-wheeler on sheer mountainsides.

"So, did he get the part?"

Deli felt a quick slip of pain between her ribs. She glanced at Lachlan, unsure whether he knew he'd been wielding a knife. "It doesn't work that fast."

He glanced back. "Yes it does."

"How would you know?"

"He hasn't spoken to you since informing you of his grand accomplishment?"

Deli lied. "Yes. A bunch."

"A bunch?"

"Mmhmm." She studied the horizon.

"So he's missing you desperately already?"

A twist of the blade. She doubled down. "Desperately."

"Sounds like you've done what you came here to do." Lachlan's knee tapped up and down. "Why stick around and make the man suffer?"

Deli couldn't tell Lachlan the truth. If he'd been in the Beast's castle when that hag bestowed the curse, he would have been turned into sentient Thigh Chafe, not, like, a candlestick. She couldn't tell him Trey hadn't responded. She couldn't say she'd spent the night awake, refreshing her phone in a dark bedroom with no reception at all. She couldn't bring herself to tell Lachlan that she was yet to be loved.

"Distance makes the heart grow fonder," she said. "I need to make sure the lesson sticks."

"Uh huh. And you'll do that by . . . turning him wild with jealousy?"

He sounded so doubtful, like the idea that Deli could make Trey jealous was on par with vegan cheese tasting like the real thing. A nasty voice deep in her head agreed.

She couldn't say *nothing*.

"Trey is pining for me already. Imagine how he'll feel when he sees me in the arms of a gorgeous six-foot-something man who looks good in tartan. He'll have to get on a plane just to keep from imploding."

Lachlan rolled his eyes. "Jesus, *The Highlander* really has a hold on you."

She recoiled at the accusation. "Don't loop me in with my mother and her special brand of bananas, thanks."

He stared at her long enough that she mumbled about his eyes being on the road.

"*You're* the one here, in Scotland, searching for a *The Highlander* knockoff, and your mother, the superfan—whom you are *nothing* like—is not."

"I don't even watch *The Highlander.* Trey just . . ."

"Trey just . . . ?"

Deli sighed. "Trey has a *thing* about the men on that show."

"Then why isn't Trey in their arms, frolicking through windswept landscapes?"

Deli was starting to feel a poking on her sore heart. "Do you need me to explain the situation again, but, like, slower?"

"Just sounds like he's the one with complicated feelings for Scottish hunks."

"Trey was upset because he thought I wanted someone"—she gestured at Lachlan's enormous self making the cabin of the massive truck feel compact—"unrealistic. He's a normal person."

Lachlan's small movements—the knee tapping, the chest rising and falling—went still for a fraction of time, like a shock had gone through him. "I'm a normal person."

Deli snorted and rolled her eyes. "Nothing about you is *normal*."

He shrugged. "At least I haven't thrown a fit because I can't reach the top shelf."

Deli let anger smother the pain Lachlan was prodding. She was tired of hurting.

"Listen, Shrek. It was perfectly reasonable for him to be angry with me when he thought my tastes were defined by some genetic outlier impossible for most people to compete with."

Deli suddenly thought of Trey's costars on *Chestnut Gardens*. Girls who had carved their faces and bodies into shapes most women would never be. She didn't fault them for it, but she faulted Trey for lusting after one or two.

She chased the thought from her mind.

Lachlan watched her, serious again. "He was *angry* with you?"

"Trey just cares about me."

"No." Lachlan's voice was dark. "He doesn't."

Deli realized she had reopened the cuticle she'd made bleed the night before. She wrapped her hand in her other fist. "You've clearly never had a soulmate. You don't know anything about him. And you don't know anything about *me*."

Lachlan's nose crinkled like he smelled something rotting. He flexed his hand against his knee and balled it back into a fist. Deli was struck with the memory of that hand pressing against her lower back, radiating warmth where he kept her steady.

"Please, I know you." He looked at her sideways. "I know that you're in love with an absolute bawbag, so you've run away from home in hopes his childish jealousy will break you out of the friend zone he's put you in for, how many years now? You're glued to your phone, trying to teach everyone in your life some kind of lesson, and in the meantime, you're running around Mo's life, using her guest room and jacket and time." He looked at her in mock curiosity. "Did I miss anything?"

Deli didn't want to think. She just wanted to bite the hand squeezing around her pain.

"I love this game," she growled. "My turn. You're the neighborhood downer who stalks through this tiny town like a guard dog no one asked for. You're screwed up from whatever happened with the gorgeous redhead you fumbled, and your daddy issues, or mommy issues, or both—but you haven't changed a thing about the pub they left you with."

For a split second, Lachlan looked shocked.

Deli always knew when she'd met another kid with . . . difficult parents. "Please. There was a layer of dust so thick on that frame I'd believe it if you told me you built the place *around* it. Did I *miss* anything?"

She wouldn't have said it, but he'd said it first.

The seat belt kept her body from flinging through the windshield as Lachlan slammed on the brakes. Graham stared at them through the glass from the practice field, eyebrow raised.

"STOP DOING THAT. I don't know what scared little boy is tantruming around in there"—she poked him once in the chest—"but I don't care. Little Lachlan isn't my problem. He's yours. And he's not getting in my way. Capisce?"

Lachlan's nostrils flared. He leaned so close to her face she could feel his annoyingly fresh breath on her skin.

"Yeah? Well, I *do* know what lonely little girl is sulking in *there*"—he pointed at her heart—"*Delilah.* And I can't wait until you get tired of playing adult and go back home to Mommy."

Whatever goodness Lachlan Scott was capable of, he hid it on the top shelf and only poured it for people he called precious or pitiful. Deli MacDonald was certainly not precious to him, and she'd draw blood before he called her pitiful.

She leaned even closer, daring him to pull back, like a game of angry-whisper-chicken between grown adults. "You're *never* getting rid of me. I'm *here*. And Mo? She's *my* family. Not yours."

"I won't let you hurt her."

"As if you could *let* me do anything."

A sharp knock on the window pierced the tension.

"Oi!" Graham cupped his hands against the glass and peered in. "Lovebirds! Let's go!"

Lachlan's door was already slamming closed behind him.

Deli and Graham watched him cut a path through the mist as he stormed away. "Christ, girl, what did you do to the poor lad?"

She crossed her arms over her chest, hushing the soft, people-pleasing part of her that cried *guilty*. "I haven't done a thing to him."

Graham nudged her shoulder with his. "I wouldn't be so sure. Come on. The boys are dying to meet you."

Deli shook out her wrists to recover from the bizarre, searing jabs of the drive as she followed Graham. She didn't know why Lachlan brought that out of her, or why she brought it out of him. It was like the air between them hissed with electricity so potent it forced a path out, one way or another. She focused on breathing the fresh air as they walked.

"The boys," it turned out, was a cluster of potbellied men in their fifties and sixties, two ripped women tossing a medicine ball back and forth, and a young man with an acne-covered face and bones practically poking through his skin, eyeing her hungrily as he rolled his socks up to his knees.

She swept the field again, hoping to find the dreamboat she'd been promised now that she hadn't heard back from Trey. She couldn't let him forget about her, and she didn't have a better plan than escalating with a fake fling. She squinted at movement through the mist.

A man with his back to her tugged his shirt over his beanie-covered head. The broad sweep of his shoulders rippled with muscle. *Bingo,* she thought as he pushed his arms through the sleeves of a ratty thermal undershirt. He turned as he pulled it over his face, and Deli got a full view of his perfect front. His muscles moved in tandem with a layer of softer body, like a man who had earned his strength, not purchased it. There wasn't a personal trainer in Los Angeles who knew how to coax *that* sort of body out of their client. Deli marveled at the sight of a real Highlander and understood what Trey meant when he'd said *unrealistic.*

"Graham!" she hissed out of the corner of her mouth. "Who is *tha—*"

Lachlan Scott tugged his shirt down and found her staring, slack jawed, as her question died like a fly getting swatted.

"Who's who, lass?" Graham began to follow Deli's line of sight. She panicked.

"Um, that!" She pointed at the pimply boy with ravenous, possum-ish eyes.

Graham sounded suspicious. "Kevin?"

"Yep. Yes. Kevin."

"Kevin . . ." He drew out the name, waiting for her to stop him. She didn't. "Is a checkout boy at Tesco's up the road. He's built on Mountain Dew and Hot Cheetos."

"Maybe he'll fill out?" Deli squeaked.

"Aye, give him forty years and he'll fit right in with that lot." He gestured toward the bald men with round bellies and a total lack of butts.

"Well, he's the best option here besides the girls, who could kick Trey's ass." She admired the women radiating power. "They'd strike fear into his heart, not jealousy."

"I see at least one other contender."

"Graham. Lachlan loathes me."

"You certainly have an effect on him."

"Yeah, blind fury and the slipping of his brain out of his ear."

"The line between hate and love is very thin, indeed. Passion has many masks."

Deli made an exasperated sound. "I already have somebody to love. Someone who doesn't have to go anger-stalking into the woods after spending a single car ride with me."

She prayed the memory of Trey tossing her mother's birthday gift away in disgust didn't show on her face as Graham studied her.

"The day is young. Could be your dream man's just running late." Graham clapped his hands together and turned toward the group. "Alright, you lot! Let's begin!"

36

Mo

Mo admired the low vase of yellow roses and deep Scabiosa on the table while she listened. Moss was wrapped around the stems, like a mother had tucked them in.

"Is William coming?"

Mo smiled and said what she always said. "William will be home soon."

"Good." Lucinda Scott sighed and leaned back in her chair. "He's such a special boy."

"He is."

"My William, he's going to go to university."

"I'm sure he will."

"Yes." She nodded, her pale hands wringing in her lap. "Bright future, my William." Mo had stopped hoping she would ask after her other son during their visits long ago. The unfairness didn't burn hot anymore. Just a dull ache. "And my husband?"

She repeated the soothing lie, like she did every week. "Just closing up at the pub. He's probably already on his way."

Mrs. Scott sat up straighter and smoothed the floral skirt of her dress with trembling fingers. Mo had just helped her zip it up the side after assisting her while she showered and evaluating her general wellness.

"I should check on dinner. He's a good man, you know. Works hard for his family."

"Of course," Mo said, devoid of emotion.

Mrs. Scott's foot began to tap. "Have you seen my son anywhere?"

"William will be home soo—"

"No, not William. Lachlan. Where is that boy?"

Lachlan's mother so rarely mentioned him. Mo leaned forward and smiled as she thought fondly of the boy Lachlan used to be. "I'm sure he'll be back soon, too. He's got an adventurous heart, that one."

Mrs. Scott looked sour. "He'll anger his father, tromping mud through the house. Staying out past dark. How many times have I told him?" She twisted around and looked through the window. Her hands wrung in her lap again, leaving streaks of angry pink across the places her fingertips pressed into her skin. Mo tried not to dwell on the silvered scars on Lucinda's palms. "It's like Lachlan *wants* to provoke him."

Mo took a deep breath to center herself. "I'll go find him, Mrs. Scott, don't worry. I'll clean him up. He'll be home before your husband, shiny and fresh."

"Well, hurry, dear, hurry!" She waved the backs of her hands impatiently at Mo, shooing her from the room. "We're running out of time."

Mo stood and collected her teacup and saucer from the table. The other sat untouched.

"Mrs. Scott?"

"Hmm?"

"He's special, too. Lachlan is exceptional."

She scrunched her eyebrows together, considering Mo's words, and Mo thought she might have an audience with the real Lucinda Scott—Lucinda from before Alzheimer's had arrived too early and sunk its teeth into her. But Mrs. Scott just looked back out the window.

"Lachlan is late."

37

LACHLAN

Lachlan tried to ignore the woman ruining his day.

Deli was perched on a rock, cheering on *his* friends. Well, fine, Kevin wasn't exactly his friend. In fact, Lachlan had dedicated more than one wandering thought to being worried about what havoc Kevin might release on the world if given the chance, but Kevin was still *his* Kevin. In his world. Not hers.

Deli probably didn't even *have* a Kevin.

"Hell yeah, Ilona!" Deli's chin chattered. Her gloved hands made muffled *poof* sounds as she clapped. Ilona grinned and launched another hammer with dizzying strength. Deli whooped. "Divine! I'd sacrifice a virgin to you!"

Kevin's neck sank into his body like a cartoon tortoise as he took a nervous step away.

Lachlan still felt something unnamable well up in his throat when he thought of the day they'd met as kids on the cliffside, and again at a train station—the wild flash of her smile, the stubborn courage in her eyes. Deli was quick. She was warm. She was resilient and brave and the sort of person who notices the shapes of leaves on trees that pass by—but her compass was all wrong.

He felt a bit queasy over the comments about her mother. Lachlan had never forgotten the sound of the woman screaming at a little girl from behind the red door of Mo's home. In any other situation, he would have already apologized profusely and tried to warm up her toes. But being around Deli stoked a fire in his bones. He was sure it wouldn't die down until it had turned her presence in *his* life—his friends, his town, his family, his pub—into ash.

It didn't matter that his mind had taken to wandering to Deli's laugh or the crushed-bramble color of her lips. It didn't matter that he'd paced behind the bar in pajamas for hours, imagining a chance to speak to that absolute walloper, Trey Evans. It certainly didn't matter that Lachlan hadn't been able to picture himself happy for years until she'd come.

Deli needed to go, and she was making it very clear that she did not intend to while she grew roots in the hearts of most of his patrons. His people. He was barely protecting his own. And she would leave them torn open when she uprooted and left.

He had to say what he did on the drive. It was for the greater good.

"Oi, Lachlan!" Graham beckoned. "Tug-o-war time!"

Lachlan coiled the thick rope and heaved it onto his shoulders while Deli fished mini bottles of sports drinks out of Graham's cooler and passed them out like she had a child on the team.

Robert, one of the three middle-aged men who weren't related despite passing as triplets, announced he had to sit out for a dodgy knee.

"That does leave us with odd numbers . . ." Graham glanced around the group.

"I'll do it."

Lachlan's jaw dropped.

Deli clapped her hand against Graham's back with more gusto than she probably would have naturally, mirroring the way Graham did it. "I'll be on your team, Graham. We can take anyone down."

Lachlan stepped forward. "She's got an injured ankle. She can't play."

The look she gave him could have branded his skin. "Did I miss the part where I asked you?"

He ignored her. "She's a liability."

"I'm *FINE*." Her volume wasn't quite shouting, but it wasn't quite not. She put her hands on her hips and did a borderline offensive imitation of an Irish jig. "If I was dreadfully injured, could I dance like an angel?"

Lachlan looked at Graham, pleading. "Graham, we don't need her."

Graham scratched his chin. "That's not yours to decide, Lachlan. Deli, you're in."

Deli mouthed *neener neener* behind Graham's back.

He arranged them so Lachlan and Deli were face to face on opposite teams. Lachlan flexed his fingers around the rope and rooted his boots into the mud. Deli glowered, with fingers so white they looked blue without her gloves.

Lachlan spoke quietly as they settled into their places. "You're gonna hurt yourself."

Deli made a *pfft* sound. "I'd be more worried about losing if I were you."

"Your confidence is inspiring."

"Thank you."

"And delusional."

"A woman beating a man in a show of strength is delusional? Hot take."

"Ilona could beat me. You?" He looked her up and down. His heartbeat picked up. "I'll take my chances."

"Your hubris will see you smitten."

"And your pride will see you fall." He felt his ears turn a touch pink.

"TUG!" Graham shouted, and the rope snapped taut. He was pulled toward Deli as she and her team yanked backward.

She cheered. "That's it, team! Tug, Kevin, tug!"

Kevin lit up at the sound of his name spoken in a positive context by a woman, and pulled with a fervor Lachlan didn't know he had. It propelled Lachlan forward again just as he was getting his footing.

"Lachlan!" Ilona growled from behind him. "Get it together!"

Deli's boot was perilously close to crossing over the stick that marked her team winning. She was the last who needed to cross. Lachlan was inches from losing.

He dug his heel into the mud and pulled with all his strength. Deli's backward momentum vanished, and she stumbled toward him as his team gave another heave.

"Over my dead body," she grunted, and resisted with renewed strength, pushing up mounds of wet soil around the soles of her boots.

A collective creaking, groaning sound came from the other team as they successfully slowed Lachlan's momentum to a stop. He could see beads of sweat on her lip. Then her face twitched with an unmistakable strike of pain. His eyes snapped to her ankle as he remembered the state of her the night he'd held her in his arms. He eased a bit. She took a small step back.

She really was going to hurt herself. "Deli, this is a bad idea."

"Cuz you're losing?"

He wanted her to stop. "I know that has to hurt."

"Why do you care, Lachlan?" Her voice was strained as her team claimed another few inches. Graham stepped back over the winner's line. "You're way too concerned with my joint health."

"Believe it or not, I don't want to see you hurt."

"I *don't* believe you."

"I'm trying to *help you*!" Lachlan rooted his feet again and halted their progress.

"I didn't ask for your help," she growled, tugging against his weight. She was only a step from the finish line, and once she crossed it would be done.

"Fine." He yanked Deli and her team forward. Graham swore as they nearly lost their footing. "Break it, for all I care."

"I wi—"

Lachlan pulled. She gasped as her eyes widened in pain.

No.

Lachlan's heart pounded through his chest as he abandoned the rope and reached for her. Deli's expression morphed from pain-stricken into triumph as she stepped backward over the finish line. Lachlan didn't have time to register that she'd been faking before the three grown adults who had been tugging behind him collided into his back with the momentum of a small rugby team. Her face changed again as Lachlan was pitched toward her.

"No no no no n—OOF."

They crashed to the ground. He caught himself on his hands on either side of her as best he could and felt his knee sink into the cold mud.

Deli lay with her eyes squeezed shut and her face turned away beneath him.

"Are you okay?" A cold, sharp grip of panic coursed through him. He searched her face for signs of pain, of a concussion, but she didn't move. "Deli, are you okay?"

Deli slowly opened her eyes. Her chin tucked into the softness of her neck while she tried to take inventory at their strange angle. Her breathing was too shallow. A red flush crept into her face—the marks of some ache she couldn't name.

Lachlan was frozen with fear. How could he have been so careless? Why did he have to play petty games with her? Why did he have to hurt people he didn't want to?

"Deli?"

"I, uh"—she stopped to swallow—"I'm not sure. I can't move."

Dread tore through him. "What hurts? What did you hit?"

"No, Lachlan, you're sort of on top of me."

For the first time, Lachlan realized how close he was—how he could see the hazel starburst in her left eye he hadn't noticed before. He was hovering over her in a half push-up with their pelvises pressed together and his knee in the mud between her splayed legs. The heat in Deli's cheeks glowed warmer. Despite the cold soaking through his clothes, his skin flushed, too.

"I'm sorry." Lachlan walked himself backward until he was off of her. "I'm so sorry."

Deli actually chuckled. "I'm fine, Lachlan, seriously." She tried to sit up and winced as the mud made a sucking sound around her torso.

Lachlan had lifted her off the ground before he knew what he was doing.

"Holy jabeezus!" Deli wheezed as he sat her down on a boulder and knelt. "I'm okay!"

Lachlan cupped her bad ankle and flexed her foot. "Does it hurt when I do this?"

"No," Deli began, but she hissed as her ankle jerked.

Lachlan's father had been right: He broke everything he touched.

"I need to take you to a hospital—"

Static electricity danced across his skin where Deli's hands suddenly cradled his face. She tilted his head up, but he kept his eyes trained on the ground. He couldn't bear it.

"Lachlan?" She whispered his name with softness he didn't deserve. "Hey, Lachlan, look at me."

He forced himself.

"It's not your fault."

His breath halted.

"Lachlan, you didn't do anything wrong. You didn't hurt me. I'm okay." She wiggled her foot between them. "See? The only thing wounded here is my pride—"

She was smiling. Deli was *smiling.*

"*—and* yours, I'm assuming, since you lost *big-time.*"

Somehow, Lachlan laughed, and a barb buried deep in his heart lost small but significant purchase. He smiled at Deli, so relieved he could have cried.

"Hey. You cheated."

She raised a devious eyebrow. "I'm wily! And you bought it."

As she pulled her hands from his face, she hooked a finger under the brim of his woolly hat and flipped it off his head. The cold rush against his damp hair sent goose pimples racing across his neck and arms, but Lachlan Scott didn't feel the chill.

All he could feel was something close to daylight on his skin after a long, midnight storm. He wasn't sure how, but somewhere, finally, the sun was rising.

And he was scared to death.

38

Deli

Deli could only imagine the sight of her—dipped in mud like a soft-serve cone in chocolate, as horrified as she'd ever been as Kevin winked and blew her a kiss behind Lachlan's back.

"Can ye give me a lift, Lachlan?" Kevin waggled his eyebrows. "I'll sit with Deli."

"Erm." Lachlan's cheeks flushed as he ran a hand through his auburn hair. It looked like a fire licking to life where the light caught the rouge strands. "I would, but I've got to get her back, and—"

"Actually, Deli, Blair has requested your company. Something about needing baking backup?" Graham squeezed Lachlan's shoulder. "You are free to ferry our wee Kevin home to his mum."

Deli couldn't read Lachlan. He'd been—they'd *both* been—sort of horrible on the drive over. But then they'd fallen, and Deli watched his eyes change, like the splintered wood of a shipwreck had swallowed up all their wildflower honey. Part of Lachlan had been right there, scanning her every movement for signs of pain. But another part of him vanished into that darkness, like something with claws had dragged him away.

Next thing she knew, she was holding his face in her hands.

When Trey had moments of insecurity, Deli stepped in, too. But Trey's ego was like being in a room with a snarling animal. She had to step between the man she loved and his own anger. If she were any less practiced, that anger would eat her alive. Deli still bore a few scars.

She knew Lachlan wouldn't have let her battle the prowling thing she'd seen in *him* for the world. But Deli glimpsed his suffering, and that was enough. She would have braved anything.

Which was, of course, unnerving.

Now he was back to refusing to meet her eye.

"I hope Blair knows I won't be appearing on *Bake Off* anytime soon," Deli said with a smile. She felt a queasiness at the news that she wouldn't be riding with Lachlan.

Tension radiated off him as he slammed the back closed and braced himself against it with both hands, breathing thick puffs of air into the cold.

Then he rolled his shoulders and stood with a mask of cool indifference.

"Then there's really no point for you to be there, but I suspect Blair will figure that out on her own." He glared at his new passenger. "Get your skinny arse in, Kevin."

Deli took a small step back at the harshness in Lachlan's tone. She thought of another man on another day—Trey taunting her with a book over her head and burying his face in her neck a moment later—and she curdled. She was tired of paying the price.

Her voice came out coarse. "Right. I forgot you're the expert on who Blair does and doesn't need in her life."

Graham sucked in a small, sudden breath as Lachlan met her eyes from under his brow. Shadow covered most of his face, but in a sliver of cloud-break light, he burned.

Graham unlocked the van. "Time to go, lass."

Deli stalked away limping.

"Oi, Lachlan," Graham called. "A word?"

She slammed her door.

Outside, Lachlan crossed his arms over his chest and looked down while Graham spoke. When Lachlan responded, palms up in a pleading sort of way, Deli thought she saw the words *wallflower* and *The Highlander* on his lips. Graham nodded, then took a breath and said something else. Lachlan's posture went rigid. Graham reached to touch him, but Lachlan walked off and left Graham's hand hovering in dead air.

Graham walked toward her shaking his head. As he reached for the handle, Deli heard him say, "Eejits, the two of yous," before Lachlan's truck roared to life and flung mud from the tires.

39

Deli

Deli stood outside her *new* friend's home in the pair of Graham's sweats she'd changed into in the back of the van, muddy clothes balled up in a bag, and she felt . . . wrong.

She missed her *old* friend. The one whose initial would grow old beside hers carved into the bark of a sycamore tree.

Chloe had witnessed all the small and different people Deli had ever been, and she'd loved them all. She had been a little girl in Deli's house, too. And Chloe had the only front row seat to Deli's many micro-heartbreaks from loving Trey Evans.

Was it asking a lot of her best friend, to answer the phone and watch her person fall to pieces over something she couldn't fix? Deli had done the same—passing notes about second-grade breakups, sobbing along with sad songs in first cars, bringing blankets and pad thai to eat on the floor of first apartments. But maybe Deli's hurt weighed too much. Maybe Chloe couldn't bear to carry it anymore.

Maybe Deli had been so absorbed in her own heartbreak she'd missed something unforgivable in Chloe's life. Now it had been weeks since she'd spoken to her best friend. It had been months since they'd been normal. And it felt like Deli's fault.

She shifted from foot to foot, trying and failing to adjust under the ache of missing Chloe—the heaviest thing of all.

Blair's front door swung open as Deli raised her fist to knock. A short, round girl who looked about ten with two long braids the color of new pennies and brilliant French-blue eyes stared at Deli from behind a screen door. A sick, sweet taste filled the air as Deli remembered another round little girl in this town—pigtails too tight, but not tight enough for her mother.

"Hi," the girl said, stone faced.

Deli always felt like she'd say the wrong thing and ruin children forever. "Hi."

"Who are you?"

"Uh . . . I'm Deli? I'm . . . Is your mom home?"

The girl put her hands on her hips and cocked her head to the side. "She might be. Depends on what you want."

Despite her general discomfort with kids, Deli did appreciate their audacity.

"Hmm." She put her hand on her chin. "I don't like doing business with people whose names I don't know. You've got mine. Seems fair I get yours."

The girl smirked. "Shouldn't have given yours so easily, then."

"How do you know Deli's my *real* name?"

"You would lie to an innocent child?"

"I would lie to a freakin' prison warden."

"Oh, so you've been to prison?" She tilted her head with a gotcha smile.

Deli playfully narrowed her eyes. "Not yet, but I've still got time."

"Penny!" Blair's voice rang from inside. "Has someone come round?"

"Yes!" Deli called at the same time Penny yelled, "No!"

Deli whispered, "Tell the truth, *Penny*."

"Just a felon, Mum! Straight from jail, by the looks of her."

"Then ask her in, Penelope! She'll be in need of a good meal!"

Penny stepped back. "Some mum you are, having your child open her home to a criminal."

Blair carried a daunting pile of laundry past with a smile and called, "Come in!"

Penny put her hands in the air as Deli slid past her into the narrow entryway. "I don't have any money!"

Deli scrambled for a comeback appropriate to toss at a child who was actively and effectively roasting her. "Oh, cuz you spent it all on . . . manners school?"

"*MaNnErS sChOoL?*" Penny mocked.

Blair appeared and planted a kiss on Penny's head. "That would be a good idea."

Penny rolled her eyes, but Deli caught her smile as she disappeared down the hallway.

"Hi," Blair said.

"Hi," Deli replied.

"So, you've met Penny."

"She's an excellent guard dog."

"She did bite a babysitter once."

"For failing her riddles three?"

"For telling Pen not to sing along while they watched *Mulan* so the babysitter could 'hear the songs.'"

"I'd bite her, too."

"Yes, Andrew and I are very proud." Blair looked her up and down. "Is this your baking outfit?"

Deli smooshed her lips together. "There was a mud incident."

Blair raised an eyebrow. "Local hazard."

"It would seem," Deli said. "So . . . baking?"

"I hope you stretched." Blair ushered her in. "It's gonna be a marathon, Chef."

"Yes, Chef!" Deli saluted as she followed Blair into a small, thoughtful kitchen that Blair moved through like it was an extension of herself. She glanced at the clock and winked.

"It's five o'clock somewhere?"

Deli retraced the *mud incident* and aftermath in her head. "Yes. Do you have—"

Blair uncorked a ceramic white bottle with a pop. "Rock Rose Gin is your favorite, no?"

Deli's mouth fell open. Chloe still had to ask what Deli wanted at the bar every single time, even though she always ordered a gin and tonic, and Chloe always ordered a vodka cran.

"How did you *remember* that?"

Blair clinked a few ice cubes into a highball glass. "I just paid attention."

Deli shoved her hands into the pockets of Graham's sweatpants, and her fingers brushed against something. She pulled out a wad of paper that might have gone through the wash. It was a brochure for a *Highlander* tour. She squinted at the photo.

Blair handed Deli a fizzing, rosy drink. "Cheers."

Deli took a sip and thrust the brochure at Blair's face. "Is that—wow, that's a good G and T, thank you—is that Graham with the guy from *The Highlander*?"

Blair glanced. "Erm, looks like it, yeah."

"Are they standing outside Lachlan's pub?"

Blair picked up her own drink and took a long sip. "I think that was a long time ago. Graham just uses the photo for advertising." She clapped her hands together suddenly. "What do you know about cakes, Miss MacDonald?"

Deli peeled her eyes from the brochure, though the image of Billy S. Burns and Graham's easy familiarity turned in the back of her mind. "I know that a stodgy cake is a sin against God."

"Correct." Blair snatched the brochure from Deli's hand and shoved it into a drawer behind her. "You'll be needing both of your hands." She tossed her a balled-up wad of fabric. It unfurled into an apron.

Grandma Rosemary used to bake when Deli was very small. She'd spend hours showing Deli how to mix dry ingredients into wet, how to beat an egg white, how to measure brown sugar. Even when Deli messed up, Grandma Rosemary fixed it. She snuck her cookies in her backpack when her mom came to get her. She'd been so elegant, in heels with a neat apron and a glass of sipping wine. Grandma Rosemary made it seem effortless.

Deli, on the other hand, only needed two gin and tonics to end up coated in flour with a streak of chocolate batter across her forehead like Rafiki had hoisted her over Pride Rock.

Penny strolled by and casually called Deli a chimney sweep.

"Could be worse." Blair shrugged. "She called Lachlan a 'grumpy old turnip.' He moped around for a full week."

Deli laughed while the smell of vanilla, chocolate, and blackberry whirled through the kitchen. "I'm with Penny. He's like if Oscar the Grouch got out of his trash can and inherited the deed to a Scottish pub."

Blair swirled her glass while the ice cubes worked up a gentle fizz. "You've been getting special treatment."

"*Special* is one word for it."

Deli did quick math based on Penny's age. If Lachlan and Blair were mid-thirties, they must have been together quite young. Maybe even high school sweethearts.

She'd been in love with Trey when they were that age, too. It had eclipsed her world. Like he was a star and she a chosen celestial body in his orbit. What kind of wanting did a young and brooding Lachlan Scott wrap his first love in? What must it have been like for Lachlan and Blair to be able to touch instead of being locked in a gravity loop—always circling? She wondered how it would have felt to have the boy she'd loved with all of her young heart span light-years to crash into her, too.

Deli only knew how to be the thing that orbits.

"Blair?" she asked. "What *is* the deal with Lachlan?"

Blair's pocket buzzed. She said that Andrew texted to say he wouldn't be home in time to give Deli a ride, as originally planned, and then placed a call to Aunt Mo.

"There!" Blair topped off Deli's drink as she hung up. "Ride secured."

"Sublime."

"Anyway, Lachlan has a good heart."

Deli's guts felt liquid. "You know, he doesn't even *know* me, and he'd already decided that I . . . what?" She heard her voice get a little louder. "That I was unwelcome at my own grandpa's home? That I wasn't good enough for Aunt Mo? Or for him?"

Blair nodded while she stared at her feet.

"BUT THEN! Then he'll snap into, like, Übernice Lachlan, and he'll be all concerned about my ankle or my head wound or something—like what?"

Blair managed to sneak in a quick, "Well, a head wound is something anyone should be concerned about."

"Who made him the boss of me? God, I've never met someone so . . ." She didn't know what to call Lachlan. "So . . . *ugh*. You know?"

"Ugh," Blair repeated with a little grin. "Ugh, indeed."

Blair pointed to a photo hanging in the hallway. In it, her younger self smiled, her long copper hair whipping around her face like a sheet of fire—a force of nature. It captured who she had been then, which told Deli more about who her friend was now. It was easy talking to Blair. Easy to know her.

"Lachlan took that photo. He inherited a camera when he was a boy, and he took to it like it had always been a part of him. He loved to take portraits. Every single one he developed was like some sort of magic. Lachlan could raise that lens and see you—*really* see you."

Deli knew what it was to translate someone else into a tangible truth—to transform yearning into a bouquet, to slip guilt into a glass vase. More than once, a soul had stumbled into the shop and told her of their person—who had gone, or who had come—and she had magicked their heart into something beautiful for one human to hand another. The photo in the hallway was like that.

And *Lachlan* had taken it.

"I've never even seen him with a camera."

"Lachlan's da was a hard man. He was the hardest on Lachlan. The plan was always that he'd stay and take over The Wallflower's Crown when it was time. Lachlan said he wanted to."

That was what Lachlan had done, as far as Deli could tell.

"All I ever wanted was this." Blair swept an arm toward her kitchen and her sofa dotted with bright toys and tiny socks. "We had a plan, and god, I loved him, but it was never easy for Lachlan. My parents . . . I have never wondered if I was loved. But Lachlan? A day's not gone by that Lachlan Scott didn't wonder what about him needs changing."

Something horrible and hot was rising in Deli's throat. If Blair noticed, she had the grace to act like she didn't.

"He'd put the camera in the attic when he was a boy, and when he found it again, something in him came to life. Suddenly, Fearnhall wasn't big enough—he'd run out of portraits to take. And for the first time, he found the courage to tell his parents he was going to leave. He told me, too."

"But all you ever wanted"—Deli cast a fond look around Blair and Andrew's life, where race cars were scattered across the floors and a rubber ducky lived by the sink—"was this."

Blair's soft sadness gave way to gratitude. "I told him I'd go with him, but he knew my heart was here. And Lachlan was making an escape. So he ended things with me. It was kind."

The two women shared a moment of silence.

Deli recalled the way he'd changed as he searched her for something he'd broken. "He didn't leave, did he? Where are his parents? Where the hell is his brother?"

"He did leave. We said when he came back we could try again, but he told me never to wait for him if it came to someone else."

Blair tapped her phone screen and showed Deli her background. It was Andrew, his eyes sleepy but laced with mischief, like Penny's cornflower blue. Their two kids were draped over him in their bed, fast asleep.

"Andrew went to school with us, too, but he was a year younger. He was shy. Then one night I went to a pub quiz where he was playing music a town over. I walked in and . . . I almost felt like I'd never heard music before. When Andrew saw me, he missed a couple notes. Turned bright red!" Blair laughed, remembering.

"And that was it?" Deli asked. "After all that time, suddenly Andrew? No thoughts of Lachlan?"

Blair looked at Deli with a tender tilt of her head. "Standing in that pub? I'd been struck by a lightning bolt that made things new. Like I'd never seen him before that moment."

Deli thought of the moment she'd met Trey, even though they were just kids. She felt that, too, in a way. Maybe not lightning, but like she'd been caught in a tide and her life would never be the same.

"If I met Trey now, there'd be lightning."

"I saw Andrew, and I knew I'd love him forever," Blair said. Deli opened her mouth to say *me too* about Trey, but Blair held up a hand. "*Because* of the way he looked *at me*. He looked at me like I was a lighthouse and he'd been lost at sea. I could feel it down to my bones, Deli. Andrew saw me in such a way that I had no choice but to see *myself* differently."

The warm place in Deli's mind that cradled thoughts of Trey chilled.

"Wait," Deli said, "if Lachlan left . . . why is he back?"

Blair blanched.

The door burst open in a riot of limbs and backpack and tiny shoes being kicked off.

"Mummy, Mummy! You'll never *believe* what I did today!" cried a little voice.

Blair couldn't smile wider. She waved through the kitchen window to a car pulling away. "What's that, love?"

"I went off the DIVING BOARD! Mu—" The voice vanished. Deli saw one giant brown owl eye, then a second as an elfish face with wispy platinum chin-length hair peered around the doorway.

Blair knelt to kid-eye level. "Kieran, this is a friend of Mummy and Daddy's."

"Hi, Kieran. I'm Deli," she said. "I love your house."

Kieran's eyes widened. "You've got a movie accent!"

"She's American." Penny slid into the small space with her sibling, eyeing Deli with a satisfied look on her face. "And a *criminal*."

Kieran's eyes got even bigger.

"Alright, alright. It's bath time for you lot. Kieran's hair will turn green. And Deli is not a criminal. She's just wearing sweatpants."

"Sweatpants from *jail*," Penny muttered as her mom herded them toward the back of the house.

Blair checked her watch. "Mo will be here in a few! Thank you so much for your help! I'm loving having you here, my friend!"

Deli watched Blair disappear down the hallway, but Kieran ducked quietly under her arm and walked silently back toward Deli. Both of Kieran's hands were knotted together in a tight ball held at the base of their throat.

After a painfully long silence, Kieran finally said in a tiny voice, "Excuse me?"

Deli tried to smile in a not-scary way. "Yes?"

"My name is Kieran, and I live here."

"Hi, Kieran."

"Erm, my friend told me to ask you a question."

Deli blinked. "Your friend?"

"He's my see-through friend only I can see. His name is Cal." Kieran sniffled, rubbed their fingers against their shirt, and said, "He wanted me to ask if you're still sad inside?"

A fridge magnet clattered to the floor as Deli took an involuntary step backward. Her jaw felt wired shut. "I . . . I'm . . . I wasn't sad."

Kieran let out a big, dramatic sigh, the way that children do, raising their arms and letting them fall by their sides. Then, much to Deli's horror, Kieran crossed the kitchen, stuck out their little hand, and wrapped it around hers.

"You don't need to be sad." Their voice was small but sure. "You are *good*," Kieran said, patting her hand. "That's what he told me. *Delilah has always been* good."

Her heart skidded to a halt. Before she could say a word, a blaring horn rattled the windows like shock paddles. Aunt Mo grinned while she headbanged to Aerosmith.

When Deli looked back down, Kieran was already gone.

40

Mo

Mo stirred her tea and listened to Lachlan pacing outside the cottage.

By the time he knocked, she had a cup of coffee waiting at his normal spot at the table.

She cleared her throat. "Do I need to post a No Loitering sign?"

The door squeaked and Lachlan peered through, scanning the room.

"She's not here." Mo watched him feign confusion. "You don't need to be scared."

"That's not—what? I just—"

"Mmhmm." Mo scooted his coffee toward him. "Could you come in before Beans pulls off a jailbreak?"

Lachlan saw Beans's head straining upward between his calf and the doorway.

"Christ, Beans. Can you not?"

The cat responded with a disapproving meow and darted underneath a sitting chair by the fire as Lachlan shimmied inside. A shower of dried mud fell from his knees as he shook his feet out of his boots.

"Took a tumble, there?"

The shift in the air was so sudden Mo's head snapped up from her crossword. Lachlan was so still he might have been made of marble—his autumn eyes wide.

"What did she say? I mean—erm . . ." Mo could actually see his Adam's apple rise and fall with the gulp he took before he attempted nonchalance. His voice came out far too deep. "Oh, so, you've spoken with Deli?"

He tried to lean against the wall and hit a raincoat, slid a few inches, and recovered. A blush rose in his cheeks. It had been so long since Mo had felt like she was in the room with this *boy* she had to fight off a smile.

"You alright, kid?"

His shoulders dropped in defeat. "Tug-o-war."

Mo raised her eyebrows, and he pointed to the muddy knees of his trousers.

"Ah."

He collapsed into his chair and reached for the coffee. "Thank you."

"Of course. And what of my niece?"

Lachlan spluttered into the mug and recoiled, blowing little droplets of brown out of his nose. "Wh-what?"

"You left with her. You returned without her. Tell me you didn't leave her to Kevin."

He ran his sleeve across his face. "Blair invited her for baking this afternoon."

"You took her to Blair's?"

He shook his head. "Graham did. Our Kevin was without a ride."

Mo smiled. "Fell on that sword, did you?"

"Aye."

"Good lad," she said, patting his knee as the phone rang.

Lachlan pretended to contemplate his mug while he obviously strained to hear her brief conversation with Blair. "Right, no problem. I'll swing by in a bit. Has Penny chased her off yet?" Lachlan's eyes tightened at the sound of Blair's laugh through the receiver. "That's my girl. See you soon!"

He fidgeted with a button on his shirt. "All good over there?"

Mo nodded, trying to keep herself from asking the things she was desperate to ask.

He didn't meet her eyes. "Does she need a ride home?"

"I got it."

"Okay, right." He stared at the ceiling for a moment before taking a huge whiff of air. "What are you cooking?"

"Bolognese. You're welcome to join Deli and me for di—"

"She's going to leave you, you know."

Mo stilled. "What?"

"Deli will leave you, Mo. Just like the rest of them."

She took a deep breath. She had wondered if this conversation would come. "I did the leaving in my family, Lachlan."

"Did you?"

"I did."

The room fell quiet, apart from the bubbling sauce and the soft rain that had begun to fall outside.

"If you did the leaving, where will you go this time, Mo? When she brings everything you left behind right back here?" He tapped the kitchen table with two fingers. "Where are you going to go when you realize Deli isn't . . . that *she* is one of *them*?"

If it had been anyone else, Mo might have been angry at the things Lachlan was saying. But anyone else wouldn't have been the person who'd witnessed her pain before, or who considered himself her protector, or who had been left behind in Fearnhall himself. And they wouldn't have been someone Mo had opened a door to find holding her niece in his arms, lost to a feeling she'd never seen on him before.

Mo leaned forward and put her hand on top of his. Lachlan needed to learn it on his own. "Did you want to wait here while I go get Deli so you can see her again, or—"

Lachlan stood and stomped away. Beans scolded him with a mighty meow for the way the cottage shook as he slammed the door.

"Ugh!" His muffled voice called from outside. "I'm sorry, Beans!"

Beans hissed from the window.

Mo rose and kissed his furry brow. "Give him some grace, my sage little legume." Beans pressed his head to her chin. "Growing pains are the pits."

41

Lachlan

Lachlan slammed on his brakes and swerved, searching his mirrors frantically for signs of the animal he hoped he'd just avoided. He'd been thinking about how he'd spoken to Deli. To Mo. Lachlan cursed himself for being distracted as he stepped onto the pavement.

He hadn't thought his day could get much more distressing. His fault, really, for underestimating Douglas.

The wee man sifted through roadside stones, facing away from Lachlan, bent at the waist. His newly bedazzled mini kilt sparkled in the sun.

Lachlan didn't shield his eyes. The damage was already done.

"Douglas?"

Douglas spun around with a palm full of pebbles. His bare chest and belly were so bright Lachlan nearly missed the fuzzy hat with antlers erupting from either side.

"You're driving too fast, lad. Could've hit a deer."

If he had killed Douglas, would that have counted?

"Mmhmm. And why are you standing in the road . . . half naked . . . *dressed* like a deer?"

"Isn't it obvious?"

Lachlan repressed many responses and settled on, "No?"

"It's such a nice day, seemed a shame to deprive the sun of this sight." He brought his arm from his head to his lower body like a game show presenter. "Considering I plan on being here awhile, I thought it kind to dress the part. Plenty of deer move through here. Wouldnae want to startle the poor *dears*."

Douglas stared at Lachlan with a self-satisfied grin on his face. Lachlan refused to indulge the pun.

"So, you're . . . sunbathing?"

"Goodness, no!" Douglas pointed to an easel *in the road* beside a small stool and crate of paint tubes. "I'm painting!"

"What are you painting in the middle of the road, Douglas?"

"Our home!"

He abruptly started back toward his canvas. Lachlan dropped his head, followed. He wondered if every small town came with an eccentric old man who preferred life mostly nude.

"You see?" Douglas said as Lachlan approached. "Look at that—worth remembering, don't you think?"

Lachlan saw . . . the farm. They were the same unremarkable hills he drove by every day, spotted with sketchy heather patches and a sheep or two. "I . . ."

Douglas turned his canvas around. "Look."

Through Douglas's eyes, it was transformed. Short strokes of greens and golds made up the grass, caught in sunlight. Speckled lavender, lilac, and magenta nestled into dark streaks, punctuating the green. Layers of blue, gray, and white adorned the sky like candy floss mid-pull, coming apart in a fragile web. It took Lachlan's breath away.

"Douglas, it's perfect."

"Oh, I doubt that. I expect it will change before it's done."

Lachlan's brow knit. "Why would you change it?"

"The season is on the brink. So is its portrait."

"But you're the painter."

"Art isn't about perfection. It's about translating the truth of things."

Lachlan thought of Douglas painting over what he'd done and felt an urgent need to save it. "Can I buy it from you?"

Douglas watched him thoughtfully for a long moment. "No, dinnae think so."

His jaw tensed. "What do you want, then? Name your price."

"The painting chooses the person, Lachlan. Besides, she's still changin'."

"But what if you ruin it?"

Douglas laughed so loudly and suddenly a sheep bleated on the hillside and ran. "Oh, Christ, my boy, don't you know? You can only be sure of two things: what you've got right now and what you don't. Being 'ruined'—that's a matter of perspective."

Lachlan stood a little straighter. "I don't believe that."

Douglas dipped a brush and squinted at the hillside. The sun had already shifted.

"Best get where you're going, lad. We're losing the light."

42

Deli

Aunt Mo pulled into a parking spot beside a garden enclosed in wild white roses.

"So, who do you know here, again?"

Aunt Mo shrugged. "I've lived in Fearnhall for a long time. Plenty of people get old and move in. Just have to drop off some paperwork. I'll be back in a second. Maybe two."

She headed into the retirement home with an official looking envelope and left Deli to wait in the car.

Deli pushed the cuticle on her thumb back with a pen cap she found in the center divider. Then she picked dried mud out of the tread of her boots. She was studying a tree in the middle of the garden—dotted with glimmers of red—when a figure appeared behind it.

An older woman in a lacy white nightgown wove barefooted through the mud in confused stops and starts. Deli searched for someone in a uniform or with a name tag coming after her, but the woman was alone. Deli got out of the car. Glossy pomegranates hung heavy from the tree, and the woman wrapped a blue-veined hand around a fruit and tugged it free. Deli cleared her throat softly. "Ma'am? Are you alright?"

She went still, the pomegranate clutched to her chest in both hands. Long strands of silver hair had come loose from a twist and now blew sideways across her face, but her eyes . . .

They burned like hearths in an empty house—fire in a hollow. Honey and amber gone dull. Still, they were unmistakable.

Deli had wiped away dust from this woman's photo.

She was with Lachlan's mother.

43

Deli

If not for her eyes, Deli might have thought she was carved from white marble. The fruit pressed against her body looked like a heart in her hand.

"Mrs. Scott?"

The woman stood straighter and lifted her chin at the sound of her name. "Ah, Maureen. Is something the matter?" Deli turned around expecting to see her aunt, but there was no one. "Maureen? Did you hear me, hen?"

She was *young* to be this sort of sick. Guilt pickled in Deli's memory and trickled down her spine as she thought of the things she'd said to Lachlan—about his daddy or mommy issues.

"I'm sorry, Mrs. Scott." Deli stepped closer. "I was distracted by the flowers. They're beautiful, don't you think?"

Mrs. Scott appraised the roses. "Nothing compared to my garden."

"Your garden must be magical." Deli drew nearer. "Are you cold, Mrs. Scott? Should we go and fetch your coat?"

She rubbed an arm with a trembling hand. "I . . ." She turned in a small circle.

Deli knew there was a blanket in the trunk of Aunt Mo's car. She spotted a cast-iron bench nestled among the wild rosebushes. "Can

I sit with you for a moment? It's so lovely here. I'd appreciate your company."

Mrs. Scott looked past the garden, searching a horizon only she could see. "I suppose. Only for a moment. My husband will be home at half six."

"Oh, perfect. Let's sit." Deli offered her a hand. A chill seemed to rack Mrs. Scott's body as the cold metal cut through the thin fabric of her nightgown. "Let me just grab the blanket in my—"

Her hand wrapped around Deli's wrist like a vise. She was not as frail as she looked.

"Maureen," she whispered urgently, "he doesn't understand. Lachlan isn't like William. He has . . . responsibilities. His father expects certain things from him. I know he listens to you. Please. Will you speak to him?"

Deli stuttered, and Mrs. Scott misunderstood her silence for a refusal.

"Please, Maureen—there are consequences for him—for *us*. His father is losing his patience."

Deli shouldn't have heard it—she shouldn't have been here. These were the rooms where the most painful things in Lachlan's life lived, and she had seen too much.

Suddenly, Aunt Mo covered Mrs. Scott's hand with hers, closing them both in warmth.

She gave Deli a meaningful look. "I'm sure Maureen will help with Lachlan however she can, Lucinda. Isn't that right, *Maureen*?"

White petals fluttered over their feet. Deli tried to help. "Yes. I'll speak to Lachlan."

Lucinda Scott looked between Aunt Mo and Deli, her lips pursed into a small O as she tried to make sense of something clearly wrong. Aunt Mo spread the blanket in her arms. She was so sure in her movements, so steady, like she'd done this a thousand times.

"They're serving smoked salmon and cream cheese sandwiches with tea today. Let's go get them before that dreadful Bernice can stuff them in her handbag again."

Lucinda stood with urgency. "Last time Bernice wafted fish for a week."

Aunt Mo whispered, "I'll see you in the car."

And Deli was alone in the cyclone of perfect snowy roses. She thought of Lachlan—so steady and unmoving, stubborn and strong—watching his mother turn into a slip of what she'd been. And she thought of what Mrs. Scott had said—how his father's anger had stalked him. Fed on his boyhood dreams. She wondered where the other son in the photo had gone. She wondered what happened to the man who'd named The Wallflower's Crown.

Wallflower. *Fidelity in misfortune.*

A wife who doesn't leave. A mother who doesn't protect. A boy, and the man he becomes, bound to a family he no longer has.

A pomegranate thudded to the ground and cracked open, scattering drops of vibrant crimson—*foolishness*—among the fallen petals.

44

Deli

Deli entered The Wallflower that night with a stomach full of lead.

"Ah! The beauties of McDonnell Cottage! WELCOME to my tournament OF DARTS!" Graham spread his arms wide. "Just in time to watch me demolish old Cairn."

Cairn leaned against the wall in the same exact outfit Deli had last met him in with his hat tipped low over his brow. He flashed her an unbothered smirk as he twirled a dart between his fingers like magicians roll a coin.

Blair and Andrew's kids sat on a couch, transfixed as Douglas made a balloon animal. Hannah was at the bar between Andrew and Blair. A framed black-and-white photo of Lachlan's parents, smiling with their arms wrapped around each other in front of the pub, hung behind them. Even in shades of gray, Lucinda's eyes were striking.

Lachlan slid a Guinness and a gin and tonic across the bar to Deli and Aunt Mo. He smiled at her, and Deli felt like she'd been dunked into warm water—caught in the caramel heat of Lachlan's eyes.

It was delusional to think there was something in the way he'd looked at her at practice, or even the way he'd looked at her when she'd just walked in. It was senseless to fall asleep imagining his arms, his heat against her body. Deli's brain, the mutinous glob, was concocting the connection between them.

How could he even be kind to her, much less be *attracted* to her, after the things she'd said? It was no wonder he'd lashed out, knowing now that she'd taken shots about a father who wasn't around and a mother who was replaying his childhood trauma in a care facility. She felt . . . disgusting. Lachlan had said things, too, but Deli needed to make amends.

"Ye shall never take what's mine, Farm Beast!" Graham boomed.

Aunt Mo leaned toward her. "This rivalry has been brewing for years. Graham's gloating has become . . . excessive."

Cairn's blue eyes glittered as he cocked his arm. A hush fell over the pub. "Kieran? What do I need to win?"

"A bull's-eye!"

"Then bull's-eye it is." He threw the dart with shocking speed, and it connected with a satisfying thud in the very center.

The pub erupted.

"God, the walls," Lachlan groaned behind her. Hannah flicked her wrist and produced a blade. She looked at Cairn.

He winked. "Go on, hen."

She sank the blade into the wall, adding a tally to a column with the letter C above it, and Graham collapsed to the floor in a dramatic heap.

Blair came over and threw her arm around Deli's shoulders as she called for Lachlan. Deli dropped her eyes. "Hey, you, I have a wedding favor to ask."

Lachlan nodded. "Of course I'll pour drinks."

"Actually, we were hoping you'd be our photographer."

He looked stricken. "Me?"

"Of course you."

"I couldn't—it's . . . I haven't touched a camera in ages, and—"

"Lachlan, please?" Blair interrupted, her voice soft. "For old time's sake?"

He stilled, and Deli felt like she was watching an important moment on a tightrope—Lachlan balancing under a spotlight on the brink of a drop far longer than it appeared to everyone but him.

Aunt Mo jumped in with a smile. "You just need a little practice. We'll sort it out! Blair, let me show you some color palette ideas."

Blair and Aunt Mo sank into a loveseat and left Deli at the bar with Lachlan alone.

She plucked up the guts. "Hey, um, Lachlan?"

His shoulders hunched up around his neck, and he turned as slowly as a person could without actually doing the slow motion bit, multiple feet away from her. *"Mmm?"*

"I . . ." She cleared her throat and tried to project a whisper. "I'm sorry for what I said."

"What?"

She added a little volume, shooting a look at the merrymakers close by. "I'm sorry."

Lachlan didn't come any closer. "What?"

"Would you just come here already?"

His voice was tight and smile fake as he approached. "At your service, miss."

Deli took a big breath in and slowly let it out between her teeth. "I just wanted to apologize for . . . what I said in the car the other day. I shouldn't have . . . I just . . ."

He stared at her with a superior glee now that he knew she was apologizing. "Go on."

"I didn't know what I was commenting on, and I shouldn't have commented on it. I was angry, and I'm not used to being angry."

Lachlan raised an eyebrow. "I find that unlikely."

Deli narrowed her eyes. "Well, I was finding you insufferable."

"Lotta feelings."

She felt irritation slip into her voice. "I'm finding you insufferable now."

"Shocking."

"Like I said," she said slowly, trying to reharness the sentiment, "I am *sorry*."

His mouth turned down in a thoughtful frown. "Alright." He raised his eyebrows. "Anything else?"

Her annoyance picked at her patience. He'd said some nasty things, too, to be acting so above it all. She slid off the barstool as she snatched her drink off the counter. "Enjoy the view from your very high horse."

He stuck a finger in an ear. "Sorry, can't hear you from up here!"

But when she spun, Douglas was standing so close they were very face to face.

"Deli, may I?" He hopped onto the stool beside her, and she climbed back up reluctantly. Lachlan had turned away, and she was grateful for the small privacy. Douglas produced a rectangular parcel wrapped in brown paper from under the bar and placed it gingerly between them.

"A gift for you."

"What?"

"It's a painting. It's yours."

"Oh my god, Douglas, that's too kind!"

Douglas put his hands on hers. "Take it home, but don't open it."

"Why?"

"I suspect it has something to tell you."

"You have something to tell me?"

Douglas shook his head. "The painting does, love. I'm just the delivery guy."

Deli pressed her lips together. "Will the painting tell me when to open it?"

"Don't take a sarcastic tone, or she may show you before you're ready."

"And what would happen if she did that?"

He looked at her with sorrowful eyes. "We would never know. And it would be a tragedy."

Silence stretched between them for a moment. Deli was coming to deeply appreciate Douglas and all of his Douglas ways.

"I won't open it until it tells me to."

He released her hands. "My work is done. Now, it's well past time for a pint."

Lachlan was already watching them out of the corner of his eye. Aunt Mo slid onto the stool on the other side of Deli and hugged her with one arm as Lachlan drew near.

"Hey, Lachlan, listen. I have a plan."

"I don't trust your plans, Mo."

"No, this one's *good*."

Deli listened in shocked silence to Aunt Mo's solution for Lachlan's conundrum.

When she was done, his tone was nearly as flat as his mouth. "I'm not doing that."

"Why not? You'll get the practice you need to feel ready, Deli's free, and your kilt hasn't been touched in ages. It'll need a day to breathe before the weekend anyway."

"And how am I meant to be *in* the photos and taking them?"

"You've got to get good at self-timer before the wedding, as I expect your buns in most of them."

"Blair doesn't want me in her wedding photos."

"Like hell I don't, Scott!" Blair looked proud of her eavesdropping. "Plus, the bride requests a few solo glamour shots just for Mo's fridge."

Aunt Mo held her hand up and Blair high-fived it seamlessly. "Think of my fridge."

Lachlan looked at Deli, and the warmth bloomed in her again. She snapped her jaw shut and stared at her hands—figuring it was better to be suddenly mute and incapable of eye contact than risk speaking while her brain was, apparently, melting.

She could feel his eyes like a laser beam. "Don't *you* have anything to say about this?"

She counted her fingers. Nine. No, wait . . . that . . . She started over.

"Earth to Deli—have you no thoughts?"

She had a lot of thoughts, but they weren't in English.

"She's struck speechless by the genius of it!" Aunt Mo clapped her hands together. "So that's that."

Lachlan's eyebrows shot to the ceiling. His face pleaded for Deli to intervene.

She shrugged and sighed. "I guess that's that."

They would go to some scenic glen, pretend to be into each other in a romantic fashion, and create photographic evidence of it in two days' time. The wedding was that weekend.

"What a time for you to be made speechless."

Lachlan handed her a Diet Coke with lemon when he saw she hadn't touched the gin and tonic. Deli had never ordered one from Lachlan before—he must have noticed her drinking it at the cottage. She took a hearty swig that ended up too hearty, and sloshed dark brown soda down her front, sputtering.

He grinned. "Though it's good to know you've not lost your effortless grace."

"And you your charm," Deli said while still dribbling. Lachlan extended a fistful of napkins before she could ask, and she snatched at them with the hand that wasn't cupped under her chin, collecting Diet Coke runoff from her face.

"You're dripping on my floor."

She stared him in the eyes, unblinking, and dipped her fingers into her glass before flicking them onto the ground. "Am I?"

Then Deli felt a tug on her elbow. Kieran blinked up at her. "Excuse me? My mum wants to speak to you, Delilah."

Deli cringed at the name, reminded of their strange conversation before. Lachlan let out a low whistle. She spun on him.

"Did you tell Kieran my full name?"

"Me?" He polished the bar top casually. "Not I, *Delila—*"

"Don't."

He chuckled.

"I told you," Kieran said, tugging on her sleeve. "My friend told me. Can you come talk to my mummy please?"

Deli followed Kieran dutifully to report to Blair, who, Deli suspected, was just giving her child a task to keep busy.

She pulled Deli into a corner. "Deli, I have to ask you something."

Had Blair seen the strange shift in Deli and Lachlan's interactions? "Sure!"

"Would you design my bouquet?"

"Oh." It was a reverent thing—a wedding bouquet. The photos could hang in their home forever. "I would be honored, Blair."

"Very good."

"Wow. Do you have any ideas about what you want?"

Blair shrugged with a big smile. "I trust you."

"Are you sure, Blair?"

"Yes. Now, if you'll excuse me, I need to see a man about a dress." Blair strode toward Douglas, leaving Deli alone with her thoughts.

Until her phone started buzzing in her pocket.

45

Deli

Deli pulled her feet up onto an armchair and held her phone between her knees and her face to see whatever had come through as privately as possible. She didn't want Blair to loop her into wedding talk and pull her away. She pushed down thoughts of Lachlan with the hope of Trey and unlocked her phone with her heart in her throat.

She needed to know that it mattered to her closest people—that it mattered she'd disappeared.

There were two texts and an email.

But nothing was from Chloe. It landed in her chest like a weight onto a padded floor—muted and heavy. An unread text from Trey beckoned from her palm, but Deli hesitated. She'd been gone nearly a month, and the gravity of it set in. She couldn't do this forever. Soon, Deli would have to go home, no matter what was or wasn't waiting for her.

She closed the messaging app and opened her email instead, ducking under the guillotine feeling in her head.

There was a message from Rosemary McDonnell.

To: Delilah MacDonald
From: Rosemary McDonnell
Subject: You need to know . . .

Hello Delilah,

This is Grandma Rosemary. I understand you've gone to visit your aunt, Maureen.

Maureen abandoned the family many years ago after being misled by your grandfather to play into his last bitter attempt to hurt me. Instead of listening to reason when Callum washed his hands of Lorraine (your mother) and disinherited her in favor of Maureen, Maureen simply cut us out.

I confess, your departure worries me, darling girl. I know you are a bright woman of your own mind, but so was Maureen, once. That town . . . Fearnhall . . . No one knows better than I how beguiling it can be. There was a time that I, too, was a young woman taken by its sea, its rain. Its poetry. However, I beg of you to remember your life here. You will wake someday to find the air is too damp, the food too bland, and the company too stuck in their ways.

Soon you will know Fearnhall is no place to call home. I only hope it will not be too late for the people and life you've left here to welcome you back.

Come home, darling. Though Maureen has caused great damage to this family, it has taken years off my life to have my child so far gone. I dare say there is a part of me who believes you might be, God forbid, following in her footsteps.

I could not survive it. Even now, I have a new knot in my chest and can scarcely catch my breath.

When will you be home? Please give me a date, and I will have my travel agent purchase you a ticket immediately.

Yours,
Rosemary McDonnell (Grandma)

Deli read the beginning of her grandmother's email again, trying to understand the scant but illuminating details. She'd never known the *full* story of her aunt's departure. She'd never heard about her mother being cut out of a will or about Aunt Mo being complicit. Across the pub, Aunt Mo's laugh rang out loud and clear as Graham wove a tale, and she wiped away tears of laughter.

Aunt Mo just made Deli feel like everything was easy.

Deli knew Lorraine and Rosemary were often complicated . . . sometimes even cruel. Her grandmother, strict and exacting, like a surgeon with a scalpel excising the tumor of unruliness and excess before it could consume the little girls she loved. Her mother, so hot and cold, creative and kind until some passing shadow, then a whip already on its way to you—searching for open skin to leave welted. But they weren't *bad.* They had their reasons and the benefit of motherhood's eyes.

Deli couldn't dismiss what they said about Aunt Mo without consideration—*she* had only known her for weeks, while they had known Aunt Mo her entire life. But the person Deli had come to know was so at odds with who her grandmother and mother had painted in sketchy strokes over Deli's life—especially a person who would do something so callous to her own sister.

She felt a pang of anger for her mother—the forsaken daughter of an absent man.

Deli breathed in slowly for ten seconds and out for ten seconds, then clicked on her texts. She debated between the two names with unread messages and felt a splotchy rash start up her neck. She clicked the text from Trey.

> Deli . . . Things are so weird now. It's like I don't know what to do with myself. Every morning I wake up and reach for my phone to text you. It feels like you're never coming home. I'm starting to think I need to figure out how to live my life without you. Tell me we can fix it? I need you. Please.

Deli felt like she'd swallowed a rock and it was lodged in her throat. Her fingers shook as she started to type.

> Yes, we can fix it. I'm so sor

Lachlan's laugh washed over the pub and caught Deli's attention like a small shell swept up in the water. Hannah held up a compact mirror to show him his reflection with a rhinestone mustache glued to his face. Douglas plucked them up as they fell one by one on the bar with Lachlan's smile, and put them back in his "bling kit."

Deli stopped typing. Her mind raced like she was leaping lily pads, but they collapsed before she could get anywhere. Each time she thought she had a handle on how she felt, the concrete things turned to mist and left her staring at her hands. She felt her breath rising in her chest, her pulse pounding in her neck—too aware of the wrong things going on inside her.

She began a new text message and typed Chloe's name.

> Hi Chlo. God, I miss you. Whatever I did, just let me fix it. I never want to hurt you. I will fix it, I promise.

Deli sent it and waited, staring at the screen, praying to see the dots that meant Chloe was responding. An entire song played from start to finish in The Wallflower. Nothing came.

Deli sucked in a breath like she'd broken some dark water's surface. She was drowning in all of the things she wanted to tell Chloe, all of the things she'd hoped to say and laughs they were supposed to share. Before her mind could catch her heart, Deli opened social media and typed Chloe's name, searching for clues about her best friend's life.

And there she was, glowing against a sunset while a man held her from behind and kissed her neck. Again, dancing in a West Hollywood club with a group of girls Deli didn't recognize, but who laughed and held Chloe's hand under strobe lights.

Deli's world had frozen while Chloe's kept spinning. She squeezed her eyes shut against the tears and willed herself to sense. She knew the snippets on Chloe's social media had always been curated to tell an only half-true story. There were always messy moments the camera didn't witness. Those were the ones Deli did.

She moved away from Chloe's page, a little reassured. Deli would have chained herself to the lunch tree before it could be cut down, and Chloe would, too. It hadn't been that long, really, in the context of their lifelong friendship. They still had time.

Just as Deli was about to exit the app, she was struck cold by Trey Evans's eyes.

He stared at her from a photo, gaze intent and lips twitching the way they did when he shared a secret just with her—but it wasn't Deli who whispered in his ear. It was Scarlett. Her pillow lips brushed Trey's skin like crimson velvet as the two of them sat in Deli's favorite booth, in Deli's favorite neighborhood bar.

The light in The Wallflower seemed to dim. Heat pricked her cheeks and neck like feathers poking through a down pillow. Deli's eyes darted from left to right, focusing on nothing, trying to track the fragments of thought careening through her mind.

So dramatic, Delilah, she thought as she found the unopened text from her mother and clicked without hesitation. *Cope.*

Hi, honey. I'm so worried about you, and your father is a mess. I know that things were hard for you back home, but we are here to help. Grandma said she'd book you a ticket back same day if you wanted! She's started slowing down since you left . . . just tired all the time. I know it would mean the world to her to see you . . . even just hear from you. She has been devoted to you all your life. I am worried for her, too.

Deli tried to scroll for the rest of the message that wasn't there. Her grandmother's email had been sent a few days before, and she hadn't gotten a new one since. She pictured Grandma Rosemary, bird-boned and blushed, turning gray under her immaculate makeup. A sea breeze swirled around her through an open window, and under the salt and brine was the unmistakable scent of rosemary.

She recited the meaning in her head.

Constancy.

Remember me.

Death.

Deli typed furiously to Lorraine MacDonald.

Mom, is Grandma alright? What's going on??

She sniffed the air again, but the smell of rosemary bushes had gone. She didn't remember it growing anywhere near The Wallflower's Crown. Her mother's response buzzed her palm.

Hi! Where are you? How are you? Grandma is driving me crazy. Last week she had 'rabies' because of 'that damn squirrel on her bird feeder.' I asked if it bit her and she refused to elaborate. I'm missing my backup.

Speaking of . . . Are you coming home soon? Grandma and I aren't the only ones missing you. I spoke to Chloe. We both agree you are just . . . struggling to come to terms with some things. Trey has been such a focus of yours for so long, we think you've lost sight of the truth. Maybe it's time to let him go, honey.

And if not, we can help you. I'll email you some of the healthy recipes I've been finding for you! There's nothing broken we can't fix. I know it's hard to hear, but I only tell you because I love you, Deli. It's for your own good.

Come home.

For her eleventh birthday party, Delilah asked if they could take some friends to the beach, and her mother had looked quite odd. Later, Delilah overheard her mom and Grandma Rosemary talking in her mom's bathroom before they knew she was there.

"She's wearing an *extra* large?" Grandma hissed.

"I'm doing everything I can!" Delilah's mom whispered, but not kindly.

Delilah was so angry at herself for the way her eyes welled up and her cheeks got hot. She wiped away the single bit of proof that she'd been eavesdropping as it slid down her cheek, as quiet as she could be until their voices were normal again. Then she took a few deep breaths, smiled, and knocked. "Can I come in?"

Delilah hopped up on the countertop and watched, content as they frowned into the mirror and pinched the skin on their hips, tugged on the skin by their eyes. She was one of them—the girls . . . even if she couldn't look at her own reflection very long for some stupid reason. Before they left, Delilah's mom told her a beach birthday was not a good idea.

"I'm sorry, sweetie," her mother cooed. "It's for your own good."

That night Delilah pulled the covers over her head to try to block out the sound of her mom's and dad's too-loud voices. In the morning before school, her dad came through the kitchen on his way out the door and said, "You better start thinking about who you want to invite to the beach, kid! It's gonna be a good birthday!" She stared at the low-carb English muffin half on her plate, slathered in some sort of butter substitute, until the sound of the garage door opening and closing had come and gone. Her mom didn't talk to her for the rest of the day.

The day she turned eleven, she wore her dad's big Eagles T-shirt over her one-piece while she played in the waves. Her mother loved Chloe's triangle shaped bikini. On the way home, noses burned and hair crunchy with sea salt, Chloe passed Delilah an earphone attached to her pink iPod mini and played "Beautiful" by Christina Aguilera. She'd even let Delilah listen to it twice in a row before she put on NSYNC.

Eighteen years later, Deli stared at her phone and realized she had been a fool.

She'd caused all of this pain to the people she loved, and for what?

Trey, hurting, begging her to come home—filling her place in their booth and his heart with someone who was there to love him.

Grandma Rosemary, waiting by a window—each sun setting sooner than the last.

Her mom, abandoned by those who had promised not to leave—searching for proof from anyone she could find that her daughter, *Deli*, would not be the third.

And Chloe, confessing to another that her best friend had been so busy carving "D + T" into the bark of a tree, she had turned Chloe invisible.

All this time, all Deli had wanted was for the people she'd chosen to choose her, to love her in the same ways. But she'd been so desperate, so *needy*, that she'd done something impulsive and selfish instead of being brave enough to just face the truth.

It didn't matter how many miles she ran—they would never love enough. Because it would never be enough. Deli was a person who *needed* too much. She just hadn't wanted to admit it.

It's for your own good.

She clamped a hand over her mouth just in time to muffle the violent sob that broke loose from her throat. Tears—hot and fast—ran down her cheeks and the contours of her fingers. She was as lost as she'd been when she'd left. A month had already gone.

Far from home, Deli MacDonald hid in a lonely corner of the world and wept silently into her favorite Eagles T-shirt, worn tired and thin with time.

"Deli?"

A shiver ran through her at the sound of Lachlan's voice, too soft and too close. She heard his clothing rustling and watched the light from her phone grow in his shadow, but she couldn't look. She needed Lachlan to go away.

He repeated, "Deli?"

She flinched at his tenderness as he knelt beside her chair to bring his face level with hers. He waited. When Deli met his eyes, Lachlan Scott was again the man who searched her for the places that hurt.

"What's happened?"

"Nothing. I'm just being stupid." Shame stained her skin under the weight of his worry, his *care.* She would never forgive herself for ridiculing the pain of the wounded boy Lachlan had been forced to be. She looked away from him, her neck straining to escape. "Ignore me."

Deli didn't expect the gentle touch of his thumb against her jaw, catching a mutinous tear before it could fall. She didn't expect how long he cradled her face in his hand, or the way she leaned her weight into him without thinking—like she'd done it a thousand times.

And Deli didn't expect him to sound so helpless as he replied, quite simply, "I can't."

46

Lachlan

For as long as he'd known Deli was returning, Lachlan wished she would go home.

He'd formed a plan, and he'd been executing it—acting as unpleasant as possible whenever he could. Sure, he'd slipped now and then and forgotten to be somewhat hostile, but that was normal, he reckoned. In fact, in his general life, he had worked hard to become the opposite of hostile, but he reasoned it was for the best, even if it reminded him of something he was desperate not to be. Lachlan hadn't considered that during his quest, however valiant in intent, he might catch his passing reflection and see his father. Each polished surface a minor resurrection. It set his teeth on edge.

Still, he soldiered on. Of course, there had been small problems with Deli herself. There had been tension he hadn't been able to unknot in time to call it adversarial, and not admiring. That was all it was—miscategorized conflicts, not connection. Lachlan was loath to admit he'd been unconcerned with dating for so long he'd had to remind himself that the body concocts meaning out of biology. Which was not the same as fact.

Though there had been *moments* of . . . confusion—Lachlan's goal had not changed.

So he didn't expect panic to crack through his body like lightning through a storm-dark sky when Deli MacDonald closed her eyes and whispered, "I think . . . After the wedding, I think I just need to go home."

Her tears wet his skin where Deli's cheek was still pressed against his palm. He felt her heart beating too quickly as his fingers brushed her neck, and his jumped to beat in time.

He searched her eyes for a clue. Had her boy hurt her? Lachlan was hesitant to call him a man. Had it been the friend she'd mentioned? Was it her family?

Or had it been, god forbid, *him*?

"Why do you want to go home?"

She sat straight up, adjusting her shoulders to angle away from him in a small but significant way. Sobered, Lachlan pulled his hand back to rest on his knee. She wiped her tears and ran a finger under each eye, then closed them and set her jaw. He didn't know how he should move—sit in the chair across from her and leave too much dead air between them for tender things to be said? Tower over her like an oaf? He heard the stream of rapid whispers Deli spoke—he realized too late—to herself.

"Stupid, stupid girl, Delilah. Selfish, stupid girl."

The sickly treacle feeling of seeing something intimate and private crept through him. He wanted to leave her alone. He wanted to build her a shelter from his arms and stand sentinel against all who had harmed her.

"I shouldn't have come here. What a ridiculous idea." She shook her head. "I just quit my life and bought a ticket and showed up! Who does that? Who just says 'Oh, hey, aunt I haven't stayed in touch with or bothered to know—mind if I take over your entire existence for a second? Oh, how long? Unclear.'"

Deli was like a dammed river finally set free, and the words poured from her so quickly Lachlan was almost lost to the current.

"Grandma Rosemary is my mom's mom. Mo's mom! You don't know her, right?" She looked at Lachlan expectantly. He tried to keep the acidity from his voice.

"I haven't had the pleasure, but I'm familiar."

Deli's face turned pleading. "I know, I know. I know how she can be, but . . . she *loves* me. She really *loves* me, you know? The stuff about my body"—Lachlan watched a patch of red creep from her neck up her jawbone and bleed into her cheek like ink—"she doesn't mean it. She's from a different time. She's in her eighties, and I run to the other side of the world—to the *one* person that would double-break her heart?"

Lachlan could guess what types of comments from her grandmother Deli was referring to. He opened his mouth to say something, but the river flowed on.

"Oh, and Trey? Some great soulmate I am. *One* bump in the road and I vanish? Like his world was going to stop without me. And now someone named Scarlett is in all our secret places while I'm on some ridiculous quest to make him jealous. As if that would *ever* work."

Lachlan's thoughts were sharp. "Why wouldn't that work?"

Her laugh was short and biting. "Please. Just look at me."

"I am looking at you, Deli." Lachlan felt the shock of her attention pulse through him. "You could make any man jealous."

She was very still, but her nostrils flared and her chest rose and fell quickly. The electric energy between them swelled until she shook her head, like a dog shaking off a nagging insect.

"And, you know . . . Chloe."

A sob stole the name from her mouth. Whatever misery Deli had been keeping back surged forward and wrapped a hand around her best friend's name in her throat.

"Chloe," Lachlan repeated.

"Yeah . . . She's . . ." Her voice broke, the tears coming quiet and constant. "She's been my best friend my *entire life*, Lachlan."

The sound of his name so unexpectedly in her mouth lit a small fire in his heart, slow and boiling, like molten metal settling into a thing to crack open.

"I just *left*. Like I owed them all nothing. My mom is right about me . . ."

"What do you mean, Deli?"

She shrugged with a wet chuckle. "There is a lot I need to fix."

Every time they were together Lachlan hunted for proof of Deli's selfishness, her callousness, her covert narcissism hiding behind the charm. He'd searched for shades of her family and for shadows of his own brother. He had been certain of little else than when it came to the wellbeing of *his* best friend, Deli was a threat. But hearing her accuse herself of the same thing he'd been desperate to prove settled the argument in his head as clearly as a bell ringing in an empty church.

Deli was not who he had thought she was.

Her breath hitched as she battled against the bleeding emotion. She closed her eyes and spoke with a sort of inevitable finality that made him ache.

"Lachlan? I don't think I'm a very good person."

And all at once, Lachlan Scott knew two things: 1. Deli MacDonald deserved better love than she'd gotten, and 2. All he wanted was for her to stay.

47

Rosemary

Rosemary McDonnell directed the arrow to the refresh button and clicked. She was the most tech savvy of her friends at the club, and she relished the looks on their faces when she mentioned navigating emails and text messages with ease. Her bloodred nail varnish shone in the glow from the screen. There was a chip in the polish on her pointer finger. She bristled.

Her inbox loaded. No new messages.

An icicle feeling cracked up her spine into the base of her skull.

"Siri," Rosemary said curtly with command, just like her mother had taught her, "call Lorraine."

She glared at the nick on her fingernail. Just painted and already falling apart.

Lorraine picked up. "Mom?"

She skipped the pleasantries. "Anything?"

Rosemary heard her daughter take a deep breath and release it in a sigh. "No. You?"

The calendar of family photos Lorraine gave Rosemary for Christmas, just like she did every year, hung limply against the wall in the dim light. She squinted.

"Nothing." Rosemary chewed her bottom lip without thinking, then stopped and pinched the skin on her hand as the voice of a woman long gone scolded her for the nasty habit. "Darling?"

Lorraine sounded sharp and frazzled—like static before it gathers into a spark. "Yes, Mom?"

Rosemary hated the smell of rain. "I'm assuming you did what I asked you to do?"

"Which thing?"

She could almost hear her daughter thinking—*needing.*

She pinched the bridge of her nose and popped the cap of a large red marker (she believed in the power of large red markers) to circle a block of squares on the calendar. March's photo was of Rosemary, Lorraine, and Delilah gathered around a table with a tower of tea sandwiches, scones, and little chocolate cups piped with raspberry cream. Delilah had come to the door in a band T-shirt. They'd nearly been late after waiting for her to change into something suitable for high tea.

Rosemary traced over her large red circle a few more times.

When Callum had left her and her girls and sent them back to California so he could wither and die in that godforsaken cottage, Rosemary McDonnell swore she'd never set foot in that village again. She'd never count the waves, the gulls, the clusters of heather from the cliffside.

She'd only broken that vow once for a noble attempt, and she had failed.

Delilah was just a girl. So impressionable.

And Rosemary could not fail again. She was running out of time.

"Your passport, Lorraine." She shook the bottle of the cherry polish she kept in her purse at all times. "You renewed it, correct?"

48

Deli

Deli was waiting for Lachlan outside when he pulled up to the cottage.

As he walked over, she gestured behind her where Hannah and Aunt Mo were inside, chatting at the kitchen table about place cards, and whispered, "Lachlan, I don't think Hannah likes me."

"She doesn't like anyone. It's the best." Lachlan pointed toward the path meandering away from the cottage, not to the cliffside, but into the gentle hills. "Walk with me?"

There was such an earnestness in the offer—such an openness in his face.

"Okay," she said, and they began to walk as the sun moved toward the sea.

For the first time, Lachlan explained that Hannah hadn't always been quiet. Once, she'd been a vibrant young mother engaged to be married, but her daughter and fiancé had vanished into thin air the night before the wedding. Hannah spent her life silently searching for her child. Most people thought she was saving her words for all the things she'd need to tell her daughter once she'd found her—all the questions she'd ask about a life she hadn't seen.

"Still," Lachlan said, offering his hand as they stepped over a patch of stones, "Hannah never gives up."

Just that morning Aunt Mo had come in from the garden, beaming, with a handful of small, spiked clove.

You do not know how I have loved you.

"That's . . ." Deli searched for the words.

"Yes," Lachlan said simply—a sweet sadness in his voice. "It is."

They came over a small hill to a massive meadow blanketed in blooming purple heather. The trail was dotted with patches of wildflowers, all miraculously vibrant and alive.

Deli laughed, taking in the sight, but Lachlan pulled up short. She heard him make an uncharacteristic sound of surprise.

When she turned back, she was struck still.

There, in the meadow, Lachlan Scott was a portrait—brushstrokes of auburn, amber, and cinnamon against the untamed Scottish wild. A gust rippled through the blooming valley, tousling his hair and turning his cheeks a pale raspberry, while the sun tipped the sea's gentle waves with gold.

Deli took his arm without thinking as they continued into the meadow full of new life.

"I don't recognize so many of these," she said. A budding bush of mustard colored flowers scented the air with coconut and almond. "What's this called?"

Lachlan nodded toward the shrub. "Gorse. Or broom."

Deli leaned closer and tilted her head this way and that, trying to commit it to memory so she could add it to her dictionary later. She felt the muscles of Lachlan's arm relax under hers. They were different from the muscles in Trey's—full and sure. Trey felt sharp all over.

Just ahead, she spotted narrow shoots of green tipped with vibrant cerulean bells.

"I wonder what these are," she said under her breath as she knelt to examine the rare blue flower, and she thought of Scarlett's delphinium.

"Bluebells." Lachlan knelt behind her and left a trail of goosebumps up her neck with his answer. Deli made a sound of squeaky protest as he reached around and plucked a stem from the ground. "It won't mind," he said. "The meadow knows me."

They stood as Lachlan held his hand out and offered her the perfect drop of blue. She tucked her hands behind her back and bent to study the pristine blossom made small in his palm. "I wonder what they mean."

"They're poisonous, for one. And it's unlucky to pick a stem—you'll anger the faeries that live underneath."

Deli shoved his arm. "You're making me a faerie target!"

He chuckled. "The meadow and I are old friends. You're always safe with me." She focused on the way the pink light was turning the bluebell periwinkle. Lachlan's hand held steady. "But I prefer the old rumors about them."

Deli risked a glance at his October eyes. "Rumors?"

"Aye." He lifted an eyebrow. "Legend says if you wear a necklace of bluebells, you must only speak the truth."

"Ha! Wish I'd known. Could have saved myself a trip and slipped one of those babies over Trey's head while he was sleeping. *Hey, you, wake up. Do you love me or not?*"

Lachlan's smile faded. "I imagine so."

"Plus, you wouldn't have wasted the last month chauffeuring around an irritating, lovelorn squatter, right?"

She tried to make her laugh light. Lachlan had a real life to get back to, just like the pieces of Deli's—waiting for her to glue them into something bearable.

He looked at the bloom in his hand for a long, long moment. "They also say that if you can turn a bluebell inside out without tearing it, to have faith, for you will win the one you love."

She reached for it, but he closed his fingers and pulled away.

"No, Deli."

"Come on," she said. "Lemme have it."

"No," Lachlan repeated. He didn't smile. "He doesn't deserve . . . He doesn't deserve it."

They stood in the meadow, looking at one another.

Deli spoke abruptly. "The sun's getting lower. We should go."

She started back without checking if Lachlan was coming, too—intent on avoiding her new, unhinged, make-believe thoughts whenever she looked the man in the eyes—but she heard his footsteps, sure and steady, keeping pace behind her. He caught her arm moments before she stepped into a patch of mud that would have claimed her shoe to the ankle.

"Deli, you're freezing." She hadn't thought to grab a coat on her way out. Lachlan shrugged out of his jacket. "Put this on."

"No, I'm fine," she said.

He wrapped it around her shoulders anyway.

It was something . . . to be enveloped in the warmth of Lachlan's body—in the cinnamon and smoke and sea salt scent of him. When they got back, Deli hesitated on the cottage doorstep.

"I . . ." she started. Then reality forced its way into her brain before she could mumble something complicated, so she walked straight through the empty cottage and out the open back door.

They found Hannah in the garden. Deli could see the peach fuzz on her cheeks and the strands of white hair loose from her braids dancing on the breeze, cast golden in the last of the light. She stepped into the wild like she was greeting an old friend. In an instant, Deli saw Hannah as she could have been—a bride, a grandmother, a woman who gathered a family around her table as it overflowed.

Deli didn't know what to call the quiet ache of realizing all the things a woman would never have. No one had bothered to make a word for that.

Lachlan stopped behind her and watched Hannah move slowly down the path, trailing her fingers along a row of yarrow with the kind touch of a companion. He touched Deli's arm, so gently she almost missed it, like he just wanted her to feel him there.

Yarrow. *Courage. Healing. Cure for a broken heart.*

Her eyes began to water.

Lachlan took a deep breath beside her. "I know," he said. His eyes were shiny in the day's final moments, too. "It's just not fair."

A tear crested Deli's cheekbone, and she didn't try to stop it as it left a cool trail to her chin and trembled before letting go. Deli had cried more easily and often since coming to Fearnhall than she had, maybe, in her entire life before. It was like the soil itself called the depths of her out, hungering for things she didn't know were buried.

Hannah turned toward them, and Lachlan jogged to sweep her into a wide, rocking hug—his stubbled chin resting on her silvered head. Then he chose a pink carnation from the garden's bouquet—like he knew it told of a *mother's undying love* and *a promise to never forget you.* He tucked it behind Hannah's ear.

Deli felt another tear leave her, though she thought it might have been for Lachlan and the happy son he never got to be.

A few minutes later, as they watched Lachlan's Land Rover disappear over the hill, Aunt Mo explained that Hannah didn't like to drive in the dark anymore. He'd come to take her to the type of appointment Hannah's daughter should have been there for.

"Hey—is that Lachlan's jacket?"

"Huh?" Deli turned away from the shrinking taillights. Lachlan hadn't asked for it back. "Oh, I—yeah. He insisted."

Aunt Mo smiled too widely for news of a borrowed jacket as she thumbed through the stack of handmade paper Hannah had come to deliver.

"Photo shoot tomorrow. I know you should rest, but . . . Scrabble?"

"Sure," Deli said as she opened the closet, patting the pockets of Lachlan's coat. She slipped her hands inside and felt something soft and small.

When Deli opened her fingers, she found a perfect blue blossom curled in her palm—whole and inside out.

49

Mo

"Do me a favor?" Mo asked as she shoved a tote bag stuffed with picnic makings into Deli's arms.

"What?"

Mo pulled her cleaning tiara from her pocket and put it on. "Remember to have a little fun?"

Deli's face scrunched in confusion. "I . . . Is that a tiara?"

"It's chore day." Mo patted her pockets for her keys. "Chores are easier to do when you have a crown."

"Why haven't I ever thought of that?"

Deli grinned, and it loosened the worry that had gripped Mo's heart since the night of the darts tournament a few days before. Her niece hadn't been her curious, vibrant self since then.

"Royal secret. Sir Beans has one to match." She reached out and booped the tip of Deli's nose. "Seriously, buddy. Have *fun.*"

Deli curtsied. "Milady."

Mo left Deli waiting for Lachlan in The Wallflower so she could bust out some serious cleaning before she had a cake tasting in the city.

Lachlan's Land Rover came around the corner and drove up the bank of The Wallflower's lane so Mo could squeeze past while he rolled his window down.

She smiled. "Hey, you!"

He nodded toward the top of her head. "Chore day?"

"Professional secret for you: Brides don't like walking down the aisle covered in mystery cat fur."

"Checks out," Lachlan said as he tried to subtly scan her car.

"I left her in the pub, and you're not sneaky."

He slapped a hand to his forehead and groaned. "What's wrong with me?"

Mo suppressed a squeal. "Are we admitting it?"

He stared at her, all pitiful. "I suppose we are."

"Yes!" She fist-pumped into the air. "Yes, yes, yes!"

"You mock my misery."

"Love is misery, my boy."

"Mo, am I a thirty-four-year-old man with a *crush*?"

"Not for long." If Mo had written a list of her wildest hopes, Lachlan and Deli being destined would have been on it.

"I don't know why you're so happy to see me fancying a girl who's in love with someone else."

"I wouldn't be so sure about that."

"Have you forgotten the entire reason she came here?"

"Why she came here is yet to be decided, if you ask me."

His brows knit together. A guarded hope crossed his face. "What do you mean?"

Mo felt the tug and push of what she wanted to say and what she probably should. "I mean that with space comes perspective, and that guy sounds like an asshole."

"*Such* an arsehole, my god."

They chuckled until the sort of charged silence that could only be relieved by things yet to come fell between them.

Lachlan reached toward her through his window, and she took his hand. "Mo, I'm so sorry for . . . for what I said about her. About you. I was afraid she would hurt you when she left, but I was out of line. And I was wrong."

Over the years Mo had told Lachlan, again and again, that his fear of becoming his father was a thing without roots. He continued to prove her right.

"Lachlan? Remember—*courage.*"

He studied their fingers, knotted together like their lives. "From Deli? Or from me?"

Tug and push. Push and tug.

"Love you, kid. Have fun."

Mo squeezed his hand, then let go, and Lachlan pulled away.

50

Deli

While she waited for Lachlan, Deli was alone in The Wallflower with Wi-Fi. She palmed the phone in her pocket. It was a bad idea. But she had to.

A video of Chloe filled her screen. She was singing along in the passenger seat of a car Deli didn't recognize. The camera panned over to a *new* man, driving with his hand on her knee.

In the last few days, Deli had thought a bit about her situation with Chloe, turning it over like a gem in a tumbler until it came out smooth. When she'd read in her mother's text that the two of them agreed Deli had forsaken everything for Trey, she'd felt entirely responsible for the distance between them. But the more she'd thought about it, the more she felt like Chloe could have carved out a minute to at least answer one of Deli's many attempts to learn what she had done wrong. Maybe Deli should have known that Chloe felt invisible, but she'd done the next best thing. She'd tried to figure it out.

Chloe hadn't helped.

As Deli contemplated the *new* man in Chloe's life replacing Jared, who'd been with Chloe on Deli's birthday, she admitted, in the darkest, private corners of her heart, that she was a little bit *angry.*

The next video was of Chloe surrounded by new friends, smiling with mimosas and big sunglasses at a Malibu brunch spot Deli had asked Chloe to go to a hundred times. *They don't have anything I like there, Deli.*

And Deli had . . . feelings.

"I've seen caged zoo tigers look less murderous."

She felt the strange and sudden halt that had begun to accompany Lachlan's presence still her mind again. He had a duffel bag over one shoulder, and he ran his hand through his thick hair, sending a fine spray of water into the air.

Deli shook the feeling off. "Raining?"

"Just barely. It should clear up."

"They drug those zoo tigers, you know."

"I know." Lachlan walked around the bar. "Fucking bastards. Caging something wild to keep it wounded?" He reached for a glass. The soda hose fizzed. "No excuse for that sort of thing."

By the time she slid onto a barstool, there was a Diet Coke with lemon bubbling gently in front of her, and she felt a surge of fondness for the man who could cause such destruction in the world with his place and his power, but who didn't believe in it. She put her lips to the glass and sipped from the rim with no hands. Lachlan shook his head, but he smiled.

"So," Deli said between sips, "what's in the bag?"

Lachlan released a deep sigh. "Well, we've got the costume—"

"The KILT?"

He rolled his eyes. "Aye. The kilt. The object of your fascination."

Deli clung to the feeling of a small win after he'd been so stubborn about the darn thing. She kept herself from doing a victory lap. "I just can't wait to see *you* in one."

His cheeks flushed. "Well, I—"

Deli realized how that sounded a little too late. "Oh, I don't mean—"

"I didn't think—"

"Just that you've been such a brat about it, and—"

"I'm sorry, did you just call me a *brat?*"

They fell quiet. Deli scanned her vocabulary for a better-suited word to describe how surly he'd been. "Would you prefer *butthead*?"

He considered her with pursed lips. "You know what? We don't need to do this. No kilt for you."

Deli made a shocked face. "Well, that's odd. Because I remember a certain someone's ex asking a certain someone to photograph her wedding this weekend, but that certain someone was all like, *Aye, no lassie, I couldnae possibly! I've no touched the witch's photo box since Culloden*—"

"Did you hit your head on a magic rock since I saw you last?"

"—and a perfect *angel* muse model appeared—"

"Can you follow my finger?" He held his pointer finger in front of her nose. "I need to check your pupils."

"—whose beauty will grace thy lens and thy portfolio forevermore!"

"At least that part's true."

Silence fell over them like a weighted blanket. Deli felt a hot blush creeping under her turtleneck, and she would bet it matched the one flushing Lachlan's cheeks.

"Camera," he blurted out.

She stared. "Huh?"

"In the bag." He slapped the duffel with a large hand, then withdrew with a worried look. "All my camera gear. I . . . shouldn't slap it."

"No, you shouldn't"—Deli swallowed—"slap it."

Another stretch of quiet pulled like taffy.

"Oh!" Deli hoisted the bag laden with Aunt Mo's mystery fare in the air. "Snacks!"

Lachlan looked like a dog who'd just heard the cheese drawer open as he slung the duffel back onto his shoulder. "What did she pack?"

"I didn't have a chance to check. Beans caught the scent."

"Of course." He held the door for Deli, muttering as she walked past, "That cat's a pain in my arse."

51

Lachlan

Deli landed a playful punch on his arm.

"I knew you'd been flinging me all over this car for your sadistic pleasure."

Lachlan *had* taken to driving a bit quickly around corners, but that was before. Now all he wanted was to surround her with things that were gentle.

"Today I won't rattle a tiger's cage. I'm smarter than I look."

Deli laughed, watching the Highlands blur through the window.

Lachlan didn't want to have feelings for her. But they'd kicked in the door and announced their name the night he'd watched Deli cry—helpless as she became her own judge and jury. Seeing the peeled-back heart of her pain had galvanized him. He'd found his hands shaking from anger. And terror. Lachlan hadn't felt so strongly about anything in . . . a long time. It was unexpected. He was unprepared.

"Erm, how have you been since the . . . the other night?"

"Since my meltdown, you mean?" Her words had an edge turned inward. "Yeah, not my best moment. Sorry you had to see that."

"There's nothing to apologize for."

"No, I shouldn't have put that on you. I'm just ridiculous." She laughed, a harsh, punishing sound. "This whole plan. If I wasn't enough for th—for *him* before, how the hell would all of this help? I just need to call it." She stared out the window with her arms wrapped around her body so tightly the varnish on her fingernails disappeared into the fabric of her jacket.

If anyone was laughable, it was Lachlan. The man falling for a woman who declared she was in love with someone else as often as she could—the woman he'd been trying to send away every brief moment they'd had. *Fool,* he thought, *thy name is Lachlan.*

"That's not true." The words were out of his mouth before he had a chance to consider them—another newness that had arrived with her. "It's a good plan."

She raised an eyebrow. "Did *you* hit your head since the last time I saw you?"

"No, really. It is. The male mind, Deli . . ." He tapped his temple. "It's an enigma. You couldn't hope to understand all its wee nooks and crannies—"

"Seriously?"

"However, you have homed in on one basic truth: When it comes to women, men are simple. Throw in an arch nemesis? You've got a trap laid well."

She was uncharacteristically quiet. Deer scattered into the trees as they rounded a curve in the road. "That wasn't even my plan."

"No, but it's mine. Listen, we'll strike a pose, get you proof that you're moving on, and in a few days?" He snapped his fingers. "I'm an incredible actor. We'll have Trevor believing I'm coming for his girl and his job."

Lachlan hated that Evans had lived off Deli's good heart so long, but still. If she thought there was still a chance the fool could be won, she might stay a little longer. Just a day.

Even a day more with her would be worth it.

The hollow, hungry ache of things unrequited chewed at his insides. Then Deli laughed, and it was the antidote.

"I can't imagine you as an actor. And I know you know his name."

Lachlan ignored the last part. "A shame you weren't around to see me play the role of Romeo in school."

She smirked, and he sketched the lines of her face in his mind. "Makes sense. You *are* tragic."

"The audience wept."

"And you're sure it's because you were *good*?"

"A granny in the front row swooned."

"Admitting you gave an elderly woman a coronary isn't convincing me of your *talent*."

"ANYWAY, we're taking these photos today, and you're gonna post them tonight when we get back. He'll be blowing up your phone by morning."

Her voice was small, unsure. "Do you really think that will work?"

From what he knew, Trey was exactly the sort of toddler to throw a tantrum when he saw someone else with his favorite toy. But Trey was what Deli wanted. And Lachlan wanted Deli to be happy.

So, even though the words stuck, barbed in his throat, he said, "Aye. It will work."

"I don't know . . ."

"It's not stupid to think he could love you, Deli. It's stupid to think he couldn't."

Deli punched him in the arm.

"Um, ow?"

"Why are you being so nice to me?" she demanded.

"I'm not."

"You are, and I don't trust it."

He looked at her scrunched nose and suspicious glare, and it clicked into place.

Deli's eyes were Highland winter, when the cool sunlight filters through the clouds and falls softly on the rain-slick green—the shimmering, iridescent dance of silver-blue streams and emerald hills. A hazel starburst, the rusting fern forests. Her lips were bramble berries grown ripe and sweet on summer vines. Her laugh like the lap of water against wood, the call of gulls over music, the millions of raindrops filtering through an ancient forest. The dark line of Deli's hair against her jaw, like the sacred place where the land meets the ocean.

Deli was the wild, fierce, loyal, earth his heart longed for. She was the land he defended, where he longed to stay and rest, but that he could lose to another. Deli MacDonald felt like home—the only place that he knew and that knew him to his bones.

His name would never be known to history, but Lachlan Scott was born, for better or worse, a man beholden to his duty. A soldier for his homeland.

How quickly this woman had claimed his heart's country.

It knocked him off his feet.

Lachlan knew what he had to do, like he had known he'd need to remember and had taken her photo before the red door. He wondered if he'd always loved her in a small, boyhood corner of his heart.

He would care for her the best he could before she needed to go, and Lachlan would never be the same. But it didn't matter what happened to him.

"You're definitely being too nice to me, Lachlan. Did my aunt say something to you?"

"It was Beans. He threatened my life."

"He does that all the time."

"But this time he meant it."

"*I* think I'm just growing on you."

You have no idea, he thought. "Yeah, that's it."

"I knew it." She grinned and turned to the rugged beauty passing by, her chin cupped in her palm and her other hand laid lazily in her lap. He could just make out her reflection, sheer over the wild land—and Lachlan decided it was true, what some people say.

Maybe you only get one big, real love of your life—one soulmate, one shot. And for some people, that love is unrequited. To Lachlan Scott the truth was quite simple: Knowing Deli MacDonald only to lose her would never be a tragedy.

What would it have been like? To have lived and died with his capacity to love undiscovered, forever cold and still? Even now, grief held an hourglass in its hand and a sign with his name in the other, but it was a price he gladly paid to have met the far corners of his heart. Deli would leave him anguished when she went, and it would be proof he had finally lived.

Lachlan would let the loss of her anoint him. He, a man who had *loved*, could call the pain holy.

52

Deli

Deli MacDonald wasn't typically a waffler.

She usually knew exactly what she thought—be it about karaoke songs, politics, or what she wanted for dinner—so much so that it was sometimes a problem. Her mother said she was born stubborn.

But as Lachlan took to the Let's Make Trey Jealous concept again with renewed passion, Deli couldn't decide if she really wanted it to work. She couldn't decide if she thought Trey would ever love her the way she hoped.

And she couldn't decide if she'd begun to wish it was Lachlan at the end of this whole thing instead.

"Right," he said as he parked. "That's us."

Deli's hair blew into her lip gloss as Lachlan got out of the Defender and closed his door behind him. They'd pulled off a winding road onto a dirt one to find the photo shoot location. Watching Lachlan navigate the unmarked, twisting paths through a place so rugged and raw and *different* from Deli's eight-lane freeways and smog-choked skylines made her feel a sad sense of wanderlust. She would be thinking back to these moments when this all inevitably ended, watching *The Highlander* in her apartment.

Get it together, brain, she thought as she unfastened her seat belt with a click and stepped down. She stared at her new boots—a gift that had appeared at the foot of her bed one day with googly eyes stuck to the box and a note about an auntie's duty to preserve big toes—and put on a smile. She squared her shoulders in a confident sort of way, she thought. *Fake it till you make it, dude.*

Then she walked around the truck and saw Lachlan's bare ass.

She was surprised the sound that came from her body didn't send birds into mass flight, but Lachlan spun around.

"S—" he half yelled, half mumbled as he pressed the kilt he was about to put on against his body. "Christ, woman, look away!"

The sight of Lachlan Scott's hot cross buns had frozen her face in whatever ungodly contortion it made to unleash a sound like a seagull dipping its tailfeathers in magma.

"Ohmigod!" She dove back into the truck. *"Sorrysorrysorry!"*

She slammed the door. Her breath was fast. The wind whistled past the still-open back.

"Jesus!" Lachlan cried as he collapsed to the ground—out of the sight of the rearview mirror, which Deli was, apparently, looking into.

She slapped a hand over her eyes. "Ow!"

"Are you alright?"

"SORRY!"

There was scuffling and more mumbled curses. She shuddered as the back door slammed shut and left her in a cotton ball sort of quiet until her door opened.

Deli kept her hand over her eyes. "Hello?"

"It's me."

"Uh huh. Is it . . . safe? Or will I be violating you again?"

She heard the smile in his answer. "It's safe."

Deli didn't move.

Warmth laced through her skin as Lachlan cupped her chin and turned her face toward him. He gently pried her blindfolding fingers loose in his and pulled them away, but he didn't let go. The light filtering through her scrunched eyelids blazed orange-red.

"Deli, I'm sorry. I should have warned you. Will you open your eyes?" She didn't. "Maybe just one?"

Deli painstakingly opened one eyeball. "I can't believe I just stood there—" she began, but the words died in her throat.

Lachlan was starting to feel unreal. He hadn't paused to put on a shirt in his hurry to comfort her after she'd ogled him like drunk-Deli ogled french fries, and he was so gorgeous it was almost funny. One of his booted feet was propped on the step to the passenger side, and a beautiful pleated kilt in deep green with threads of cream and a turquoise green draped over his thigh to the knee of his bracing leg. He was breathing so easily, despite his bare chest's size.

"I thought I'd have a second while you gathered your things so you wouldn't even know, and I didn't want to announce it and be creepy about it but—" Lachlan shook his head. "Doesn't matter. I should have warned you."

"No." She was struggling to speak. "'Smyfault."

Lachlan's eyes fell to her hand in his, and he pulled back like she was a snake. He probably didn't want good ole porn-stache Deli touching him, and she couldn't blame him.

Lachlan coughed. "I should finish getting dressed."

"And I will keep my eyeballs to myself."

She was hot around her ears and, if she was completely honest, a little bit in her unruly nethers. She couldn't remember the last time anyone but Trey had awoken that particular beast. It felt like betrayal.

"Judas," she whispered toward her bits. "Shut up."

But it also felt good . . . and *new*. Moments of tension with Trey were charged with a familiar danger—and when she really thought about it, loving Trey was asking a question on repeat: Have I done enough? He would dangle the carrot, slip her secret moments of assurance, and then let her fall—and Deli always landed on her feet. Her sore, sore feet.

She focused on rearranging her features into something casual and grabbed the bag of snacks as she got out. Lachlan slung the duffel over his shoulder. His full outfit was straight out of her imagination—a vest over a crisp shirt, a fur pouch slung around his waist, a knife tucked into his boot. She bounced her eyes away to keep herself from ogling. Deli had never been an ogler before.

"I've got the snacks!" She made her face smile normally.

Lachlan actually smiled normally. "My hero."

He led her to the type of trail a couple of hobbits would have loved that disappeared between soaring peaks. They walked awhile as the off-and-on sun broke through to light the slopes and turned the veins of water running down the rock faces quicksilver blue. Ahead of them, a stream cut their path in half.

"Here," Lachlan said, reaching for the bag of food she was shifting uncomfortably on her shoulder. "Stay here, I'll help you across." He carried both bags across the stream in two long steps using a single stone in the middle and set them on the dry ground.

Deli spotted a series of stones she was pretty sure she could use without help and made a confident leap just as Lachlan turned around. One boot sank into the mud to the ankle and remained there as her foot slipped right out, but she managed to land on a dry rock with the other. She stood like a flamingo, in the middle of cold Highland water, with her foot exposed, in her only pair of good socks.

The silence between them was very, very loud.

Lachlan breathed in.

"Don't," she warned.

He stuck his bottom lip out and raised his eyebrows.

"I said don't."

He dropped his head to hide his grin.

She flexed her woolen toes in preparation for her next jump to a water-slick stone.

"Oh, no, we're not doing *this* again."

"I can figure out rocks on my oWWNFRNG!"

Her declaration turned into a wheeze as Lachlan quite literally stepped into the water and swept her off her feet.

"I've met your ankles, Deli. They're lovely, but I wouldn't call them robust. Now, are you fixing to complain, or are we past this?"

Thick white clouds with graying bellies wandered across the sky above him, and she thought of the way the stars framed his face the night she'd fallen in The Wallflower. It occurred to Deli that if she hadn't met Lachlan Scott, she might have never known what the sky looked like from somebody's arms.

She might have never seen the world differently.

"Good." He carried her across the stream and set her on her booted foot. "Now, can you keep your balance while I retrieve Cinderella's slipper?"

"I'm a very good hopper."

"Hop away, princess. I'll be but a moment."

She hopped. Then he was kneeling in front of her.

He patted his knee. "Foot."

Deli obeyed. She watched his hand hesitate before cupping the back of her ankle. There was such a startling intimacy in the way he cradled a simple, tired part of her body that so often hurt, she was overcome with a rogue wave of emotion. Lachlan didn't see the tear that shocked her by running down her face. He was already guiding her toes into the neck of her boot.

Deli's chest *ached.* She looked up to the sky as a soft breeze blew a strand of hair across her cheek, mimicking the path of the next tear to cool on her skin. The clouds looked heavier and softer than before. It wouldn't be long until the rain was too much for them to carry.

Lachlan slid her heel into place and patted her foot affectionately as he looked up smiling. She wiped the tear away with her thumb, and it took Lachlan's smile with it.

"What's wrong?"

Deli was filled with warmth. She lifted the hand on his shoulder to his jaw and said, "Nothing's wrong."

And at that moment—while the wind rustled through the grasses and the water sang over rocks, while the clouded sun turned Lachlan's eyes to topaz held to the light, while she felt far enough away from her real life . . . Deli actually meant it.

He grinned. The scruff moved against her skin.

"So is the kilt, like, a kink thing, or—"

Deli's eyes went wide in self-horror as she realized she'd escalated from ogling to groping. Lachlan laughed at her expression and covered her hand with his own, keeping it in place against him, and her teenage dread changed to a sort of adult oh-well-ness. Then Deli laughed, too.

It felt so good, like it had been locked away. Deli kept laughing until her head was thrown back in snorting laughter. Her whole body shook and her eyes brimmed with the absurdity of the day, the month, the impossibility of the fantasy scene she was living.

Lachlan's other hand spread wide against her back as he stood and buried his face into her shoulder, and the part of her that *thought* about everything was tackled by the part of her desperate to *feel.* She ran her hands through his hair and held him in the sensitive hollow of her collarbone, and they stayed there a little longer with their bodies pressed together, alive with joy.

When they finally managed to catch their breath, Deli leaned back just enough to shrug. She nodded toward the bag of snacks that lay forgotten in the dirt.

"I could really use, like, an entire wheel of cheese right now. Think she packed any?"

Lachlan wiped away a final cry-laughter tear and nodded. "I'd stake my life on it."

53

Deli

"Looks like Mo packed you a surprise."

Lachlan held out Aunt Mo's leather jacket, and they walked until he stopped her and took a few steps back to survey the location. Deli took her denim jacket off and slid the leather one on. It was soft with familiarity and comfort. It never tugged or pinched.

Just like everything else in Aunt Mo's house, it never hurt.

Deli thought of her life back home—of how impossible it was to meet her family's ever-shifting standards, of how Chloe had vanished, and of Trey. Trey, who was happy to have Deli as his best friend and support, his partner in so many ways—but who, she was starting to think, may never want to be hers.

For the first time in her life, Deli MacDonald wondered if perhaps she wasn't falling short of the love she wanted. Perhaps the love she wanted was falling short of her.

The thought of it turned her chest into a sudden, stabbing vise. Then a bird nearby chirped for a friend or a lover while the small waters trickled on and the wind tousled Lachlan's hair as he straightened the collar of Aunt Mo's jacket, and the pain got a tiny, beautiful bit smaller.

Lachlan knelt and pulled the knife from his boot to cut a cluster of heather free.

"Here." He tucked her hair behind her ear and pressed the bouquet of white and lavender into her palm. His voice was soft. "You're gonna break his heart."

Deli shook her head. "I don't know if there's much of a point. I think maybe . . . it's time for me to let Trey go."

For a long moment, Lachlan became a study in strained intensity. Finally, mercifully, he spoke.

"Even so, will you still help me dust up? I haven't touched a camera in ages."

"Of course."

"Alright, stand just there." Lachlan turned Deli's shoulders gently into profile and appraised the scene. "Don't move."

She watched him retreat toward the camera, his calves defined and shoulders broad as he cut a path through a fairy-tale sort of place—a place where he belonged. The light was starting its journey from day to night as he knelt to the viewfinder, rotated something on the lens, and looked back, and Deli was hit with the strongest sense of déjà vu she'd ever felt. It was impossible, but she could have sworn . . .

"Alright," he called. "Here we go!"

And Deli . . . froze. She felt very alone all of a sudden, standing in the wild magnified under a lens. Lenses were never very kind to her.

Lachlan walked back to her with a frown.

She wrapped her arms around herself. "You should have had Douglas be your model. He's got the gams."

"Douglas does have great legs, though he pales in comparison."

Deli's laughter came out sour. "I'm sorry I'm not photogenic."

His frown deepened. "Who told you that?"

"Tyra Banks."

Lachlan's gaze remained. He didn't laugh. Deli felt the truth rising like a bubble.

"My mom." She tried for a Lorraine impression. "*It's simply math, Delilah. Calories in, calories out.* It was all anyone could talk about when

I was growing up—" Deli studied her palms before she pressed her fingernails into them. "She had her reasons."

Lachlan didn't speak. She released a pent-up breath and looked to the sky.

"I'm always a bit too . . . I think I was born just a little disappointing. All the time, in every way. It's like I get *so* close to getting it right, then—" She snapped her fingers. "I thought coming here might prove I was wrong—that maybe I was being hard on myself. My mom and Trey and Chloe would realize that I wasn't so bad. That they, you know . . . But . . ." Deli shrugged, surprised to find her eyes were perfectly dry.

At the pity in Lachlan's, she felt shame and regret curdle her words before they could even be carried away.

"Oh god, sorry. What an overshare. Forget I men—"

"My father wanted me to take over The Wallflower."

He'd begun so abruptly she heard her teeth collide as her mouth shut.

"I was the oldest son. He had a temper. He wasn't . . . He loved us, but he was a complicated man. I tried to distract my wee brother, hide him away, stand over him while he slept, but I couldn't hide my mum. I was so angry Da was just allowed to *be* that way. Cruel."

He watched his hands turn to fists.

"He had all these rules. I had to be home, washed, and sitting for supper before the sun went down. Anything I did, he acted like withholding punishment was a mercy, and everything I did was wrong. So I stopped trying. I was reckless. One night I stayed out well past sundown to take a"—his eyes flicked to hers—"long walk. I could hear him yelling from down the street, and I got so angry I felt like I was gonna explode. So I tracked mud in on purpose with a big smile. Then I saw that he had my mum by the arm. She begged him to let me leave. But he didn't even *look* like my dad anymore. He smiled at me with these black eyes, then punched Mum in the face."

Deli's hand flew to her mouth.

"He knocked her into the wall, and a framed photo of our family fell off and shattered. I should have stopped him, but I was too scared to move. He pushed her down into the glass on her hands and knees and said, *See, boy? Look what you've done. You break everything you touch.* So . . ."

Lachlan stared at a fixed point behind her.

"Mum still has the scars on her palms. I fell in line."

Deli opened her mouth to say how untrue it was, but stopped at the look in his eyes.

"I met Mo soon after that night. She gave me project after project, putting things together—creating and making and fixing with my hands. She taught me kindness. She tried to show me that I could be trusted with things that were precious. I don't know who I would have become without her. Or maybe I do."

A thousand thoughts vied for Deli's attention. *I met your mom. What happened to your dad? Where's your brother now? Did my aunt talk about me? How did you survive it? How do you keep going? How do you love somebody when love is a weapon?* But what came out was, "Fuck that guy."

His laugh was genuine. "Indeed."

"How old were you? When he hurt your mom?"

The look in his eyes was pleading, and the thing that had been gnawing at her since Aunt Mo's email was more frantic than ever. "About thirteen."

"What did you want to do before The Wallflower?"

"Photography."

"Did he ever hit your mom again?"

Lachlan shook his head, his eyes wandering toward the sky. "No, he never did. He did a bit of groveling, renamed the pub for her, he said, and she forgave him. Started playing along, even. But I think it was my growth spurt that helped. He knew if he hit her again, it might be the last thing he'd do."

The light was starting to tint pink where it painted the lazy clouds traveling in packs across the blue.

Deli looked at the heather in her hand. *Wishes come true. Protection. Healing from within.*

"Lachlan, do you know what wallflowers symbolize? What they say?"

He shook his head.

"Fidelity in misfortune."

Lachlan watched a passing cloud. "Loyalty. Duty. Those are good things."

Deli saw his pulse jump, so slightly, under his jaw. "Loyalty to what? To whom? How long?" He dropped his eyes to hers, and she hoped she was talking to the boy inside the man. "And at what cost, Lachlan? When does fidelity become a betrayal?"

Deli stared openly at Lachlan as rose gold sun fell across his face. Even his sweep of eyelashes seemed to glow like they were made of cinders.

"I met your mom. It was an accident. She was just there standing in the garden, lost, and you . . ." She tried to speak fast enough to outrun the panic that flooded Lachlan's face. "You have her eyes."

His head dropped like the rope that held it up was severed with a blade. Deli knew what she said next could slam the door on whatever trust they'd built, but it had to be said.

"It wasn't right that she let you believe your dad's anger was your responsibility. She should have protected you, Lachlan. It wasn't fair."

"She didn't know any better. But I knew better, and I made the wrong choice. I live with it. I'm past it."

"Bullshit," she said. "Lachlan, you didn't break *anything*. And you didn't deserve to be told you did."

A long look passed between them.

"Your mum was wrong about you, Deli."

For a moment, Deli thought Lachlan was about to say something huge and important. Instead, he reached for her hand and squeezed it, lingering before letting it go.

"The light is leaving and the rain is coming. Let's do the ones together first, then I'll snap a few closer portraits of just you to brush up on details if we have time." He turned and walked toward the camera.

Deli exhaled in a gust, shaking off the weight of the childhood pain two adults hadn't learned how to carry.

"Oh, I got you something," Lachlan called. He returned, holding out a cashmere scarf in the pattern of his kilt. "You don't have to wear it. It's just a silly thing."

She took it from his hand. "Your family's tartan?"

He shrugged. "I thought it might sell it a bit more."

"I love it." Deli wrapped it around her neck, savoring the feel of cashmere against her skin. "How's it look?"

Lachlan adjusted it with both hands, tucking it under the lapels of the leather jacket and hiding the tag. The cold had colored his ears pink. "It suits you."

She reached for something light to say. "I bet you say that to all the girls."

Lachlan's smile turned somber. "Deli, there are no other girls."

A tingling feeling coursed through her. He'd said *other*.

They went through a series of poses as Lachlan triggered the camera via a remote control concealed in his hand. Each time they moved, she could feel it to her bones. Normally Deli felt a sort of permanent lag between her brain and her body, like they were two unrelated departments in a corporate office. But his arms around her from behind, his breath on her neck sent a buzz across her skin. It was easy to follow and fall into him. She forgot to worry about how her clothing hung or how her chin looked from different angles. She simply . . . was.

"Alright," Lachlan said after taking a few tight shots of their feet together sitting in the brush, her hand on his kilted knee. "Are you ready for your close-up?"

She stood, fidgeting, until he took a few paces away and raised his camera.

"What should I do?"

Lachlan peered at her over the lens, his eyes a flash of gold against the changing sky.

"Just be yourself!"

The memory that had been fluttering around in the back of her mind broke free.

And suddenly, Deli MacDonald was nine years old again on a heather-sown path leading to Aunt Mo's red door, bloodied and wind chapped and alive, looking at a boy named Lachlan and his camera.

54

Deli

She knew she recognized those eyes.

It was Lachlan all along.

"It was you!"

"What was me?" he asked, camera still raised, shutter still clicking.

"That day I almost fell to my death off a cliff."

The camera dropped, and Lachlan was thirteen again, too.

His words came out a wanting sound—like wind through a hollowed tree. "You remember?"

She walked toward him. "Have you known this whole time?"

His smile came slowly, like it didn't want to scare a timid thing away. "Aye."

Deli laughed as she ran and threw her arms around Lachlan's neck, thinking back to the feeling of freedom the day she ran to the cliffs, then the feeling of familiarity the day she got off the train.

He held her with his arms around her waist. "I never could forget the way your mum yelled and you didn't cower. When I got home that night and my dad hurt my mom, I got scared. So I'd think of you sometimes. The memory of you was this phantom of courage, like a guardian angel, in a way."

Lachlan had met a version of her that she'd forgotten herself, and he'd kept her alive. Suddenly, it didn't seem so impossible—the way she'd gravitated toward him the whole time she'd been in Scotland, despite the ups and downs. Lachlan, just like Aunt Mo, *saw* Deli in a way she hadn't in a very long time.

"Wait," she said as his words caught up with her. "The day we met was the day your dad hit your mom?"

He nodded.

Deli remembered him now, using his own jacket to wipe the blood from her hands, spending his own time to walk her home.

"God, Lachlan, I'm so sorry."

"There's nothing for you to apologize for, Deli. Nothing."

"You've . . . you've taken care of me. But I've been messing your life up since the day we met."

"Listen to me." He reached under her chin and tilted it up toward him.

"I'm not a courageous man, Deli. I have a small life, and I've made my peace. But being with you, no matter the circumstance, makes me believe that maybe it *could* change. That *I* could change." The last rays of sun found them. "You breathe life into everyone you meet."

Though her heart was pounding, Deli felt a sort of supernatural calm. There was a reason she'd come here. Trey's confusion, Chloe's absence, her mother's critiques—they'd all sent her running to Scotland.

Back to the place and the girl she'd forgotten, and to the boy who never had.

"Lachlan, you don't have to be what someone wants you to be, you know that, right? You're not a little boy anymore." She touched his cheek. "You're allowed to change."

Tears transformed Lachlan's golden eyes to beveled glass, like amber windows scattering sunlight high above consecrated ground.

Deli felt like she was hovering over her own body, watching the girl below like it was on-screen, as she leaned toward him. He stilled for a long moment, then moved so slowly the waiting ached. His breath was shallow as warmth touched her ears, her cheeks, her lips. In the fraction of space before the kiss, when she could feel electricity passing between them like they were gods playing with lightning, a raindrop landed on her nose. Another landed on Lachlan's cheek. The last of the sunlight was swallowed as clouds sealed the sky above them.

They held their breath with an impossibly small space between them. Drops began plinking against the camera equipment he needed for Blair and Andrew's wedding.

She whispered, "Out of time?"

Lachlan pressed his forehead against hers and closed his eyes, winding one hand into her hair at the nape of her neck. He let them breathe together for one breath, two.

"Yes." Lachlan tilted his face slightly and brushed the tip of his nose against hers, and for a second, she thought he might kiss her anyway. Then he looked up, his jaw cutting a rigid line against the sky. "Out of time."

55

Laurie

Five thousand miles away, Laurie MacDonald was typing like a woman possessed. She'd sent message after message to Delilah, and only got a response when she'd thought her grandmother was dying. Laurie hadn't heard from her since. Delilah was drifting.

Maureen had already left Laurie once, and she'd be damned if she sat back and let her only daughter leave, too.

She fought the urge to scream at the sound of her mother's pointed nails clicking against her table.

"Tell them I'm not eating red meat."

Laurie sighed more deeply and loudly than most people would say was necessary, but Rosemary McDonnell wasn't most people's mother. "Yes, Mom, I already wrote that."

"And tell them I have to have herbal tea, no caffeine at all, *at all.*"

"No caffeine."

"And tell them I'll need extra blankets for my—"

"MOM! I got it. Okay? I'm well aware of all your *limitations.*"

Rosemary looked a lot like she was being forced to suck on a whole lemon, and Laurie winced under a sudden wave of guilt.

"Fine," Rosemary snapped, "but don't get all huffy with me when we're sharing a threadbare quilt because you forgot to warn them about my sensitivity to cold."

"It will be fine, Mom."

"You're only as 'fine' as you are prepared, Lorraine."

She hated the name *Lorraine*. It hung over her like an axe, demanding perfection somehow, like the word itself wore Chanel suits and expected her to be valedictorian. Only her sister and her dad had embraced it when she decided to go by Laurie in high school. Every letter she'd kept from her father, postmarked by Royal Mail from Scotland, was addressed to Laurie, not Lorraine. Except the last one.

She still remembered the smell of it in the fireplace, sealed in its envelope, while Rosemary watched over her shoulder. *Lolo*, scrawled in his handwriting on the front, was the last thing to curl up and burn.

Laurie did wonder, sometimes, with twenty years of hindsight, if she'd been wrong to listen to her mother instead of reading her father's last words. Even if he had left her.

They sat in a tense silence punctuated by the clacking of Laurie typing the email into existence while a horrible aching tide tugged at her insides. She reread what she'd typed, and a flash of anger burned through her, evaporating the tide all together. A swooshing sound sent the email on its way.

"There," Laurie said. "It's done."

Rosemary looked her daughter up and down and made a tutting sound. "Well, what are you waiting for, Lorraine? We have a lot of work to do."

Yes, Laurie thought, *and it's about time everyone did their fair share.*

56

Mo

Mo tasted a slice of chocolate-raspberry cake while she wrapped the baby hairs at her temple around her fingertip. The cold sweat from her nightmare had turned them curly.

In the night, she'd seen a young girl walking with bloody knees and a bluebell—growing taller and more tired, following a golden thread that ran slack through the middle of the flower like a bead on a string. She walked until she could see the ocean, and there, by the sea, stood a boy—his eyes lit by the glow in his chest where the thread buried itself and anchored. The girl reached out toward him.

An ink black horse reared between them, and she saw the rider's hand with cherry red nails gripping an onyx dagger. The blade slashed downward and thrust up, then the world folded like it was made of origami paper. The boy clutched at his chest where the golden thread had been severed as the girl was swallowed by darkness.

Mo's foot tapped against her stool in the bakery as she took another bite. *Not good,* she thought, barely tasting it. *Definitely not good.*

"I think the lemon raspberry."

"Good choice." The baker winked and carried the crumb-covered sampling plates back toward the kitchen.

On any day before this one, the news that Lachlan was enamored with her niece would have sent her floating into the sky with excitement. But last night she'd had the dream, and as Lachlan confessed his heart on the road, Mo felt the thread beginning to pull. Even from where she sat tasting cakes, it tightened—like she could reach out and pluck the invisible thing.

Just do it, Mo, she thought.

She opened her email and found exactly what she'd expected. An onyx blade.

Maureen, she read, her eyes flying over the lines as quickly as her heart was beating. If she hadn't had Deli, she might have tried to run. But Mo was determined not to make the same mistakes.

"Love's a beautiful thing, isn't it?" The baker entered totals into her cash register.

"Nothing quite like it," Mo said, still alone after a lifetime of running from hoofbeats.

57

Deli

Lachlan plugged the camera into a laptop behind the bar while Deli shivered in wet clothes.

"Let's get you something dry to change into while they load. I won't take no for an answer. You get the behind-the-scenes tour."

Their almost kiss in the Highlands had tipped the fragile plane between platonic and *not*, and Deli didn't know what to think or feel or do. She followed Lachlan through the swinging door, up the stairs to the apartment he called home over The Wallflower's Crown.

Lachlan moved easily through the cozy space. It was clean, straightforward, and intentional, just like him. He handed her a flannel button-down that was the sort of soft only a well-loved shirt could be.

"This should fit. Take whatever you want from the closet." His clothes were still wet, his kilt suit weighed down. Lachlan held up a pile of folded clothing in his hand. "I'll be downstairs whenever you're ready."

She waited to hear Lachlan's footsteps retreat back to the pub before she stepped up to the mirror and began to peel away her wet clothing. Trey had never left Deli entirely unattended in his apartment. He watched her in his territory with those hawk eyes, tensing if she threatened his curated perfection with her messiness.

Lachlan's shirt, black-and-green checks turned fuzzy, hung comfortably over her hips. She snagged a pair of socks from his top drawer and slipped them on before padding down the stairs. Then she took a running start and burst through the swinging door, sliding across the polished wooden floor with her arms out like she was riding an extra-gnarly wave.

"BoooYAAAHHHHH—"

Lachlan jumped, spun, and started to say "What the fu—" as she sock-surfed into the countertop.

"—AAHGHRF."

He leaned against the counter with a grin. "Worth it?"

She rubbed her hip. "Totally."

"I just sent the first batch of photos to you."

Deli scrambled for her phone buried somewhere in her bag. She bounced on the balls of her feet while the photos loaded. "How do they look? Anything good?"

Lachlan took a moment to respond. "Yes," he said as the photos appeared. She clicked on the first one. "They're remarkable."

She barely recognized herself—cast in lavender light, the best details of her brought forth. It wasn't the Deli who usually showed up in photos. It was the Deli who occupied the quiet, unobserved moments of her life—who slipped bunches of flowers out of vases in her kitchen to change the water and trim the stems while singing the same songs she had for twenty years, who stuffed her face into fresh laundry from the dryer, who liked to sit in coffee shops and listen to the first dates at other tables. It was the truth of her. It was magic.

"Lachlan, how the hell did you do *this*?" She held the screen toward him with a disbelieving laugh. "Those social media filters have nothing on you. What did you change?"

"I didn't change a thing about you." His voice was resolute. "I wouldn't."

She stared at the Deli in the photo. A stranger she'd never seen, yet someone she'd spent so much time with—like a long-lost person you've always loved.

Aunt Mo had another photo of her as a little girl pinned to her refrigerator. Deli couldn't imagine a world where her mother would pin that little girl on her fridge proudly. The thought cramped painfully in her body—scar tissue remembering a wound.

Deli swiped to the next photo.

She was kneeling to tighten her shoelace, and Lachlan was behind her, waiting. It was how he looked at her when she wasn't watching—something in the set of his shoulders, the tilt of his body blocking her from the wind, the clench of his jaw and the soft fire of his eyes.

"Oh," she said, and she risked a glance. There, behind the bar, in worn out jeans and a navy woolen sweater, his eyes burned. "You were right. You *are* a good actor."

She flipped to the next close-up of them from the waist down, trying to ignore the hot drip of Lachlan's attention lighting her from the inside out, pulling her away from her life as she knew it. In the photo they were boot to boot, his hand resting on her lower back, pulling her into him. Hers hung at her side with a small clutch of heather.

Another crop of Deli standing in front of him, laughing with her eyes squeezed shut. The smile on his face while he listened transformed him—the hard edges made soft with affection.

She gulped as quietly as one could. "A *really* good actor."

"No, Deli. I'm not."

She could hear the plea in his voice to look at him. But if she did, things might never be changed back. If she did, Fearnhall, the fever dream of her time there . . . Lachlan? They'd all be *real.* For better or worse, forever. Her heart pounded.

"Thank you for these, Lachlan."

"I should be thanking you. I do actually feel better about the wedding this weekend."

Deli opened her social media and selected the photo of her holding the heather to post, but thoughts of making Trey jealous or making Chloe curious or making her mother feel the sting of her absence were gone. She simply wanted to proclaim her own life—because somehow, despite living twenty-nine years, Deli was realizing she might have done very little living.

"That's good . . ." Deli said, distracted. The photo posted, her feed reloaded, and suddenly she was looking at Trey and the breathtaking blonde Deli had met in the elevator, slightly blurred in the darkness of a late-night Los Angeles party. Trey looked roguishly at the camera, his half grin like a baited hook, while Scarlett pressed against his chest and looked up at him with her thousand-watt smile.

Deli didn't know if Trey really *did* love her, underneath it all. But she did know Trey would never post a photo like that of her. Not unless she carved herself away to, quite literally, fit into his expectations.

Lachlan sounded far away. "Deli?"

"Um"—Deli's voice was hoarse—"sorry, can I have some water?"

Concern creased his brow. "Of course."

There was something both bolstering and disorienting about being in a place, with people, doing things that no one she had known and loved her whole life would ever see. It was resoundingly lonely in one way—to be writing chapters Chloe would never read, living small moments no one would remember—and entirely freeing in the other—to exist, for once, unobserved. There were no judges in the audience, holding up a diagram of who she was supposed to be and pointing out where she'd fallen short.

Deli wasn't sure who she was or who she was going to be, but the space and time had given her the seed of a new perspective. Whether or not she was forever falling a bit short of Trey's or Chloe's or her mom's love was really, at the end of the day, up to them.

Deli was tired of trying.

She took a breath as she navigated to her texts as quickly as she could. She couldn't lose her resolve.

Trey, I think I fell in love with you the day I met you, and I think you've known that all along. I need to find a way to get over you. It's time. It's been time. I'm sorry. I'll miss you.

She hit send.

Deli could hear her heart from inside her body, shivering from the cold prickle of fear that comes when something unforgivable has been done. She tossed her phone onto the counter, her hands shaking as it skittered away.

"What did I do?" she whispered to herself. *"What did I do? What did I do?"*

Lachlan spun at the sound and was there in less time than Deli thought a human could move. He bent to her eye level. "What happened?"

She practiced the feel of the words in her mouth. "I just told Trey . . . everything."

Lachlan's eyes widened. "Everything?"

She nodded. "I told him . . ." Part of Deli wanted to stop talking, let it be unreal for a little longer. But it was time to tear down the curtains and let the light in. "I told him that I need to get over him. And that we shouldn't be in each other's lives right now." The air seemed to shift around Lachlan, though his face stayed inscrutable. She ran her fingers into her hair as the supercut of nearly fifteen years of memories with the boy, then man, she'd always imagined loving burned up like film in her mind. She was on the verge of tears. "Oh my god, Lachlan, what did I do?"

"What do you need, Deli?"

She shook her head. "I'm fine."

But then she wondered what it might be like to say something else. In a new place, with a new man, having just cut a thing out of her heart and let it float away down a river, Deli stood on the bank and thought she might try something new.

"I'm not fine," she said.

"You don't say." His voice was soft.

"I don't know what I need."

He considered her a moment. "I do."

Deli was so surprised by his hands on her waist that she threw her arms up like she was being arrested. He started walking backward, guiding her until she was standing with her back pressed against the bar.

"I'm unarmed."

He smiled. "Jump on three."

"Heh?"

"Three."

Deli jumped as he sat her on the bar top she'd watched him meticulously polish and fuss over for a month. "Lachlan, the bar! The shiny, shiny bar!"

"Mmhmm," he said as he headed back behind it.

"I'm not allowed to sit on the bar. I'm barely allowed to touch the bar." She twisted around to look at him over her shoulder, switching from the left to right as he passed behind her. "The owner is very crotchety about it."

Lachlan uncorked a bottle of warm looking liquid and reached for two short glasses. "I think he'll give you a pass tonight." He came back around to her. Deli took a glass from him as he set the other on the bar and scooted the stool next to her away, then lifted himself to sit beside her.

The glass wafted smoke from her hand. "I don't like whisky."

"Tonight, you need it." He began a toast, and Deli thought it was a poem at first. "To the wild women. To the courageous women. To the caged bird finally free. To the hope that the fog of him, of *them,* will pass, and you'll be able to see yourself clearly, Deli."

Nobody had ever spoken to her that way. The world narrowed in until it was only the two of them. "How am I supposed to see myself?"

Lachlan's voice was steady. "Like I do."

"You barely know me," she whispered.

He held her gaze. "I'm proud of you."

Deli MacDonald had spent most of her life thinking. Thinking about other people, thinking about their feelings, thinking about how to make them feel better. She thought about good and evil, and if those hundred-year-old tortoises got sad when their bird or lizard companions were born and died and died again, and of all the ways she had fallen short.

So when Lachlan leaned toward her, his fingertips brushing her cheek in an unspoken question—she decided not to think about what the right thing or the smart thing or the considerate thing to do was. She decided not to think at all.

Which was how she found herself with her fist knotted in the front of Lachlan's shirt, tasting the smoke on his lips.

58

Lachlan

The entire way home, Lachlan had cursed the rain. It was typical for him, really. A moment so close to perfect—gone before it arrived.

As he paced behind the bar, trying not to think about Deli in his bedroom—Deli slipping out of the black tights stretched sheer against her thighs, slipping into something that was his—he considered his life so far. He'd spent most of it trying to stay out of people's way. He'd tried to be helpful. He'd swallowed a lot of things he probably should have said.

Lachlan sometimes wished things were different but accepted that life was what was handed to you. He did his best with what was offered, and he never asked for more. Even when the thing he wanted most in the world was pressed against his forehead, a hairbreadth from his lips—the rain had come. And he'd accepted it.

When Deli burst through the swinging door in his flannel and socks, sliding into the room the way she'd slid into his world, Lachlan reconsidered. She'd stoked the fight, the want, the passion in his heart from cold ash to roaring flame. Deli was bright and vibrant and brave. She was who she was—born knowing.

What sort of man would let the woman who'd proven his heart was a phoenix believe she was unworthy when he could do something about it? Or, at the very least, try?

So, as he watched her eyes glass with the hurt of realizing the people she loved hadn't loved her well, Lachlan gathered his courage. He listened to her tell him she was brave enough to let her heart break if it was the cost of knowing she deserved more.

He lifted her to the bar top, poured her whisky, and decided it was time.

He was done wishing things were different.

In the moment before their lips touched, Lachlan Scott had never been more terrified.

59

Deli

Deli, who had spent the majority of her twenty-nine years loyal to a boy named Trey Evans—who was going to love her back one day—hadn't kissed many boys.

At Bree Jackson's thirteenth birthday party, tucked away in a corner out of sight of the parents monitoring the mini golfing preteens, Carlos Ramirez kissed Deli for the first time in her life. It was stiff and sloppy and they were going at different paces, but Carlos had been staring at her in social studies for months with his dark velvet eyes and fast-talking mouth, and she'd floated home on the memory of him saying, *Wow, that was awesome.* The handful of others that came after were sometimes better, a few times worse, but for the most part, the same.

On a bar top in a pub in Scotland, Deli MacDonald learned that anyone could mash their faces together in dark corners, but a *real* kiss was the closest thing she'd ever known to magic.

Lachlan didn't just kiss her, he kissed her like a secret whispered, then a truth declared. He kissed her like a love song strummed, then an orchestra's crescendo. Rain thrashed against the windows, and just as Lachlan's hand skimmed from her thigh to the hem of the shirt he'd probably worn a thousand times—thunder clapped, and they were plunged into darkness.

Lachlan slowed his lips against hers. His thumb traced her cheekbone.

"Stay here." He kissed her forehead and nearly her mouth, then pulled himself away at the last moment and jumped down from the bar top to disappear into the back.

In the dark, the spell was broken, and her thoughts—which she'd hoped she had successfully banished—were coming back in full force.

Deli felt very foolish. Exposed.

A flicker in the fireplace caught. Lachlan appeared in front of her with tealights and matches, eye to eye with her as she sat on the bar. He stepped between her knees and kissed her quickly, and Deli felt herself go stiff. Lachlan scanned her face before he moved to the tables and lit candles until the room filled with soft, warm light.

"Hey." He spoke quietly as he found his way back to her, not intimately close, but close enough. "You alright?"

She forced her lips into a smile, but her jaw felt wired shut. Lachlan touched her knee tentatively, a gesture of comfort, and even then she flinched. He froze.

Deli wrapped her arms around her body.

"Lachlan, I . . . Nobody's ever wanted . . . I mean—" She took a big breath to gather her strength for a burst of honesty—a window to her shame. "I don't need you to say anything; I'm not fishing for compliments here, it's just this is the last stop before you're disappointed. And I don't want to go there."

As he listened, his face shifted from concerned to something darker—maybe angrier, maybe hungrier. She needed to rip the bandage off.

"If this goes farther, than, you know"—she gestured between them—"this . . . you're not going to like what you see, okay?"

Lachlan held her gaze for a second, then another, and she felt her chin jut out like a child issuing a challenge, her arms still tight around her chest. He dropped his hands to his hips and his head toward the ground, obscuring his face. She could see his shoulders, taut with tension, rising and falling with his breath. The silence was miserable. She wanted to melt into the floor to escape.

"I know what you look like, Deli." His voice was new—gravel and firewood and goosebumps. It was unfamiliar and terrifying. It left her aching to touch him. "And I assure you, I like what I see."

She tried to accept what he was saying. She really tried.

"You can't know that, Lachlan. And I can't believe you."

"If you can't believe me . . ." Lachlan stepped closer. "Will you let me prove it?"

He reached toward her face and caught her chin gently in his hand, pausing to read her expression.

"Will you let me show you?"

It took all of Deli's courage to stop herself from stopping him—to let herself have something that she had not earned. She nodded once.

He placed a hand on her knee, this time with purpose, and pried it sideways, then stepped in and pushed her other leg open with his hip, eliminating the space between them. Lachlan ran his hand up her thigh and jumped to her lower back, pressing her toward his body, and she felt herself arch toward him before she could think. She sucked in a surprised breath.

Lachlan's lips dusted her jaw. His whisper was smoke against her ear. "I do want you, Delilah."

Her name on his tongue—the way he made it sound like *hers*—would have been enough.

"From the moment I saw you get off that train, and every moment afterward." He pulled her closer to him, and her thighs enclosed his hips as his breath coaxed chills from her skin. "Will you let me prove to you how much I want you? How much I have always, always wanted you?"

Lachlan met her eyes, and her sea of fear felt smaller under the heat of the thing that passed between them. He ran a hand through the hair at the base of her skull and tilted her head to position her lips. She closed her eyes as his nose brushed hers, and he whispered.

"Let me?"

60

Lachlan

For most of his adult life, Lachlan had been in a sort of half-on state, making it day-to-day, prolonging the inevitable.

Now, Lachlan Scott was finally alive.

He moved slowly, easing Deli back into their connection. Lachlan felt at home in his body, Deli didn't. Lachlan trusted his body, Deli didn't. There were a lot of voices fighting for space in her head, all with opinions about what made her wrong.

Lachlan didn't need to use his voice to tell Deli the *truth.*

He teased her lips apart with his and let a low moan rumble from his chest until she pressed herself into him. Lachlan had kissed his share in the past, he'd had his passion—but he'd never kissed someone who made him feel like his life had just begun. Now he kissed Deli like it was the first kiss to ever be, attuned to her like they had all the time in the world.

Her hesitancy gave way to hunger. He grinned and cradled her head with the hand that wasn't running up her back. The damp ends of her hair tickled his skin.

God she was soft. Her hair, her lips, her body.

His blood pumped urgently through him and turned him hungrier with each heartbeat. He kissed her harder, and she moaned softly into his mouth. Even just that, the sound of her pleasure at a simple kiss, made Lachlan want to bury himself inside her—but he quieted the swelling fire that wanted to consume. He needed this to last.

He would show her she was worthy of worship.

Deli unbuttoned the top of his old flannel—which had never looked as good as it did on her—and it slid off her shoulder. Lachlan broke away from her mouth and drew back to hold her gaze while he brushed her dark hair away from her skin. He couldn't believe she was really with him. He couldn't believe she was real.

He longed to show her his gratitude. As he pressed his lips against the soft corner of her jaw and her throat, he imagined how her eyes would look—pupils blown wide, trying to focus on him again after they'd rolled back in her head. He kissed lower with just enough pressure to pull another moan.

"Lachlan . . ."

"Delilah," he breathed into her neck.

He'd always loved the sound of his name when she spoke it, the way her accent stretched the vowels in new ways. But hearing his name in the voice he was coaxing from her now was like hearing it for the very first time.

Lachlan tingled under her touch as she trailed her fingers down his back. It was like Deli could spark electricity when she wanted to—like she could sear lightning into him. She tugged up the hem of his jumper.

"Are you gonna help me, or what?"

He smirked. "I thought you'd want to 'do it yourself.'"

Deli looked him up and down, setting him ablaze in the wake of her wild green eyes.

"Tonight?" she said. "I don't want to do *anything* myself."

That was all he needed to hear.

Lachlan pulled his jumper over his head and crushed his mouth against hers again, trailing his hands down her lower back and under her body. She wrapped her legs around his waist to squeeze him against her. In the thick air of the pub, so warm compared to the rain-soaked night outside, he could smell the different layers of her—the perfume on her neck, the soft coconut of her hair, and the heady, heavy scent of her body coming alive under his touch.

He was thrumming with pent-up wanting. Lachlan left her mouth to kiss down her throat, skimming the sensitive skin with his teeth and tongue as he slid the flannel off both of her shoulders.

"Hey . . ." Deli kept her legs around his waist but pushed him back.

He blinked hard, dragging himself back to reality. "Is this alright? Is this too much?"

She crossed her arms over her chest. The flannel hung on by the last center button, threatening to fall entirely away. The lace edge of a black bra peeked out of the tatty fabric, and her bare skin glowed like moonlight under the red tracks he'd left with his mouth.

"You're less naked than me." She slipped a bra strap off her shoulder and let it fall—an ember threatening to spark. "Doesn't seem fair."

Lachlan exhaled in a half chuckle, half growl—relieved and desperate to keep her from putting her clothes back on.

"As you wish." He tugged off his white T-shirt.

"Now let me look at you." She unwrapped her legs and pushed him backward a step.

In the same little pub where he'd spent most of his life, listening to the familiar fire and rain, Lachlan stood with his arms spread wide, feeling brand fucking new.

"God, you're hot," Deli said. "You're, like, really, really hot."

His chest heaved with his breath. It was taking all his focus to hold back the animal part of him that longed for the hunt—for the feast.

Deli swept her eyes once more, painfully slow, over his entire body. When she finally met his gaze, she was a goddess atop a mountain, waiting on a desperate sinner to atone on his knees.

And he was desperate.

Eyes locked, Deli smiled, and Lachlan felt the anticipation coax his heartbeat to rise. He held his breath for one second. Two. Then she nodded.

Lachlan had her off the bar and in his arms in a second. She crossed her ankles around his waist as he supported her from underneath. He buried his mouth in the soft skin of her chest, and he couldn't stop the low moan that escaped him as his lips found her breast, his hands felt her body. Deli knotted her hands in his hair and pressed him more firmly against her, whispering "Oh my god," as he walked her toward the place he'd lay her down.

As he lowered her onto a table, the vase holding a sprig of the honeysuckle vine that had sprouted out back wobbled and tipped with their impact.

"Oh no!" Deli reached behind her to find the rolling glass before it fell to the floor. "This little guy almost met his end."

Lachlan looked at the glass in her hands, so cold and brittle compared to the girl sitting on his table with perfect lips and red splotches growing up her neck. He grinned and snatched the vase from her grip. Then he threw it across the bar.

"Fuck it."

"Lachlan Scott! Who's gonna pay for that?"

"Never mind that. I know the owner. Lovely guy." He leaned down and nipped at her lip, bit it just hard enough to pull her toward him, and released. "Besides, I'd do a lot worse for a lot less if you asked me, Deli."

Deli touched the lip he'd just bitten and sucked it between her teeth before it bounced back into place. She looked at him from under a sweep of dark lashes—all heat and swelling lushness. *God,* he thought. *Thank god.*

"Fuck it," Deli echoed, and she blew out the tealight and tossed the votive over her shoulder. By the time it shattered, Lachlan had hooked a hand under each of her knees and pulled her forward so she was sitting on the very edge of the table.

"Tonight," he whispered as he placed a hand on either side of her, splayed against the polished hardwood, "I want you to know *exactly* what it feels like"—he kissed her and pressed her backward until she had to catch herself on her elbows—"to have someone take care of you."

"Hoookay," she rasped into his mouth as Lachlan pressed her onto her back and held his body above her.

"You said you didn't want to do *anything* tonight." He kissed her lips, her neck, her collarbone. "And I'm good at following directions."

"I remember." She gasped as he slid a hand under her shirt. "So, you'll do the doing?"

Lachlan grinned, letting the exquisite, fluttery feeling of her humor collide with the wanting. "I'll do the doing."

He slowly shrugged the flannel off her body and dropped it onto the floor. He felt her stiffen. Her eyes were squeezed shut.

"Sorry," she said, suddenly crossing her arms over her body.

"Don't apologize," he said. "Do you want to stop?"

"No, no, I don't think so." Deli made a sound somewhere between a sigh and a laugh. "I just need a second to adjust."

There she was—in his pub, on the table he'd built with his own hands, nearly topless and flushed with the heat he'd kissed into her skin. She was as beautiful as she'd always been, but now she was colored with desire. Her lips were even fuller. Her eyes were even clearer, like the crystal waters of a forest lake dappled with white light.

Lachlan couldn't imagine moving through life believing that he was less worthy of good things, of pleasure, of love, because his body didn't look the way complete strangers' bodies looked. He couldn't imagine telling his daughter she needed to starve or carve away at her skin and bone. He couldn't imagine ever telling a woman he loved that the body she had, the *one* body she had to carry her through life, was lacking, and reason enough to not love her anymore.

Lachlan hoped she'd hear him, even if he never touched her again. "Deli? You, too, you know." She looked at him, at war in herself somewhere, and he'd never meant anything more. "You're allowed to be free."

In the beat of silence, he soaked in the feeling of her—the relief of standing under all her light. Then she kissed him. A bolt of heat rolled through him in a wave, and he was at its mercy. *Her* mercy.

She ran her nails down his back, raising gooseflesh where she touched.

Lachlan slowly traced a line from her waist to the clasp of her bra.

He whispered into her ear. "Yes?"

He could hear the smile in her response. "Yes."

It fell away as Lachlan laid her back down and kissed her collarbone to her sternum, and then each breast—taking her into his mouth, cupping the other in his hand. Deli moaned his name and tangled her fingers into his hair, tugging and intoxicating.

Lachlan stood and lifted her legs so that her ankles were hovering over his shoulders. He gripped her by her thighs and pulled her, hard and without warning, until she was flush against him. She let out a surprised breath that turned to a quiet pining sound as he began to move against her. His body was humming with energy, begging. He slipped a finger under the elastic of her lace-trimmed pants.

"May I?"

She covered her eyes with her hands and laughed. "Oh god, fine!"

He lifted her body off the table just enough to slip them out from under her. Lachlan watched her eyes and kissed the inside of an ankle, down her leg as he hooked them over his shoulders and lowered himself to his knees.

He licked her inner thigh and closed his lips over the place, growling deep in his throat.

Deli raised her head off the table.

"Tell me to stop and I'll stop, no questions asked," Lachlan said. "But I want to." Her chest was rising and falling quickly, skin like snowdrift and petals. He loved seeing her like this—giving in to her body and pleasure. "Deli, *I* want to do this until your eyes roll back in your head. Until you forget everything—everything that takes up space in your mind—but *my name.*"

Deli looked at him for a beat, then dropped back to the table with a grin. "Then do it."

"Fuck yes," he growled, and he sank into her warmth.

She shuddered and moved under his touch. He slid his hand up her body until he found her fingers and wove them with his own. The way she writhed, the sounds she was making—listening to Deli moan his name and feeling her under his mouth was better than any sex he could remember. She gasped at his tongue dipping inside her, ground against one of his fingers, then two. He wanted to remember the taste of her—coming alive as she deserved, *feeling* how he wanted her as he knelt between her legs—for the rest of his life. His hand and mouth worked together to call every part of her into her body beneath him—to wind her so tightly that when he released her, it would be shattering. Unstoppable. Unforgettable.

"Lachlan, *oh my god, don't stop—*"

Deli's back bowed and her thighs tightened around his head. He groaned into her as her pleasure built and broke over—legs shaking, hips rolling with her fist knotted in his hair. Lachlan was still licking and kissing her when her convulsions finally slowed, like they would never have another place to be. He didn't want more from her. Her breath coming fast, her heat beneath him—that was more than enough.

Listening to her panting, he decided there was nothing he'd rather do than make Deli feel good.

Lachlan Scott was best when he was a man in love.

"Lachlan?"

Her voice called him from his haze. She sat up, her legs still hooked over his shoulders. He marveled from his knees.

"Yes? I'm right here. What do you need? Water?" He nodded toward the rows of liquor bottles behind the bar with a smirk. "A drink?"

"I need you," she began, tilting his face up by the chin. He could fall into her eyes and never have his fill of the way she was looking at him now. "To *fu—*"

"GUESS WHO?"

They whipped their heads toward the pounding on the door just as the lights blared back to life with a hum. Deli shielded her eyes with a hand.

"Lachlan, I know you're in there!"

No, he thought. He recognized the voice. *It can't be . . .*

61

Deli

"Fuck me," Lachlan muttered.

"Who is that?" Deli whispered, seated on a table with her boobs out, quite unacceptable for polite company.

A key scraped against the lock. Lachlan moved in a half crouch, collecting various flung garments.

"It's pure baltic out here! *Let me in!*"

"Here." He tossed her bra and underwear at her. "Go through the back. My office is unlocked." He threw his flannel over his shoulder in her direction-ish while he bent for his own discarded sweater.

The stranger pounded on the door. "Did you change the locks? Typical!"

His accent was so familiar, but it wasn't someone from the local crew in Fearnhall.

Lachlan's face was stricken with panic and . . . regret? Guilt? He spoke low and urgent, pleading. "Deli, I'm so sorry, but you have to hide."

"Hide?" She blinked as she slipped the flannel onto her arms. A minute ago he was changing her entire opinion of the cosmos and her place in it. Now she was an old-timey mistress? A shameful booty call? Something ugly in her started to bloom.

"Should I leave the money on the nightstand, or—"

"Deli, *please*," he cut her off. *"Go."*

She stood, stung, but reached up and ran a hand through his hair, tucking it back into its standard casual unruliness. As she turned to go, he caught her hand in his, kissed the inside of her wrist, and pressed her palm to his cheek.

Lachlan closed his eyes, exhaling slowly, and Deli was struck a bit speechless again. By the cut of his jaw and the curve of his lips—the deep rose in his cheeks and dark flame in his hair. She'd never forget those eyes finding hers while he was on his knees, glowing with intention and desire—like he was lit from within and she was looking into a room ablaze. He was dripping honey. Liquid gold. The steady flow of something rare at its most pure. Being near him, being *with* him, was some kind of magic.

She made a mental note to tell as many lurid details she could recall if she ever got the chance to grow old in a retirement home with proper ladies in need of scandalizing.

The door shook so violently the man outside must have shoulder-checked it. Lachlan grew so agitated that she was struck with a terrible thought. It tumbled out before she could stop it.

"Are you ashamed of me?"

"What?" Another impact outside nearly rattled the place. "Go! Please!" he hissed.

Deli grabbed her phone and bag from behind the bar and bolted through the door to the back, then turned and pressed her ear against it. The dead bolt slid. Rain and wind came rushing into the room behind the stranger. His footsteps reverberated across the wooden floor.

She'd never heard Lachlan sound threatening before. "What are you doing here?"

"There's that charm." She heard a sound like he'd clapped Lachlan on the shoulder.

Lachlan practically snarled, "What are you doing here, William?"

William?

"I needed a drink." His footsteps moved past Lachlan. "And anyway, there's no place like home."

No place like home? She pictured the Scott family hanging on the wall. The missing little brother.

"Can you not?" Lachlan sounded almost petulant. "That's the most expensive bottle."

William chuckled, low and rich from his chest, and she heard the telltale scrape of glass across wood from Lachlan's sacred space behind the bar. The air tasted stale and achy—like dust on a forgotten photograph, or a scar dully lamenting a fall long ago.

"Please, Lachlan." Liquid poured. "*I'm* not the one he would have been worried about handling his best stock."

Lachlan was silent. A sour note streaked through the space, and Deli could feel the sting of this stranger's words on his soft heart. She wanted to know who had interrupted her impossible night and who she might have to fistfight. She knew from the look in Lachlan's eyes when he recognized the voice that she should really just stay out of sight. But she figured curiosity had killed a lot of cats, and Deli was no better than the exquisite Sir Beans. She'd be a dick to think so. So, she peeked.

William stood behind the bar with his back to her. He was even taller than Lachlan was, but with shoulder length, thick, sandy blonde waves and broad shoulders that pressed against his very expensive looking camel coat. He stood casually, one leg tucked in front of the other, propped against the counter and holding a glass. Lachlan braced himself against the bar where he'd kissed her not long before. William took a sip of the whisky and held it up to the light. His hair fell back from his face as he admired the contents.

Deli's breath caught. *No effing way . . .*

Lachlan glared. "Do you have any idea how much I charge for a pour of that?"

"You're the businessman in the family." William shrugged and took another sip. "I'm just the entertainer."

Deli's phone lit up in her hand as it connected to the restored internet, glowing blue in the dark. She rushed to tuck it under her shirt.

"Family." Lachlan's laugh was short and bitter. "Surprised you still consider yourself a part of this one."

William snorted. "Doesn't it get strange, spending every day standing in the very spot he died?" He took another slow drink from his glass, draining it with a dramatic *ahh.* "You're starting to sound *just* like him."

"At least I'm here."

"So am I."

"For how long this time, Will? How long until you disappear again, and I have to come up with a good reason you're on the telly every night but she can't see you?"

There was no way Deli was seeing what she was seeing and hearing what she was hearing. Perhaps there was an ancient Scottish curse that gave American women hallucinations if they dared defile anointed land—like the local pub—by bouncing their baps about. That had to be it, because there was no way, *no way*, that was—

"How many times, William," Lachlan continued, "are you going to break Mum's heart?"

Deli's phone chimed under her shirt.

She scrambled to turn the volume down. William poured another glass from the expensive bottle as Lachlan shot a glance toward the crack where her eye peeked through. She saw his widen.

"At least you inherited Dad's taste for guilt trips *and* whisky, Lachlan."

Her phone chimed again as it downloaded missed messages, and William grew still. The text she'd sent to Trey just before she'd lost service—the one sealing the fate she'd been terrified of for years—scrolled in her mind. Her hands shook as the screen opened to where she'd left off. A new message banner showed one from Trey.

Deli, you can't be serious?

Notifications started pouring in. An email from her mother. One, two, three texts from Trey as she finally turned the volume off. She clicked on the message.

Deli, Please, I'm so sorry I've been such a dick. Can we talk?

"Is there someone here?" William asked.

"No!" Lachlan answered too quickly. The floor creaked.

I can't lose you. Talk to me. I need you. Please.

Trey, saying what she'd longed to hear for most of her life, coming in a minute too late? Or was it too late? Her hands shook as she tried to make sense of everything happening at once. The phone clattered to the ground.

"Will, no! Wait!"

The door swung open—revealing Deli 50 percent dressed, 90 percent disheveled, and 100 percent in shock. William's frame eclipsed most of the light while he looked her up and down, and a slow smile spread across his face.

All she could say was, "It's *you.*"

Because she *did* know him. That voice had been declaring love and war into her living room the night she decided she was going to come to Scotland. The night this all began.

Billy S. Burns, the star of *The Highlander*, was William Scott.

Lachlan's *brother.*

And William Scott was standing over her—less oily, but just as impressive—grinning like a cat who'd just spotted a tasty canary, despite Lachlan's attempts to *hide her*.

"Aye, it's me." He had very white teeth. "Who, *exactly*, are you?"

"Deli—" Lachlan yanked the currently unkilted television star back from the doorway. "I . . . Are you okay?"

William surveyed her over Lachlan's shoulder. He had to be taking in her mussed hair, his brother's shirt, and her bare legs. She felt her ears turn hot.

William smirked. "I'd say she looks like she's doing just fine."

Deli had never seen Lachlan so . . . pained. She saw it in his face, and it broke her heart.

His brother finding her was his nightmare.

He spoke, resigned. "William, this is Deli." Deli raised a hand. "And Deli"—Lachlan closed his eyes—"this is William. My brother."

William popped his head onto Lachlan's shoulder with a shit-eating grin.

Lachlan looked as guilty as a dog who'd torn up the sofa. *Good,* she thought, *you should.*

"Deli, I'm sorry—"

William interrupted him with a hard pat on the back.

"Where are your manners? We have a guest! Come join us for a drink. On the house!"

Deli widened her eyes at Lachlan to scream *absolutely not* as non-verbally as possible. She thought she heard the sound of the door-knob behind the two towering (*actual*) Highlanders in front of her as Lachlan's brother wrapped his arms around Lachlan's waist and lifted him *off the ground* to tug him backward.

"William!" Lachlan growled.

"Lachlan!" Deli called.

"Deli?" The door slammed open, punctuating Aunt Mo's voice like an exclamation point. "We've got a problem."

The boys swiveled. Lachlan elbowed William in the stomach and dropped to his feet as his brother released him with an *oof.*

Her aunt smiled. "Hi, Will. Good to see you."

"Aunt Mo!" Deli grabbed her phone off the floor and stuffed it into her bag as she pushed through the door toward her aunt.

"*Aunt* Mo?" William looked between them before sliding his gaze to Lachlan.

"Hey, kid." Aunt Mo winked at Lachlan, whose face lit up like a torch. "Will, I see you've met my niece. And, Deli? Your mother and grandmother are here."

62

Deli

"Well, I have bad news and I have good news, missy."

Aunt Mo started up the road, and Deli watched the amber glow of The Wallflower's Crown grow smaller through the rain-streaked window.

"Can we start with the good news?"

Aunt Mo chuckled. "The good news is, I haven't seen Lachlan that mortified before, and I now have something to dangle over him for the rest of his life."

Mortified, Deli thought. *Ashamed.*

"Glad I could help."

Aunt Mo let the quiet sit for a moment. "Do you want to talk about it?" Deli hadn't realized it, but she'd been expecting her aunt to be angry. "I know I'm Lachlan's friend, but I'm your aunt. So if you want to talk about it, I'm safe."

Deli turned the word *safe* over in her mind. In the cold, starless Highland night—while she could still feel the touch of Lachlan's lips on her thigh, her collarbone, her mouth—the realization that she'd been looking for someone to call safe her entire life hit her like a blow to the stomach.

She thought of the tears she'd shed after that night at Trey's, leaving Technicolor droplets on her screen as her finger hovered over the button to call her mother.

"Fine. Yes, okay? We kissed or whatever."

"YES!" Aunt Mo whooped as she drove.

Deli told her aunt the tamer details of the night. About the shoot, about realizing Lachlan had taken the photo that Aunt Mo had sent. She felt the flame of embarrassment trying to claw its way up her skin, but as Aunt Mo listened, nodded, and commented along the story, it got easier and easier to douse it.

"Then *William* is there. When were you going to tell me about that, by the way?"

Aunt Mo's brow creased with guilt. "It was Lachlan's to tell."

"I trusted him the way I never do. He asked me to. *Begged* me to. Then he *hid* me, Aunt Mo. As soon as the international-Scottish-heart-throb-weird-tension brother showed up."

"I know. I know. I don't think he meant to be hurtful."

Deli knew her reaction was too big, but it wasn't about William—not really.

She took a breath. "Regarding what you said about my mother and grandmother, may I just ask . . . What the fuck?"

"Ah. Yes. The bad news."

"You don't say?"

"They are"—Aunt Mo checked her watch—"about twenty minutes away."

"That's impossible." Deli shook her head. "They hate it here."

"And yet."

She scoffed. "What could possibly make them visit the place they've talked about like it was the last circle of hell after twenty years?"

"My mother and sister have never been good at letting go with grace."

"You've been here for two decades."

"Oh, it's not me they are interested in retrieving. It's you."

Deli's heartbeat picked up. "I've been gone, like, barely a month."

"Exactly."

"That's nothing."

Aunt Mo pulled in front of the cottage, put the car in park, and took off her seat belt. "A month is enough time to *change*, Deli. A month is a lifetime."

"I haven't changed."

It came out on instinct—like blocking a ball from getting into a net. She thought of the time she'd come back from summer camp and told Chloe she didn't want to always be the bad guy when they played make believe. The time she'd told her mother she couldn't come early to cook for Christmas because she had to work. The time she'd told Trey she'd met a long-haired drummer with chipped black fingernails at a café and given him her number before he skated away on a longboard.

Wow, you've really changed, Deli.

"I hate to break it to ya, buddy, but yes, you have. And I've been so proud. I know how hard it is to get enough space from our family to grow."

"That's not what I'm doing here," Deli snapped.

Aunt Mo spoke softly. "Isn't it?"

She hadn't wanted to pull an Aunt Mo and disappear. Though . . . she had noticed that her days felt lighter, that her inner voice felt clearer. She had made fast friends and learned to trust their affection without having earned it. She *had* let a man who wasn't Trey Evans kiss her like the world was ending.

The Deli MacDonald from a month ago couldn't have done any of it.

"Deli." Aunt Mo shifted her body to face Deli in the dark car. "Do you know what happened between us? Our family?"

Deli knew this story ended in a little cottage on a cliffside. "Just how it ends."

Aunt Mo took a deep breath. "From the day I was born, I was difficult for my mother to understand. I would fight her over every bow in my hair, every ruffle sock. I got along too well with my dad."

"Grandpa Cal?"

"We were peas in a pod, and your grandma punished him for it. I tried to protect him."

Deli could picture her aunt clearly, small and fierce. But she couldn't picture her mom.

"Was my mom like the evil stepsister to your Cinderella?"

Aunt Mo laughed, but it died quickly. "No, no—at least, not at first. I tried to protect her, too. But your mom was more fearful, and *our* mom was . . ." She shook her head. "Fearsome."

Deli's throat was getting tight. "What happened when Grandpa died?"

"Your grandpa was the only person in our family who I felt like understood anything about me.

"Then he died. I'd never known firsthand how grief unmoors you. How easily you can be swept away. It was like . . . I suddenly didn't know myself, even after so many years of having to be so sure of who I was. I was . . . adrift.

"The thing about my mom, Deli—your grandma . . . she held me as I cried. She told me things would be okay. My partner—" Aunt Mo paused. She closed her eyes. "Beth, she tried to warn me. She tried to tell me that my mom hadn't just *changed* overnight and was safe now, but I didn't listen.

"Then we got the will. The lawyer read off that the cottage was mine and only mine, and my mother looked at me like she wished she could make me disappear."

Deli's stomach turned sour. "I can't even imagine what my mother would say to me in that scenario."

"Mine was not kind."

"What did Grandma say?"

"She accused me of manipulating my dad to steal what she'd rightfully earned. She said he only loved me because I was a liar."

Deli recoiled. "That's awful, Aunt Mo. You didn't deserve that."

"She demanded I relinquish my claim to the cottage and give it to her so she could split it between your mom and me when she died. She demanded to know what Lorraine had ever done to deserve my 'hatred.' She said, *He's trying to hurt me. He's hurting your sister. That cottage belongs to the family. Don't you want to be a family?*"

Deli tried to imagine what it must have been like. Whatever else she was, Aunt Mo was brave. "But you didn't do it."

Aunt Mo took a deep breath. "I told her no."

"And how did that go?"

"First, Mom tried to ice me out, hoping I'd come crawling back. She sent your mom to tell me how badly I'd hurt her. When that didn't work, they took the offensive. They called constantly, they wrote emails. They even showed up to my apartment. That's how my mother met Beth."

Deli had wanted to ask about the pretty strawberry blonde in the Polaroid on Aunt Mo's fridge, but every time she'd gotten close, she got this feeling—like it would hurt. So she hadn't. "Did she know about her before?"

"Only Laurie knew, and it was a big enough thing that I didn't think my sister would tell. I was wrong, of course. She'd told our mom everything."

Deli was angry. Angry at her grandmother, angry at her mom. "What happened when they met Beth?"

Her aunt smiled. "They regretted it."

Deli grinned. "Not their biggest fan?"

"Beth . . . was a force. She was fearless and loyal and she loved me. She'd get so angry when people killed spiders, but if someone hurt me?" Aunt Mo laughed. Ruefully. "Beth wasn't scared of Rosemary like everyone else. She told my mother exactly who she was. After that, I don't know who she hated more—Beth or my dad."

"Didn't you leave California really soon after Grandpa died?" Deli would never forget how it had felt to go from a Scottish funeral to a Scottish vacation, to learning her aunt was moving far away forever.

"I couldn't see a way out. They wouldn't give up. My mother packed up the things my father had left behind and threw them away before I could get to them. His old writing desk, his notebooks of poems, the photos from his childhood. Gone. They started harassing Beth, too. Then one day Beth came home in tears. An anonymous parent had complained that they didn't feel comfortable with a lesbian teaching their children. She'd been fired."

"They couldn't. Right?" Deli didn't know how to wrap her mind around the thought.

"I drove straight to my mom's house, and of course my sister was there. I didn't want to believe it, but I got one look at Laurie—at her face—and I knew. Sisters know. She'd told our mom where Beth taught, and my mother had done it."

"That's . . ." Deli searched for the word. It didn't exist. "That's fucking horrible."

"I had to protect her. Unless I fell into line, Beth would always be a target. Because she loved me. I couldn't . . . It would have never been fair to her. So I went as far away as I could."

The final pieces of the puzzle clicked into place in Deli's mind. Aunt Mo had left Beth behind because her family refused to let her be happy. To let her be free.

Deli had never left a call, email, knock, or request from her mom or grandma go unanswered for more than a day.

She'd been in Scotland for a month.

They were coming to drag her home, and she had just learned what lengths they would go to force a black sheep back into the fold. Or, at least, according to Aunt Mo.

What if they had done it? What did that make them?

And what did it make her? What was Deli if there was a part of her—no matter how little—that couldn't wait to see them? That wanted them to say she belonged?

She had barely managed to get out of Lachlan's clothes when she heard a car pull up outside.

63

Lachlan

Will's smirk hovered near the lip of the whisky bottle. "She seems nice."

"Get out."

If looks could kill, Lachlan would be standing over his little brother's dead body, not watching him slobber into his most expensive stock. Lachlan would be following the tug in his ribs to run into the rain after Deli and stop her. To explain.

"Lachlan, please. This is my dad's pub, too."

"You don't get to say that. You did nothing for them. For us."

Will sighed and rolled his eyes toward the ceiling—resurrecting the hot static of anger Lachlan felt every time Will fake-cried to win an argument as kids. "I have offered a million times—"

Lachlan cut him off. "I'm not letting you turn this place into a joke."

"But you'll let it die?"

The scattered papers across Lachlan's desk flashed in his mind. The numbers—sinking farther and farther into the red. "I'll figure something out."

"Just like Dad did?"

Lachlan scowled. He hated William for saying it. Hated his father for leaving him a pub in a dying town without a plan. Hated himself for staying the course.

"Lachlan, listen." Will's voice softened. "We have a problem, and we have a solution. Tourism is the only thing that's gonna save The Wallflower—hell, this *town.* It's crumbling." Lachlan met his eyes for a moment, but they slid away like flint striking flint. "I know how this is going to sound, but—do you realize how many women will travel here just to sit where I've sat? To wonder if I've drunk from the same cup?" Will dropped the kidding tone. "If you make this the home of *The Highlander*'s Billy Burns? You'll survive."

A coil of the bar's sealant peeled up under Lachlan's fingernail. The bar he and his father had sanded together by hand. The sealant he'd finished himself.

"I won't let you turn our family's home into a temple to your vanity."

Will set the nearly empty bottle down with a clunk. "It's *your* pride that needs minding, brother. Not mine."

It drove Lachlan a little bit mad that Will wouldn't be baited to anger. His brother was always, infuriatingly, unbothered. Lachlan Scott was bothered by many, many things.

He snatched the bottle from under Will's resting hand and took a swig. "What are you really doing here, William?"

"I heard there's a wedding."

Whisky burned Lachlan's nostrils as he coughed. "You're invited?"

"Of course." Will shrugged, kicking off his shoes right there behind the bar. "*I* didn't break her heart."

"Ha ha."

"I *was* worried about you, brother. Watching the ex–love of your life—who's way more fit than you are, by the way—marry someone else. I thought I might have to fly out a girl from LA to take your mind off it." Will smirked at the way Lachlan's lip curled in disgust. "But you seem to have found quite the beauty."

"Shut up about her," Lachlan snapped. He didn't care that he sounded like a teenager.

"Oooh." Will wiggled his eyebrows. "Sore spot?"

"Fuck off, William."

Will sat at the bar like a patron while Lachlan poured himself another dram. "Mo's *niece*? Isn't that like . . . incest?"

"William, I mean it. You're here for the wedding, fine. You'll be gone by Monday. I won't allow you to mess with Deli. She's not a pawn in"—he gestured between the two of them—"whatever this is. It needs to stay between us. Leave her alone."

Will looked him up and down. "Whatever you say."

This wasn't how the night was supposed to end. There were things Lachlan needed to say, needed to do—there was a way he needed to finish what he'd started.

What had she asked? He'd been distracted. Did she think he was ashamed of *her*?

Lachlan felt the acid sting of knowing something was going wrong but not knowing what in his throat.

Will rapped his knuckles on the bar.

"So, you got an air mattress, or do you fancy a wee cuddle?"

64

Mo

Rosemary and Lorraine stood, hands clawed upon hips, like twin judgmental towers.

"Well, Maureen," her mother said, standing in her tiny living room. "Don't you have anything to say?"

How could Mo say *I hate you* and *I've missed you* and *Where have you been* and *Why are you here* and *Get out* and *Please don't leave* at once?

Rosemary McDonnell was smaller, frailer than the last time Mo had seen her. It was rattling. But Mo felt smaller, too.

"Maureen?" Laurie sneered, repeating the name their mother had given Mo. She tossed a glance toward the mostly full glass of whisky Mo had abandoned to get Deli. "Ah. Taking after Dad?"

A firework of anger flared in Mo's chest as her sister reached for the old *Mom says Dad's an alcoholic* refrain. But just as she took a breath to defend her father, Deli stumbled through the doorway, struggling with a massive suitcase. Beans was by her side in an instant, and Mo was pulled forward through time—from the child she'd been to who she was now. An adult who had made her choices—facing two other adults who had made theirs. For the sake of her niece, Mo would be who Deli needed her to be. At least, she would try.

"Mom"—Mo smiled—"and Laurie. It's so good to see you."

"Really? Because we were never invited for a visit," Laurie snapped.

Deli placed her body between Mo and Laurie, smiling and slouching somehow, like she wanted to shrink. "Neither was I, technically. We've all just invited ourselves! Poor Aunt Mo, right?"

"Yes." Laurie ran a finger down Mo's wall and rubbed it against her thumb with a repulsed look. "Have you enjoyed my stolen daughter?"

"Mom," Deli started, "Aunt Mo didn't ste—"

"I have." Mo raised her voice. "Every single second. Deli is welcome for however long she likes *whenever* she likes." Laurie's eyes widened like she'd been slapped, then flicked to their mother, to Mo, and finally to Deli—who was staring at Mo with shining eyes. Mo was ready to be the bad guy if it meant being Deli's protector. "Deli really seems to belong here."

Laurie's hatred nearly bored a hole into Mo's face. She swiveled on her heel, stalked into the bedroom where they'd once whispered secrets in the dark as sisters, and slammed the door.

Rosemary sighed. "Thank you very much for *that*, Maureen."

Deli moved like she might follow her mother in before she stopped and stared at her boots. Beans rushed to weave between them, and Mo could *almost* see Popsicle smeared across her dimpled cheeks. Mo could almost see the little girl.

"Hey." Mo spoke out of the corner of her mouth. "Wanna play a game? Drink every time one of them sighs?"

Mo picked up Beans McGee as a wry smile broke across her niece's face. Deli scritched the top of his head with ten fingers as Beans flattened his ears, closed his eyes, and purred. *It's gonna be okay,* Mo thought. *We're gonna be okay.*

"So this is what you left us for?" Rosemary held her arms out to her sides and performed a slow, dramatic twirl in the middle of Mo's home. "I'd forgotten just how *claustrophobic* it all is."

"Huh," Deli said. "I think it's perfect."

Mo's eyes almost bulged. For a moment, a memory stole her away—a slick of poppy hair, the gleam of Beth's canine bared in warning, the shock on Rosemary's face as her crimes were read aloud. It slid down her back like an ice cube.

Rosemary gave a pitying laugh. Deli asked, "Grandma, what are you doing here?"

Rosemary leaned casually on the counter. Mo didn't like the way her mother moved, like this was *her* home—like she'd never left. "Can't an old woman visit her daughter? And granddaughter, it seems, since you've moved in, *apparently*."

Mo felt a tear begin in her somewhere. "After twenty years?"

"No time like the present." She plucked the wedding invitation Mo had designed for Blair and Andrew from the refrigerator. "How lovely. I do enjoy a wedding."

65

Deli

When medical dramas were at the height of their popularity, teenage Deli used to sit with her eyes glued to the screen, holding her hand flat like a pancake, admiring the natural stillness she'd need to become the best surgeon around.

Now she felt the tremor rattling her fingers echo all the way to her heart.

"I can't believe you're dragging me to a witch's house."

Deli clenched her hand, then shook it out before turning the key in the ignition of Mo's car. "Hannah's not a witch, Mom. She just has a forest path behind her house, and I need some big branches."

Lorraine held up a finger, adding one for each thing she said. "Doesn't speak, magic forest, mind reader, spooky hair and no makeup—"

Deli's stomach flipped, threatening to expel the breakfast Aunt Mo had forced on her. She thought of Aunt Mo's impossible garden, blooming with things that shouldn't grow. She thought of Douglas, of Hannah. Of an imaginary friend named Cal.

"Well, everything in Fearnhall is sort of magical. Hannah's just quiet. And aging gently."

Lorraine laughed. "Please. Aging is a war. You're either winning or dying."

Her mother flipped the mirror down and tugged at the edge of her plumped lips, running her tongue across her unnaturally white teeth. Agreeing to let Lorraine join felt like Deli's first bad choice in a horror movie—like she was halfway down the basement stairs.

"You don't have to come, Mom. Aunt Mo and Grandma could use your help."

Lorraine snapped her head toward Deli. "Do you just not want to spend time with me?"

Deli didn't have to look to know her mother's chin would be puckered or that her eyes would be glassy with rejection. What she said next would decide the entire day. *Blair's* big day. She couldn't be the one to ruin it.

"Of course I want to spend time with you. I just don't know if you'll have fun. I want you to have a nice time."

Lorraine savored the silence as she decided if her daughter's plea was enough. "I always have fun with you, Delilah."

"It's Deli."

Her voice was little more than a whisper, smothered by whatever blanket Lorraine MacDonald was throwing over the fire Deli had been kindling in her heart for weeks.

Lorraine responded with an eye roll–sigh combo and reached for the radio. An accented voice sang about going five hundred miles for someone they loved, but before they could promise five hundred more, Deli's mother turned it off.

"God awful *noise*."

66

Lachlan

The day of the wedding, Lachlan rose before sunrise. The last time he'd shared a bed with his brother, they'd both been much smaller with much younger backs—though William's propensity for stealing the duvet and defending it with donkey kicks had persevered into adulthood. Two nights of spooning had proven so.

He wouldn't have slept anyway. Lachlan spent both nights tormented—tossing and turning with thoughts of the dewdrop curve in Deli's upper lip, of the soft skin near her eyes where laughter left its mark. He hadn't seen her since the night they'd been interrupted. Mo had filled him in on the family situation, and of course, he now had William to contend with, so he'd thought to give Deli a little space. He wasn't sure why she'd looked so hurt, but he did know panicking and asking her to hide wasn't his best move.

He was anxious to see her. He missed her.

He was terrified.

You break everything you touch.

Lachlan sawed the last branch he needed from one of the ash trees in Hannah's back garden. He was nearly done with the first of his wedding duties, and the sun had hardly risen. Once he was done, he'd return to working on the beer garden at The Wallflower. He'd been renovating it in secret for weeks. Finishing that would take the rest of the day.

That was good. Lachlan wanted to be busy.

He ducked into Hannah's home just as she hung the phone back on a wall. He heard Mo's tinny voice say goodbye, and was glad he'd missed the moment he might have been offered the phone. He was avoiding—no, giving space to—Mo, too.

There were two glasses of cloudy lemonade on the counter. He reached for one. Hannah slapped his hand.

"Ow!" He curled it to his chest. "What was that for?"

Hannah looked him up and down and raised an eyebrow.

Lachlan tried for the lemonade only to be slapped again.

"Fine!" He shook out his fingers. "Fine. Deli and I . . . we . . ."

Hannah nodded.

"I'm giving her space."

This time she made contact with the side of his head.

"Seriously?"

Lachlan leaned backward on his stool at the sound of tires outside. Lorraine MacDonald was in the passenger's seat of Mo's car. And *Deli* was driving it.

"Deli's here?"

Hannah grinned. He'd been set up.

"You and Mo?"

She winked, and Lachlan had to fight to keep the panic from his face. He didn't want Hannah to know every instinct was telling him to run.

"Do you know Deli's mum, Lorraine, is here? She's not—"

Her dark eyes hardened.

"Ah. So you're familiar? Hard to believe that's Mo's sister."

Lachlan took a deep breath. Deli parked, turned the car off, and returned both hands to the wheel. Lorraine's mouth was moving. A lot.

"Should I stay?" The words came out quieter than he intended. Hannah slowly pushed the lemonade he'd been denied across the counter until it nudged his hand.

"Yeah." Lachlan took a sip, his eyes glued to Deli. "I thought so."

Hannah wiped her hands on her dungarees, squared her shoulders, and headed for the front garden. He listened as he nursed his glass, straining to catch Deli's voice on the wind, but there was only Lorraine's, midsentence as she swung a leg out of the car.

"—really, Delilah, if you want Trey to choose *you* and not that child-bride, running away to this godforsaken place *cannot* be easier than a treadmill or something."

Lachlan's anger rose, then his stomach lurched at the horrible familiarity of it . . . anger and silence and someone he loved.

"Oh, you must be Hannah!" Lorraine MacDonald smiled as she took to the cobblestone walk. One ankle wobbled. She spoke with a hint of the distinct way people speak to toddlers and the elderly. "Delilah has told me *sooo* much about you." She stuck a hand out to shake.

Hannah snorted and spat into her palm, then locked Laurie's in a vise grip before she could recoil. Deli got out of the car behind them. The lemonade glass hovered just below Lachlan's lips as he watched Deli glance down toward her body and tug at the fabric of her shirt, pulling it as far as she could from the slope of her belly.

He finished in a single gulp.

Laurie rummaged through her purse, produced a wet wipe, and furiously rubbed her palms. She looked like one of those smiling dolls with eyelids. "My daughter tells me you have a real green thumb, huh?"

"Mom." Deli caught up to them.

"Oh! That's right! The"—she gestured at Hannah with a judgmental waggle of her fingers as she dropped her voice to a whisper—"*thing.*"

"Hannah, I'm so sorry," Deli said as Lachlan stepped outside. Laurie tried to drop the wrinkled wipe into her purse, but it tumbled onto Hannah's lawn. Her eyes locked on to him.

"And *who*, exactly, are *you*?"

Deli turned, prepared to put out whatever fire her mother was starting next. Her face drained of color when she saw him. She mouthed his name without making a sound.

Lachlan.

It wasn't a greeting.

"I'm starting to see why my sister favors the rain," Lorraine MacDonald purred in his shadow. "I'm Laurie, Delilah's mother." She held out a manicured hand like a dog with a limp.

Lachlan forced his eyes away from Deli. He pinched her fingers between his as lightly as he could and shook once. "Lachlan."

Her smile flickered. "Don't you kiss to say hello around here?"

Lachlan fought the urge to withdraw as she wrapped a hand around his bicep and tapped her cheek with one bedazzled pink fingernail.

"Mom." Deli glared with laser focus at the five acrylic talons pressing into his skin.

"Delilah, you didn't tell me there was such a gorgeous specimen tromping around this little place!" Laurie squeezed, and his skin went white under her nails.

"Can you stop fondling him, Mother?" Deli snapped, tugging at her mom's shoulder so Lachlan's arm came free.

She pouted. "I wish I knew what I did to deserve such relentless criticism, Lachlan."

Behind her, Deli scoffed and rolled her eyes up to Lachlan's. His breath caught in his chest as she smirked at him. She mimed wrapping her hands around Laurie's neck and mouthed, *Oh my god,* and Lachlan had to cough to cover his laugh. A fragile thread pulled taut between them.

It was a funny thing—how a person might not realize they were drowning until they'd come up for air.

Laurie tracked Lachlan's gaze to her daughter as Deli wiped the smile from her face.

Lachlan was too stunned to react as Laurie pressed a hand to the space between his pecs and began to trail a fingernail down his body. He caught her by the wrist just before his belly button. She barked with laughter and looked back at Deli—whose mouth still hovered somewhere between open and closed. "Doesn't he look like he belongs on *The Highlander,* Delilah?"

The thread snapped. Lachlan dropped Laurie's wrist like he'd been burned. She brushed past him and into Hannah's house without an invitation, and Hannah touched his forearm as she stalked after her unwelcome guest.

"Deli, I—"

"Don't." She folded her arms over her chest and shrank from his outstretched hand. "Please. Just don't."

Lachlan searched her body as she stared at the ground, like he could find some bleeding wound—stop it, bind it, heal it. His arms ached to hold her, to wrap himself around her and absorb the impact of her mother's blows. Of his.

Deli lifted her chin, defiant and proud, but her eyes shone a sea glass jade.

"So, how's your brother?"

He looked down. "I'm sorry. I'm so sorry. I know I should have told you."

"Uh huh . . ." Deli pouted in thought and pinched her chin in her fingers. "That your brother was *the star* of the dumbass show that inspired this dumbass idea?" Deli's arms swept toward the Highland hills and sea. "Maybe ONE of the times that I mentioned it?"

"Yes."

"What are you even doing here?"

"I had to get some branches."

She blinked at him. "*I* have to get some branches. Dogwood."

"I just needed ash tree."

She flinched, like the words had struck her somehow, then recovered. Her eyes narrowed. "Where's your truck, branch boy? I didn't see it when I pulled in."

"Cairn and Douglas have it."

"Why didn't they use Graham's van?"

"Graham is picking up the out-of-town relatives."

He stared at her. She stared back.

"Deli, can we . . ." He glanced over his shoulder to be sure they were alone. "Talk?"

The sound from her throat was something between a laugh and a sob. "Talk? You want to talk? About what?"

He winced. "I know the night didn't end well—"

"Oh?" Deli cut him off. "Which night, Lachlan? The one where I poured my heart out to you? And you kissed me? And you . . ."

She trailed off. He watched embarrassment flood her cheeks as she waited for him to say something, but his teeth felt glued together.

Deli nodded. "Okay. Do you want to know what the best part was? The best part was being a full-grown woman getting *stuffed behind a door*. Then peeking through the crack with a breeze on my bits only to realize that your *brother* was the very man I'm pretty sure my grandmother *masturbates* to!" This time her laugh was disbelieving. "A little warning would have gone a long way there, pal. You know what my grandma looks like, right? *Quite* the mental image."

"Do you really want me to imagine—"

"NO!"

He swallowed.

"Why?" she said.

The silent tension swelled between them as Lachlan's head swarmed with things he wasn't sure how to say.

"Just . . . why?" Her voice broke on the last word.

Because I'm a moron? he thought. *Because I'm afraid—all of the time? Because William wins everything. Because my father always said . . .*

Lachlan opened his mouth to speak. He just had to say something. Anything.

Deli's eyes turned so green when she cried. Sea glass drifting toward the open ocean—treasure fumbled by a fool.

Because I can't lose you. He just had to say it. *Because I love you.*

She waited. And waited. And Lachlan couldn't do it.

Deli spoke instead. "I understand. You're . . ." She hesitated and stared at the clouds for a long minute. "You didn't want to have to explain, you know . . . *me*. You're ashamed of me. And you regret it."

She shrugged as she said it, like the thought was a simple truth to be acknowledged and disregarded. Like the idea he wanted to *hide* her was a common thing—a penny in the street not worth bending down for.

How could he have overlooked how that would have felt for Deli? She hadn't told him she was *over* the man she'd been in love with back home—she'd told him that it just hurt too much. She told him that the man back home had left her in such uncertainty for so long that she couldn't do it. She couldn't keep feeling unsure.

Lachlan had kissed her. He'd convinced her that he was nothing like the guy who'd been hurting her and that he could hold the places that hurt. He'd convinced her to trust him.

Then his brother had shown up, and he'd completely panicked. He wasn't a man anymore, he was a child—except instead of hiding *William* from their dad, he was hiding *Deli* from *William*. William, who would see her as a pawn in a game. William, who took whatever he wanted and never looked back. William and his selfish, petty ways.

No matter how much time passed or how hard he tried, Lachlan was a coward.

He'd stood by and said nothing when his family's baggage had threatened to hurt her. Or perhaps it was worse. Perhaps he really was just like his father—content to hurt the woman he loved as long as his own pain stayed buried.

You break everything you touch.

It was *Lachlan* who was unworthy of *her*.

"Deli . . . no."

"It's fine, Lachlan. You can say it."

"I'm not ashamed of you—"

"I told you, do you remember?" Deli walked toward him, angling to pass without looking up. "I told you you'd be disappointed."

He grabbed her arm. "Deli. Please. Let me explain."

She went rigid at his touch, staring forward before snapping her head up. She glared, daring him to say something that could salvage this. But all Lachlan could think of was the look in Deli's eyes when she'd realized that he'd promised to care for her but wouldn't.

People always said you forgot a dead loved one's voice eventually. Lachlan could never forget his father's.

Everything you touch.

"That's what I thought." Deli jerked her arm from his hold, then gasped, "Mom!"

Lachlan spun around. Laurie leaned in the crooked doorway of Hannah's home—lemonade in hand, watching the two of them with calculating eyes.

"Delilah, did you bring me here to do all the work while you do whatever"—she waved her hand at the two of them—"this is?"

"I'm coming right now," Deli said, and she pushed past Lachlan.

"Delightful." Laurie ran a finger along the rim of her glass as Deli moved past her into the house without looking back. For a long, uncomfortable moment, Laurie watched Lachlan pine after her daughter.

"You remind me of someone," she said at last.

He was suddenly very tired, all the fight drained from his bones. "Someone good?"

She shook her head. "Someone dead."

67

Mo

"Mom!" Mo swatted her mother's hand. "For the last time, stop touching things."

Rosemary scowled, rubbing the spot, and Mo watched her mother's paper skin glide over the blue-green veins.

Rosemary went back to tucking sprigs of lavender into simple folded napkins. "Where is the ceremony taking place today?"

Mo spoke around the needle she held in her teeth as she pinched another fold into the chiffon draped over the floor. "Here."

"I'm sorry?"

"They're doing the ceremony here. At the cliffside."

A response didn't come. Her needle nipped in and out of the sheer fabric, bunching and loosening in Mo's hands.

Mo had always loved family harmonies—the way family voices blend and anticipate and layer. She remembered her mother's cadence, her sister's lilt. The way Laurie turned up the edges of her words and thoughts, like a paper aging in the sun. The way her mother spoke in staccato—heels clicking across marble floors.

Mo always sang the harmonies.

She was surprised to find, twenty years later, she still could.

And even though what Laurie and her mother did could never be unsaid or undone in Mo's heart, the house she'd grown up in was almost full for the first time in so long. She'd pay for it, she knew that. But for the moment, she cherished the quiet bustle of her kitchen that morning as she forced breakfast on Deli and was scolded by her mother about the temperature of the tea. She'd stood in the window, soapy dish in hand, and watched her sister wander out the back door all the way to Mrs. Peevis and tuck a daisy into her fur.

She just wanted a life with a front porch light glowing softly and steadily when the moon rose, and everyone came home.

"How selfish of you, Maureen."

Mo jerked her head back. "What?"

"Letting those children get married *here*, for your vanity?"

Mo looked around the room, like a clue might be peeking from her cupboards. "Okay, Mom—I'm lost."

Rosemary rolled her eyes and shook her head, flattening her palms against the smooth wood of the kitchen table she used to set as a much younger woman. "Do they know this is a place only fit for endings?"

Despite her many unflattering traits, Mo had always admired the way her mother could translate the things most people hide from the light into language. Mo's father was always a poet in love. Her mother was a poet in pain.

She wondered whether Rosemary ever got credit for that.

"It's not like the land is haunted, Mom."

Rosemary watched Mo seriously. "A brilliant thing died a violent and early death right here"—she gently patted the table—"and it is here it was buried. The ghost in this house has touched every bit of our lives since we put it in the ground. Am I wrong?"

Mo's life in the cottage flashed through her mind. Her parents' fighting, her father in the rearview mirror. Then his funeral. Deli crying as Lorraine took her home. Mo's first night alone without Beth.

Hot, prickling tears gathered along Mo's lash line. To her shock, her mother leaned forward in her chair until she could place a hand on Mo's shin and gently squeeze her leg. Her grip was still strong.

"What do we call this place, then, my girl, if not haunted?"

Outside the sun broke through the clouds and slanted through the kitchen windows, and Beans hurried to bask in the sunny spot on the floor. The California sun used to make squares on her black-and-white-checkered tile, and sometimes Mo would find Beth napping with Roni on the kitchen floor—her citrus-kissed hair spilling into the grayscale, her freckled hand in fur.

Tires came up quickly outside.

Mo cleared her throat as she rose. "That's probably Lachlan."

"Who's Lachlan?"

"Hellooooo? My darling!" Douglas's voice cracked as he cooed and fearlessly reached for the high note.

"Not Lachlan," Mo managed a moment before the door burst open to reveal a potbelly and spindly legs peeking from under a long, pleated kilt. Douglas's face was hidden behind the two massive bottles of bubbly he held up in front of him.

"Peekaboo!" He parted the bottles like curtains on a stage, twinkling eyes scrunched in mirth. "'Tis a beautiful day, indeed, my Mo! Oh!" he cried, rushing to set the bottles on the counter. He spun to strike a pose with shoulders and head back, a pointed toe in front of him, and his hands on his hips. One eyebrow lifted with the side of his mouth as he looked Mo's mother up and down. "You must be Rosemary."

Rosemary looked briefly shell-shocked before she rearranged her face into cool superiority. She stood and smoothed her skirt just as Cairn's shadow from the doorway fell across her feet.

"Rose."

Mo couldn't remember the last time she'd seen her mother taken aback.

"Cairn?"

Cairn rolled a toothpick from one side of his mouth to the other, his bluebell eyes shining. "You're lookin' well, Rose."

Rosemary's cherry nails fluttered over her midriff before clasping in front of her body. "You do, too."

"As glamorous as I've heard, I see." Douglas floated over and lifted one of Rosemary's hands in his, bringing it to his lips. "Such a shame I was away those years you were here. But a pleasure to meet you at last."

Mo braced for the acid comment her mother would produce for soft, sweet Douglas, but Rosemary's smile was real.

"Douglas, I presume?"

Douglas took a quick step back, crossed one ankle over the other, and bowed. "At your service."

"Yes, a shame," Rosemary mused. "Perhaps if I'd made more of an impression, you all wouldn't have stolen away my daughter." Her tone didn't match her words—still wistful and soft. Mo opened her mouth to protest, but Douglas beat her to it.

"Perhaps if you hadn't stolen away young Callum's heart, all of our lives would be different now." He watched Rosemary meaningfully. Mo got the feeling she was missing something. "Alas, however the story was written, I am glad we are here for *this* chapter."

"Perhaps."

Cairn cleared his throat in the doorway. "Where do you want this, Mo?"

Mo jolted to life at the sound of her name. "Oh, you can put it—wait. What is it?"

Cairn jerked his chin over his shoulder as Douglas clapped his hands together in glee. "Come darlin'," Douglas said, offering his arm to her mother. "Have a look."

Mo followed Cairn out the door and squinted into the filtered sunlight. A towering archway stood behind the truck. She gasped at the glory and shape of it—two separate pieces made of entangled branches, reaching up and toward each other but not quite meeting. It reminded

Mo of the arms of two lovers, one's fingers about to brush the soft, pulsing skin of the other's wrist.

"Holy hell." Mo knotted her hands in her hair. "It's incredible!"

Cairn gave a noncommittal shrug. "Was mostly the boy. His wood, his design. I was the assistant."

"Lachlan?"

Cairn nodded. "Ash cut from Hannah's grove."

Mo smiled, full of fondness. "Let's get it to the cliffside."

"First things first." Cairn disappeared behind the truck and reemerged carrying a large box with a light tinkling.

"Champagne flutes? Kitchen counter, please, Cairn."

He nodded. "Excuse me, Rose."

Her mother pivoted sideways as Cairn walked past, and she swore she saw a blush peeking through her pressed powder. "I'll help," Rosemary muttered, and followed Cairn into the house.

Mo had the feeling she was seeing back into time. "What am I missing, Douggie?"

Douglas put an arm around her shoulder and kissed her forehead. "I suspect we are witnessing a remembering. Alas, I wasn't there."

Mo pursed her lips. "If only you hadn't been traveling the world, we'd have the gossip. Why'd you have to be so hip when you were younger?"

Douglas recoiled. *"Younger?"*

"You're right, please forgive my past tense."

"Forgiveness is very hip."

Mo grinned. "Bitchin', even."

"So totally bitchin'." He walked to the archway. "Come on then, you and I can handle this. Let's leave the kids to catch up."

68

Deli

"Where's your mum, kiddos?"

Penny pointed down the hallway at the same time Kieran squeaked, "She's soooo beautiful, Auntie Deli!"

Auntie Deli. Her heart felt like a thing with wings.

Blair was sitting in a cushy armchair, removing the last large curler from her hair. She found Deli in the mirror and grinned.

"Dude. Andrew might pass out up there when he sees you."

Blair laughed. "That would be a little bit funny. The tartan's on the bed."

Deli grabbed the folded swath of Andrew's clan tartan she was going to weave into the archway. "Where is the blushing groom?"

"He's off with Will." Blair met her eyes in the mirror, a bit sheepishly. "Have you gotten to meet him yet?"

"Oh, have I ever." An insta-blush flushed her chest at the memory of William staring down at her sans clothing on the floor of his family's pub. She tested the strength of the women-talking-with-their-eyes thing.

Blair made an *eek* face. "It wasn't mine to say."

Deli sighed. "I know."

"He drives Lachlan crazy."

The longer she'd been in Fearnhall, the stronger Deli's intuition had grown with the cottage garden's potential poetry. It was almost like the flowers whispered to her, and each time she cross-checked with the book from Aunt Mo, she had already known.

When Lachlan told her he was gathering ash wood, it had nearly knocked her down.

With me you are safe.

She hoped Blair didn't see the slip in her smile. "Yeah, that became clear."

"Will's always been *such* a wee brother. But he's harmless. He's actually a lot of good fun if you get the chance to pal around. You might think he's a hoot. Just don't let Lachlan see."

Deli's heart gave little skip. "Why not?"

Blair rolled her eyes. "I imagine he'd be quite jealous."

"Um, there's a lady at the door," Kieran announced from the hallway.

Deli blanched. She'd begged her mother to wait in the car.

"Who?" Blair asked.

"It's Lolo," Kieran stated.

Deli felt like roots grew through her feet.

"Who?" Blair asked again.

"My mother."

"Huh?" Blair's voice trailed after her as Deli booked it down the hall.

Lorraine ran her finger through a thin coating of flour on the countertop. "*There* you are, Delilah."

"Mom, you promised you'd wait in the car."

Blair came into the kitchen with her warmth swirling around her feet like morning mist.

"Hiya! Are you Deli's mum? I'm Blair." She held out her hand.

"Laurie," she replied with a sugary smile. "Are you the bride to be?"

Penny leaned against the doorway and gave Lorraine a judgmental look. "Did you *actually* just walk into our house, or are you taking the piss?"

Deli loved Penny the watchdog.

"Young lady, that's well enough. Off with you." Blair shook her head as Penny went down the hall, but she was chuckling under her breath. "Sorry about her. Born fiery, that one. I do hope she never loses it, but it can make for awkward hellos." Blair didn't realize Lorraine wasn't laughing. "Mo didn't tell me she and Deli had family in town!"

"Yes." Deli's mother looked like she had smelled something foul. "Deli's grandmother is here, too. We didn't realize there was a wedding this weekend. Though we *did* pack something formal—just in case."

"Oh, you *have* to come!" Blair clapped her hands together. "Please!"

"If you *insist*."

Deli snatched the keys from her mother's hand. "Let's go."

"So dramatic." Lorraine laughed, looking to Blair to join in. It was Blair's turn not to.

A small voice said, "Bye, Lolo."

Lorraine stared at the child in the hallway with saucer eyes. "What did you say?"

Kieran walked over and handed Deli's mother half of a peeled clementine. Her face drained of color.

"Bye, Lolo!" they repeated as Lorraine retreated to the car.

Her mother rode quietly, cradling the orange in her hand.

"My dad used to split a clementine like this for me and Maureen to share."

Deli shuddered at the memory of Kieran calling her Delilah—asking questions on behalf of an imaginary friend named Cal.

"Huh."

"Yeah," her mom said as she turned the citrus over and over. "Huh."

69

Deli

Deli poured champagne into the waiting flute and clutched it between her fingers like the last life vest on the *Titanic*.

She'd barely had any time to get ready. Quick makeup, a swipe of cranberry lip gloss, and a messy half-up bun was all she'd managed after flower prep and before she was due for hostess duty. At least Aunt Mo had taken care of the dress and bought her an emerald sweetheart thing in town.

Aunt Mo came back in from seating guests and clapped. "Alright, lads, you're up!"

Deli unwrapped the boutonnieres set aside for the groom and his men, pinning them one by one. William's grin was devious at best.

Deli lifted his lapel. "Don't smile at me like that, William."

"Call me Will," he purred. "And like what?"

"Like you've just found your new favorite toy."

William bent his head to her ear as she positioned the boutonniere. His fingers brushed her wrist. "What if I *want* you to be my new favorite toy?"

"I'd say start talking money or stop breathing on me."

"Sharp wit and curved . . . edges?" He winked at her. "I'd happily go broke."

She pushed a pin through the fabric and into the stems. "Wow, you need an actual job, dude."

Deli thought she saw the flash of headlights through the window, and her whole body buzzed with the adrenaline of expecting Lachlan to walk in. William threw his head back and laughed so loudly she almost jumped.

"I really like you, Deli. I see what he sees."

Will's slimy pretense was gone. He was Lachlan's little brother, out to play a game. She straightened his lapel, ignoring the pang in her chest. "Yes, I'm a delight."

Aunt Mo lined up Andrew's groomsmen by the door, including Andrew's brother with a guitar in his hand. "Well? What are you waiting for? Giddyup, fellas."

Will paused in the doorway. "Wait, I almost forgot—you look absolutely lovely, Mo."

Her impatience melted with a grin. "You can kiss my ass another time, kid."

Will chuckled. "And *you . . .*" He looked Deli up and down. "Deli, you are ravishing."

She rolled her eyes. Will walked confidently out to the ceremony.

For a moment, Aunt Mo and Deli were alone.

"Have *they* seen him yet?" Deli asked.

"Oh, yes." Aunt Mo took a sip of champagne. "He politely asked them to refrain from photos until after the ceremony."

"Oh, I bet they *loved* that answer. I can't believe he's officiating."

"I can't believe our mothers are hitting on the officiant."

"Probably throwing a tantrum about having to sit waiting with the peasants instead of walking down the aisle."

Aunt Mo snorted as the sound of an engine came up outside.

"Here comes the bride!" Blair called. She was breathtaking in a simple satin gown so softly kissed with blue guests might not have noticed anything but the way her hair burned especially fiercely.

At the look on Deli's face as she took in her friend, Blair laughed, radiating joy.

"We're flower faeries!" Kieran chirped and twirled in their ruffled skirt and jacket.

"Yes!" Deli feigned a gasp. "I almost forgot!" She pulled the baskets filled with the electric blue petals of her favorite delphinium from the top of the refrigerator and knelt eye level with the kids. "This is very serious business, okay? Do you swear to petal that aisle to the best of your ability and let no grown-up, child, dog, or butterfly distract you from your task?"

"We do!" Kieran and Penny said in chorus. Deli stood and saluted. They saluted back as she handed them their baskets. Then Deli gave Blair the bouquet.

"Deli MacDonald, you're a *genius!*"

Deli sagged in relief. "Oh, thank god, you like it. I made sure to only put the ones with the very best meanings in."

Blair couldn't wipe the smile from her face as she touched a milky petal. "They have meanings? What about this one?"

Deli was particularly fond of the bloom, but after seeing Lachlan that morning—after he'd just said nothing . . . it felt strange in her hands. "Dogwood. *Love undiminished by adversity.*"

"What's this one?" Kieran pointed.

"Larkspur. It means *lightness* and *ardent attachment.*" She continued, pointing to each flower, "Chamomile daisy for *innocence* and *energy in adversity*, Forget-me-not for *faithful and best love*, eucalyptus to *watch over you*, peach cabbage roses for *gentleness* and for *closing the deal*, Baker's fern for *magic and fascination*, and sweet pea for *blissful pleasure*"—she winked at Blair—"and *thank you for a wonderful time.*"

Blair's voice was thick with emotion. "How can I ever thank you, Deli?"

Blair had just absorbed Deli into her life, into her family, without any tests or hoops to jump through. Deli hadn't really known a friendship like Blair's before. And though it was young, it had taught her something new. Something very important.

"You have given me more than you can imagine." Deli pointed to the last small, blue-purple flower. "Periwinkle. *Early friendship* and *fond recollections*."

Blair gripped Deli's forearm, and Deli returned the gesture. They could just hear the plucking of guitar strings from the cliff.

They sent Penny and Kieran out first, both with deadly serious faces and petals at the ready. Blair hugged Aunt Mo.

"Mo, you are—and I mean this with every bit of me—the *best.*"

"Go on, then." Aunt Mo pulled Blair's hair behind her shoulders and let it fall. "Get married."

Neither Aunt Mo nor Deli heard the soft click of the back door as Blair and the kids walked out of view.

"She's . . . so beautiful," Deli said.

It was Lachlan who responded, "Yes, she is."

He stood behind them, back against the door, draped in formal family colors. He met her gaze, and it was like he'd fired a cannonball of mixed, nauseating feelings into her chest. She stumbled a half step back until she bumped against the counter. He clenched his hand into a fist.

"Mo," he said as he broke their connection. "Sorry I'm late."

"Is it done?" Aunt Mo asked as Lachlan bent to kiss her cheek.

"It's done." He stood back, holding her shoulders at arm's length, taking in his friend in her smart high-waisted trouser suit. He took Aunt Mo's hand and twirled her. "You are a vision."

"Thank you, my love. Let's go." She gestured to his camera bag tucked by the door.

"Blair's cousin managed to come to the wedding. She's a professional." Lachlan shrugged.

"That doesn't mean you're off the hook, kid." Aunt Mo beckoned as she walked out. Lachlan trailed behind with his eyes fixed to the floor.

"Wait." Deli barely whispered the word, half hoping he wouldn't hear her, but his body went still. She reached above the fridge and brought down the last boutonniere. Forget-me-not and purple verbena. *Hope in darkness,* she thought. *And regret.* "Blair told me it's for you, specifically."

Lachlan hesitated. "I . . . I don't know how to put it on."

"That's why I'm here."

He crossed the room to her slowly and stopped a sterile three feet from her. She felt her temperature rise anyway. She held her arms out, about six inches short of him. "Should I . . . put it on with telepathy?"

"Telekinesis," Lachlan said.

Deli smirked. "Nerd."

Lachlan sighed and looked down. Deli closed the space, torn by how easy it was to fall back into rhythm with him like nothing had changed.

She stuck the black heads of the boutonniere pins behind her teeth like she'd done a million times before. She could feel his heart beating against the back of her hand as she positioned the boutonniere.

"You're shaking." Lachlan's hand fell over hers.

She gasped at the shock of his touch and the last pins in her teeth clattered to the floor, rolling in lazy circles in the silent room.

When Trey had shown up on her doorstep and kissed her, Deli had barely felt anything. It was so quick, and then it was over, and she hadn't wondered why the feeling of it hadn't stayed in her head.

Since Lachlan had kissed her on the bar top, the feeling was all she'd thought about. It wasn't just the heat and the wanting of it—it was the feeling of trust, of intimacy. The way he'd cradled her head and moved with her, like he had attuned to the things Deli needed but could never seem to say. He had made her feel *safe*. Kissing Lachlan was *belonging*.

She could almost feel him on her mouth as her hand rose on its own. The moment her fingers found his face—her nails disappearing into the thick hair at his temple—she moved toward him, and she didn't have to imagine anymore.

Lachlan's lips found her throat as her hands wrapped around his neck. He threaded his fingers into her hair behind her ears and walked her backward, whispering her name as he kissed her jaw, the corner of her mouth.

As she collided with the counter, his kiss could have convinced her she was the last woman on earth. She didn't recognize her voice when she sighed his name. It was the most natural thing in the world to kiss him back—to pretend there was nothing to say.

She didn't know how long they were there—hands tangled in hair, chests heaving and lips desperate. When he finally pulled away he stooped to press his forehead to hers and whispered, "God, I missed you."

Of all the many years Deli and Trey were so emotionally connected with lives intertwined, he had never shared a photo of them together on any public platform. Her mother and often grandmother responded to any mention of Trey's resistance to their connection with the suggestion of weight loss. And of course, she had tried. But eventually Deli learned that some bodies simply aren't thin ones, and hers was perfectly reasonable.

In most ways, she no longer felt like she needed to change—but that coiled, hissing shame lived under her skin and spat at anyone who wanted to *touch* her. Like if they felt her softness with their own hands, some illusion of her would drop, and they'd see her for what she really was. Someone who, despite being compatible in every way but one, was made, fundamentally, unlovable.

Deli had racked her mind for reasons Lachlan's face had gone pale when William showed up. She didn't expect anyone to understand how impossible it felt to scrape away a truth she'd carried in her bones for the majority of her life and ignore her biggest fear. She didn't expect anyone to believe that it had taken all her courage to let Lachlan touch her, and to *believe* him when he said everyone else had been wrong. That, to him, Deli wasn't falling short.

Then, at the first chance, he'd treated her like an indulgence to be ashamed of. A dirty little secret he didn't want his brother to know.

Deli wanted to be someone new. She wanted to be someone Lachlan could be proud of. But the girl she'd always been had arrived on a plane with her mother, shaking her head at the Deli who should have known better, waiting in the dark to whisper, *I told you so*.

"Every second, I've missed you," Lachlan said. She'd believed him once—telling her things alone in quiet rooms when there was no one else to see.

Deli answered him with the tears she lost the fight to keep from falling.

He pulled her to him, wrapping an arm around her shoulders and gently cradling her head against his chest. Deli clung to their last moment.

"It's okay," he whispered as he gently swayed on his feet, rocking them to a song that didn't play. "You don't have to say anything. It's my fault. I know. It's okay."

He kissed the top of her head and crossed the room to the door before she could think.

Deli felt like she was drowning. "I . . . I don't know what to say."

"I am sorry, Deli." He pulled his camera out of the bag and slung it over his shoulder. "For everything."

"I—"

"You're the most beautiful thing I've ever seen."

Deli's knees nearly buckled. "You haven't seen the bride yet," she managed with a laugh. She felt frantic and unmoored, but he stared, resolute.

Lachlan spoke clearly, strong and final. "It will always be you."

He left her standing in the kitchen—undone and unsure of anything at all.

70

Deli

Deli had seen more grand wedding ceremonies in her life, but she hadn't seen any more beautiful.

The arch was draped in billowing chiffon and long swaths of tartan, and the blues and periwinkles she'd woven through the ash wood popped against the slate sea and sky. Andrew stood like a pillar in deep hues of forest green and gray, while Blair burned against the horizon—the white smoke of her skin and the hearth of her hair alive and wild among the blue.

Their vows had been lovely and simple. Andrew revealed himself to be a poet, penning a declaration to Blair that had Kieran beaming and Penny hiding her face.

"Look at what you've given me," Blair said simply. "I could love you until my dying breath, and it would never be enough."

Andrew burst into tears.

Will announced they were married and led the crowd in a toast as they laughed and kissed and danced back down the aisle to rousing cheers.

"Deli!" Aunt Mo caught her hands and spun, twirling them in a girlish circle and laughing as the last of the guests rolled away from the cottage in a caravan to The Wallflower's Crown. "Let's get crackin'. Poor Lachlan will be fending the partygoers alone."

"Where's my mom? And Grandma Rosemary?"

"Graham offered to take them."

"They agreed to that?"

"Once they saw Graham."

They both chuckled, soaking up the feeling of it being just the two of them again as they climbed in Mo's car and started down the road.

"Speaking of Lachlan . . ." Aunt Mo tread carefully, letting the question float unspoken for Deli to catch or leave to drift away.

She sighed. "I don't know."

"Did he tell you he's sorry?"

"Yes."

"Did he tell you he's *really* sorry?"

"Yes."

"Did he tell you he's in love with you?"

If Deli had been driving, she would have swerved into a ditch. "Did he tell *you* he's in love with me?"

Aunt Mo looked pained. "I've known him a very long time, Deli."

"What is *that* supposed to mean?"

Aunt Mo's cheeks blew out against her pinched lips.

"No! You don't get to drop something like that and go all pufferfish!"

"What have you told *him*?" Aunt Mo demanded. "How do *you* feel about Lachlan?"

"I—" Deli's voice fell. "I don't know."

"Well, buddy, I suspect he knows that, too."

They were quiet until the roof of Lachlan's home came into view. They could hear the rowdiness from the road.

Deli cleared her throat. "I've loved Trey for so long."

Aunt Mo nodded. "How does *Trey* feel about you?"

Deli thought about the way he'd happily accepted her affection and devotion for years and years and never wondered if it hurt her. "I don't think he cares."

"Lachlan cares."

They were pulling into the parking lot.

"Lachlan . . ." Deli tried to find the word for what he'd done. Promising not to be ashamed of her, and breaking that promise. "Lachlan lied."

"Deli." She put the car in park. "You and I are not the only ones with a family who made it hard to be loved. Lachlan is learning, too."

Aunt Mo squeezed her hand and got out. "Well, are you coming? William is in there with your mother."

Deli scrambled for the door. "Oh god, and yours!"

71

Deli

If she hadn't walked through the doors herself, Deli wouldn't have believed she was in The Wallflower's Crown.

Candlelight twinkled from every shelf of the bar, every table, the mantel. There were flowers in mixed vases, clustered in color blocks, dotted around the pub. Deli hoped Aunt Mo had been able to muster a few arrangements from the buckets she'd cut while Deli did the bouquet and archway, but she hadn't expected her to be so successful.

Her aunt was absorbed into a conversation instantly, so Deli laughed with Douglas and played darts with Cairn and sat in silence with Hannah and arm wrestled with Graham—trying to avoid Lachlan while he was avoiding her. Drinks were poured. People danced and toasted. The fire burned.

When she finally ran into Aunt Mo, Deli squeezed her in a huge hug. "You outdid yourself! The flowers look beautiful!"

Aunt Mo shook her head. "Not I."

Lachlan came through the doors behind them with his bicep curled around the firewood he balanced on his shoulder. His dress shirt was pulled up so Deli could see a slim line of his skin just above his belt. She looked away.

Aunt Mo smiled at him. "Deli was just saying how incredible the flowers are, and so was I! I didn't know you had this in you."

Lachlan surveyed the room over their heads. A shadow of pride flickered across his face. Pride, and something else that hurt enough to cover up a wince with a smile. "I didn't know I had it in me, either."

"How did you decide where to put what?"

He hesitated. His Adam's apple bobbed.

"I asked myself what Deli would do." Their eyes ricocheted off each other.

Standing in all Lachlan's flowers, she thought of the meadow and the garden—his hands leaving the most delicate petals unharmed. She'd marveled at the way he held things she considered precious with reverence. What a rare person he was—always *choosing* to be kind.

In a room Lachlan had painted with petals like a declaration or a plea, Deli wondered why she'd ever rejoiced in the pain Trey inflicted with his jealousy.

A bud vase with a single stem of bluebells sat alone on the bar.

Have faith, for you will win the one you love.

For a single moment, the woman she'd been becoming overcame the one she'd been. "Lachlan, can we tal—"

"BROTHER!" William broke through the crowd and squeezed his brother's shoulder. "Come on, now! It's not every day both Scotts are pouring at The Wallflower, eh?"

"Will, I need a minute." The Lachlan watching her as he answered his brother was the same who'd been sure he'd broken her bones—the one who blamed himself for his mother's scars. She felt a knife in her throat at his shame.

"I know the bride's your ex, but no moping at the party."

William tugged on Lachlan's free bicep until he stumbled toward the bar, a silent plea in his eyes.

"Oi, William, don't be a right wee dick!" Graham called as he stepped into the room from the back, and Deli caught the glow of light and the sound of laughter from where he'd come. As far as she knew, it was only a spare bit of space for mingling and an extra bathroom.

She turned to her aunt. "Is there something back there?"

Aunt Mo grinned and handed Deli a glass of red wine she plucked from Hannah's passing tray with a wink. "The garden was boarded up since his dad died. He's been working on it for weeks now."

She moved through the pub, trying not to attract attention, as Cairn issued a challenge to the Scott brothers over who could pour the best pint. Deli had nearly reached the door when it swung into her.

Lorriane and Rosemary strode through with eyes like hawks, and as they found the tall, blonde, Hamish-y object of their desires, Deli's full glass of wine splashed against her chest and ran down the length of her dress.

She stared down, transfixed by the way the drops of merlot seemed to be making small choices about their paths down her body with each rise and fall of her breath as their trails faded behind them.

Lachlan's voice almost sounded warped as he called her name, like she was underwater. Rosemary and Lorraine called for William at the end of the bar, but Lachlan pulled his brother back and obscured their view as he stepped around him. Rosemary and Lorraine swiveled and finally registered Deli wearing her entire glass of wine.

Deli had never been the poet of her family, but as she stood alone, once again doing a shoddy *Carrie* impression in a new dress while being stared down by her mother and grandmother, she figured there must be some lesson to learn she kept missing.

Rosemary and Lorraine stood before the exit from the bar with their hands on their hips. Her grandmother's brow creased in concern, but her mother spoke first.

"Oh, Delilah. Maybe you should just wear black to formal events so you don't ruin any more dresses with the whole clumsy thing. Plus!" She gave a wide smile. "Black is flattering!"

Then Deli watched in half wonder, half horror as Lachlan loomed behind them and issued a simple command.

"Move."

Lorraine MacDonald was not used to being told to do things. She started to say, "Excuuuse m—" but was cut off as Lachlan put his hands on her shoulders, physically moved her out of the way, and stepped to Deli.

Deli looked at her dress. "Well, eff."

"Eff," he repeated and handed her a clean towel. Her heart leaped at Lachlan's smile.

William's shadow fell over his brother as he took in the scarlet stain down Deli's front. "I always loved a lady in red."

Something primal passed over Lachlan's face as Deli scrunched her nose and her mother wrapped a manicured claw around William's arm.

"Delilah has always been one for drama," she said with an airy laugh.

Grandma Rosemary pried her daughter's hand from the famous bicep by the wrist. "She got that from you, darling."

Aunt Mo appeared beside Lachlan with two new glasses of red. Deli took one and toasted Aunt Mo, then watched her aunt dump her wine down her front.

Grandma Rosemary gasped. "What on *earth* are you doing, Maureen?"

Aunt Mo winked at Deli. "Following my heart."

Deli took in her ruined dress and her aunt's pristine outfit, stained maroon to match. Her giggle grew into a real laugh as Aunt Mo wrapped an arm around Deli's waist and joined in. Aunt Mo's eyes squeezed shut in joy, and Deli marveled at her face—touched by time and full of grace. She heard her mother sigh.

Lachlan cleared his throat and tried to speak quietly. "If you need anything, Deli . . ."

William made a sort of mocking sound, and Lachlan glared at him before stalking off.

"Oooh." William wiggled his fingers like a child telling ghost stories. "Scary."

"Anyway," Lorraine said, reaching for William again, "as I was saying—"

"Deli?" William ignored her mother as his massive hand wrapped around Deli's glass and passed it to Aunt Mo, who was happily wearing her own. "Fancy a dance?"

Deli blinked stupidly as William pulled her through the small crowd. Lorraine's mouth fell open, and her eyes tracked Deli's path like one of those haunted castle portraits of dead rich people wearing velvet.

Deli caught the flash of Lachlan's eyes just before his brother led her through the door to the garden with her hand in his.

72

Deli

Deli stepped out of the pub and into someone else's fever dream.

In Lachlan's garden, towering silver birch trees arched over a space twice as large as the pub itself, leaving a wide swath of twinkling night sky. The crescent moon lent its glow to the dance floor where a local band played, flanked by an eclectic mix of tables, sofas, and fluffy armchairs. Warm strings of twinkle lights wove up the white bark and through the leaves of the birch guardians. And the ground was covered in blooming flowers, grown wild and strange just like the cottage's impossible garden.

The archway from the ceremony had been moved to the secret oasis. The wedding cake Aunt Mo had chosen sat on a small table beneath it—a simple white buttercream adorned in black wild bramble.

Blair's laugh showered Deli from the dance floor like a warm summer rain as she watched Douglas and the kids doing the funky chicken in unison. Andrew danced slowly with a woman who was surely his grandmother, his head on her cheek.

Deli stilled on the path, taking it in.

William's voice was laced with teenage mischief. "Are you turning me down, Deli?"

Deli dragged her eyes from the glimmering, endless night where the people she'd come to love laughed and spun under the moon. He looked pointedly at her unmoving feet.

Deli narrowed her eyes. "Why are you doing this, Will?"

"I'm simply asking an enchantress to dance."

She pulled her hand from his. "Lachlan."

William smiled like a child caught doing something naughty, tilted his head, and raised an eyebrow. "Oh, yes, my brother. I *did* ask about the two of you, but he was tight-lipped. Is there . . . something going on?"

She took a deep breath. "It's complicated."

"With Lachlan, it always is." William sighed. "With me, it's just a dance." He offered his hand again. "Besides, I see my big brother so rarely. Would you deny me my god-given right to be a pain in the arse?"

Blair spotted them and waved for them to join her on the dance floor. Deli glanced over her shoulder at the closed door. Lachlan wasn't there, and Deli was either going to have to dance with an ultimately harmless man with her friend at her wedding or go back inside and face her mother and Lachlan.

"I'm not a good dancer." She took his hand.

"Don't worry." He swept her onto the dance floor. "I am. And it's just a bit of fun."

73

Mo

Mo was proud of her work. It was a beautiful wedding.

She was deeply ashamed, however, of her family.

She was pretty ticked off, too.

She tried to let it go as she turned her back to her family and leaned against the bar with Deli's glass of wine, sipping as she thought. Deli was an adult. Maybe it wasn't her job to get involved. Maybe Mo just needed to keep her head down until her mother and sister got tired of cloudy skies and finally left her alone.

Lachlan was busily pouring shots at the end of the bar for a handful of rowdy groomsmen and cousins to take out to the garden, but his eyes kept darting toward the back door. Mo knew the feeling. After a few minutes, she couldn't keep herself from listening as Rosemary and Laurie kept speaking in hushed tones.

"Remember her birthday?" Laurie said. "I'm telling you, Mom, it's like any time the attention is on me, Delilah can't handle it."

Mo had heard enough.

"What is WRONG with you two?" she demanded as she turned.

"US?" Laurie pointed her thumb between her chest and their mother's. "We weren't the ones so desperate for attention we would pour perfectly good wine all over ourselves *Flashdance*-style!"

"Laurie, you didn't even *pretend* to be concerned!"

"Please." Laurie rolled her eyes. "This is her new stunt. She practically lapped it off her chest."

Mo's jaw dropped. She stared pointedly at her sister's cleavage, pushed up and tumbling out of her too-short, too-low dress. "*Deli's* chest? Have you seen yourself today?"

Laurie studied a cuticle. "I don't know what you're talking about."

Mo mimicked her sister's voice. "Ohhh, *Hamish!* Please! Sign my ever-so-aaaammmple bosom!"

"Really?" The word came out in an incredulous huff.

"Yes, *really—*" Mo began, but her mother cut her off.

"Girls, enough."

Mo hadn't heard her mother's Because I Said So tone in so long it sent a nostalgic, yearning fissure through her heart.

Laurie balked. "I'm not doing anything! It's Maureen!"

"Maureen, I raised you to be a lady—not a wine-wearing troll who says *bosom*."

"Ha!" Laurie jeered.

"And Lorraine?" Their mother scowled at the neckline of the nude bodycon dress Laurie had squeezed herself into for a wedding in a pub. "Put your tits away."

Mo chuckled as Laurie sucked in a sharp breath and stared at their mother with her bottom lip protruding. Another strange pang rang through her, lost and wandering—like a thing trapped too far in the future, unable to get home.

It sobered her. She took a few breaths. "Mom, what are you doing here?"

She could have sworn she saw fear pass over her mother's face before it hardened into impassivity, but she hadn't known her mother in a very long time.

"I know you'd hoped I'd die before this day, Maureen, but, alas, I am still your only mother. Don't I have a right to see my daughter? See her life?" She paused and cast a pointed gaze around the small pub.

"Doesn't Lorraine deserve the chance to save *her* daughter from the same fate?"

All her life, Mo was not allowed to be angry. She wasn't allowed to rage at the endless flow of small injustices with a mother who was never wrong, never the bad guy. If she confronted Rosemary, the explosion that followed would always leave her torn open while her mother would be unscathed.

So Mo had learned to smother the sparks that threatened to catch. She became a thing that couldn't burn. Like stone.

It had been twenty years since she'd been forced to choose between leaving Beth behind or dragging her into her mother's blast radius. The ghost of Beth's plea rattled in the attic of Mo's heart.

Let me in, baby.

God, Mo had loved her. They'd had such little time.

Why can't you just let me in?

The flame tore through Mo, desperate for oxygen.

She glared at her mother. "Whatever rights you had to me, to *my* life, you lost. You have no right to judge me or the people I actually call family."

Laurie stepped closer with a mocking laugh. "Ha! *These* people?" She sneered at Cairn and Hannah playing cards near the fire.

"*These* people," Mo said, her anger rising, "would have never done what you did, Laurie. You were supposed to be my *sister.*"

Laurie jabbed a finger into Mo's shoulder. "I AM your sister!"

Mo should have suffocated the flame and said something to pacify. But there, in The Wallflower, burning with twenty years of resentment, Mo looked her sister in the eyes and said, "You *used* to be."

The sentence dropped between the three of them, landing on the floor with a deafening sound. Mo caught Lachlan's eyes from the far side of the bar, his body rigid and his ears tuned. On another night, she would have been by his side to comfort him after the arrival of his brother and the fallout with Deli. But they were both being hunted by their ghosts, and hers were threatening to ruin a wedding, wearing pub-inappropriate heels.

"Maureen, ENOUGH," Rosemary bit. Her whisper was a hiss. "What, *exactly*, are you accusing us of, Maureen? What new imagined slight have the great villains of your life committed to excuse your father and your betrayal?"

Mo snarled, "I will never forgive you—*either* of you—for what you did to Beth."

Her mother's cheeks paled. Laurie seemed to shrink. For one impossible moment, the three of them teetered on the edge of the world.

Then Rosemary McDonnell spoke, and sent them all falling.

"How do you know about that?"

No apology. Not even the courtesy to deny it. Mo should have confronted her that day so long before. There was so much she should have said.

"How do I *know*? We knew how awful people could be, so we were careful. Beth and I kept our life to ourselves. I only told one person where Beth worked and what she did." She spun on her sister. "But you couldn't just be my sister. You had to be Mommy's Little Helper. Right, Lorraine?"

Laurie's eyes narrowed, her jaw set and her head dipped like a thing stalking prey—her desperation consumed by resolve. Mo had seen it before many times in their life—the flip of a violent switch.

If Laurie MacDonald thought she might get hurt, Laurie aimed to maim.

She brought her lips closer to Mo's ear and wielded her words like a blade. "I did her *a favor*." She pulled back with slow control, studying Mo's face to harvest the pain she'd sown.

Mo barely recognized her own voice. "What the *fuck* did you just say?"

A cheer rose from outside as the local band started a new song.

Laurie reared back for another strike. "Poor Maureen, always running from anything hard. You would have left her eventually. At least

Beth still had some good years to give someone else." Laurie sighed. "You were always too much like Dad, you know that? But your hero left us to rot away in this excuse for a town while Mom struggled to give you everything. *Everything.* And here you are, limping around like some martyr, waiting to die alone . . . just like *him.*"

Her words clamped around Mo's throat. She couldn't breathe. She barely managed to choke out, "I'm not alone."

"Delilah isn't like you, Maureen. She's loyal. Just because you never had a daughter doesn't mean you can have *mine.* Besides, have you forgotten?"

Mo heard the phone ring behind the bar. Lachlan answered, then responded with a very sharp, "You want to speak with *who*?"

"You broke your niece's heart. You left her, *too,*" Laurie spat. "Perhaps Deli needs to be reminded. This has gone on long enough."

As Laurie started for the door, the knowledge of what was about to happen to Deli propelled Mo's feet forward, despite the way her body fought to stay still.

Mo had to protect her. She wouldn't leave Deli again.

A shaking, too-thin hand caught Mo by the wrist. Her mother trembled in front of her, silent and colorless, eyes so wide and vulnerable it made Mo sick.

"Maureen, I—"

"Are you proud of her, Mom?" Mo growled. "Your perfect little girl is *just like you.*" She snatched her wrist away and stormed after Laurie as she disappeared through the swinging door. Lachlan caught her eyes for a desperate moment as he slammed the phone back onto the receiver. She didn't have time to explain.

Mo and Lachlan called her name at the same time.

"Deli!"

74

Lachlan

The last time Lachlan Scott had stood up for a woman he loved, it ended in shards of glass splintering his mother's hands and her resentment splintering his heart.

In so many small ways he'd sacrificed something precious to preserve peace and called it noble. Blair's dignity, his passion, his family's self-respect—all dead on an altar to civility while Lachlan put up no fight at all. He'd been a cowering boy, calling himself a man.

When Rosemary and Lorraine came to Fearnhall, it was like missing pieces had arrived to a complicated puzzle. They all fit together—noses, nailbeds, voices overlapping—yet they were entirely different. Lachlan had come to understand that the choices the four had made, spread over decades, had a clear pattern.

Two were led by courage. Two were dominated by fear.

Those women stood over Deli and Mo, mocking them in *his* home.

He let *his* brother lead her away.

His brother, who fled their family as soon as he could and left Lachlan behind to cope. It didn't matter that their mother was sick. It didn't matter that their town was crumbling. William had no sense of duty or integrity. He was charming to your face and then turned selfish . . . a man who *used* people for his own end. It was why he'd tried to keep William from finding her, that first night he'd come home. Deli wouldn't be safe if William knew she was someone Lachlan loved.

But Lachlan had failed to keep her safe. And he'd been so ashamed, he hadn't even found the words to explain.

When he'd watched his brother take her by the hand, he'd said nothing. Again.

Then the phone rang. Lachlan couldn't believe what he was hearing, and Mo began to chase her sister into his mother's garden, where he'd left Deli to his brother, and he knew it might already be too late.

You break everything you touch.

Perhaps if he'd been less of a coward at any one of the many chances he'd had in his life, none of what he knew was about to happen would have ever happened. Perhaps if he'd been braver sooner, no one would have gotten hurt.

As he abandoned the bar where his father died, pushing through the door to what had once been his mother's sanctuary, Lachlan Scott made a choice.

Even if it was far too late, he would still change.

He would choose the people he loved—damn peace and damn the fear.

No matter the cost, Lachlan would never be a coward again.

75

Deli

The night was starting to feel like everything would be okay.

Deli nearly cried with laughter as she spun in circles. She had no idea what she was doing, but she was having a great time doing it as she danced the ceilidh with Blair and Andrew's families, Douglas, and the kids. The band played "The Flower of Scotland," and a rowdy group of kilt-clad cousins, groomsmen, and tipsy aunties went wild singing along with so much passion Deli picked up the chorus and a secondhand distrust of the English by the end. Then the music changed, and William's hand appeared over hers as his other materialized around her waist—and they were slow dancing.

He grinned at her like he knew he was pushing it. Still, neither her family nor Lachlan had followed them out. It was better than all the . . . than everything waiting for her back inside.

She rolled her eyes at him. "You're ridiculous."

"And you're delicious," he murmured into her ear.

"Gross," she said, but she smiled. It was nice to be a girl twirling on a dance floor with a boy she'd never pine after—made simple for a moment. He spun them in a dizzying arc and she laughed. The sky was miraculously clear, the night unseasonably warm. Blair and Andrew rocked back and forth beside them while Douglas held Kieran's small frame up in a dramatic waltz and their little feet dangled. The band played a folk song's melody that was hopeful. Reverent.

Under the glow of starlight and friendship, Deli felt, for the briefest moment, that she might still belong there.

William twirled her back toward him for a dip. Her balance shifted as he lowered her body toward the floor, and she saw clouds beginning to eclipse the sky.

Her mother's yell was so unexpected she wasn't sure she'd actually heard it.

"*DELILAH!*"

Two more voices called her name.

"*Deli!*"

Lachlan and Aunt Mo chased behind Deli's mom as they poured out onto the dance floor. Everything was upside down.

"What is *this* supposed to be?" Lorraine's heels stepped inches from Deli's brow.

"What are you talking abo—" She realized William hadn't pulled her up, and she summoned every chin she had to look at the man who'd frozen in place, his eyes locked on something coming toward them. "Um, Will?"

Her phone, which she'd given to her aunt for safekeeping, as she had pockets and Deli did not, started ringing in Aunt Mo's pocket as William brought her to her feet.

Lachlan's shadow fell over them. "Get. Away. From her."

William raised an eyebrow. "Are you mad?"

"She's not one of your toys, William."

Deli was lost. "Wait, me?"

Lachlan looked at her quickly before homing in on his brother again. "I said, get away from her."

William rolled his shoulders. Then he smiled, and Deli knew she'd missed something very important about the Scott brothers.

"Make me."

Lachlan launched at his brother, but Deli wedged herself between them and brought Lachlan to a full stop. His chest heaved against her palms.

"Boys, stop it!" Aunt Mo started toward them like she was going to haul them away by their ears, but her hand went to her pocket and she stopped as Deli's phone rang again.

Deli pushed against Lachlan's chest. "What the *hell* is going on with you?"

"Has he told you?" Lachlan demanded.

"Told me what?"

She spun to look at William, but he looked as confused as she was.

Lorraine grabbed Deli by the upper arm, her nails pinching as she yanked her away from Lachlan and William. She batted her lashes. "Trust me, William, it's not worth all this fuss. Besides, we're going home."

Deli balked. "Who's 'we'?"

Aunt Mo stared at the phone in her palm. "Deli . . ."

"Stay out of this," Lorraine snapped over her shoulder as the ringing ended and picked up again immediately.

Deli pulled her arm free. "She didn't do anything, Mom. Leave her alone."

Lorraine's jaw fell open and she took a half step back. Her eyes ran from Deli's head to her toes and back. A raindrop landed on Deli's cheek.

"Deli?" Aunt Mo said. "You . . . you might want to take this."

"Don't you dare defend *her*, Delilah!" Her mother blocked her path. "Not to me!"

Deli kept moving toward Aunt Mo. "Mom, relax—"

"NO!" Lorraine's shout echoed around the garden as chatter fell silent.

Deli froze, every nerve recognizing the danger then. Lachlan shifted his stance the slightest bit toward Deli's mother. Deli spoke through her smile, quiet and slow.

"Mom, please—"

"NO!" It was a roar. "You don't know your precious Aunt Mo, Delilah. Do you know what happens after she makes you feel special? The second you disappoint her—"

Lachlan began to say something, but Aunt Mo held up a hand to silence him. The phone rang again, and her face contorted with worry.

"—she abandons you."

Deli looked between them, bewildered. Aunt Mo didn't interject.

"Tell me, Delilah—weren't you lonely for your hero over the last *twenty years*?"

Thunder shook the sky. The treetops shuddered with the sudden storm's first rain. Hurried voices began to call for people to head inside as guests peeled their attention away.

Deli's instincts tried to kick in from a lifetime of surviving—placate the beast. Get out of the way. Stay quiet.

But there on the dance floor, as the sky began to weep, there was nowhere to hide.

After a month in a different world, Deli had let her guard down, and her mother's blows left her reeling. She tried to find her voice, but it was buried. The only word she caught hold of was a hollow sounding plea, like it had been scraped out from the middle.

"Stop . . ."

"You don't *belong* here, Delilah. Your grandmother and I—we're the ones who have kept you safe, attended to your every need. What has Maureen sacrificed for you? You will never be enough for her."

Deli's blood was pounding in her ears. She swayed on her feet.

Lorraine frowned. "She didn't love you enough to stay. And you want to be like *her*?"

Lachlan stepped between Deli and her mother.

"Enough."

"You," Lorraine growled.

He was a wall of sheer rock. Unmoving. "Aye, me. And your sister? She's *my* family. You won't speak another word against her while you stand in *our* home."

Aunt Mo gave Lachlan an *attaboy* smile like her sister hadn't just eviscerated her for fun.

Lorraine was still for a moment, then her face softened. She held out a hand to Deli. "Delilah, honey, it's time."

And suddenly, her voice belonged to a woman who was tender and patient and kind—quick to laugh and quick to comfort. It was the voice of the person who'd pressed cooling rags to Deli's sick forehead, who'd shaped her pancakes like dolphins and taught her how to tie shoes with bunny ears and patience.

It was the sudden arrival of her mom. Her actual *mom.*

"Come home, sweetheart. We've missed you. We need you. You belong with us."

All her life, Deli felt like her head had been forced under. She'd never found dry land, paddling and paddling to get moments of air before she was tumbled back into an ocean of things she'd never be or do. She'd never found rest. Her life was one of striving.

Then a few words from her mom and . . . suddenly, land.

She took a small step forward.

Lachlan's arm blocked her path. His eyes were fixed to her mother, churning like storm waters turned golden.

"You don't deserve her."

He said it with such conviction, Deli almost believed him.

Lorraine took in the man standing between her and her daughter, astonished. "What?"

Deli's phone chimed again as the heavy clouds blotted out the moonlight.

"I said"—Lachlan shielded her body with his—"you don't deserve her. You act like she's a burden."

He looked back at Deli over his shoulder. Though he spoke to her mother, his eyes were only for her.

"You don't see her. You have no idea who she is. Deli is *kind*—do you know how rare that is? She's smart and curious and funny. She meets every challenge with humor. She makes everyone feel important. And my god—"

Lachlan smiled, and it was like a floodlight spilling into a dark room. She wanted to bask in it. She wanted to cower.

"Deli is *brave.* I knew the moment I saw her—"

Memories of a day long ago. Her scraped knees. Lachlan's gentle hands putting her back together.

"—if I lived an entire life beside her, it would not be enough."

For a single, shining moment—it was just Deli and Lachlan. A girl who knew only how to stand alone and a boy who wanted only to stand beside her—tethered together despite the ocean, the losses, the time.

Lorraine's laugh sliced through it.

"Oh god, you're in *love* with her? You poor, pathetic boy."

Blair stuck her head out of the pub, waving the landline in her hand. "Will! Someone keeps calling for you. PR or something? They say it's an emergency?"

Will hesitated.

Lorraine shook her head with a smile. "Delilah doesn't love you, Lachlan. She's in love with someone else. Someone who sees her *potential,* not who settles for . . ."

Deli's mother looked at her—and Deli caught a glimpse of her fear. Her mother's guilt. Her love. Her secret self-loathing.

". . . this."

Deli's phone rang again. She forced her eyes from her mother to her aunt's outstretched hand.

Lachlan's focus didn't sway. "Get out of my pub."

Lorraine was gobsmacked. "What did you say to me?"

Deli touched Lachlan's hand and heard the sharp intake of air as their fingers brushed.

"Lachlan, it's okay."

Then, right there in front of her family and his brother—while the clouds surrendered their last grip on the rain—Lachlan cupped her cheek in his hand, pressed his forehead to hers, and said simply, "No, Deli. It's not."

If the raindrops that found her skin were cold, she didn't feel it. She only felt the very old, aching thing wake up in her heart and stir—to lift its eyes to the light and fight through the pain of something so bright finding something so long in the dark.

Aunt Mo's voice was soft and urgent. "Deli? I just know you've been waiting for this call."

Everything felt like a movie as Deli took the phone from Aunt Mo's hand. William stole away to answer the urgent call of his own. As the screen lit in her palm, Lachlan touched her shoulder.

His face was shadowed. His voice changed. "Deli, I'm so sorry. I never meant for this to happen."

Before she could ask what he was talking about, she heard the special chime she'd set only for texts from Chloe. Her stomach was in her throat as she clicked on the text—a photo sent, *finally*, from her best friend.

It was a screenshot from an infamous celebrity-gossip magazine. A gritty photo showed romantic light cast onto the handsome face of Billy S. Burns as a mystery woman was pressed to his chest. He wore a secretive, flirty smile as he whispered in her ear and tucked a strand of her raven hair touched with golden firelight. What it didn't show was her pinning a boutonniere on his chest.

The title read:

WHO HAS STOLEN THE HIGHLANDER'S HEART?

All Chloe said was:

Is that really you?

And Deli just wanted to know—more than who had taken the photo and more than why—was how, after a lifetime of friendship, that could be *all* Chloe had to say?

Deli felt something double over inside her, struck by a killing blow.

William burst from the pub and started toward Deli in the rain.

"No." Lachlan moved to intercept his brother. "You've done enough."

William ignored Lachlan as their shoulders collided. "Deli—"

Lachlan caught his brother's arm, an unstoppable force meeting an unmovable object, and the two towering men struggled to keep their balance on the rain-slick dance floor.

The phone rang again. She read the name of the person desperately trying to reach her . . . the person she'd desperately been trying to reach.

Trey Evans.

Two days had passed since she'd told him—not that she was over him, but that she needed to move on. And it had been two days since he'd written frantic messages begging her not to go. She hadn't gotten the chance to even think about it in the aftermath of Will's and her family's arrivals. It was like her hand moved on its own as she held the phone to her ear.

"Trey?"

"Deli? Thank god!"

Lachlan and William were locked in some half-falling, half-wrestling struggle.

"God, it's so good to hear your voice, Del. You have no idea. I've been going crazy."

Deli's eyes widened as the Scott brothers' momentum carried them off the dance floor and sent them stumbling toward the archway.

"Listen, I've been thinking a lot. And . . . I can't lose you, Deli. I can't. Come home to me?"

"Trey, I—" was all she got out before William escaped Lachlan's grip and shoved him backward. Lachlan's feet couldn't find purchase on the slick grass and fresh mud. Rain ran down her phone in rivulets, seeping into the speaker. The last thing she heard was Trey's crackly voice before the phone went dark.

"Deli, please? Please! I lo—"

She dropped the phone. "Lachlan!"

There was a snapping sound as Lachlan's body collided with the archway. Dogwood petals sank to the ground and were pinned by the rain. Deli ran toward him past a trail of white buttercream smeared across the ground.

Back on the dance floor, Lorraine spun on her sister. "Look what you've done!"

Aunt Mo's voice came out steel. "I suggest you think about the next thing out of your mouth, Lorraine."

"Lorraine! Maureen! Delilah!" All of Rosemary's girls turned to see her standing in the doorway, hand braced against the frame, pale as the moon. "I need to speak with you three."

"Grandma?" The air turned to ash on Deli's tongue. "Are you alright?"

A lull in the storm fell over them like a blanket. Rosemary's voice was so loud in the pocket of quiet.

"You should all know"—Deli thought she saw her stumble—"I'm dying."

The other two rolled their eyes at the announcement of another illness. But Deli didn't.

Lorraine sighed. "Oh really? What is it now, Mom?"

Rosemary answered without emotion. "Cancer."

"Inspired," Lorraine snorted.

A sharp crack shook the night as silver lightning sliced through the sky, and Deli watched a surreal scene unfold in black and white. Her grandmother, Rosemary McDonnell—bitter and witty and critical and constant—collapsed into the rain.

A scream tore from her mother's throat, and Deli felt the concrete slab she'd built her life upon crack in two.

76

Deli

"MOVE PEOPLE!" Blair called as she held the door open while Andrew cleared William and Lachlan's path.

"Mom?" Lorraine jogged to keep pace with the brothers as they carried Rosemary toward the parking lot. "MOM!"

Deli had sprinted ahead with Aunt Mo. She threw anything cluttering the back seat of Aunt Mo's car onto the drenched asphalt while Aunt Mo turned the key in the ignition.

"Go!" Deli closed the door and hit the top of the car with the flat of her palm. Aunt Mo's tires squelched against the wet gravel as she wrenched the car back toward The Wallflower. The rain sent dark ribbons of Deli's hair streaming into her eyes as she jogged behind.

"I said, I'm *fine.*"

Deli nearly cried out at the sound of her grandmother's voice. It had to be a cruel trick of the wind. She'd seen her collapse. By the time Deli caught up, Lachlan and William were massive shadows backlit in the yellow glow of the pub's window as they stood over the open door to the back seat.

Lachlan started toward her as she closed in. on the car. "Deli . . ."

She pushed past him and yelled at her mother standing beside the passenger's seat, "Mom, get in! We have to *go!*"

"Tell that to your grandmother!" Lorraine barked back.

"She's—"

Rosemary's voice, now coming from the back seat, was unmistakable. *"I'm fine."*

"Grandma?" Deli ignored the sting as she dropped to her knees on the asphalt to search for her grandmother's face where she lay across the back seat. "You're okay!"

"Sure, minus the cancer," Lorraine muttered from above them.

Rosemary propped herself up on her elbows. Even with her hair flattened and a swipe of mud on her chin, she was the most elegant woman Deli knew.

Her grandma smiled. "Don't frown like that, you'll wrinkle."

Aunt Mo twisted in the driver's seat. "Mom, I think we should still go to the hospital."

"Agreed," echoed Lorraine.

Rosemary tutted. "I just need a shower and stronger ankles. The cottage will do."

Deli reached for her hand. "Are you sure you're okay?"

Grandma Rosemary squeezed it. "Absolutely."

"Okay." Deli stood. The rain had softened. In her head, she started sorting through the many pieces that needed picking up. "I think I should apologize to Blair."

Lachlan cleared his throat. "Go, Mo. Get Rosemary home. I'll take Deli when she's ready."

"Thank you," Aunt Mo answered.

"Mom, put your seat belt on, for god's sake," Lorraine said as she disappeared into the passenger seat. A moment later Deli watched as the car pulled away, taking the silhouettes of her family with it.

She stared into the dark, shaking in her ruined dress. Hot tears threatened to fall.

Enough, Delilah. She needed to be practical. *So dramatic.*

She took three long breaths, each steadier than the one before.

Then she pushed through the brothers before either could say a word, grateful for the wall of stifling heat on the other side of the door to chase the chill that had grafted itself to her bones.

Inside, Douglas was perched on a chair, telling the room a dramatic story.

Blair threaded her way to Deli. "Is she alright?"

"She's alright. Well, I mean, I think she's alright. Aunt Mo's taking her home. Blair, I'm so sorry—"

"Shut up." Blair crushed her in a hug so warm and honest it threatened to break the retaining wall she'd already erected in her heart. Deli pointed at the watery grit she'd left staining Blair's quick-silver satin.

"Blair, your dres—"

"Deli, it's just a dress."

"I'll take it into town. I'll pay for it to be cleaned."

"Deli MacDonald, you're about to go in time-out."

"Oh." Deli blinked. "Mom voice."

Blair nodded. "I'm sorry you had to see that. Now, are you okay?"

Deli tried to take inventory of herself, but she felt . . . nothing.

"I don't . . . know?"

"Mmhmm. And is Lachlan in love with you?"

Lachlan hadn't actually said he loved her. It was Lorraine who'd used that word, and she'd used it like a weapon.

"I . . . don't know?"

"Of course he is, I was only asking to be nice. The more important question is . . . do you love him back?"

The suggestion of Deli loving Lachlan felt like being plunged into frigid water. Her time with him played in her mind like a wonderful, horrible, irresistible, unfinished movie of arguments and pining and pain and promise. And still . . .

He made her laugh. He made her reconsider. He kissed her like he'd been put on earth to do little else. He had made her feel safe enough to let go. He'd said things to Deli that she'd waited her entire life to hear. And he'd stood up for her to her mother.

But first he'd been ashamed of her—and it made her question everything.

And there was Trey. Trey, who she'd loved for many years. Trey, who'd been a best friend. Who missed her. Who didn't want to lose her. Who had been about to say . . .

"What?" Blair asked flatly.

"It's just . . . Trey—"

"Oh my god, fuck Trey Evans, that bawbag!"

Douglas fell silent mid-squawk with a leg and his arms still in the air like a giant crane as the remaining well-wishers turned their heads toward Deli and Blair. A bony hand wielding a walking stick poked through the cozy cluster, and the white wispy curls of Andrew's grandmother followed. She scowled, looking scandalized.

Then she yelled, "Aye, fuck Trey Evans! The fanny!"

Everyone with a drink held them into the air. "AYE!"

Blair nodded. "Nan is wise and has known many men in the biblical sense. You should listen to her."

"Was she a pilot? A touring musician?" Deli peeked over Blair's shoulder to get a glimpse of the grandma with a prolific list of past lovers. "A stripper?"

"A nun."

"I *have* to meet her."

Blair took her hands. "Deli, I can't tell you how to feel. But I can tell you this: Tonight, I learned that Lachlan never really loved me. Tonight, I learned what it looks like when Lachlan is in love. Because he is in love with you."

Deli shook her head. She didn't want to listen.

She had no idea what to do. She'd only known Lachlan for a month, but she'd known *and* loved Trey for years. He'd been everything she wanted—why she came here in the first place. He'd even been about to say he loved her. Trey was about to tell Deli he *loved* her.

But then . . . then Lachlan, and the difference in how she felt about herself when they left a room, and the way he'd been a part of everything without Deli even knowing from the start. When Lachlan hid her from his brother moments after he'd been more intimate with her than anyone else—moments after she'd given up on Trey for the way he left her suspended in insecurity—it had hurt Deli. *He* had hurt her. In a real, wounding way.

But he didn't seem ashamed of her on that dance floor. He'd protected her, claimed her in front of everyone. Though it could have been about his brother, not her.

"Maybe Lachlan was just . . . jealous seeing me with Will—which was nothing, by the way, but apparently enough to tackle him for—"

Something clicked into place in her head, halting her thought before it finished. The way Lachlan had watched her and William together like it was a crime—like he'd do *anything* to get them apart.

A photo had been leaked to the press, sending hounds after whoever William was "seeing."

He'd put his hand on her shoulder just as she was about to find out about her picture flooding gossip magazines and apologized for it. *I'm so sorry.*

Lachlan's voice made her jump. "Am I interrupting?"

"Yes," Blair said while Deli said, "No."

But the truth was, Deli's mother had torn her fantasy apart, then Deli watched her grandmother faint into the mud, and all the other decisions and heartbreaks and hopes became so, so much smaller. Her family had come.

And now they had to go.

"I've got to get back to my grandma, Blair. But I'm so sorry for my disastrous family. I feel like I ruined your wedding."

"Please, it was better entertainment than we could have paid for around here," Blair said. Deli turned to leave, but Blair didn't release her hand. "Hey, *I* love you, too, you know."

A pang of guilt shot through Deli, colliding with what she already knew.

"I love you, Blair."

She hoped her friend couldn't hear the louder word beneath her love.

Goodbye.

77

Lachlan

Lachlan had loitered outside The Wallflower's Crown long after Will had stalked off, avoiding the moment he had to go inside to get Deli. He had a sinking feeling that by the end of the short ride to Mo's, things with Deli would never be the same.

Maybe not. Maybe things would be okay.

He was trying to be optimistic.

But he'd opened the door and watched Deli say a clipped goodbye to Blair, and now she was storming out of The Wallflower with her arms crossed over her chest. She didn't even look at him. He jogged to catch up.

"Are you cold?"

"No."

She shot the word like a bullet, and he heard it in her voice. Anger, pain. It tore through the parachute holding his hope above the waves. Though his legs were so much longer he had to take wide strides to reach the passenger door so he could open it for her. He reached for the handle.

"No." She opened the door so quickly he had to stumble backward to avoid being knocked to the ground. She got in and slammed it closed.

Lachlan's hands shook as he walked to his side and slid into the truck, useless to comfort her in her pain. He couldn't imagine how Deli must be feeling after all that had happened in the last few days, especially the last few hours. He closed his door, muting the sound outside to a fuzzy gray. He counted a second. Two.

"Are you alright, Deli?"

"I'd like to go home now, please."

He looked away. "Right. Of course. Sorry."

She snorted at the word as he turned the key.

"What?"

"Nothing." Deli looked out the window. "It's just funny."

He drove all the way to the main road before he asked, "What's funny?" He flipped on his indicator. Its hollowed clicking sound was too loud.

She shrugged. "That you're sorry."

Lachlan *was* sorry. Sorry for ruining her work on the archway. Sorry for scaring her. He was sorry for embarrassing her in front of her family. He was sorry for ever letting William into her life and sorry for trying to hide her from him. He was sorry he'd promised to keep her safe and had let her down. He was sorry he'd ever tried to stand between her and Mo. Sorry he'd misjudged her so harshly. Sorry for the way he'd treated her from the moment she got off a train.

He was sorry he'd seen her break for freedom twenty years ago and forced his way into her life. He was sorry he'd become another thing to escape.

"I *am* sorry."

"Sorry I found out about your little plan?"

"Huh?"

She shot him a scathing look that could have rivaled what he'd seen from her mother.

"It's a little too late to play himbo, Lachlan." She stared back out her window and added in a half mumble, "God, it's so annoying that you're smart *and* hot."

"Okay, I know I've done a lot of things wrong, but I'm not *playing* at anything."

She stared at him with her eyebrows raised. When he didn't go on, she shook her head.

"Wow, that's it? I'm a little disappointed. Guess the acting chops went to Will after all."

Lachlan readjusted his grip on the steering wheel. If he had hackles, they would have been raised.

"See?" Deli gestured toward his hands kneading the wheel. "You *have* to get a grip about your brother. The lengths you've gone to . . . ridiculous."

William had risked exposing her to invasive, endless media scrutiny—to deep dives into her life and hate mail from his rabid fans. He'd risked exposing their town—exposing Mo and her cottage—to teeming masses of sightseers who would trample Fearnhall underfoot and never look back. William had staged those photos for another fifteen minutes of attention, no matter the fallout for everyone else.

"His behavior was unforgivable."

"Seriously? Okay, one—you don't get to decide that for me. And two? That doesn't give you the right to—" She cut herself short.

"To what?"

"To do what you did!" The words exploded from her.

Her anger hovered in the air. Lachlan almost never got calls to The Wallflower's line. He'd hung up on the reporter before they'd finished saying, ". . . in a green dress with dark hair," and had torn after his brother. Seeing Deli dangling in Will's arms, unguarded and vulnerable? His rage slid into place like blinders, and then there was scrambling, and slipping, and finally a crack.

A shattered picture frame.

White petals, browning in the mud.

And a thing that he and Deli had built, lying broken.

Lachlan was suddenly sure that if he spoke, he would hear his father's voice.

"Listen." She started to reach for him before staring at her own hand in the air like it was someone else's and pulling it back into her lap. "Whatever bullshit is between you and your brother? Just, please, leave me out of it."

They rode in silence for what felt like a very long time.

The glow of Mo's cottage tinted the windscreen. Lachlan could hear the ticking clock.

He parked and reached into the back for the leather jacket Deli had left in his room that perfect night that was pierced and left bleeding. As he twisted, he felt the place his ribs had collided with the archway throb, felt the tear in the skin of his arm tug. In the dark cab, Lachlan felt all the things he'd hurt come back to him. He sucked in a breath of pain and pressed a palm to his chest.

Deli's eyes went wide with worry. "What's wrong?"

"I'm fine." He tugged his sleeve over the wound.

"You're hurt?"

Hearing the alarm in Deli's voice was so much worse than if she'd been apathetic. Her affection, her concern—just more he'd taken.

"Just let me look at it—" She reached for his arm, but he pulled it away. They stared at each other in the dark.

She started to reach for the door.

"Wait—"

He caught her wrist and his skin crackled. Her body stilled. He let go.

"Take this."

He set the jacket in her lap and her face went blank. She smoothed it with her palms.

"Deli?"

She hesitated. "Yes?"

God, there were too many things to say. Disgrace clamped its hand over his mouth. All the time he didn't have overflowed as he silently began to cry, leaving streaks down his face where they caught in the moonlight.

He steadied his breath. "I meant every word."

Deli watched a tear dip into the hollow of his cheek, but she didn't respond. Lachlan chose the last thing he'd say to the person he'd always loved. The person he always would.

"I promise, I never meant to hurt you."

"I believe you."

The despair in her whisper could have drowned him on dry land.

Deli didn't move, and neither did he. They sat together in the silence. Finally, she spoke, and he was sure the wrenching cry of pain that chased her words would stay with him forever.

"Lachlan, what if she dies?" Deli doubled over in the front seat, trying to mute her grief with her hands. "What am I gonna do if she dies?"

He ached to help. To do anything to make it stop for her. All he could do was watch. As her breathing inched its way back to normal, Lachlan would have given his soul to send her forward in time to a place where it all was over. She closed her eyes until she'd stopped crying.

Then she spoke a death knell—a dove shot from the sky.

"I just don't think I belong here."

She got out and closed the door behind her.

Lachlan watched Deli walk all the way up the path with stones still sunken into heather. He narrated it over and over in his head—memorizing the pale glow of her skin, the hair curling at the base of her neck, the soft fabric falling over her shoulder. She bent on the doorstep, hand to her mouth in a silent sob, before standing up tall, rolling back her shoulders, and slipping into Mo's jacket, and he branded it all into the flesh of his heart. As she stepped out of his life and into the cottage where her family of women were grappling with another unjust goodbye, Lachlan pressed the feeling of her into his mind.

He didn't care that it hurt.

Lachlan had wasted so much time forgetting the truth of Deli once—the girl made of fire and kindness and courage.

He would never forget her again.

78

LAURIE

Laurie secretly resented the fact that she fell in love with a man named MacDonald. She'd spent most of her life looking forward to walking up the aisle a McDonnell and walking back down with a name like Simpson or Goldfield or Finch—free of any family stain.

Ever since she could remember, Laurie couldn't wait to be someone else.

But here she was, at the same table in the same godforsaken cottage by the sea, and nothing had changed at all.

She watched as her sister helped lower their mom into a kitchen chair before settling opposite her. Their mother had sat briefly in a shallow bath of warm water to stop her shivering. It felt ridiculous that they were about to have this conversation in pajamas.

Mo spoke. "Okay, Mom. How bad is it?"

"It's cancer, darling. It's bad."

"Did the doctor tell you what type? What stage?"

"She may have mentioned it. I wasn't listening."

Laurie slapped the table with both hands and slumped backward. Mo held up a palm. It was infuriating and comforting, all at once.

"Mom, please. This is serious."

"I crawled into a tin can and hurled my crumbling body to my ex-husband's glorified tent on the other side of the world to be here, Maureen. I know it's serious."

Mo's cat, Lord Peas or something, jumped into their mom's lap and began purring. Laurie watched a chipped red fingernail rake a path through the cat's calico fur.

"Okay. Alright." Mo pinched the bridge of her nose. "How did *you* picture this conversation going?"

"Well," Rosemary mused, "I pictured a single glistening tear, perhaps a group hug. No blubbering. Lorraine gets snotty when she cries." Laurie felt the haphazard bandage she'd slapped into place around her heart start to give. "And I expect you'll come home while we put my affairs in order."

Mo's breath escaped her in a rush.

Laurie's mouth popped open with a sound loud enough to startle the cat. "Maureen *come home*? And stay with who?"

"Us, of course."

"Us?"

Her mother kept on like she couldn't hear the escalation in Laurie's voice. "Obviously, Lorraine. Or do you think I should stay in my home alone while this disease eats up enough of me that I can't stand? Die of thirst and starvation?"

"Mom, please—"

"I'm sure the housekeeper would find me eventually," she said with a thoughtful expression. "On account of the smell."

Laurie flinched and slid her hands into her lap, rubbing the pink grooves in her palms where she'd pressed in the contour of the wood.

The last time she'd felt so small, she'd been in the exact same place.

It was the day Laurie first realized that she *felt* more than other people. She never understood why she seemed to be the only one who simply couldn't take it—why she could feel everybody's bad feelings, all of the time.

She and her sister lay in their Scotland house room, honey and cinnamon ringlets tangled together on the same pillow.

"I don't want to talk about it, Momo," Lorraine whispered.

"If Mom and Dad are getting a divorce, we *have* to talk about it, Lolo."

She rolled to face the wall. "No."

"Don't be a baby."

The disgust in her little sister's voice peppered Lorraine's face like hot oil.

"I'm not being a baby. I just don't want to talk about it."

"Why not?"

"Because it hurts."

Lorraine felt her sister's annoyance before she heard it—a thrumming pulse of pain in her muscles like when their dad tuned a guitar string.

"Everybody hurts about this stuff, Lolo. We still have to face it."

"It's not going to happen!" Lorraine bit, drowning out the pain for a moment.

"It is, Lolo." Maureen's sudden wave of grief rushed her so cold it burned. "Trust me . . . it is."

Lorraine tried to fight the tears that threatened to betray her. She was *not* a baby. "Stop. My skin hurts."

"What do you mean your skin hurts? From what?"

Laurie rubbed at one of the massive welts on her forearms no one could actually see. "I told you. From this. And from when they . . . from earlier."

She gasped as a thrash of Maureen's anger landed right on top of the sore spot she'd just tried to press away. The old welt and the new rose, hot and stinging.

"Grow up, Lorraine! It hurts me, too, okay? But if we have to choose between them, we have to stick together. I'm trying to figure that out right now. But you are being dramatic, like always! Aren't *you* supposed to be the big sister?"

Every new word felt like a thing Maureen shot at her out of a gun, ripping holes through her skin no doctor would ever see. Her sister didn't understand. She didn't know that disgust was like burning oil; annoyance, a bad chord; anger, a whip. Disbelief, a bullet. Of all the ways she hurt, not being believed was the worst one. That, and the way disappointment ruptured in her head like a volcano. Disappointment was like her brain popped. She pressed her fingers to her temples, trying to breathe.

"Sometimes you have to just suck it up, Lorraine. Like Mom says."

Lorraine snapped, "Oh yeah? At least Mom actually *loves* me, Maureen! At least she doesn't have to keep punishing me and forcing me to be good!"

Maureen's bad feelings after Lorraine's outburst should have flooded her, but Lorraine's own anger rose up like a cleansing fire first. It burned, keeping her sister's feelings at bay, and when it finally died, all the other wounds from the day were barely there. They were so dull she could actually fall asleep. When she woke, she could hardly remember them at all.

She'd found the secret to surviving.

It wasn't until it all came true, just like Maureen had said it would, that Lorraine met a pain she couldn't forget. She'd wailed and pressed her small hands against the rear window of the car, clawing at the glass as her father turned his back and closed the door to his cottage before she was even out of sight.

The day he abandoned her, an animal moved into the place where her heart used to be and ate it all up, but it was always hungry, even while it slept. The best she could do after that was try to stop other people from rattling her bones, breaking her skin. The best she could do was to try to keep it sleeping.

Over four decades later, Laurie had never spent a day without worrying about someone else's feelings being too loud.

She still hated this cottage. Every time she was here, everything hurt *more.* It was like the soil itself wanted to watch her suffer. It was like the ground was cursed.

Laurie noticed for the first time how much *older* her sister looked as she watched fault lines appear in Mo's lips as she spoke. "I can't just move to California, Mom."

"You 'just moved' to Scotland."

"I have a life here. A business. A cat."

"None of which stopped you before."

"That was different. I was younger."

Their mom looked at Mo seriously. "So was *I*."

The cocktail of Mo's grief, fear, and sadness exploded at Laurie's feet like a dropped bottle. She yanked her slippered toes off the ground on instinct, but it didn't help. The feeling, like bits of invisible glass and lemon juice, found her skin anyway.

Laurie had never been sure if Mo knew about what had happened with Beth. It wasn't like Laurie *wanted* to hurt her—she just wanted to stop hurting, and it had been getting so loud. She had hoped her mom would be quiet if Laurie just gave her a secret. The second Mo decided to say it all out loud in that pub, the beast in her chest roared awake.

Maw snapping and spittle flying, it gnawed through the cage of her ribs and started eating everything else. She felt like she was being erased from the inside out.

Laurie had only carried the best of her intentions with her. But pain could drive a person to do things they never thought they could. She didn't really remember what she'd done at the wedding to stop it. She only knew that by the time she'd slammed a lock on the thing's cage and backed away slowly, she'd looked up to see her mother collapse in the doorway.

It didn't matter that Laurie had been good. It didn't matter that she'd spent her entire life trying to placate her mother's disappointment before it could leave marks.

She'd done everything right, but her dad left. Her sister left. Her daughter might be leaving, too.

And now her mother was dying.

As Laurie sat at the table where she'd first learned the word *divorce*, she felt like she'd been skinned alive.

Then Deli stepped through the door and stood in the last spot Lolo McDonnell had ever hugged her dad. She thought to herself how very much Deli looked like the thirty-year-old sister she remembered, how very much she would love to rest her daughter's head in her lap until she fell asleep—anything to take away the heartbreak that racked her baby's face. Laurie wanted to apologize.

Then she recognized her father's jacket.

The last thing Laurie would remember from that night was the way the beast roared back to life as the first lick of Delilah's grief found her broken skin—and the invisible breaking of her bones as the beast ate Laurie up and took over.

79

Deli

"Well, it's about fucking time," Lorraine snarled.

Deli scooped the words her mother hurled at her off the ground and tossed them over the dam in her head where she'd thrown everything else.

"And take off that jacket."

Aunt Mo said, "It's my jacket, she can wear it if she wants to."

"It's not *yours*, Maureen."

Deli walked to the table, heels clicking against the floor, and dropped the worn leather into her mother's lap without a word. She slid into the last chair beside her grandmother, who sat silently petting Beans.

If Deli MacDonald had known that her great-great-grandfather had built the table they were gathered around as a gift for his only daughter's wedding, perhaps she would have felt something beautiful. If she'd been able to go back in time and watch that young woman spend hours by the fireside, cutting and stitching the squares of a quilt for her little boy who was afraid of thunder, maybe Deli could have felt some reverence.

If the world was fair at all, Deli would have known the cottage on the cliffside had seen so many sacred moments it had become hallowed ground.

But all she knew as she joined the last of its daughters was that she felt nothing at all.

Aunt Mo leaned toward her. "Deli, are you alright?"

"Leave it, Maureen!" Lorraine's anger was deafening. "*My* daughter is fine!"

Deli watched a spot on the ceiling.

"Laurie, she's soaking wet and clearly freezing—"

"If Delilah can choose to run away, she can choose to change her clothes. She has made it clear she certainly doesn't need a mother."

"Jesus Christ, you're a monster tonight, Lorraine! What is *wrong* with you?"

Deli hardly noticed the way they both stood, chairs scraping, and yelled over one another so loudly Beans jumped from her grandmother's lap and hid under the armchair.

"Grandma?" Deli spoke directly to her. Nobody else noticed. "Are you really dying?"

"Yes, Delilah, I am." Deli studied the grooves of the table, nodding to herself. "I'm not positive *when* that will happen, but—"

"It doesn't matter," Deli interrupted. "It all ends the same."

Rosemary took her hand. "Sweetheart, what do you mean?"

Deli shrugged. "We're going home."

Her mother and aunt fell suddenly silent. Aunt Mo threw her hands in the air, spinning in a circle, and her mother slapped the table and gestured.

"*Thank you!* Finally, Delilah—some sense."

Earlier, when Deli's mother had torn through Blair's wedding, Lachlan's home, and onto the dance floor, Lachlan had tried to protect her, and she'd thought she might love him, too. She'd thought she might be somebody she wasn't.

But it didn't matter.

Because as she stepped inside and saw her mother, aunt, and grandmother sitting at the table, she'd known something bigger. Bigger than how he made her feel real. Bigger than if he'd hurt her, or if he'd leaked some photo of his brother to spite him or chase him off at her expense. Bigger than if he'd fallen for a phantom Deli who didn't really exist.

Her past and future were already decided.

It didn't matter if they loved each other. It didn't matter if they always would.

None of it mattered, because it all would end the same.

She'd been pretending to be someone deserving of things she hadn't earned, and he'd fallen for a person who only existed in Fearnhall—not in the real world. Deli couldn't live in a fantasy forever.

She didn't know how long they had been yelling.

"Deli has a *life* here, Lorraine!"

"Please, she barely has a life in Los Angeles."

"Why do you have to suffocate everything she has? Why can't you let her be happy?"

"You sound like a lunatic, Maureen."

Her grandma reached for her hand again. "Delilah, please. Look at me." Deli tried to look. Her eyes weighed a thousand pounds. "Are you happy here?"

Maybe Trey would just let things go back to the way they were and forget this entire situation happened. Maybe Chloe would accept an apology. It didn't matter whether she'd been happy, or that when she'd woken up that morning she'd felt like she might be someone new. It was too late.

"It doesn't matter, Grandma."

"What about that boy? From today? He seemed . . . well, he seemed to be quite fond of you, darling. Is he someone special?"

Lorraine was listening to them again. "He's pathetic, Mom. You saw it."

Aunt Mo's face turned to stone. "Watch *your mouth*."

Deli stood without a word and retrieved a wineglass, a bottle, and the corkscrew before sitting back down and beginning to twist.

Lorraine continued, "What's she gonna do, Mom? Throw her life away like Maureen? Marry someone like *Dad*?" The wine splashed into the glass, sloshing crimson up the sides. "Though I *am* glad I didn't have to bribe you with Trey, Delilah." Her mother sat back into her chair and scooted in. "I thought I was going to have to keep his engagement covered up long enough to lure you home."

Deli stilled, wineglass halfway to her lips. "Trey is engaged?"

"Grandma and I ran into his mother the other day. She said he'd asked her for the family ring to propose. That Scarlett just snatched quite a pretty penny out of the Evans family's pocket."

Deli took a sip.

Trey, who had never chosen her back.

Chloe, who had vanished without warning after a lifetime.

Lachlan, who deserved better.

And her mother.

Her mother.

Her *mom.*

She would go home and try to be the daughter her mother had always needed. Maybe her mom would forgive her for the way she'd quit early after only twenty-nine years of trying.

Deli took in the cottage around her—the cold fireplace, the worn chairs, and the old quilt that belonged to someone else.

"I can't do this anymore."

"What?" Lorraine snapped.

Deli stood with the full wineglass in one hand and her skirt in the other, pushed through the door, and walked into the stormy night.

Her days in Scotland were numbered.

It was always going to end the same.

80

Rosemary

Rosemary McDonnell had never fallen before, not once, despite having been an age where falls are common for some time. Claire had fallen at their weekly bridge game, and Shelley had fallen at the largest fundraiser of the year. She'd even had to be rushed out by paramedics—hit her head or something, it was all very dramatic and, frankly, *typical* for Shelley—but not Rosemary. She *considered* every step she took.

Until now.

"Let me see that."

Lorraine gave her a quizzical look but passed her Callum's jacket. The feel of it in her hands took her back in time.

She got out of her chair while Maureen and Lorriane fought on and on. She slipped her feet into her good-traction shoes and pressed against the door.

"Where do you think *you're* going?"

Rosemary turned to look at her oldest daughter—the one most like her, perhaps. They would have to pin her down to halt her steps now. "I'm going after her."

When Rosemary was a younger woman, she played tennis against the other girls at the club dressed in pressed white skirts—perfectly pleated without a wrinkle or spot. With each win, she earned a nod of approval from her mother and, if she was lucky, a passing grunt of acknowledgment from her father. Rosemary barely broke a sweat as she played every morning, and she'd glance at the balcony dripping in bloodred bougainvillea where the mothers were drinking mimosas, hoping hers would nod.

One night Rosemary was walking home from a show with a bachelor from the club—who was perfectly reasonable, if entirely bland—when she felt like she was struck by lightning. Callum stumbled out of a pack of men with shirts and jackets made loose with whatever activities young men do that young women didn't speak of, and their eyes met.

She felt something hot and urgent rip through her—like a tether in the center of her had been excavated and tied to the center of him. Callum walked right up to Rosemary, and she pulled her hand from the man who had paid for the fur coat she was wearing to place it in Callum's instead.

But it was neither love nor lust that made her run away with him. It wasn't even the way Callum spun magic out of words, or the way the wild sea and sky of Scotland poured out of him in his passions. In truth, Rosemary married Callum McDonnell because of the look on her mother's face and the sharp glint of her father's attention when their daughter invited an untamed poet for dinner.

She married him because her parents *noticed.*

Now, squinting at the slippery trail that led to the cliffside, Rosemary felt a seething anger toward her younger self.

"Stupid girl, Rose," she hissed under her breath, picking her way carefully up the path toward her granddaughter. "Look what you've done."

Delilah's silhouette was the spitting image of the girl Rosemary used to be—dark against the twilight sky and the silver streak of the Scottish sea. She couldn't count the number of times in her young life she'd sat just there, tennis ankles dangling over the crescent strip of land, watching it be swallowed at high tide.

Oh, she thought with a devastating suddenness, *it never stops.*

"Delilah!" she called. "You'll catch your death!"

For a moment, Delilah only stared blankly.

Something was broken, and it was Rosemary's job to fix it.

"Grandma? What are you doing out here? You'll slip!"

She came alive again and jogged toward Rosemary without any idea of how young she really was. The wineglass she'd taken was sloshing as she moved, spilling through her fingers despite her attempt to cover it with her hand.

"Oh, hush." Rosemary waved her concern away. "You're wasting good wine. We'll need it to stay warm."

"We should go in. It's too dark."

Even in the last of the light, Rosemary could see the mascara-streaked skin under Delilah's eyes, so pale against her freckles. When she was just a child, all innocence and ideas and magic, Rosemary would watch Delilah sleep sometimes. Her eyes would dart through the land of her dreams as that delicate skin moved with her adventures—the same freckles, like they'd been blown out of the palm of a passing god, landing carelessly on a little girl who would carry the marks her whole life.

When Rosemary was a little girl, *her* mother had kept a long tape measure in her nightstand, and every day, after she brushed her teeth and before breakfast, her mother would wrap it around her and mark down the numbers in a small notebook. Mother adjusted meals. She made her clothes that fit and flattered her figure. She cared so deeply about Rosemary's body, about her *rightness*, and she spent a great amount of time dedicated to the pursuit.

It wasn't an easy job. Rosemary was born with a certain unruliness about her. Her body insisted on getting bigger whenever she wasn't in strict control. Her mind seemed to wander. She wanted so badly to be a good daughter, but she had bad thoughts of disobeying constantly. She was, it seemed, at her core, *wrong.*

Of course her mother loved her. It wasn't Mother's fault that Rosemary was too soft, and her critiques could cut Rosemary to the bone. She spent a lifetime trying to make Rosemary acceptable to a good man so she could focus on bringing up a family, and that was a safe, neat life. Her mother only wanted Rosemary to be safe.

But she couldn't keep her daughter safe from the cottage by the sea and her own reckless heart.

Callum was loud and alive—a riot of color, sound, and bloodrush. Under the neons of Hollywood Boulevard or the flickering firelight of a cottage pounded with Scottish rain, Rosemary had never seen someone so beautiful. She marveled at his poetry—how he could reach into the air, pluck a feeling or fear from the sky, and translate it into words that gave voice to the great task of being alive. Callum spoke the language of the heart in a way that Rosemary never could, but when he translated it for her, it was a sacred intimacy. Like he was a prophet with precisely one disciple.

Yes, in the early days of their marriage in the cottage by the sea, Rosemary McDonnell was in love.

But her mother still needed her, and they had to return home. Against the cold, white marble, Callum looked less like a person and more like a blemish. His laughter rattled. His muddy boots left imprints in the foyer. His filthy jacket lay draped across the back of a chair—a streak of gore in the pristine gallery of her mother's perfection. Under Mother's gaze, Callum's touch made Rosemary flinch.

In the California mornings, Rosemary would wake with Callum's arm draped across her. She would roll away to slip on her robe, her slippers, and report to her mother's room.

That was how she found out she was pregnant for the first time.

Rosemary's hips and waist measurements had grown by a full inch. Mother placed a hand on either shoulder. For a moment, Rosemary believed her mother might kiss her, might hold her close. But her mother was not a woman who indulged in the guilty pleasures of womanhood—the giddiness and the gaudiness of things. She was practical and efficient, and so was her love.

What she whispered into Rosemary's ear was kind, really. She was right, after all. Rosemary had thrown away everything on a whim, and now there was certainly no going back.

It was the first time she regretted marrying Callum McDonnell.

The day they were told their second child would be a second daughter, Callum did not come to bed. In the early hours, as she picked up the wooden horses and doll clothes, she found him snoring at his desk. The empty bottle of whisky and the tipped glass stained the pages of his notebook amber and confirmed what she already knew. Callum's handwriting tumbled across the paper. She could feel the roiling heat of him left burning in ink. She almost recoiled as it sparked against her hand.

Had Rosemary been able to understand, she might not have decided she no longer loved Callum McDonnell that day. She might have remembered the man who had once said she was the only thing with a tide he would follow, damn the moon and its light, as he kissed her on the cliffside of a dark and raging sea. But Callum spoke the language of the riotous, windswept heart. If he didn't translate, Rosemary couldn't hear him clearly.

By the time she decided she no longer loved him, she hadn't heard him clearly in years.

Callum had never helped in Rosemary's considerable effort to teach their first daughter the way that girls must behave by the time Maureen arrived. He resented Rosemary for every cookie snatched off a plate, every stubborn hair pinned, every denied request to play in the dirt. *Let her be,* he would beg, insisting that Lorraine didn't need any changing.

But Callum didn't know what it was like to be a woman in the world.

Callum had no idea at all.

If Lorraine was a molehill, Maureen was born a mountain. Messy, loud, and hot—all pink cheeks and full-chested wailing. Lorraine's soft brown eyes would widen like a doe's while Maureen threw food off her high chair or tore bows from her hair.

Rosemary hadn't loved him for some time by the time Callum came to her with his tail between his legs and uttered the word *divorce.* Still, she raged against it. Why should he get to call *her* a failure? She'd done everything right! She'd pushed him into getting a respectable job, she'd given birth to his children and raised them. She'd even turned a blind eye on Callum's affairs. And Rosemary had had her chance with someone, too! Someone who made her wish she'd met *him* first. But it was Callum who had found her, and Rosemary did the *right* thing.

They screamed in the bedroom of the cottage, which was leaking and musty no matter the season. When they finally stood panting, staring hatefully at each other across the mattress where they'd spent their first night as lovers, she heard the quiet sob of her eldest daughter beyond the door. Lorraine sat on the kitchen chair with her knees pulled up to her chest and her doe eyes shiny. Maureen stood in front of her with her arms spread like a guardian, glaring at Rosemary with Callum's eyes.

Rosemary was yelling before she could think. "I told you not to track mud into the kitchen! Look what you've done!"

Lorraine made a yelping sound like a dog and buried her head into her knees. Maureen snarled her lip and narrowed her eyes—burning blue coals set too deep in the cherub face she should have already outgrown.

"It's okay, girls," Callum drawled softly, as though he hadn't spit venom moments before. "Your da will clean it up. Go play!"

He stepped between Rosemary and her children, and she felt a hatred twitch from elbow to fingertip. Maureen ran from her place in front of her older sister and flung her arms around her father's legs, burying her head into the soft layers of fabric he patched and never replaced. Callum bent down and kissed the top of Maureen's auburn head, which was already losing its penny undertone, closer each day to a muted brown.

"Go on, you," he said. Maureen walked to the door and put a hand on the knob.

"Lolo," she called, and cleared her throat as her small voice gave. "Come on."

Lorraine watched her mother, trembling, thin, and unmoving.

Callum hissed, "Do you *see*, Rosemary? Do you *see what you've done*?"

She loathed him. "Go and play hero, Callum."

He ran a hand through his sandy hair and took the smallest step back from her. "Who are you?"

Rosemary's voice was steel. "I am their *mother.*"

Callum took Maureen outside, and Rosemary was left with Lorraine. She slid from the chair, went to the cupboard where they kept the broom and dustbin, and whispered, "I'm sorry, Mama." Then she began to cry.

Many, many years later, young Delilah came into the cottage from the cold, covered in blood and mud without a single tear.

"Reckless girl!" Lorraine barked, pushing Delilah into the kitchen chair rather more forcefully than she needed. "Look what you've done!"

Lorraine pressed a hot cloth to the stained knees, chastising, and Rosemary witnessed her only granddaughter refuse her gathering tears.

Maureen stepped between them just so. "Don't blame Delilah for *gravity.*"

"Would you like to replace her ruined clothes, *Maureen*?"

"It's just a T-shirt, *Lorraine.*"

"I'll never get the blood out."

"I'm sorry, Mama," Delilah whispered.

"*Sorry* can't erase a stain, can it?" Lorraine spat back.

Maureen held a Popsicle out to Delilah, but Lorraine snatched it away and scowled.

"Delilah, this isn't sugar-free. You know that."

As her granddaughter's tears finally spilled hot and fast, Rosemary felt something hit her chest like a battering ram. And suddenly she heard Callum's voice again, crackling through time like acid down her spine.

Do you see, *Rosemary? Do you see what you've done?*

But soon after they returned home, and things had returned to normal, Rosemary had forgotten (perhaps, she thought now, intentionally) that Delilah might have been inheriting something she had never intended to pass down.

Now, at eighty-something years old, Rosemary could see the thinness that had begun to declare the presence of time in Delilah's eyelids—crinkling to eclipse the freckle-stars in worry—and she had the most peculiar feeling. Desperate and panicked, like something was happening. Someone was taking something, but she wasn't sure who or what.

"Damn the light, Delilah," Rosemary said, cupping her granddaughter's face. "We need to talk."

As she walked arm in arm with Delilah back toward the place where the land met the sea like the past met the future in a sudden and violent rift, Rosemary closed her eyes, only for a moment. She could feel her mother's hot breath on her ear.

Stupid, reckless girl. Look what you've done.

81

Mo

Mo watched her dying mother follow Deli into the dark. The creak of the door as it swung home, slow and determined, rang in Mo's heart like the tolling bell of something inevitable.

"She shouldn't be in the rain," Laurie said quietly. "She'll get sick."

"Mom is gonna do whatever she wants, Laurie, just like always."

Mo's hands shook. She pressed them to the countertop and leaned her weight against it, closed her eyes, and counted the seconds as she breathed in. Breathed out. She was alone with her sister for the first time in many, many years. "Did you know?"

Laurie's reply was high and reedy. "How could you even ask that?"

Mo leveled her sister with a look that said all the things Mo couldn't.

"No, okay, no." Laurie slumped into her chair. "She's been more tired and less, I don't know, sharp? But I figured it was one of her 'ailments.'"

Old wounds ached, reopened. The vibrant, horrid slash of a wedding turned into a battleground stung fresh. Mo studied the backs of her hands, so much like her mother's. "How *could* you act like that tonight, Lorraine?"

"I don't know what you—"

"If you want to play games, get out of my house."

Her sister squirmed at the table. "Fine. Maybe I said a few things that went . . . too far. But I wouldn't have had to if you hadn't pushed me! If you hadn't taken her in the first place!"

Twenty years. Twenty years between them, and Laurie was the same.

"Whisky?" Mo asked. "It's good stuff. Lachlan brought it."

"Ah, *Lachlan*, the kilted wonder boy."

Mo stilled long enough to say, "Last warning, Lorraine."

"Fine."

She pulled two glasses from the cabinet and blew into each to clear the dust that wasn't there, but she knew Laurie hated dust. Then she sat and let the chair take the weight of her—of everything. Mo took a long sip. Laurie held her glass between her hands on the table and didn't lift it.

"Mo," Laurie said in a small voice, "what are we gonna do?"

Her sister, soft and fragile and so easy to bruise, needing Mo to get her through the loss of a parent. Asking Mo to stop the impact before it happened. Asking her for the impossible.

She wondered, for the thousandth time, if she'd let her sister down—if everything that happened in Laurie's life could be traced back to that night and two little girls whispering in their beds.

"What we always do, Lolo," Mo said. At the sound of their childhood nickname, tears traced the grooves of her sister's face. Her *wrinkles*, this little girl. Time was a slippery thing.

Time . . . Mo thought, *and grief.*

"We're gonna survive." Mo reached for her sister's hand. "I'm with you."

"You're not with me," Laurie choked too loud in the subdued space, like a bark. She snatched her hand away. "You *left* me! And you *never* came back. You are a person who *leaves*."

Mo recoiled as her heart pounded and heat crept up her neck. She was trapped in time, somewhere between being here and being there, and she had to get out. Her eyes darted toward the door.

"See?" Laurie's laugh was stiff as she gestured toward the exit. "Even now."

Though she'd never said it aloud to anyone, Mo's greatest regret was leaving Laurie behind. She chose to save herself, and she left her sister to find a way to survive. Soft and sensitive, alone with a woman who didn't know how to love if she wasn't squeezing so tightly she left a mark. And it had cost Laurie dearly. It had cost Deli. It had cost them all.

At her core, Maureen McDonnell wasn't sure if she was a good person.

"I'm sorry," Mo rasped. "I'm so sorry, Laurie."

"For *what* exactly?"

"For leaving you with her."

Her sister stared with the burning resentment she'd been nursing for years. "It was awful," Laurie said, her voice dark. "It was *awful,* Maureen."

"I know—"

"Don't you dare," Laurie cut in. "You made me *choose.*" Mo winced. "Between my *only* sister and my mother. Because *you* left, Maureen. You made the great escape to this shitty house that our shitty dad left to his perfect daughter—the one who didn't remind him at all of the woman *he* married. He left you with a home. And he left me with the woman he chose to be our mother."

Mo's hands shook. "I did come back once."

Laurie's entire body went stiff. *"What?"*

"About a year after I left."

"What do you mean?"

"I came to your house. None of you were home. Mom showed up as I was leaving."

"She saw you?" Laurie asked.

"She told me nobody wanted me there. That I was dead to her. To *you.*"

"I never said that!"

"I know that now, but then? It was all still so fresh. I was still heartsick for her love."

Laurie made a face. "You knew what she was like."

"I know, but . . . Laurie, my biggest fear was that if I left you behind, you'd hate me. And when she confirmed it, I just . . . Then she said that Deli had seen a photo of me and asked who I was. And I . . ."

"Oh . . ."

"I left." Mo shrugged, tears running down her face. "Because what if it was all true?"

"I didn't know, Mo," Laurie said softly. "She told me you didn't want to see me."

"Ha! I suppose we should have seen that one coming."

"I suppose so."

Mo took another sip from her glass. Laurie's was still untouched.

"And now she's dying," Laurie said simply.

"Now she's dying."

Laurie looked at the ceiling and released a long breath. "I don't know how to feel about that."

For a beat, the two looked at each other, all the unsaid and forbidden things on the tips of their tongues.

Twenty years before, Mo McDonnell had seen no way to survive her family other than to escape it, and so she had. But the Mo that stood in her fraught oasis now, with the sister who had betrayed her, who *she* had betrayed, too—she knew better. Love could be a gnarled and knotted thing that would strain and pull until it was handled with deft hands. Mo had run away, and the love had never released its vise grip on her. It had snarled and spat and demanded to be known.

All these years later, Mo knew that *she* could be the person who held hurting things with open palms—who could love something for what it was and what it wanted to be, not for what it should have been if things had been fair and just.

Mo knew now that her sister was scared, and that Mo could learn to love her with proper expectations. She could protect her own heart at the same time.

Love and grief were the same thing, really . . . depending on the light.

And Mo suddenly knew that for this chapter in her life, twilight had come.

She broke into a laugh, deep and long, and felt the tension loosen in her chest as Laurie joined. The two of them shook with the absurdity of the night—the absurdity of the way there are no hard and fast rules about when you give up on the people you love—the way cruelty and admiration dress the same. Mo raised up her glass.

"To peace: May we find it, may we know it, may we keep it."

Laurie raised hers, too. "Here's to hoping." She took a sip and winced. "God, I don't know how you and Dad drink this shit. I just can't stomach it."

Mo smiled.

"So . . ." Laurie began again. "Did you see *her*? When you came back?"

"I . . ." Mo could almost hear her heart suffer another crack, like there was a real candy shaped thing in there being broken. "I tried."

"And?"

"And Beth was with someone else. I saw them getting out of her car—"

"The old Beetle!" Laurie interrupted, beaming, a flash of the sister Mo used to make daisy chains with outside. "I loved that car. The little flower vase was always full!"

Mo smiled even as her memory of Beth turned her eyes misty. "Beth would pick anything she found. Wildflowers, weeds. She'd steal poppies off the side of the road even though it was illegal to pick the state flower. She said they were nature's, and nature could give her flowers if it wanted to." It surprised her how well she could still mimic Beth as she added, *"'Plus! I'm a taxpayer!'"*

Laurie chuckled. "I remember . . . the poppies matched the paint. All that orange."

"Her favorite color."

A silence stretched between them in the wake of the evening's carnage. The fight, the screaming, the rain, and their mother. Deli—wandering out into the night.

And two sisters, finally saying things that had never been said.

"Laurie?" Mo whispered. "I did the best I could."

Laurie stared, unblinking.

"I didn't want to leave you," she choked out a sob. "I did the best I could."

"I know," Laurie said. "It's okay, Momo. It's okay."

Mo began to really cry, and Laurie squeezed her hand once then withdrew.

"I loved those little white flowers," Laurie said. Mo kept crying, but Laurie acted like she wasn't. It was a small act of grace. "I think they were in Princess Diana's wedding bouquet? What were they called again?"

"Lily of the valley," Mo said. "I got them for her in May. They're her birth flower."

"I just thought they were so pretty and delicate. So feminine."

"Deli told me they mean *the return of joy*."

"The return of joy?"

"Yep."

Mo remembered the first time she'd given them to her love—how tenderly Beth had taken the stem—how reverently she had accepted Mo's heart in her hands as she professed that Beth had been the return of *her* joy.

"Huh." Laurie drew circles on the tabletop with her fingernail. "When Mom dies, let's order them for her funeral."

Mo spit out the drink in her mouth, and the sisters laughed together in the little house where they had weathered blow after blow, doing their best to survive.

82

Mo

Mo settled into her favorite squishy chair in The Wallflower's Crown. Lachlan set a steaming mug of peppermint tea down and sat across from her. As always, she was buoyed in the company of her friend.

"So, your mum is really dying?"

"Soon, apparently."

"And are you going back?"

"I think so."

"How long would you be gone?"

"No idea."

They shared a bittersweet smile. So much time had passed in very little time at all.

"Right. And what do you need from me?"

Mo knew that Lachlan thought there was no hope with Deli, but Mo also knew he was wrong. Lachlan loved Deli the way Mo loved Beth.

Without end.

"I need you to look after her."

Lachlan's eyes widened. "She's staying?"

Mo shook her head, watching the steam rise from her mug. "I don't know." She blew on her tea, mulling over the decision that had just become clear. "I'm going back with my mom. And my sister."

Lachlan's face creased with concern. "Are you sure?"

Lachlan was protective. But Mo's choice wasn't about Laurie and Rosemary.

Laurie had always been too much like their mother, and Mo, just like her father. She'd thought of her McDonnell blood running strong as a good thing—evidence that she was not like the others. It wasn't until quite recently that Mo had wondered if, perhaps, she was a bit *too* like her father. One sister left behind and bitter, one sister gone away and alone.

No, Mo wasn't going because she'd been asked. She was going back because of the cycle she needed to end.

"I'm so proud of you, Lachlan."

He made a face.

"You have chosen to be an extraordinary man. You didn't just wake up one day and accept how the world had shaped you." She watched his beautiful eyes turn glassy. "And you will never be your father." He reached for her hand, and she took it gladly. It was the great joy of her life—to have Deli and Lachlan rely on her for comfort, friendship, and laughter. "If Deli stays?"

"I will always take care of her."

"I swear, Lachlan Scott, if you don't let her care for you, too, I'll sic Beans on you."

Lachlan laughed through his tears. He stood and pulled her into a hug.

"I love you, Mo."

"I love you, too, kid. And so does *she*."

Mo felt Lachlan's chest hitch softly. She rubbed his back as they stood, swaying lightly in the boy's pub.

"You both deserve to be happy, Lachlan. *Choose* to be happy." He nodded, wiping a tear from his cheek, and she smiled. How could she not? "Okay. Now. How about a round of Battleship?"

83

Deli

Deli heard a soft meow from the corner of her room.

"Beans! What in the . . . ?"

She toed the suitcases until one nudged back, and she unzipped it. Beans leaped out and aborted his plan to stowaway with just hours until she was leaving for California.

"Chicken," she said as she scratched his head. He closed his eyes and rubbed his face against her boot. "I'll miss you, too."

Knuckles tapped on her door.

"Hey," Aunt Mo said. "You got a second?"

"Sure."

"Great." She threw a bright orange knit cap at Deli. "Don't forget a towel!"

Deli followed the same path to the water she had the day she'd arrived. She'd gone numb since everything happened. When she'd walked away from Lachlan, every step was a stitch torn from the seam of her. By the time she got to the front door, she'd let a final tormented cry slip through her grasp, and then she'd just . . . stopped.

One second she was being pulled under the dark water, and the next she no longer needed to breathe. She supposed it was what she'd always done.

As Deli and Grandma Rosemary had talked on the cliffside, she'd been numb. Her grandma asked if she loved Trey anymore. If she loved Lachlan. If she felt at home in Fearnhall or if she felt like she belonged back with them. All the words strung together without purpose.

"I don't know," she'd said. "I don't care. It doesn't matter."

"What do you mean, it doesn't matter, darling? Please. Don't come home for me, Delilah," her grandma said. "You still have time."

Of course she was going home.

She'd ruined everything she had in California, but she couldn't stay in Scotland. She'd come on a selfish whim, and the best people in the world welcomed her into their home. And what had *she* done?

Ruined a wedding.

Broken a good man's heart.

Brought the cancer back into Aunt Mo's life.

She'd let everyone down, but of course she was going home. Her family needed her.

She would miss Aunt Mo so terribly—it was a punishment fitting of the crime. Come screw up her life, never see her again. That sounded fair.

Deli didn't realize she'd waded into the sea until she was waist deep. She hadn't felt the cold. As she got all the way to her aunt, she still didn't.

"Look at you! No fuss at all this time! Have you been swimming without me?" Aunt Mo's smile barely faltered in the face of Deli's detachment. She twirled in a circle, kicking underwater with her arms spread wide and face turned to the sky. "I *will* miss this place."

Deli's heart lurched in warning. "What do you mean, Aunt Mo?"

"Though I'm looking forward to some warm sand to nap on."

Deli couldn't believe what she was hearing. Her teeth started to chatter. "You . . . you can't *leave*?"

"Why not?"

Aunt Mo's tone was light and airy, like it was joy holding her up, not physics.

"You have Beans! And Mrs. Peevis! And the cottage! Your event calendar is booked for the summer. And who's going to take care of—"

The name wouldn't abandon her mouth.

"—Lachlan?" Aunt Mo asked.

"You don't have to go. I'll call you when things with Grandma get . . . When you need to come. I'll take care of it, Aunt Mo."

"It's not your job, Deli."

"But I can do it! And they need me. My mom needs me."

"Do they?"

If Deli had taken a second to *think* about how her choices would have impacted others before she had run away like a child, she might have seen it coming—the ending where their family's baggage burst from the grave and clutched Aunt Mo by the ankle. The ending where Deli dragged her down.

Stupid, reckless girl.

"I'm so, so sorry, Aunt Mo. I should have left you alone."

Deli's aunt studied her face, and Deli turned away.

"Deli," Aunt Mo said, "look at me."

The numbness was coming back as the cold retreated. Deli turned to face the woman she'd let down, ready to stomach the truth. The water lapped against the rocks, and a gull overhead cried out, and Aunt Mo's eyes were nearly the same color as the navy-gray ocean.

"Even if you'd brought an invading army, a plague, and a pack of homophobic dance moms to my door, I would have taken them all for the chance to have you back in my life, Deli.

"The thing is, I didn't leave well. You didn't bring my sister and mother with you. They were always there. It's well past time for me to clean up my mess, and I owe you the apology, not the other way around. I'm so sorry for that."

Aunt Mo wiped a tear from Deli's cheek she hadn't known was there.

"But this is your *home*, Aunt Mo. You belong here."

"It's your home, too."

Deli started to protest, but her aunt stopped her.

"As for the rest? I was hoping you'd take care of the cottage. And of course Peevie, and Beans, if you'll have him. You're perfectly capable of stepping in for any and all events—it would bring me so much joy to call it a family business.

"Everyone here *loves* you, Delilah. They really, truly love you. You have a family right here if you want it. And Lachlan?"

Aunt Mo tipped Deli's chin up so they were square on, face to face.

"I've lived long enough to know that you two won't find anything better. Understand?"

The tears were coming softly. They tugged on Deli's composure. She nodded.

"And hear me now, Delilah MacDonald, because the next part is the hard part. Your mother loves you. She *loves* you. But she cannot change. Some people think love is something you earn. My mother never understood how to choose differently, and neither does yours—"

Deli caught her breath as Aunt Mo's words moved into the same room in her heart where Grandma Rosemary's cliffside plea had been locked away.

"—but we do. I can't tell you what to do, Deli, but you will always have a home with me, no matter where or when. You do have love here. Someone who wants to care for you. I know it's not the same, but different is a *choice.*"

Deli's heart was pounding. It was all too much. She pressed her hands to her temples. "It *hurts.*"

Aunt Mo pulled Deli's hands into her own while they bobbed in a rising tide, lifted by the pull of the moon over a world that kept turning.

"Any love lost is a love that needs grieving. But Delilah? Some love comes easy. Letting someone love you, even when you haven't *earned it,* doesn't make you a bad person. Okay?"

Deli cried. "Okay."

"And as for me belonging here? I get to decide where I belong. And *so do you.* Got it?"

Deli watched a cloud drift across the iron sky over an endless sea. "Got it."

They swam back to shore with only hours left.

Deli didn't know what to believe.

84

Deli

Deli walked and walked, trying to decide.

She ached for her life before Scotland. She used to be so sure.

Deli remembered reading about a memorial in Edinburgh to honor the dog who lay by his owner's grave until the day the dog could join him in the ground. She'd cried as she gazed at the photo of his small statue, nose rubbed brassy by millions of grief's pilgrims—a hero for those whose loyalty would not yield to death.

Who was she if Trey only loved her when someone else might take her away?

And who was she if Chloe didn't love her at all anymore?

Deli wasn't left behind by death's cruel choosing. She was an old dog with tired bones, unwanted and abandoned in an unfamiliar place, hoping for a way home.

And she suddenly knew without any question—there was no path *home*. Her life as she'd always known it was a haunted house—pale and empty except for her and her imaginary friends. Trey was asking another girl to marry him when Deli had thought for so long his heart lie waiting for his head to see the light. How silly she'd been to think Trey would ever wake up.

She thought of her mother and felt her knees threaten to go weak. Her mother, whose unconditional love she pined for in the very core of her. If only she'd never tasted it, she might have found peace in the empty place. But her mother did love her, and Deli did have all-consuming memories—moments of being a girl with a mom who never bit. It wasn't that Deli was entirely neglected that caused her phantom heart to ache. It was that her mom loved her *so much,* Deli feared it made her animal.

Still, her stupid, reckless hope refused to stay unborn. Each time, Deli passed it, so vulnerable, to her mother's hands. Each time, Deli's hope was left bleeding, ready to be buried.

It all, of course, had led her to Chloe. A family she had chosen and that kept on choosing her. Sometimes, in the wrong light, Deli looked at her best friend and saw her mother—but then a cloud would shift and Chloe still loved her, and everything was fine.

Deli didn't grow up in a house where people *knew* her. But Chloe did. Chloe knew Deli's first crush, where she hid the keys to her fuzzy diary, and which Powerpuff Girl was most like her. Chloe knew Deli's favorite color when they were six, then twelve, then fifteen, then twenty-five. Chloe knew that when Aunt Mo left, Deli had drawn a map in the clover-speckled dirt and made a plan to escape, too. SATs, driver's licenses, bad bangs, and first rent checks—there wasn't a bit of Deli's life Chloe hadn't witnessed. There wasn't a single other person who'd known every Deli that had once lived, back through time.

If Deli MacDonald had built her life upon pillars, Chloe had been one of them. Now it had crumbled, and Deli was scrambling for purchase in the world as she fell. How much easier it would have been to know what to do now if she could call her best friend and talk it through. How quickly would Deli make a decision if she hadn't been so wrong about the best friend she'd loved so long? Best friends are different than romances. Chloe had moved into Deli's heart, and Deli had never planned for what would happen if she left.

If Deli hadn't watched the person she was *most* sure of in her life drive away and leave her on the side of an unfamiliar road, would she already know if she should stay or go? She had been so, *so* wrong in a way she'd never even thought to question. Deli wasn't reliable.

Deli, and whatever broken part of her chose which people to love, could not be trusted.

Even so, she would have given the world to sit under the lunch tree again.

She wanted to find that little dog and lay in a graveyard beside his small warm body with a heart shaped crooked like hers. Two living beings, loyal to ghosts.

And there on the road alongside the sea, Deli sat on the ground and gave in to the anguish. It was the sort of thing that swallowed up every inch of space in a person—an onslaught of hungry, desperate longing. Deli cried until her fingertips went numb in the cold. She wrapped her arms around her middle and rocked herself in a patch of white clover. She listened to the water and let the wind carry her tears in wild paths and away. She stayed there until she felt a sudden warmth and wet on her hand.

"Angus! You scared me. Are you lost?"

The dog walked a few feet up the road and paused.

"You want me to come with you?"

Angus huffed. Deli slipped her phone from her pocket, hoping for service, but found none. She saw a small mailbox ahead of them and walked toward it. Angus's eyes were focused as he flanked her, like he was driving her somewhere with urgency. Her heart picked up as she neared the mailbox and read.

CAMPBELL FARM

"Angus—what's wrong, boy? Where's Cairn?" Deli jogged behind Angus toward the bend ahead of her. The wind came to life and brought a smell so familiar but so out of place she couldn't name it. Then she saw, and she knew.

A great plume of wildfire smoke was rising from the hills of Cairn and Douglas's land.

85

Deli

"CAIRN!"

Deli raced up the unpaved path toward the fire. She could see the silhouette of Cairn's buggy at the top of the hill—harsh black against the smoke behind it—and what looked to be the bent knees of someone lying on the ground.

She had to fix it. She had to get to him. Rocks skittered down the path when her feet slipped. Adrenaline pumped through her as she crested the hill.

It was Cairn, lying in the grass with arms flung above his head and face turned toward the sky.

Angus shot past her as she closed the gap.

Deli hit her knees beside him as Angus licked his face. Cairn moaned, moving slowly. Her hands flapped uselessly over him. "What hurts? What happened?"

"Huh?" Cairn sat up in a half crunch. "When did you get here? And why?"

Deli's mouth fell open. "I thought . . . I thought you'd fallen or the smoke had gotten you or"—she waved a frenzied hand at the growing, suffocating wall, far too close for comfort—"Cairn, your farm is on fire!"

"I know."

"You know?"

"Aye. I know."

"Then why aren't we running? Or trying to like . . . put it out?"

"Well." Cairn sucked his teeth and propped himself on his elbows. "Because I started it. And I don't have a bucket that big."

She stared. He stared back.

"Okay, Cairn, but, um . . . why did you light your own land on fire, CAN I ASK?"

He tilted his head. "How else would I do it?"

"Do what? Destroy everything?"

"No, darlin'. *Save* it."

She tried for a smile and felt her eye twitch. "IT'S. ON. FIRE."

"Yes, Deli. *Fire.* Good."

She threw her hands up. "But Angus came and found me! He thought you were hurt. You're not hurt?"

"Did he, now?" Cairn ruffled the dog's fur. "No, Deli, I'm not hurt. Was just admiring the clouds while I waited."

"Waited for *what*?"

"For the heather to burn, of course."

She whipped around to see the heather, *all* the heather, ablaze. There was an ugly black scar in the fire's wake—ashes where there had been life. She fought the impulse to run to it.

"But . . ." Deli sounded small, like a child. "It was so beautiful."

"No, it was beautiful last year. That was all dead."

Deli's alarm surged. "No it wasn't! There was still color, Cairn. There were spots where it was living. It was going to survive and you just . . . You *killed* it!"

Cairn studied her face.

"Deli, if you'd tried to pull that heather from the ground, the flowers would have come off the plant and turned to dust in your hand. Most flowers—they have their day in the sun and they go soft. Turn back to the soil. But heather goes hard, holding on to time that doesn't belong to it anymore. It dies with clenched fists. Do you understand?"

Here was Cairn, a gnarled thing himself, tending to her soreness. She shook her head.

Cairn nodded. "Sheep are the only things that can stomach the stuff. It's why so much of this land is left to the sorry old lot who farm them." He chuckled softly. "But they don't eat enough, and it chokes the earth. I *have* to burn it. Because the soil needs to churn, and the new needs to grow. Even if it seems unkind, or it doesn't look dead, it was time. It would suffocate its own seeds if I didn't help it move on."

"It was already d—" Her voice broke and the first tear fell. She inhaled jerkily. "Dead?"

"Yes, Deli. It was already dead."

How long had she been watering something that was already dead? Bringing it sunlight, trying to nurse it back to health because there were still parts of it that seemed alive. What was she supposed to do? Bury something . . . *someone* still blooming? Leave her haunted house with her mangled heart in a suitcase, and burn the whole thing down?

She sat back and pulled her knees up as she buried her face in her hands. Angus lay beside her, his nose wedged between her thigh and belly. Then, to her true surprise, Cairn wrapped an arm around her and gently pulled her toward him until her head fell onto his shoulder.

The last of the dam inside her was swept away as she wept and Cairn ran his hand up and down her upper arm, leaning his cheek against her hair. In the flickering shadow of the fire, Cairn's penchant for long, quiet stretches was finally welcome.

The light began to turn toward dusk—promising to sink her last moments into the horizon.

"Cairn? How do you know?"

"Know what, darlin'?"

"That something new will grow?"

The wind changed, and the smoke shifted, and sunlight fell upon the three of them, sitting in the grass. Cairn dropped a grandfatherly kiss onto her head.

"Because it always does. You just need to make it room."

86

Lachlan

Lachlan should have known.

But he was thinking about the envelope he'd left on the kitchen table—about standing on a cliff's edge, looking down to where two orange caps floated in the sea. He should have seen it right away, but he didn't. His thoughts were with someone else.

"Whisky, neat," the stranger said. It was a statement, not a request.

"We've got plenty of whisky." Lachlan rubbed a nonexistent spot out of an already sparkling glass. "Which would you like?"

"Whatever's most expensive."

Lachlan chuckled to himself as he reached for the highest shelf.

"Something funny?"

"Not at all," he said as he popped the cork from the bottle and turned to face his guest. "We just don't get that answer much around here."

The man cast a glance toward where Hannah, Andrew, and Douglas sat playing cards by the fire and teasing each other gently. "Obviously."

Lachlan already couldn't wait to never see the man again. He pushed the glass across the polished wood. The stranger took a sip.

He held the glass up to the light. "At least this place has *one* thing going for it."

Lachlan raised an eyebrow. "First time in town, then?"

"First and last."

"What brought you?"

The man contemplated the glass with sudden nonchalance, all traces of coldness replaced by a charm and ease. "A girl. I'm here to bring her home."

Then he knew, and Lachlan felt a great caving in his chest. The accent, the affect, the way he'd answered. This had to be the man Deli was actually in love with. *This* was Trey Evans.

Lachlan cleared his throat. "A girl?"

"What else?" Trey's mouth curled up to reveal too-white teeth.

Lachlan could hear his heartbeat in his ears. "Who's the lucky lady?"

"She's my best friend," Trey replied, setting the glass down on the bar and meeting Lachlan's eyes. "She makes me a better man."

"Sounds like one of a kind." Lachlan saw Hannah look up from where she sat and go still.

"Well, yeah, in a way. But *this* is the girl I just broke up with to come here."

Trey thrust his phone toward Lachlan. A girl who couldn't have been older than twenty-two stared at the camera in a sultry pout, draped in a barely there dress that Lachlan could not imagine a single woman on earth moving comfortably in.

"See?" Trey said. "Hot."

"But like you said," Lachlan said, holding back the torrent of dislike and dread, "nothing compares to the real thing."

Trey sighed. "Yeah, 'love.'" He rolled his eyes, and Lachlan wanted to pluck them out of his face. "I just thought I had a little more time before I had to settle down with the one with the good personality, you know what I mean?"

Of all the times in his life that another man had assumed Lachlan would happily participate in the shared degradation of women because none were present, none had made him angrier than the man Deli was in love with referring to her as "the one with the good personality."

He wanted to reach over the bar and stop Trey's talking with his hands around his neck. At the very least, he wanted to throw him out, heavy emphasis on the *throw*, but he couldn't. This was the man she *loved*. Lachlan had already hurt her enough.

It wasn't for him to decide.

"Can't say that I know what you mean, no." Lachlan's fingers twitched toward a fist. "Why now?"

"Huh?"

"Why 'settle' now?"

Trey drained his glass. He tapped the rim while he gave a little chuckle, but his eyes were hard and sharp. "Can I get some service over here?"

Lachlan reached for the bottle.

"She left me." Trey sighed as Lachlan twisted the cork. "Just ran off one day to this godforsaken place." Lachlan began to pour. "I thought . . . I mean, I knew she was sort of in love with me, so I thought she'd be around. But then she boarded a plane to *Scotland*, of all places, and now she's stopped answering me entirely. Won't take my calls."

Lachlan looked up. "She won't?"

"Jesus, man!" Trey shoved away from the bar as a pool of whisky trickled off the edge.

Lachlan wiped at the spill with a towel and tipped the overflowing glass into the sink. "My mistake," he said as he slid it back toward Trey. "It's on the house."

Trey stood across from Lachlan, staring. The air got tight. Waiting.

"What did you say your name was? Something about you is . . . familiar."

Lachlan held his gaze. "I get that a lot."

Trey's mouth twitched up. He sipped and spat back into the full glass.

"Sorry, *friend*." Trey set the soiled whisky down and plucked a thistle out of the bud vase on the bar. "I've got a date." Then he turned and walked out into the drizzling gray.

Hannah stood and crossed her arms over her chest.

"I know," Lachlan said. "But it's not up to me."

Andrew gestured at the glass still swirling with the thick contents of Trey's mouth. "That was a good bit of whisky."

"Nah. I keep a bottle of the cheapest swill on the top shelf. He didn't even notice." Lachlan dumped it in the sink.

He held his shaking hand out in front of him and flexed it once, twice. He couldn't believe he was letting that man go to the woman he loved. Lachlan pressed the heels of his palms into his eyes, fighting back the panic. He should warn her about who Trey really was, but what if she already knew?

What if *that* was what Deli thought she deserved?

Strong fingers wrapped around either wrist and pulled gently.

"Hannah, please, I—" he began, but he fell quiet as she touched his cheek. She held out her sketchbook, flipping past a pretty strawberry blonde woman with orange nail polish, an old man sunning on a beach, and a puppy. Then she opened to a drawing of Deli the night she'd first sat in his pub.

The night Hannah had chosen Lachlan's deepest desire to draw. The night Lachlan had fallen in love.

His throat was too tight to do anything but whisper. "She doesn't want me."

Hannah tore the page from the rest, folded it into a square, and tucked it in Lachlan's shirt pocket. As the sketch found a home above his heart, Lachlan swore he felt it spark.

87

Deli

Deli neared the cottage where her bags were packed, replaying her conversation with Grandma Rosemary on the cliffside.

"Listen, here," Grandma Rosemary said after she'd lowered herself to the muddy ground and hung her feet over the edge, like a woman who'd never been sick a day in her long life. "Delilah, there are many things to say."

"You don't need to, Grandm—"

"Hush." She pressed an elegant finger with a slightly chipped nail to her lips and took a swig of the rained-down wine. "This may be my last chance to set things right."

Deli took the glass back.

"The silly thing about dying, if you're lucky—which I do consider myself—is that it gives you brilliant vision, but so few days to see. Don't cry, darling." Grandma Rosemary ran a thumb under Deli's left eye, and Deli could feel her hand shaking. "This is life. And I need you to pay attention. That's important. God, Deli, I wish I'd paid attention."

Then, in just thirty minutes, her grandmother did what Deli would come to understand as one of the most courageous acts she'd ever see. Rosemary McDonnell named the many things she believed she'd gotten wrong.

"Do you remember when I used to throw you tea parties? With that miniature plastic set I got you for your birthday?"

Deli nodded as she passed the wine back over. "Except we had juice instead of tea."

"Yes, well"—Grandma Rosemary held the wineglass up to the moonlight, tilted the dark liquid back and forth—"besides the taste, I was terrified of what caffeine would do to you. You were already so wild."

"I know." Deli watched the charcoal horizon going black. Her grandmother passed her the glass. "You always made me brush my hair."

Then Grandma Rosemary gripped Deli's wrist and clutched her hand. "I should have never made you brush your hair, Delilah. I mean it." She touched the dark, dripping ends of what had been Deli's curls with an adoration reserved for things set apart. "Oh, Deli . . . I should have never made you brush your hair."

They had walked arm in arm back to the cottage, but they didn't go inside. Grandma Rosemary wanted to search for something she'd buried in the garden.

"You really haven't seen it? Just a small pile of stones, about that high?" She kneeled to show the lost marker's height, squinting into the dark.

"No, Grandma. It's been a long time for something like that to still be here."

"What a shame." Grandma Rosemary looked so fragile under the silhouette of Highland mountains. "You think you'll stay who you are when you're young forever. And those special moments that stop time . . . You think, of course, you could never forget them. God, how much I have forgotten, Deli. How many versions of me I have forgotten, too."

Just before they went inside, Grandma Rosemary took Deli's hands. As she met her grandma's eyes Deli could *see* who her grandmother must have been as a little girl. And Deli knew she would have spent hours with her in the garden, telling tall tales and dreaming up worlds.

What was it called, she wondered, to ache for a childhood friendship forbidden by place and time?

"You still have time, Delilah. Time to *live*, like you truly mean to be here. I was too much a coward, it turns out." Rosemary laughed, her faded lipstick cast pink in the window's glow. "But you? I have never been more sure I've known a lion's heart." Grandma Rosemary pressed her palm to Deli's chest. "Delila—Deli? My brilliant, wild girl . . . Please tell me it's still in there?"

They had booked flights home that night. Grandma Rosemary insisted on paying and selected the refundable option for Deli's ticket. Now, as she walked through the magical garden and while heather smoke still tinged the air, leaving was less than an hour away.

She slipped in the back and went straight to the room she was sharing with Aunt Mo while the family was there to hide in case they were around, but the cottage was empty. Deli decided to spend her last moments adding the final flowers from Scotland to her dictionary.

She had just finished white clover (*will you think of me?; I promise)* when her aunt, mother, and grandmother came in with rustling shopping bags from their last minute trip for "suitable airplane snacks." She kept quiet where she sat in her room.

"Where's Delilah?" her grandma asked.

"Out for a walk," Aunt Mo said.

Lorraine sighed. "If she makes us miss our flight, I swear to—Oh! What's this?"

There was a rustling sound, then one like paper being ripped.

"Where did these come from?" Lorraine sounded suspicious.

But Aunt Mo's voice was warm. "They must be from her and Lachlan's photo shoot."

"Isn't she beautiful?" Grandma Rosemary said.

Deli's eyes widened and her pulse quickened at the thought of anyone else seeing those shots—the way Lachlan had looked at her.

He rolled through her heart like thunder.

"Hmm," her mother mused. "These are good photos of her, actually. Maybe I should use one when I send the follow up to that gossip magazine."

"What?" Aunt Mo's voice was hard.

Deli heard a photo hit the ground and her mother's response.

"What is *this* doing in here?"

"What do you mean 'follow up,' Laurie?"

"Hmm?" Her mother sounded distracted as she turned another page. "Oh, I sent off those photos of Deli and William."

Deli went still. She had blamed Lachlan—had thought he had been so wrapped up in the tension with his brother that he'd used her as a pawn in an endless chess match and told himself it was for her good. But if it wasn't Lachlan . . .

She thought back through his reaction on the dance floor, his reaction when he thought William was going to walk in on them . . .

Lachlan, as a boy hiding his brother in quiet rooms.

Lachlan, as a boy who couldn't protect his mother.

Lachlan stepping between her and a parent's rage. And she had punished him for it.

But perhaps more than realizing it was her mother who had sent the photo for some reason Deli was sure she didn't deserve, it was hearing her mom call her *Deli*, not Delilah—only when she thought Deli wouldn't hear—that finally made it clear.

The three women jumped at the sound of Deli's bedroom door slamming against the wall with the force of her anger. Her mother tried to hide the photos behind her back.

"It was *you*?"

Lorraine's cheeks flushed. "Oh, hi. We didn't think you were home."

"*Why*, Mom? What could I have possibly done to deserve tha—" Deli saw the envelope, torn and discarded, on the table. Something blue and papery was still inside. She pushed past her mother and picked it up.

Her name was written on the front in Lachlan's handwriting. Inside was a small note and something that drifted into her hand.

Deli,

May you know a love deserving of you.
May you see yourself as you are.
May you forever be free.

In her palm was a pressed, single bloom with scalloped edges. A Scottish bluebell, turned inside out. Deli knelt to retrieve the photo her mother had discarded where it lay upturned between them.

"Now, Delilah, I know the way you get! Don't be upset at *me.* It's not my fault I had to go to such lengths when you refused to listen to reason!"

Deli held a new print of the first photo Lachlan ever took of her—a larger and sharper shot of the little girl and the cottage by the sea. She could *see* him behind the camera.

Just be yourself!

She spun on her mother. "Those are not yours."

Lorraine gasped and jerked the photos away as Deli reached for them. They flew from her grip and scattered across the floor.

Grandma Rosemary's tone was sharp as she said, "Lorraine, *please.* Control yourself."

The three unexpected knocks on the cottage door were sharp, too.

A voice Deli could have recognized anywhere called her name. Lorraine's face lit up with recognition. She strode to the door while Deli remained glued to the spot.

How? How could he be there?

"Oh my god! What a sight for sore eyes!"

If someone had asked Deli to guess what was about to happen, she would have never gotten it right. Even though she heard his voice. Even though she could kind of *see* him on the other side of her mother. Even though she knew, logically, he was there. There was simply no part of her that could believe Deli MacDonald was living in a timeline where Trey Evans was, once again, standing in her doorway.

Lorraine threw her arms around Trey Evans's neck as he smiled and laughed, but his eyes went straight to Deli. Ice shot through her in jagged lines that, for once, only felt cold.

"Trey, what are you doing here?" Deli asked as he stepped in, ignoring the hissing cat hiding under the couch. Trey plucked a photo from under his shoe. Deli watched his eyes splinter as he held the print of Lachlan's kilt and her hand clutching a small bundle of heather.

Protection.

"Deli, hi."

"Trey, *what are you doing here?*"

Trey reached for her arm, but she recoiled just enough that he stopped.

"Um, can we talk in private, please?"

She cast her eyes around the small home. "There is no private here."

"Outside, then?" he whispered. "I need to talk to you."

Deli narrowed her eyes in sync with Aunt Mo. "Uh, sure."

Lorraine tapped at her watch. "We need to leave in a few minutes!"

Deli followed Trey out the door and closed it behind her. He stopped on the heather-sown path and turned, holding out a thistle. "This is for you."

She didn't want the bloom that cried *retaliation*. She couldn't believe what she was seeing. Trey, *again*, finding her at the eleventh hour when he was sure she was about to quit him. This time, on the other side of the world. And this time while he had at least a girlfriend, probably a fiancée, back in Los Angeles.

"Again, Trey," Deli said. *"What the fuck are you actually doing here?"*

"Aren't you happy to see me?"

"Aren't you engaged?"

"Well, I . . . not yet . . ."

"Trey." She said his name in the way she always had when she needed him to hear her.

"You haven't answered my texts or my calls."

"So you . . . flew to Scotland?"

"I needed to see you."

She threw her hands in the air. "Why, Trey? What do you need from me that you don't already have? What *more* could you possibly need from me?"

A peal of thunder rumbled above as Trey Evans did the last thing she expected. He dropped to one knee with a small box in his hand.

"Marry me."

The vintage wedding ring that his mother had once carefully shown her—passed from daughter to daughter—sparkled against red velvet.

Deli's eyes moved between the ring and Trey's face, over and over, trying to understand. She saw him do a micro eye roll as he waited. He cleared his throat.

"Alright, alright. You were right. We've never been just friends. Only, I didn't realize how serious your—*my* feelings were for you until you were gone, and it was like someone had severed my arm overnight."

A picture of someone axe-chopping Trey's arm off in his pristine bedroom bounced around her brain.

"I missed you. I told you that, to be fair—I think I texted you? It doesn't matter—not important. Then I saw that photo of you with someone else and I just . . . I knew. I knew something was different. I knew I loved you. And then a few days ago that article about you and *him* came out, I knew I couldn't let you get away from me."

Trey dropped his head. When he looked at her again, finally sure of what he wanted, with the eyes made of ice and sky she'd loved for so long, Deli was sure, too.

"Will you marry me, Delilah MacDonald?"

Everything she'd ever wanted, finally hers for the taking.

She felt so much relief as she told Trey, "No."

His smile turned brittle. "What?"

"Umm . . ." Deli tried to read his expression. He may not have heard her. It was getting windy. "Did you really not hear me, or . . . ?"

His nostrils flared. "What do you mean, *no*?"

"Is that . . ." She paused, squinting. "Is that a real question?"

Trey stood in an abrupt jolt. He waggled the ring in front of her face, then snapped it closed and shoved it in his coat pocket with an almost comical frown.

"I mean, seriously, Deli—what are you thinking?"

She was thinking so many things. He wouldn't like most of them. "I'm thin—"

"Do you even *know* how many girls would kill to be in your position right now? And you said you loved me! That you've"—he mimicked her voice and air quoted—"'always loved me.' What happened to that, huh?"

He paced back and forth on the small walkway and ran his hands through his hair. There was so much product it stood in highlighted peaks after he pulled it through his fingers.

"I've been good to you, okay?" Trey's voice was turning high and needy. "You know, I've turned down Chloe like *three* times!" He held up three fingers. "Three!"

As soon as he said it, it all made sense. Chloe had never been good at being happy for Deli if Deli had something Chloe wanted. Of *course*.

"And it's like—what? Am I not *good* enough for you? You get a little attention from an inbred country giant and you think they'll be lining up for you out there? Well, trust me"—he snorted—"they're *not*."

Trey tried to slice through her with his eyes, to level her with the look that always made her take it back, talk him down.

"*Think* about this, Delilah." He poked himself very hard in the temple, many, many times. "THINK."

But Deli didn't need to think. She finally, finally knew. She chuckled, and the look on his face turned it into a laugh.

"Don't laugh!"

Trey squared his shoulders bravely and angled himself to look up at her with desperate, sad eyes. He delivered his line. "I don't even know who you *are* anymore, Deli."

"I know." She put a hand on his cheek and kissed the other. "Isn't it *great*?" She spun around, reaching for the handle.

"Wait . . ." Bravado leaked out of his voice. "Where are you going?"

"Trey, when I come back out here, I don't want to see you anywhere near *my house*."

"But!" He was the most baffled looking man alive. "We can still be friends, right?"

Deli stared in open astonishment at Trey and his . . . everything. She couldn't believe, after so mortifyingly, heartbreakingly, unbearably long, she was free.

"Absolutely not."

Then she turned to face her mother and slammed the door on Trey Evans.

"HAVE YOU LOST YOUR MIND, DELILAH?!" Lorraine's face was turning red. "Trey has been magically convinced to *propose* to you, and you *turn him down*?"

Deli walked straight past her.

"Grandma?"

Rosemary McDonnell wrapped a hand around each of her forearms, pressed her forehead to her granddaughter's, and whispered, "You still have *time*, Delilah." Deli saw her grandmother cry for the first and the last time. "Don't waste it."

Deli nodded. "I love you. So much."

Grandma Rosemary beamed and cupped Deli's cheek, brushing a thumb across the freckles beneath her eye. "Oh, darling. You have *no* idea."

Deli turned to Aunt Mo as the tears began to gather. "Aunt Mo?"

She stepped forward with a wicked grin. "Yes?"

"Sir Beans will be expecting postcards. Lots. With palm trees and shit."

Aunt Mo tossed Deli a small, silver key ring. "Everything you need is already written down."

"What are you talking about?" Lorraine snapped. "What's going on?"

Then Deli faced her mother and took her in—a scared little girl who hated the cottage for everything it took from her. She wished she could take that pain away, but she couldn't. She couldn't go back and undo the things that had happened in her mom's life.

She could only choose her own.

She closed the gap between them in two strides and wrapped her arms around her mother, who went completely stiff. Deli breathed in the smell of her shampoo. It had always been the same, her whole entire life.

"Mom, I love you. I *love you.*" She placed her hands on her mother's shoulders and looked her in the eye. "But I deserve better."

"Well, I don't know *what* you're talking about, Delilah, but—"

Grandma Rosemary cut her off. "Oh, Lorraine, would you give it a rest?"

Deli opened the door as her mother spun on Grandma Rosemary. She slipped the keys in her pocket and peeked over her shoulder at her aunt, who was waiting with a grin. The air smelled like rain. Aunt Mo shooed Deli away and winked, mouthing, *Go go go!*

She got so far before her mother noticed, Deli could barely make out the sound of her voice.

"Delilah MacDonald, *get back here*!"

But Deli wasn't listening.

Not anymore.

88

Lachlan

About an hour after he'd first arrived, Trey Evans walked back into Lachlan's pub, dripping in Scottish rain, trembling with anger.

He did not say hello. "Drink."

Lachlan poured another glass of cheap swill. He tried not to hope. "Back already?"

"Obviously," Trey growled.

Across the room, Hannah was watching intently, her eyes narrowed.

Lachlan slid the glass across the bar. "Did you tell her you love her?"

Trey's eyes snapped up from the thistle he still twirled in his fingers. "None of your fucking business."

Lachlan kept his voice level. "So, it went well, then?"

Trey's fist flexed open, then closed, then wrapped around the glass and brought it to his lips. He drank, wincing, but he didn't stop, and he swallowed hard.

Then he reared his arm back and threw the glass against the ground. The sound of the shattering brought all the dull chatter in the pub to a standstill.

"Another."

Lachlan had spent his entire life proving he was not a violent man. He forced his hand to stay steady as he reached for a new glass.

"That." Trey pointed at the tartan fabric Lachlan's father had proudly pinned to the wall of The Wallflower's Crown. "I knew I recognized it from Deli's picture." He leaned toward Lachlan and said so low it was nearly a whisper, "I knew I recognized *you*."

"It's nice to have fans."

Trey's smirk was vile. "You have no idea."

The door to the back creaked as it swung open.

"But I do."

William Scott strode into the silent pub and towered over Trey with a wide smile. He slung a rag over his shoulder and leaned casually on the counter, as always, at ease on a stage.

Trey Evans sounded like he was choking on his tongue. *"You."*

"Hiya, Trey. You're gonna have to pay for that glass."

"What are you doing here, Scott?" Trey snarled.

Lachlan looked sideways at his brother.

"This is my brother's pub, Evans. Where are my manners? Lachlan, Trey. Trey, Lachlan. Trey and I know each other from the biz—lotta time at auditions in the old days. We used to get calls for the same stuff, you know."

Lachlan smirked. "Is that right?"

Trey was silent. His eyes were murderous.

Will's smile only widened. "Well, I don't audition much anymore. Last one I saw you on was for *The Highlander*, right? But good old Trey's still out there, trying his best."

Lachlan stuck out his lip at Trey. "Aw. Must be tough never getting what you want."

"I *do* have what I want," Trey spat through clenched teeth.

"Apparently not, or you'd be with her. Not here with us, throwing a tantrum."

Trey Evans stood and squared his shoulders.

"That bitch?" Trey said. "You think I care that she didn't want to marry me? I was doing her a favor. It was charity."

Will stood to his full height and began to roll up his sleeves.

Trey had said *marry* him? A rush of relief ran through Lachlan and collided with the ache in his heart. She'd said no. She was safe. She wasn't with Trey. That could be enough.

Even if Deli wouldn't have him, Lachlan could make that be enough.

Trey laughed, low and venomous, and watched Lachlan with a quirked head in a cruel sort of curiosity. Lachlan knew his brother. He knew that whatever happened next would get Trey exactly what he wanted—*attention.* He tried to catch William's eye, but he was watching Trey. Ready.

"I don't know what she thinks she'll find here, but Deli MacDonald isn't worth my—hell, *anyone's* time."

Lachlan shifted his stance.

"As if anyone could sweep *Deli* off her fee—"

The sound of a fist hitting a face rippled through the air, fleshy and solid. Trey Evans dropped to the ground and went silent.

Hannah shook her hand out as she stared down at the pile of wet designer clothes and pitiful man at her feet. "He talks too much."

Will's jaw hung open. "Jesus, Hannah, what a fuckin' line!"

Lachlan burst with laughter as he rushed around the bar and swept her into his arms. "Welcome back."

"Put me down, boy," Hannah said. "You're making a scene." He twirled her one more time and set her on her feet. "What are you still doing here?"

All the regulars were gathered in a semicircle. Lachlan realized if it hadn't been Hannah who landed the quieting blow, it would have been someone else. Someone else who loved Deli, who loved Mo, and who loved him. This was his family. And Lachlan felt, perhaps for the first time, that no matter who came or went, he would never be alone.

Then something Trey had said hit home.

. . . what she thinks she'll find here.

Here.

Could that mean?

He dug the keys from his pocket and tossed them to Will.

"Lock up for me?"

"Aye." Will grinned. "But we'll not be done till we've drained the last of this!" He reached behind the bar and hoisted a mostly full bottle of Lagavulin.

"That'll cost you." Lachlan smiled as he put on his coat.

"It's on the house, or my name's not SCOTT!" Will roared. The small but hearty crowd cheered.

Lachlan pushed open the door, but Hannah grabbed his arm.

"Lad," she said, low enough for just them to hear, "all this nonsense about her not loving you? It's just that. Nonsense."

"She rejected me, Hannah. She might again. I'm just going to make sure she's okay."

"No," Hannah said softly. "She rejected *herself*. But now?" She gestured toward Trey, who was beginning to stir. Graham and William were standing over him, and Lachlan was tempted, only for a moment, to stay and watch the two toss Trey Evans into the mud. "Now she's ready."

"Ready for what?"

"For the way love *changes* you." Her voice was as warm and sure as he remembered. "The question is: Are *you*?"

Lachlan imagined what happened next, and the two roads he could take. He could be brave, or he could be safe. He thought about what it would feel like to spend his entire life knowing that he hadn't said what he should have.

He'd made himself a promise once. He intended to keep it.

He would carry his gentle heart, and he would never let fear make it hardened.

As he stood in the threshold of The Wallflower's Crown, named for his mother's fear and the place where he'd watched his father live and die the life of a coward, Lachlan finally understood just how unalike they really were.

He grinned at Hannah. "I think I am."

"Good." Hannah smiled. "Then go."

"Wait." Lachlan turned back toward the stairs. "One more thing."

A few minutes later he came down to a chorus of hoots and whistles. He paused and took one more long look at the people who had always loved him.

Then Lachlan Scott ran, heart in his hand, into the falling rain.

89

Deli

Deli MacDonald knelt at the cliff's edge and watched the blood trace a path from her knee to her formerly white sock. She'd run like she was still nine years old, and her ankle had seized in the cold.

"Well. At least the rain's cleared," she muttered as she lifted a long stem with a starburst of bright purple flowers toward her to look. It was growing through a patch of blooming heather. "I wonder what you are?"

"Wild mountain thyme." The sound of his voice behind her sent goosebumps across her arms, like always. "You and your ankles will be the death of me."

Deli stood and turned.

Lachlan Scott was a thing made of magic. His family's tartan wrapped his hips as he walked toward her. The light of the sun dipping into the sea lit his skin, his hair, his eyes on fire against the indigo storm clouds behind him.

"You're bleeding."

Deli grinned. "You're wearing a *kilt*."

"So I am." He paused on the path below her and looked up with one knee bent. "I'm trying to dress the part. See, I'm looking for someone. Legend says if one searches the Highlands, they're bound to find a mythical sort of woman—"

"She sounds hot."

His laughter made her feel lighter. "You have *no* idea."

Deli propped a hand on her hip. "Oh really?"

"Hmm." He stepped closer. She felt the blood rush to her . . . well. Everything. "She's got these eyes. Like endless summers, birdsong, and sea breeze. They could drive a man to do unmentionable things."

Lachlan took a step nearer with each thing he listed.

"She sounds fake."

"And her hair—god, it's soft. Ink stroke and midnight."

Deli swallowed. He was only a few feet away.

"Her smile feels like coming home. It's like . . . finding a tree to read beneath with just the right curve."

"Oh, so she reads? Nerd."

"Speaking of curves . . ."

The way Lachlan *beheld* her—like she was some precious, priceless thing he coveted? She'd never wanted to be a mind reader more in her life.

"She's . . ."

His eyes simmered.

". . . *perfect.*" Lachlan took one last step to meet her, but he didn't touch her. "Do you want to know the best part about her—this magic girl of mine?"

Deli didn't trust her mouth. No, her brain. Her mouth *or* her brain. "Mmhmm?"

His fingers brushed her jaw.

"Everything else."

He dropped suddenly and knelt before her.

If her face matched what was in her brain, she looked horrified. "Oh no. Not again."

Lachlan grinned as he touched her knee, then her ankle, so softly she ached.

"Are you alright?"

The whirlwind of her life since arriving in Fearnhall washed over her, and though Deli was now much closer acquainted with grief, she knew it was the truth when she said, "Yes. I'm alright."

He took her hand as he stood and brought it to his smiling lips.

"So," she said, "if your mystery woman is out roaming the fields—"

"And sheep farms and talent shows."

"—what are you doing here with me?"

"Hoping I found her." Lachlan's smile turned a bit sad, but recovered. "And I thought I'd better check on you. A very angry little man stopped by the pub."

Her hand shot to her mouth. "No."

"Oh yes, he was a ray of sunshine."

"Oh god. What did he say?"

Lachlan shrugged. "I can't remember much before Hannah knocked his lights out."

"HANNAH WHAT?"

He closed his eyes like he was picturing the scene in his mind. "I'll still be thinking about it on my deathbed."

They laughed. He pressed one finger to her chest, just above her heart. "I ask again"—he tapped the spot lightly—"are you alright?"

Deli didn't have to hesitate. "I am now." Lachlan wrapped his arms around her and they swayed. "Wild mountain thyme, huh?" she asked into his chest.

"Aye. Do you know what it means?"

Deli looked up at him. "Do *you* know what it means?"

"It can mean *action* and *affection.*" He looked at *her* with such affection it made her want to cry. "It speaks of *healing*, *bravery*, *death*, and *daring*—"

Deli was in awe of the enchanted soil—the way it produced exactly what needed to be said, to be grown, to be harvested, again and again and again.

"—and, of course, *a good sleep*."

Deli grinned. "That's important."

Lachlan nodded. "A wee flower with a mighty voice."

They watched the sun sink lower for a moment. "How'd you know all that?"

His chest rose and fell against her. "I have been doing a bit of studying."

"Why?"

Lachlan pulled back and tucked her hair behind her ear. The look in his eyes was the one she'd seen in their photographs together. "So I could speak your language."

If a million men told Deli they were madly in love with her, that would still be the most romantic thing she'd ever heard.

Lachlan let her go and fixed his eyes on the horizon. "When do you leave?"

"I dunno," Deli said. "It's a little early to book flights. Grandma's still kickin'."

He kept his face stoic. "Does that mean . . . ?"

"I do remember telling you," Deli said as she laced her fingers through his, "you wouldn't be able to chase me off."

For one agonizing moment, Lachlan said nothing. His face turned pained. He studied the blooming thyme and heather, then met her eyes.

"You know I'm in love with you, don't you?"

She closed her eyes as she smiled, soaking in the moment, memorizing the details to write down later so she would always be able to visit who she was when she was a young woman in the cottage by the sea. Deli leaned toward him, and his lips were so close she could almost taste electricity on her tongue as his free hand came under her chin. Then the sky flashed as lightning streaked through the clouds, and with a clap of thunder that shook the cliffside, it opened.

Lachlan still balanced her jaw on his fingers, still tilted his mouth to mirror hers. Deli had been wrong about him. Of all the things Lachlan handled with care, it was with her he was most tender. His whispered question asked so much more than it sounded.

"Are we out of time?"

Deli couldn't believe her luck—for all she'd lost, look what she'd found. "We've got all the time in the world."

His lips brushed hers, and lightning exploded.

She paused. "Um, except maybe we should spend that time not on the highest point in the area during a lightning storm?"

Lachlan nodded once. "Yep."

"And, Lachlan? This time, let's take the short way home."

90

Deli

Deli led Lachlan inside.

"Oh god!" She knelt to pick up his photos where they lay cast over the ground. "I'm so sorry, my mom—"

The photo she held struck her silent.

Lachlan's hand ran through her hair while a bunch of heather hung by her side and their mouths hovered inches apart. The mountains soared behind them under a swollen sky, her hair and the hem of the kilt tugged by the same wind. It was captured so well Deli almost expected to see them move.

She remembered the words he'd said to her mother—her mother, who'd *actually* sent the photos of her and William. She remembered the way he'd stood up for her in front of everyone.

"I'm sorry, Lachlan. For everything."

He held up a hand. "There's nothing to forgive, Deli."

"There is, and I am. I thought the worst of you because I couldn't confront the worst in me, and that had nothing to do with you. You didn't deserve that."

"It's not your fault. I know why you did."

"Yeah, I suppose." Deli thought of the ways all the people before Lachlan had made her feel like she was something to be a little bit ashamed of, and how quickly she'd assumed Lachlan was telling her the same. "Even so, it wasn't right to pass unfairness that happened to me on to you. And I *am* sorry."

He tilted his head with a small smile. "It's okay."

Deli suppressed a chuckle at the softhearted boy trying to accept an apology. "You know that I trust you, right, Lachlan? You know I don't worry about you hurting me?"

He studied the ground. "I shouldn't have said those things just now. I don't want to pressure you, or for you to do something just because I told you I loved you. I'm sorry. You don't need to do anything or say anything, okay?"

Deli stared at the man—at a total loss for how to say what she wanted to and make him hear it. Then she grabbed her shears and went into the garden. Just as she'd hoped, she found everything she needed, no matter how unlikely.

When she wedged her way back through the door with an armful of flowers, Lachlan was rising from a freshly lit fire.

"Sit," she said before he could run to her aid. He didn't move. "Sit . . . please?"

He eyed her suspiciously, but he pulled a kitchen chair out at an angle and sat with one knee dipping under the table's edge. Sir Beans McGee jumped into his lap.

"Okay, just don't say anything until I say you can. Capisce?"

Lachlan nodded, and Deli began to drop flowers on the table, one by one, to say what she needed to say.

"Hey, *you, with the beautiful eyes, your unhappiness kills me*, so let me give you this *love letter.* There are no words to express my *gratitude* and *good luck* since you've come into my life. You bring me *play*, you make me *laugh*, and you *make me think. You are tender and loving*, and *I feel you being kind* every day. Honestly, I think it might be *fate*, from the day you *held my hand and strolled with me* on the cliffside, you have *warmed my heart.* But it is so much more than that. Lachlan, *when I'm with you, the sun shines*, and *you are the only one* who makes me feel like

I'm full of possibility. *I burn* when I'm with you. I think *you are perfect.* And I know that *change* is scary, but I hope you'll *take a chance with me. Have pity on my passionate heart,* and at least *smile for me*?" She paused to frown with her bottom lip out until he grinned. "Or better yet, will you *believe me* when I *tell you,* Lachlan . . . *I am falling in love with you*?"

Deli stood with empty arms over her heaping love letter made of petals and leaves. Lachlan studied it silently, his attention jumping from bloom to bloom, still hesitant.

Deli trailed her fingers along the edge of the table and slowly approached him where he sat in the kitchen chair until she was standing between his legs. Beans gave a small meow of annoyance as Lachlan's hand stilled in his fur.

She ran her fingers into his hair. "If you can't believe me . . ." She stroked his cheek with her thumb. "Will you let me show you?"

Deli dropped her hand to his knee and ran it up the length of his thigh. "How much I want you, Lachlan?" She drew close enough to whisper against his ear.

"Will you let me prove to you? That I want this? Us?" She brushed the tip of her nose against his as she moved to whisper his plea back to him in the other. "Let me?"

Deli pulled back to take in his beautiful, impossible eyes. "You can answer now. That is, if you'll still have me?"

"Aye." The guilt in his voice was gone. *"I'll have you."*

Relief and wanting rushed her. She waited, cherishing the way he looked at her.

"Lachlan?"

"Yes?"

"The cat is in my spot."

Beans landed three feet away with a reproachful sound.

And Deli was on fire.

She hooked her legs over his to straddle him as he wrapped his arms around her. His hands pressed into her back, and he kissed her. He kissed her like the night was endless, like the stars scattered across the sky the night he'd carried her into this house. She rocked her hips against him as he buried his face into her chest, kissing up to her collarbone, to the hollow between them. She gasped when she felt the warmth of his hands under her shirt, his lips on her neck, as he pulled it over her head.

He traced the line of her neck to her chest and held there. She unclipped her bra.

God, it felt good to be wanted.

Deli knotted her fingers in his hair and pulled his face toward her, and it was all the permission he needed. Lachlan pushed her backward so his mouth could find her belly, and he made a sound of pure pleasure as his lips met the softness of her body. He ran his hand up her side to her breast, and she gasped when his thumb brushed her nipple. He smiled against her skin and kissed higher until he hovered below her other breast and stilled. She waited, chest heaving.

"Say my name." His voice was so heavy with wanting, with an animal drive, she could nearly taste it. Cinnamon, iron, and woodsmoke. His eyes burned up at her.

Her grin was wicked. "Make me."

He licked his way to her nipple and closed it in his mouth as he gripped her other breast, and her back arched to press herself harder against him.

"Oh my god." She sucked in breath. Her hips rolled against his lap. "Lachlan . . ."

He moaned in pleasure into her skin and broke away, then trailed his hand down her front and slipped it under the waistband of her leggings while he watched her face. Watched her lip quiver as his touch moved closer. Lower. Intent.

"Say it again."

Deli's mouth opened farther as his finger found its mark, sending a spasm through her body as she panted. Lachlan nodded slowly, eyes on hers, and he added another fingertip to move in slow circles. He reached farther down and traced the place she desperately wanted him to go.

"I said, *say it again*," he demanded.

"Lach—"

He sank his fingers into her as her head fell back.

"—lan!"

"Yes," he growled.

The word rumbled from his chest and into hers as he drew her body back to him and sucked at her neck, just over her pounding pulse. He knotted a hand in her hair while the other worked inside her. She ground herself against him, begging for release as he moved faster—pressed harder.

She moaned as the heat gathered, hotter and needing. "Don't stop. Please don't stop."

Deli felt herself getting tighter around him as he brought her closer. Closer. *Closer.*

Then he stopped, and she tried to move against him herself until Lachlan pulled her head back with the fist in her hair—not rough, but not softly, either. She ached for him like she'd never known as his eyes moved to her mouth and then back. His chest rose and fell in ravenous breaths. She could feel him underneath her—feel how hard he'd become through his kilt.

"Delilah?" Lachlan said as he twitched a finger against her and watched her shudder.

"Yes," Deli panted, pinned in place by Lachlan's intention. It felt so good—being with someone who didn't need her to be in control all the time.

The look in his eyes was dangerous. Devastating. Delicious.

His voice alone made her body beg for him.

"Say my name."

She obeyed. What started as *Lachlan* turned into the sound of a wave of pleasure breaking from the place he touched her. Deli writhed in Lachlan's lap. Each breath was a moan, his name every time, until her head rolled back around and he caught her jaw.

Lachlan slipped his hand out of her. He held her still as he brought two fingers to her lips and waited.

Deli grasped his wrist, and as she slowly guided his fingers into her mouth, she ran her other hand up his inner thigh. The tartan fabric bunched as she found the base of his shaft as she brought his fingers deeper. His abs contracted as she skimmed the length of him while she closed her lips around his fingers at the knuckle. He inhaled and held his breath.

She began to suck and closed her hand around him at the same time.

"Fuck, Deli," he moaned in a desperate breath. She moaned, too, sliding her hand up and down in time with her head—savoring her taste as she watched his mouth open wider, watched his eyes grow larger.

He caught her hand and pulled his fingers free. Then he slipped them into his own mouth, dragged them back out, and kissed her like he'd never get to kiss her again.

Their lips didn't part as he carried her to the center of the room and knelt to one knee on the rug. There, before the fire, they tore their clothes off and flung them away until they were skin to skin. He held himself above her and looked into her eyes with so much raw *feeling* it made her lightheaded.

Deli wondered if she'd loved him every day since they'd met somehow—the way your bones know the ground of home.

She guided him between her legs with one hand and touched his face in the other, marveling at the freckles dusted like ash across his skin.

"Lachlan?"

"Deli?" he whispered.

She tried to think of how to say it all at once.

"All my favorite days as *me* have been since I met *you*." She kissed him and nodded. "I trust you more than anyone."

He kissed her so tenderly she blushed anew, then he pushed into her, slowly at first, then all at once, and Deli suspected that every part of him was perfect for her. Lachlan moved, and it was magic—stretching and hitting spot after spot that spun her into ecstasy. Even while she was more vulnerable than she'd ever been, Deli was safe.

"Oh god, Deli," he groaned into her ear as she clenched around him. Their pace grew more urgent, and he pulled himself up to look at her.

She was hungry for him. She gave a wicked smile. "Lachlan, I want *all* of you. Don't you dare stop."

What a thing it was, to be finally out of her mind. She let whatever restraint remained fall away as she raked her nails down his back—pulled his hand to her breast. His body convulsed in time with hers as he cradled her head—mouth hot and panting her name against the spot behind her ear.

Deli MacDonald didn't claim to know too much. She didn't know if she'd made the right choices, or if she'd made the right mistakes, or if she was just a random character in the greater story of life.

But there was one thing she knew for sure.

"Hey, wanna hear something wonderful?" she whispered.

Lachlan smoothed her hair away from her eyes, pressed a kiss to her temple. "Yes?"

"I think I'm where I'm supposed to be."

91

Deli

"A little to the left."

Lachlan tilted the painting.

"Other left."

He hung his head and did as told.

"Stop!" Deli held up her hands like a frame, peering through with one eye. "Perfect."

Lachlan marked the spot and hammered nails into the wall to hang the frame.

"Tell me again *why* you want to hang this mystery painting while it's still wrapped?"

Deli looked up from the flower recipe she was planning for a wedding next month.

"Because Douglas made it."

"And you trust this to be something suitable for polite company?"

"God, I hope not."

"Why aren't you unwrapping it?"

"Because it's not time yet."

"It's not time yet."

"Nope."

"How will you know when it's time?"

Deli looked up and shrugged. "I'll just know."

Lachlan kissed her forehead. "I'm sure you will."

Deli grabbed his hand and brought it to her lips. Things with Lachlan had progressed quickly, but to them it just felt like they'd always been. In the eight months they'd been together, he'd never wavered. Even in her grief or her anger or her fear that still reared its head in the quiet sometimes. Lachlan was so sweet to her—so endlessly loving no matter how hard she could make it for her to be loved—now and then she fought the urge to run.

But she never did.

She tilted her head backward until it rested against his belly and traced circles on his hand with her thumb. "Can you go feed Mrs. Peevis?"

"Of course."

He slipped on his winter coat and wellies and disappeared with a blast of late-November wind into the still-blooming garden—full of every part of meaning a poet could need to write. Deli ran to the kitchen window they kept having to prune out of wisteria and gorse, and spotted Lachlan reaching for something in the grass.

Deli yelled through the glass, "ALSO, CAN YOU REFRESH HER FLOWER CROWN?"

He kept walking with his back to her and held up his clenched fist full of white daisies, off to adorn a giant Highland cow who liked to nuzzle against his chest. Daisies. *Gently given, gently received.*

"THANK YOUUUU."

Deli smiled to herself as she watched him from the kitchen, thinking about all the ways she loved to make Lachlan laugh and roll his eyes. Sometimes both at once. She'd often forgone the more traditional *Hey, you up?* and instead left flowers with arguably spicy intent, like devil's bit *(scratch my itch)* at his doorstep or on his pillow. More than once, she'd answered Lachlan's call for him to ask "why in the *National Treasure* nonsense must he decrypt a bouquet booty call," and could he just come over? Once, they'd locked the pub and stumbled upstairs, kissing and tearing at buttons the whole way until she was sitting on his countertop while he kneeled between her knees. In the throes, with her hands knotted in his hair and his face buried in her business, he'd mumbled something about how much he loved her taste.

"You like it?" she'd asked.

"Yes," he'd answered in a rasp.

She'd tugged his eyes to hers with her hands in his hair, forcing his stillness, savoring the surprised look on his face.

She glared, voice like ice. "That's 'Yes, *Chef*.'"

He'd closed his eyes, pressing his lips together to stifle his laughter, then went back to work as Deli chuckled until she couldn't make coherent sounds anymore.

Then there were the moments that were even more intimate than the way Lachlan gave her a safe place to become acquainted with pleasure, like the way he made it safe for her to learn her heart—her grief. He held her in his arms while she cried herself to sleep thinking of the best friend who had changed—or who she'd never really known—and who was gone. He patiently told her how he felt about her every single time she wondered if she was good enough.

Lachlan wanted to be with her in the light of day, the dark of night—in the depths and in the heights. He just . . . wanted to *be* with her. He never asked her to name something or to give him a timeline or an answer. But he'd made it clear that for him, the only option was her. He wasn't waiting on something better. He didn't need any more. He already had what he wanted.

And Deli came alive with someone who let her love him fully. She'd never had more fun. She'd never been more excited about what she might find or learn each day—with or without him. Deli had spent months on her garden dictionary. She'd painted a mural on the back of The Wallflower overlooking the new gathering spot. She'd laughed and played and professed her heart, and Lachlan was her partner in all of it.

Except, of course, the laugh-till-they-cried hours of hikes and pub nights and laundry days Deli spent with her brilliant friend Blair.

It had almost been a year since Deli came to Scotland with a heart left in pieces by the people she had truly loved. And even though the wrecking ball of that invisible grief—all the memories and time and growing up that were synonymous with their names—would sometimes hit her like a blow to her stomach, Deli hadn't gone back. She had decided to let love be easy.

She was choosing differently.

The day after Aunt Mo left, Deli opened her new bedroom closet to find the leather jacket with a letter in its pocket. It had all the details she'd need to run the house and manage the event business, as well as her Grandpa Cal's birth records with a printout about the right visa. Aunt Mo had also written just to Deli—about how thankful she was they were back together, and who Aunt Mo believed Deli to be. And Deli knew, even though she didn't have Chloe anymore, she did have a best friend who could really, truly *see* her. One who was on a parallel journey as they both tried to untangle and understand the bad of their family from the good.

It was not an easy thing—to find the parts you thought were *you,* only to learn so much of you is made of reactions to someone else. There weren't any quick how-tos on how to decide what you could forgive, what you needed to change, and who, if anyone, was to blame.

But they were doing it. And they were doing it together.

Deli spoke with Aunt Mo on the old landline all the time—twirling the cord around her finger and watching Lachlan grimace as it got tangled time and time again. She'd only spoken to her mother once, and it had been tense and happy and aching—like always.

Grandma Rosemary sounded strong when they talked. The doctors expected she'd be in good health at least until the new year. Deli and Lachlan would go to Los Angeles in a month for Christmas, and Grandma Rosemary would buy him a stupidly expensive watch he would never use, and it would warm Deli's heart.

Deli looked up as the phone rang. She didn't have a call planned until later when she and Aunt Mo would recap the latest episode of *Love Island.*

"Hello?"

"Delilah, it's Mom."

Deli's mouth went dry at the taste of her mother's grief. "Grandma?"

Her mom began to cry. "She's taken a turn."

"How long?"

"Come home as quickly as you can, baby."

Deli stood for a long time in the same place. Lachlan knocked the toes of his boots on the mat at the back door. He had a daisy tucked behind his ear.

"Peevie wanted us to match—"

He saw her face and left muddy footprints across the kitchen floor until she was in his arms. The first wave of Deli's tears after she learned her grandma was almost gone came and went while Lachlan held her.

She sniffled. She had a feeling. "Let's open the painting."

He looked down at her and cocked his head. "Now?"

Deli nodded. "It's time."

She stood back as Lachlan carefully peeled away the paper Douglas had taped against the frame months before. Whatever it was, it would hang over a photo of Deli tying her shoe in the Highlands while Lachlan stood behind her, a photo of Aunt Mo in Lachlan's pub surrounded by their family, and a drawing Kieran had made of a field of purple flowers.

Lachlan gasped as the paper fell away.

The painting of the Campbell Farm was teeming with life, but the sky was marred by a streak of black and gray. The smoke rose from the hills where a fire licked down the hillside, setting the heather ablaze.

Deli thought back to the feeling as she'd sat beside Cairn after he'd set the fire—like everything she'd known about love and what it made her was eaten up right in front of her.

But Cairn was right about how death could be a friend and how loyalty could be a foe. Deli's life had bloomed in ways she'd never known to imagine since she'd let Trey and Chloe go. She'd been freer than she'd ever felt since she'd turned her back on a life that felt safe in exchange for one that held promise.

Heather—*protection*—sometimes needed to burn.

"I have to go back."

Lachlan peeled his attention from the painting. "When?"

"Soon. Tomorrow."

"So it's time."

Her chin started to quiver. "It's time."

Lachlan stood behind her and wrapped his arms around her shoulders as he rested his chin on her head, and they swayed before the painting, which was always meant to hang right in that spot.

"Do you need me to come with you?"

Deli could still smell the smoke on the hillside. She could still feel the grass beneath her as she'd wept onto a friend's shoulder.

"No, I can do it myself. I'll be okay."

"Are you sure?"

"Yes. You're still training Blair."

"Please, Blair doesn't need any training to run the place. But I should make sure wee Kevin doesn't catch wind of the tour buses full of women coming to see the famous birthplace of Hamish the Highlander."

Deli chuckled. Lachlan and William had agreed to give the thing a shot after Deli told him it was her mother who had put Fearnhall on the map, and that shot had hit its mark.

"I still hate that my brother was right."

"I know."

They took a moment just to breathe and soak it in.

"If you get back and find I'm missing, Beans killed me and ate my body."

"That seems fair. This is *his* house."

"Agreed."

When Deli boarded a flight the next day, she didn't feel like she was headed home.

She felt like she was leaving it.

92

Rosemary

Three days before Rosemary McDonnell died, she circled the date in her calendar with a large red marker, capped the pen, and thought, *That's that.*

Then she'd collapsed.

By the time she woke the next day, Delilah was already on a plane. The next time she opened her eyes, Delilah was there in Rosemary's hospital room with Lorraine and Maureen. The three of them didn't know she was awake as she watched from her bed, machines beeping and things whirring and her body aching everywhere. But all that was just a kerfuffle—nothing could distract her from taking them in one last time.

Deli and Laurie sat in chairs while Mo sat cross-legged on the floor around a small hospital table with cards fanned in their hands.

"UNO!" Laurie pumped her fists in the air in victory as Mo rolled onto her back and Deli threw her cards at her mother. Laurie giggled. "Don't hate me cuz you ain't me."

Deli made a frustrated sound. "You're cheating, you have to be cheating."

"Nope. God just loves me."

Mo said, "I question his taste."

Rosemary braced for the anger to flare, for the sharp words to cut. Instead, they laughed. Laurie's laugh, and Mo's laugh, and Deli's—her three favorite sounds in the world.

Rosemary smiled as she fell asleep in a room with her happy, laughing girls.

She never woke up again.

93

Mo

The day of her mother's funeral, Mo McDonnell woke up from a dream.

She was sitting cross-legged on a black-and-white linoleum floor when a clementine bounced out of a dark doorway and rolled right into her hands. She peeled back the skin to find each transparent crescent had a white bell shaped flower floating inside.

It was a cruel dream. Mo had searched for Beth for months when she returned. It shouldn't have surprised her that the woman she'd loved twenty years ago wasn't in the same apartment, or that when she'd peered through the window, the kitchen floors had been done over with stone. Beth was always private, so there was no trace of her on social media. No one knew where she'd gone. It was a long shot from the beginning.

There had been a lot to coordinate for the funeral. Rosemary had insisted in her will on the color "Heartbreaker Red" for her casket. The light streaming in from the stained-glass windows caught the flecks of glitter in the paint and sent starbursts reflecting across the church. Tumbling plumes of flowers erupted on either side, cascading to the floor in a waterfall of soft petals. Mo only recognized a few of the many Deli had meticulously chosen—snapdragon, stock, peonies, zinnia, and of course, rosemary sprigs. Paola and the girls at the flower shop had taken extra care. The steps up to the casket were lined with tea candles and bud vases, each holding a single stem of lily of the valley.

"I'm so sorry for your loss," someone said, and Mo ceased her meditation on the casket equivalent of a Shelby Mustang.

"Thank you." An older man she'd never seen before grasped her hand between his two. He had a mole right between his eyes that had sprouted a trio of white hairs.

"She was a force, that woman," he said, chin quivering.

"She was," Mo agreed. Laurie sniffled loudly beside her as the man shuffled toward the hot rod where her mother lay.

"Another ex-lover?" Mo asked out of the corner of her mouth.

"Oh god, probably," Laurie said with a sigh. "I see why she never bragged about that one. How much longer do we have to stand here?"

In the week since their mother had passed, Mo hadn't cried. She had been stoic and steady—standing firm amid the rushing flood of grief that had swept her sister away.

"You can go. I'll greet the last few stragglers on my own."

Laurie looked at her with doe eyes. "Are you sure?"

Mo put a hand on her sister's shoulder. "Don't worry about it. I'm good for a few more handshakes. Look"—she flattened her other hand in the air between the two of them—"steady as a rock."

"But . . . what will people say if I'm not here? It's not proper. Mom would—"

"Laurie," Mo said, "Mom's busy. She won't notice."

Laurie threw her hand over her mouth to stifle her laugh.

"Besides," Mo said with a shrug, "if she's haunting anyone, you know it's me."

Laurie took Mo's steady hand in hers and squeezed. She looked at Mo the way she used to when they were children and they shared a secret. "She's definitely haunting you."

Mo smiled. "Go."

Laurie slipped away toward the back of the church. Deli was back there somewhere, putting the final touches on her eulogy. When she'd first said she'd like to be the one to give the speech, she and Laurie were a bit taken aback. But the more she thought about it, the more perfect it felt. Deli was a woman coming into her own. One chapter began, and another ended. That was how it should be.

Mo could see a few late cars pulling into the parking lot through the open doorway. *A few more minutes,* she thought. She tugged on her top and smoothed down her hair. She stared at her shoes until the outline of a man's broad shoulders fell across her simple, practical loafers.

"Lachlan?"

"Mo." His voice was thick with emotion as she was crushed in his embrace.

"I thought Deli said she told you not to come on her account?"

"Aye," her friend replied, still holding on to her. "But we're not here on her account." He looked toward the church's entrance. Mo followed his gaze and nearly screamed.

Hannah stepped forward from the throng of tartan that had appeared in the doorway. Mo hadn't heard Hannah speak in many years, but her voice was still warm and husky and comforting.

"We're here for *you.*"

Mo was rushed then by the rest of the crew that often sat around the fire in The Wallflower's Crown. She was bolstered. Her family had come, and that made all the difference.

Mo took a hard look at the man whom she had loved like a brother, like a son, like a nephew—and she thought what a shame it was that there weren't words for a friendship like theirs. *Love* was so limiting. People were capable of so much more than that.

"I hope there's food afterward," Lachlan said as a tear escaped the corner of his eye. She reached up and wiped it with her thumb.

"You're such a softy."

"Don't tell anyone."

He kissed the top of her head. His calves—strong and sure under the hem of his kilt—stood out against the sea of legs in black dress pants as he walked toward the front of the church. Lachlan went straight to the open casket where her mother lay, leaned down, and whispered something to her before taking a seat.

Mo pictured her niece catching a glimpse of her love in full dream-boat attire in the second row and being forced to maintain her composure. She was looking forward to that part.

"Mo?"

Out of the blue, even though it had been over twenty years, Mo knew instantly that lightning could strike the same place twice. A white-hot chill ran from her toes up her spine as her hands started to shake. She smelled summer. Mo had looked everywhere for her. *It couldn't be . . .*

Beth's voice was the same, too—and to Mo, it was still a symphony.

"Mo . . . I wasn't sure if I should come, I saw the obituary, and—I'm so sorry if I—should I go? I can g—"

Mo threw her arms around the woman she'd left behind with her heart and finally felt herself fall to pieces. She'd made a wonderful life, but being back in Beth's embrace, even for a *second*, reminded her of what it was to feel like she could trust someone else to hold things together. Beth was brilliant and capable and kind. Beth had loved her the way no one else ever had. And Beth held her up while Mo could be a daughter in a world without her mom.

She felt like all the time between them was collapsing—like twenty years hadn't gone by, and like Mo had never left, and like they were still twentysomethings holding hands in a bright orange slug bug under palm tree–lined streets. Mo felt like maybe it was just a Saturday morning, and they were having breakfast in the sun—a silk scarf in Beth's hair—and that afternoon Mo would get on one knee and ask Beth to marry her.

All this time later, she still had the ring.

"Oh, Mo, I'm so, so—" Beth cut herself short as she spotted the casket. She dropped her volume and said, "Jesus, Mary, and Joseph, that thing *should* be buried."

The sound of their laughter echoed through the vaulted stone walls. If people turned to tsk, Mo would never know. And she'd never care. She'd heard Beth's laugh again.

Mo held on to the feeling with all her strength. If they could just stay there long enough, swaying gently in the cold doorway of a church the day she would bury her mother, Mo could rewrite the last two decades and *will* the next five together.

She could *will* the return of joy.

She knew it was impossible, and even so, Maureen McDonnell decided to believe she would never have to say goodbye to Beth O'Sullivan again.

94

Deli

"Rosemary McDonnell was not easy to love—to understand, or pin down, or wrap your arms around. Her margins were messy, despite her crisp blouses and marble floors.

We do not have many good stories about complicated women. They're not often allowed the roles of heroes or leading ladies.

Women who are *easy* to love are simple. Predictable. Compliant.

My grandmother was none of those things.

She was born with fire in her belly when little girls were supposed to be quiet and demure. But no matter how hard she tried, Rosemary smoldered.

And sometimes her love could burn. It could lick down her arms and scorch the things she held so tightly. Sometimes being loved by Rosemary McDonnell felt like being trapped in a house on fire.

But sometimes? It felt like the sun. Like the sun had come after years of darkness. Being loved by my grandmother could feel like being touched by the softest, warmest light there was.

On her best days, she was pure sunlight. I'd like to believe if she had the choice, she would have spent every single second looking over the people she loved—helping them blossom. Helping them thrive.

Maybe it's not fair to be loved by someone like that—to never know if you were gonna bloom or be burned at her touch. But it also couldn't have been fair to only have a chained up heart that wouldn't go out. Maybe the unfairness happened to us all—most of all, my complicated, dimensional, wild-hearted grandmother, who thought herself a failure for burning her whole life.

Is it jarring to talk about her like this? Yeah, I know. But to *really* love someone, you have to see them. And to capture a woman like Rosemary—to paint her portrait and coax her out of words—is not a task for the fainthearted. She was a lioness. An untamed wind. And she would have scolded me in the car on the way home if she'd heard me tell you that she was an easy, simple, soft thing.

Frankly, I'm afraid she'd haunt me in a pair of Jimmy Choos.

Some of you knew her as a friend. Some as a lover. Some as a mother. And I'd bet some, even, as an enemy. I think she'd enjoy *you* being here the most, sitting in a church while I monologue about a woman you are *still* thinking about—she would call that a win. I'm sure there is more than one person here who got into a tussle with Rosemary McDonnell and limped away, nursing a wound they didn't know was possible, while she smiled and straightened her dress.

She liked to win, didn't she? Never afraid of a fight. Especially when love felt so often like a battle. I know I've come away bloody. Her daughters have, too.

When my grandmother loved someone, she made sure they couldn't wander too far. She lived her life trying to protect.

And yes, Rosemary hung on a little too tight.

It's such a task to *become* when you're on a short leash, isn't it?

That is what makes me the saddest today. Not that she's gone, or rather, done up exquisitely in this ridiculous, on-brand bombshell of a casket, but that she was a dimensional woman who wasn't allowed a dimensional life—to learn a dimensional love. She did the best she could with what she had. She did the best she could with what she knew.

But . . . what a waste.

Because the truth of Rosemary McDonnell, my grandmother, is this:

She was brilliant. And in another life she could have been a million and one brilliant things. Maybe she should have never been a wife or a mother, but a pilot—with wings to take her wherever adventure called. Maybe she should have been a scientist, who took that signature bulldog fight straight to the problem and latched on until she discovered a cure. Maybe she should have been a novelist—tucked away in rooms full of oak, writing about the string of lonely men who still pined for her in echoing places.

She was hungry. For life, for art, for experience. There is a world, I imagine, where Rosemary McDonnell had baguettes with French butter in Paris, cappuccinos and table wine in Roman squares, Dutch cheeses from a wrapped cloth on the canals of Amsterdam. There is a world where she wore smudges of paint on her skin from the hands of the artist who called her muse. There is a world where she stood at the bow, splashed with sea spray as a scarf whipped in the wind behind her, her cherry lips pulled wide with joy.

There is a world, I imagine, where she knew her hunger wasn't wrong.

There is a world where Rosemary was a living, messy thing covered in bruises and scars from the times she tried and failed and tried again.

And still, even in *this* one, she was a force of nature. She could change you forever with a single, breathtaking, brutal day of being wrapped in the fire of her arms.

So no, I cannot tell you my grandmother was easy to love. And neither, I think, am I. But she didn't have any wild women to look up to and consider a hero. Thanks to her, I do.

The night my grandma told us she was dying, I was so mad. I was *so* mad. Then she braved a storm—literally—to sit me down and ask my anger its name.

My grandmother, with her eighty-something-year-old body and her defiant, courageous heart, sat with her feet dangling over a cliffside beside me, passing a wineglass that was half rainwater back and forth. And she took my chin in her hand, and said:

'Promise me, Delilah—you will choose. No matter how scary life gets, you have to be who you are on purpose. *You still have time to choose.* So, *choose.*'

No, Rosemary McDonnell was not an *easy* woman to love.

And thank god, *thank god*, for that."

EPILOGUE

Deli woke up alone to the sound of Scottish rain falling gently on the roof of the old cottage. There, in the space between waking and sleeping, she wondered about all the other people who had ever woken up in that room. She wondered about the lives they had lived and the people they had loved—the things that they had lost.

She squeezed her eyes shut and took a long, deep breath. She could just smell the sweet smoke of the fireplace. Lachlan must have left it burning for her before he left. The thought of him stacking the logs as quietly as he could—blowing gently into the kindling so Deli would wake up to a cozy house—fell over her like a winter quilt. She still couldn't believe Lachlan was real sometimes. And that he was choosing to be hers.

Deli stretched across the bed and made a morning squeak-yawn sound as she rotated her wrists and ankles. She swung her legs over the side and threw back the duvet with a little flair for no reason other than for flair's sake, which she thought was reason enough. The knotted, old wood floor creaked under her socked feet as she shuffled into the kitchen.

In the center of the table there was a simple cream paper folded once in half. A dried and pressed stalk of heather, a stem of lily of the valley, and an inside-out bluebell were tucked inside. All still vibrant, though they hadn't been young for a long time.

Deli closed her eyes and privately thanked the strange pulse of magic that had called her to Fearnhall and still gave her endless flowers—the magic that had given Aunt Mo a home and a dream about Deli on her twenty-ninth birthday. And, of course, the magic that had filled the life of a boy named Lachlan and kept him safe until Deli could catch up.

She opened the card. Written in black ink with bold strokes, it read:

> *Good morning. The kettle should still be warm, and your favorite mug is clean.*
>
> *Peevie asked me to leave you a matching daisy crown, so check her stable. Don't forget to eat the cheese Cairn brought over—it's in the fridge beside Blair's cake.*
>
> *I spoke to Beans about behaving, but I can't guarantee it took. Godspeed.*
>
> *Have a particularly excellent day. Let me know if you fancy a wee bit of company.*
>
> *P. S. 30 looks good on you, Delilah.*

Deli lifted the note to her nose and breathed in. Smoke and cinnamon, like she expected. She imagined Lachlan's hands and the particularly excellent company they would offer her later. She thought of his eyes and wondered if she'd ever feel cold again.

She held the paper to her chest as she went to the robin's-egg blue refrigerator covered in a thick layer of postcards and magnets that made up the story of Aunt Mo's life. Deli paused at a postcard from Aunt Mo *and* Hannah. Hannah had packed for a longer trip than the rest when she'd flown to California in December. She'd found a clue about the disappearance of her daughter and fiancé, and she intended to follow it. Apparently, Beth was an investigative journalist, and she had agreed on the spot to help Hannah find answers.

Deli carefully plucked a magnet from the cluster and pinned the note from Lachlan against the freezer door. As she opened the fridge for a bit of breakfast cheese, Beans launched a full assault and tried to throw his round body *into* the dairy drawer.

"Greedy legume!" Deli removed him while he half purred, half protested.

She braced against the fridge to shoo him away with a foot, and the impact sent magnets and photos clattering to the ground. One picture wedged under her right sock. Beans assumed the role of perfect angel and rushed to curl up on the bit of glossy paper he had no idea was a photograph.

She earned another meow-scolding as she pulled it out from under him.

And Deli saw a little girl, nine years old, standing ankle deep in lavender heather on the path to a bright red door. Her shorts were bunched up where her thighs had gathered them, and her lopsided pigtails blew in the Highland wind. Her arms were stretched out wide, and her pale stomach was just poking out under the too-small T-shirt, and a trickle of something dark was running from her knees down her legs, but she didn't look scared. Instead, her eyes were squinted shut and her head was thrown back—mouth open wide with the wild call of a girl crying freedom.

Deli wiped her tear away tenderly and watched the morning's light catch in the drop clinging to her finger.

As she pinned the photo back to the refrigerator, she was overwhelmed with a fierce and unfamiliar love. One that stood tall and proud, and promised to keep that little girl *little*. One that promised to keep her wild. One that promised to keep her *free*.

Deli touched the picture to softly trace the outline of her younger body. She pressed two fingers to her lips and then against the portrait of that wild-hearted daughter, and she whispered, "Happy birthday, Delilah."

Then she turned to pour a cup of tea as the rain carried on washing away the marks of the day before—the way it always had and always would—and the smoke curled up from the chimney, vanishing into the sky.

Recipe for Rosemary's Portrait

Snapdragon	*A force of will; Gracious Lady*
Lily of the Valley	*The return of joy; You make my life complete*
Alstroemeria	*Very powerful bond*
Amaranthus	*Unending love; Unfading; Unending friendship*
Delphinium	*Transcends space and time; Wit*
Freesia (Pink)	*The honorable character of love; Mother's love*
Tea Roses (Hybrid)	*I will remember, forever*
Stock	*You will always be beautiful to me*
Peony	*Unrealized wanting; Desires unrealized*
Rosemary	*Affection, Remembrance*
Rose (Pink)	*You are so very loved; Thank you; Joy everlasting; Elegance*

Recipe for Lachlan's Letter

Variegated Tulip	*You with the beautiful eyes*
Currant	*Your unhappiness kills me*
Agapanthus	*Love letters*
Bells of Ireland	*Gratitude; Good luck; Whimsy*
Pink Hyacinth	*Play; Playfulness; Harmless playing*
Delphinium	*Hilarity; Openhearted; Wit; Transcends space and time; Lightness; Levity*
Love in the Mist	*You make me think; Perplexity; Kiss me*
Peach Rose	*You are tender; You are loving*
Flax	*I feel you being kind; Fate*
Cosmos	*Hold my hand and take a stroll with me; Joys in life and love*
Spearmint	*Warm feeling*
Daffodil	*When I'm with you the sun shines; You are the only one*
Iris	*I burn; In love I burn; I burn with love*
Allium	*You are perfect*
Dahlia	*Change is coming; Always yours*
White Violet	*Take a chance with me on love*
Jonquil	*Have pity on my passionate heart*
Prince William	*Smile for me?*
Red Tulip	*Believe me; Declaration of love*
Lilac	*The start of love; Falling in love*

A quick note about the flowers . . .

The history of people using plants and flowers to send messages is long and colorful. While Deli's journal is nowhere near a complete collection, you will see many entries share similar meanings with others, and many have meanings that are varied and contradictory.

The truth is, there has never been one consolidated source of truth—across cultures and times, but also across streets. At the height of popularity in Victorian England, there were so many different understandings of what meant what, it caused serious miscommunications.

Imagine sending your lover orange lilies to stoke a little *desire* and *passion,* but they think you sent flowers at them to threaten *hatred* and *revenge.*

Yikes.

It's likely the reason the whole practice fell out of style. That being said, I suggest you use your heart and best context clue deduction to match meaning with mention in this particular story. If you want to adopt the habit in your own life, do a little research and do your best. I'm sure a Victorian ghost won't get super offended over your use of orange lilies and decide to haunt you.

Have fun,

Devrie

Deli's Dictionary of Flowers

This book's heroes include . . .

The fine people at Hotel Julius, who quite literally kept me alive during some of the hardest parts of learning how to write a novel on the job. Like so many male authors before me know, it was only possible with a domestic partner (or, in my case, two) to run everything else in the world while I typed for thirty-eight hours straight. Thank you for being my fake spouses and monitoring my hydration levels while leaving encouraging doodles.

Melody, who makes everything beautiful, who makes me orange cakes with lemon drizzle, and who knew me well enough to dare me to race her to the finish line. You are why I crossed it.

Ryan, whose steady care and endorsement of my nonsense made it easier to write a dreamboat.

Kathleen, whose humor and twenty-year friendship made her the perfect person to ask questions like, *Which of these synonyms for* squeezed *is not disgusting but still horny?*

Braelyn, who has been my partner in adventure for over ten years, and who is so often my cottage on the cliffside.

Kelli, who has been my proof that something new will grow.

Boog, who spent many patient hours sitting by this story's side during the messy middle.

Sara, who held my head above water when I couldn't float, and whose shared sense of whimsy, exploration, and morality has been a precious touchstone for a tired heart.

Bub, who entertained countless nonsense calls full of silly, rambling nothings so my subconscious could have its top-secret Noodling Hours.

Brianna, who believes in me so hard, I have to believe in me, too.

Niamh, David, and Caitlin, who made a place five thousand miles away easy to call home.

Dylan, who saved the day and adopted me when I was all alone, and whose wit, warmth, and generosity are a portrait of the heart of Scotland. This book wouldn't exist without you.

Cameron, who helped me swear correctly, and who has loved my friend with such steadfast joy and integrity, I am confident my main characters could totally be real.

Amanda, who made me laugh until I cried while helping me swear correctly, and who I'm sure I've played horsies with in another lifetime's front garden.

Karalyn, who left a book about flower language on my porch when I was a kid, and who has become the sort of friend I can only describe as kindred. She's got such a head for knowin'.

Olaf, who made an adventure out of a chapter full of loss, and whose laughter, friendship, and fearless love of fun make up so much of the magic blooming in the garden. No thanks for Dolores, who owes Olafs a day of life back, for what? Love of boats? Sad. Olaf would never.

Amy, who slid into my DMs and kicked this whole thing off.

Megan and Charlotte, who are the closest thing this story's got to white knights, and who stuck with me despite so many track changes I may have crashed your computers.

To all of you who read this, who liked a video, who sent birthday money. To all of you who saw something in me worth rooting for. To all of you who toast to the wild women, too. This story would have never been told without you. We should all totally go wild swimming.

To me, who has burned a lot of heather. Reminder: You told this story, and it is good. Reminder Two: Don't give up on the good that's still yet to grow.

And to Scotland, whose cities have given me safe places to try being someone new, whose Highlands have reminded me that I am free and I am small, whose people have helped me up when I needed help the most, and whose magic is the closest thing to real I think I know. Slàinte.

Thanks, like *love*, is just too small a word.

A special thank you for sharing some inspiration to Kate Greenaway, Vanessa Diffenbaugh, Dale Harvey, S. Theresa Dietz, and Rachel Henry.

About the Author

Devrie Brynn Donalson is a slinger of words, lover of wit, and teller of stories great and small. She got lucky when she ran away to Scotland and its magic gave her the courage to do something new. Now Devrie is a writer, speaker, and performer known for her authentic and relatable balance of heart and humor. She loves a cold Scottish day and a warm California night, plus flowers, cheese, and dogs. She is the author of *You're Gonna Die Alone (& Other Excellent News)*. For more information, visit www.devriewrites.com.